FAMILY TIES

Malcolm Goldsmith

For People

For inspiration & help
& above all, for friendship

Malcolm.

Family Ties

A 4m Publications book
www.4mpublications.co.uk

Copyright © 2008 Malcolm Goldsmith

ISBN 978-1-906557-01-0

Also By Malcolm Goldsmith

In A Strange Land: People with Dementia and the Local Church
Hearing the Voice of People with Dementia

Knowing Me Knowing You
with Martin Wharton
Knowing Me Knowing God

Communicating with the Public
So, you're on a committee now . . .
Developing Teamwork
all with Michael Kindred

Quiz Quest Challenge
Play the Quiz Quest
Master the Quiz Quest
all with Michael Kindred

Understanding Inequality
with Neville Chamberlain & Eric Forshaw

FAMILY TIES

For Eliza, Jonny, Josie, Frank and Charlotte,
all learning what family ties are about.

With thanks to Kate, who encouraged
me to make a start and Marion, for sharing
me with a non-existent family for three years.

D amn, damn, damn!
Libby drove faster than usual. She normally drove quite slowly, she had to in London, but when she got out into the countryside she drove faster. Today, however, she was late. Today of all days. The annoying thing was that Libby was never late, she was well known for being punctual. But it's not every day that you run over a cat and that is precisely what she did on the outskirts of London. Although technically she ran over it, it was more a case of the wretched creature committing suicide. With no warning, for no apparent reason, this bundle of black fur suddenly rushed out under her car. There was nothing she could do to save it. In a matter of a second or two it changed from beauty in motion to a squashed mess on the road. It took almost an hour to sort things out and for Libby to regain sufficient composure to be able to continue, but an hour today was an hour she could barely spare.

She glanced at her watch, she was almost there now. She just hoped that she wouldn't get lost. She was lunching with her mother and her sister Victoria and family, though she doubted if any of them would feel like eating, she certainly didn't. It was bad enough before the episode with the cat but now she had absolutely no stomach for food. She saw the hotel sign and pulled into the car park. She waited for a few minutes before she got out, needing to compose herself as she was still very shaken and she wanted to exude an air of calmness to cover up the emptiness she felt inside. Above all, she wanted to cope.

Her mother looked up at her as she entered the room, her face drawn, the strain was telling and she looked much older than her sixty eight years.

"You're late," she said. "I didn't expect you to be late today, none of us did."

She decided not to tell them about the cat.

"I'm sorry," replied Libby, "it just took longer than I expected, anyway, I'm here now. Have you ordered?"

"No, we were waiting for you, but you were late."

Victoria's husband Bill grinned as he spoke and instantly she knew that her mother must have been going on about it and driving them mad.

They all picked at their lunch, endeavouring to engage in conversation but everyone's mind was elsewhere, they merely went through the motions. It was a relief to get it over with, return to the car and move on.

Spring had arrived, the day was bright and sunny, the blossom was out and the trees looked magnificent. She parked her car and mingled with the others as they made their way forward. The lawns were immaculate and there was a profusion of flowers with the yellow of the daffodils giving way to a host of other colours. There were so many plants, as though each one was vying for people's attention. It was a beautiful place and the day was almost perfect; but these were the grounds of the crematorium and today Libby's sister Maggie would be consumed by fire. Had a bird flown into the Little Chapel, as sometimes happened, it would have seen row upon row of subdued people. The contrast between the confident explosion of life and colour outside and the gloom and shades of despair inside could hardly have been more marked.

'God, this is awful, the man knows nothing about her.'

Libby wasn't sure if she actually said the words aloud or just thought them. She shot a furtive glance around her to see if anyone had reacted. Apparently not thank goodness. Beryl, her mother, sitting at her side was staring straight ahead at the coffin. She was so still she was almost statuesque in her grief. Libby thought she could have been made of marble and as such would not have been out of place in a graveyard. But there would be no graveyard, no burial with a stone and a place to visit in years to come and lay flowers; just this functional building euphemistically called the 'Little Chapel', built over the rooms which no-one ever saw, where the great ovens devoured bodies from morn to dusk. The building had little to commend it. It had been constructed in a minimalist sort of way in order not to cause offence. It succeeded in offending no-one and thereby pleased no-one as a result. Even the large candles, which were brought out or hidden away according to taste, were not real candles but canisters of butane gas, shaped to look like candles and lit by the superintendent from his cigarette lighter when the hearse came into view minutes before the service started. The chapel had an off-putting smell; a mixture of flowers and warm stale air which seemed to harmonise, almost but not quite, with the atmosphere of what might be called 'enforced spirituality'. It was stifling, in a word, deadly.

Libby was beside her mother on the front row, by the aisle. On her mother's other side sat Libby's older sister Victoria who was struggling not to cry, her hand held tightly by Bill. He was a good man, who had established a happy and dependable marriage over almost thirty years. She could remember their wedding day as though it was yesterday. She had been a bridesmaid along with Maggie. It was the first time that she had been to a wedding let alone been a bridesmaid and they were both so excited by their long green dresses.

The image disappeared from her mind. She tried to put all other thoughts aside and concentrate on what the minister was saying. They were intended to be words of comfort but they were, for her, a string of platitudes and nonsense. Did anyone actually ever listen to the words at funerals or were they some sort of mantra which a priest was called in to intone on such occasions, as though it was the saying of them which was important and not their actual meaning?

In the row behind Libby sat Maggie's three children and moving back further, in the row behind them, was Mike, their father, together with Jenny, who had been his partner since the year after Maggie disappeared from his life but not from his thoughts. He looked drawn, his face pale, his eyes glazed as he realised that she would never now come back to him. His heart was empty and his mind numb. He wondered if he should have been sitting with his children, giving them some sort of comfort, but the idea had never occurred to him when he entered the chapel, in any case, what comfort could he give them? Had he ever really been able to comfort them?

Maggie's older sister Victoria's three children filled the next row. There was a gap behind them of four or five rows before the non-family mourners filled up the rest of the chapel, which made the family seem strangely isolated, as though they feared in some way the illness which had destroyed Maggie's life and which just might be contagious. Better to leave a safe zone. On the other side of the aisle there was a respectful emptiness at the front but people then filled up the remaining pews so that there were perhaps eighty or ninety people in all. Who they were was a mystery to Libby, but then so much of Maggie's life had been a mystery to her.

She wondered if there was anything that had kept Maggie and the rest of the family together apart from Beryl's constant and enduring love. The family was all that Beryl had and it was all that she lived for. Take away the family and her life was empty, meaningless and unimaginable: but now Maggie, her youngest, was dead. Here they all were, brought together in a contrived sort of way. They looked so small and vulnerable in this 'Little Chapel' which was, in fact, quite large. They didn't know what to do, where to look or what was expected of them.

"Of course, death must come to us all and so we need to learn how to welcome it as a friend, safe in the knowledge that God has prepared great things for us and is waiting for us to join him..."

Libby tried again to listen to the priest's words, they sounded trite and she found herself asking whether it was at all possible to take seriously the words of man who was wearing a grubby white surplice in need of a wash and iron and who, moreover, was wearing *brown* shoes beneath his black cassock. She never trusted men who wore brown shoes; she never had, but didn't know why. She inwardly protested that this man, whom she had never met before and who certainly had never met Maggie, that was quite obvious, should be taking the funeral of someone who, over the years, had brought such pleasure – and pain – to so many people. Maggie was vivacious, attractive, flirtatious, and so full of life. She was a character whom it was impossible to ignore, but here in this banal little ceremony she was being treated as the lowest common denominator, she was every woman, every person, any woman, and any person. But she was not 'any person'. And why should it be 'our' dearly beloved sister when it was not his sister? Anyway she wasn't always so dearly beloved, although sometimes she was, oh yes, sometimes she was. Libby fought to hold back the tears, but hold them back she did. She had not yet cried over Maggie's death.

The Reverend Graham Whittingham was tired. This was his fifth funeral of the day and at each of them he had sung 'The Lord's My Shepherd'. In four of them he found that he was the only person singing. He was on a rota of clergy who took services at the crematorium when families had not asked for the local vicar or minister to take them. Normally the funeral would have been taken by Maggie's vicar but the parish was waiting for someone new after the abrupt departure of the previous one. The Reverend Whittingham was on duty each Tuesday. Sometimes there was only one service to take but today was different, this was number five and there was another one after this. He glanced up at the wall. Immediately in front of him but out of sight of the mourners was a clock and beneath the clock was a notice in large letters "Ministers are respectfully reminded that services should last no longer than 20 minutes. Thank You." He was doing fine, only one hymn and a couple of prayers to go and he still had eight minutes left. He announced the hymn, saw the organist who was also hidden away from the mourners put his newspaper away, pop a toffee into his mouth and begin to play. Everyone stood up and mumbled their way through 'Abide with Me' led, slightly out of tune and ahead of the beat, by the Reverend Graham Whittingham, scruffy, overweight and coming wearily to the end of his fifth funeral of the day.

His mind was already on other things. His wife was complaining that he was out every evening and neglecting the children. He was seeing the Bishop in a few days and was hoping he might be offered a new parish but he knew that it was probably unlikely as he hadn't exactly set the world alight in his present one. Added to all this he had a touch of indigestion and needed to suck a Rennie.

Victoria clung to Bill, he had been so understanding these last few months. He never complained when she left him for days on end whilst she looked after Maggie. He coped without her, phoning every evening and sometimes during the day, keeping the home running and still managing to keep working. In fact, over all the years she had known him, he had never once suggested that she should devote less time to her family and more time to him and his needs. He understood, that was the nice thing about him, he just understood.

She was older than her two sisters, well half-sisters if the truth be told, but it never seemed to be like that. She had no memory of her father and she supposed that was the reason why she had such a close relationship with her mother; she must have been the only thing that Beryl had in those difficult days after her father's death. Over the years there had developed a sort of mutually protective bond between the two of them. She had carried this sense of responsibility into her relationship with Maggie. She had always felt responsible for her ever since, as a ten year old, she had assumed a pivotal role in her upbringing. Of course this sense of responsibility on Victoria's part waned as Maggie grew up and led her rather chaotic life, but when the illness came back again a few months ago there was no question but that she would go and be with her, nursing and caring for her until the end came in the hospice. She was in the next room when Maggie was born and she was by her side when she died.

She was a crossword addict and this passion had helped to keep her sane whilst sitting by Maggie's bedside in those final weeks. As she stood, the tears slowly trickling down her cheek, the priest pressed the hidden button and the dark blue velvet curtains came together and slowly removed the coffin from sight.

"We commend unto thy hands of mercy, most merciful Father, the soul of this our sister departed, and we commit her body to be consumed by fire, ashes to ashes, dust to dust..."

Victoria was crying not only for Maggie, she was crying for the past and her memories of their shared childhood. She was crying for the present, anxious about the effect that all this would have upon Maggie's three children and wondering if her mother would be able to cope, especially after her recent bouts of depression. She was also crying for the future because she could not imagine a future without Maggie.

Beryl stared at the coffin for the whole of the twenty minute service. She dreaded the curtains closing around it and tried not to think about what would happen to it once it was out of sight. It was a nice coffin, light oak, the best that she could afford, and she had thought long and hard about what the plate on the lid should say. In the end she went for simplicity: *Margaret Arkwright, 1940-1978, God Bless.*

Maggie had reverted to her maiden name after she walked out on Mike. Beryl still couldn't believe that she was really dead. It seemed only yesterday that she was a little girl, running round and round in ever decreasing circles and collapsing on the floor amidst peals of laughter. Laughter, yes, that was her abiding memory of Maggie, she was always laughing. She laughed when things went well and she laughed when things went awry, she never seemed to be able to take anyone or anything seriously, not until this final illness and then it was too late. Maggie had given Beryl more trouble, more anxiety and stress than either of the other two girls, but she had also given her such love and joy and sheer pleasure. There had been no half measures with Maggie; life was sunshine or thunder, celebration or despair. And now she was dead. That was so unfair. No mother should have to attend the funeral of her child; no mother should have to experience the death of two husbands and a child. Beryl felt herself to be at breaking point and she had to fight hard to keep in control of herself, to keep back the black billowing clouds of fear and depression.

It had been a difficult few years, what with Libby being overseas and Maggie going off with that crazy man from Spain. Beryl had been at her wit's end trying to help Mike with the children. The arrival of Jenny into his life had been a problem for her. On the one hand it meant that there was someone else around to help with the children and she had to admit that they seemed reasonably fond of her, but somehow it seemed wrong seeing someone else in Maggie's place, in her home, her kitchen, her bedroom. It was all very difficult to come to terms with. Whether that was what triggered off her depression or whether it was Maggie's next liaison she couldn't tell, but she had never been the same since then, never felt well, always tired and lethargic and rather gloomy. It should be her in that coffin, no one would miss her. For it to be Maggie lying there, still, cold and drained of life... Beryl couldn't find any way of coming to terms with it and doubted whether she ever would.

Frank never saw his daughter Margaret, named after the King's younger daughter but always known as Maggie. In fact he knew nothing about her as he was away in the war and then killed before the news of Beryl's pregnancy reached him. His elder daughter Elizabeth, named after the other princess but always known as Libby, was a toddler when he went off and he never saw her again. Beryl often wondered if his death had in some way contributed to Maggie's problems. It can't be easy for a young girl never to have known her father, and whilst Libby seemed to have coped with having no father, Maggie hadn't. Perhaps Beryl had clung more tightly to Maggie, spoilt her, just because she was the last thing that Frank had given her and therefore she needed to treasure her all the more. There was little doubt in Beryl's mind that her attitude towards Maggie had always been different from her attitude towards the two other girls; not that she loved them any the less, but it was different. There was something special about Maggie, something that others didn't have. As the years passed by she sometimes wondered if the way that she had brought her up had contributed to her later problems. Was she responsible for her inability to take things seriously, her reluctance to accept responsibility for her actions, her disastrous relationships with men, and her abandonment of those lovely children? Beryl was not given to asking such hypothetical questions but this particular one did raise its head with a remarkable frequency. There could be little doubt that there was something slightly unusual and different about Maggie. Very often she was lovingly and exhilaratingly different, but she was different nonetheless, for instance, take all this church stuff. That sort of thing had never featured in Arkwright family life and it was unlikely that she had caught the habit from any of her men friends. Still, it seemed to play an increasingly important part in her life and apparently had given her a lot of comfort and support in the years when her health deteriorated, but Beryl still didn't understand it.

Maggie was often teased by the others and called 'the little princess' as she strutted around the house as a child. She somehow always managed to have everyone else running around after her and invariably in any conflict it was her wishes and her will that would prevail. Looking back, it could be said that the whole household was actually built around Maggie and around what she wanted. Not that the others seemed to mind, it was not in any way that their wishes were ignored or neglected, it was just that inevitably Maggie was always central to the family, providing the laughter and the drama, enriching the lives of them all and occasionally, just occasionally, giving a hint of the troubles to come.

For Beryl, Maggie was an extension of her own self in a way that could never have been said of her other daughters. They grew up and grew apart quite naturally, but with Maggie it was as though she had to be forced apart, prised away from her. Such was the joy of the relationship and such was the pain. There had only been two or three occasions when that special bond had been strained or threatened, and each time it had been restored by Maggie turning up with flowers, chocolates and always, always with a hug. Until the break when she went to Spain. That was a separation that Beryl had never been able to come to terms with, it had scarred her permanently and she suspected that it had done the same for Maggie, but they had never talked about it. Never talked about it and yet they had always talked about everything until then.

Beryl sat, oblivious of the words of the priest, unaware of her two daughters sitting on either side of her, lost in a world of grief that seemed to grow more acute as each moment passed. Her eyes stared at the coffin, and as the curtains removed it from her sight, she knew that a curtain had been drawn across her life and she would never be the same again.

Mike was also lost in his thoughts. He still loved Maggie with a love that was beyond his powers of understanding. He found it difficult to reconcile this fact with his acknowledged love for Jenny. He struggled with the idea that he could love them both; one dead and the other alive, one so feckless the other so reliable. This tension was uppermost in his mind when he saw an ant running along the ledge in front of him, on which people placed their hymn books. He stared at the ant. Why should it have life when Maggie's was gone? He looked at the busyness of its running and the focus of his senses was on the ant rather than on the words that were being said. When he could stand it no longer he picked up the hymn book and with a bang squashed the life out of the insect causing the people around him to look at him with surprise. He turned bright red with embarrassment when he realised what he had done.

Within minutes mother and daughters were standing by the door shaking hands with people and exchanging a few words.

'Yes it was a great shame'. 'Yes, she had suffered, death eventually came as a great relief' and 'you will be joining us for a cup of tea, won't you?'

They hugged people they had never met before, they smiled and joked as though this were an everyday occurrence and held back their tears as they embraced Maggie's children.

As they stood there exchanging pleasantries, the hearse was arriving for the Reverend Graham Whittingham's next funeral, his final one for the day, and he braced himself for 'Abide with Me' and 'The Lord's My Shepherd' yet again. The organist was standing outside the rear entrance having a quick cigarette with the superintendent and no doubt having a quiet joke at his expense. He tried to do his best and he knew that his best was not all that exciting; it was just that he didn't know how to do any better.

They made their way to the nearby Granada Hotel where they had booked tea and sandwiches for forty. How many people would actually turn up was hard to guess but in the event, forty was a good estimate and there were plenty of sandwiches and biscuits plus gallons of weak tea or strong coffee. The Granada had seen better days. It was a large imposing Victorian building set in rather nice gardens which had recently been invaded by concrete and tarmac to enlarge the already spacious car park. It was a centre for commercial travellers during the week and for weekend dinner dances and seemed to smell permanently of stale tobacco even when the windows were open, as they were today. Its proximity to the crematorium meant that on most days one or two funeral parties would make their way there for the customary refreshments. There were two large lounges, linked to each other, which meant that it could cope with a hundred or so people, but twenty could be accommodated just as easily without people feeling isolated or crowded. It was a place to wash your face after the tears, to straighten out your clothes, take a big breath and begin to face the world again after the formalities of the funeral were over. The Granada prided itself upon what it called its 'discreet dignity and service'. The staff were used to dealing with funereal grief and met their guests with the appropriate degree of cheerfulness or dignified withdrawal, an art form that staff in many other hotels had yet to master.

People gathered in small groups talking with an intensity which betrayed their unease and uncertainty. The two sets of children, Maggie's and Victoria's, were by the window of the large sitting room and clearly enjoying being in each other's company again despite Victoria's three being a good ten years older than Maggie's. Bill was with Mike and Jenny, deep in conversation about Margaret Thatcher's education policies. Bill, as a self-made man was an ardent supporter of Mrs. Thatcher whilst Mike and Jenny were somewhat to the left in the Labour Party. Victoria was trying to encourage her mother to have something to eat. She had drawn up a few chairs around Beryl's table and they were talking to Mrs. Braithwaite, a neighbour of many years.

"It was a lovely service," said the neighbour without much conviction and Beryl nodded her agreement but said nothing.

"I think that was the same vicar who took our Ethel's mother's funeral," she continued.

This comment about people she had no awareness of, nor any interest in was received by Beryl in total silence but it did not deter Mrs Braithwaite.

"I love that hymn 'abide with me', I think I'll have it when I'm called up higher. Of course Crimond is my favourite, we had it at our wedding, that we did."

On the other side of the room a group of a dozen or more people who all seemed to know each other but no-one else stood talking amongst themselves; they were from Maggie's church. Six or so women came partly to pay their respects to her but primarily because they went to every funeral and to every funeral tea. They could almost be described as professional funeral goers. Few things escaped their notice. They knew which hotel served the best sandwiches (not the Granada), who the priest was who took the service, how fast or slow the hymns were and whether the flowers were up to scratch. Two of them were sisters, they always went with each other and they shared a mutual loathing for each other. Their assistant organist was with them, she could play the piano and was called upon when the organist failed to turn up, so also was the leader of the Mother's Union, an elderly spinster who frowned upon children. The rest were ordinary members of the congregation who seemed to have a genuine fondness for Maggie.

"I was wondering if Father Peter would turn up," said the sometime organist, referring to their former vicar who had suddenly left the parish about a year ago.

"Surely not," said both of the sisters together, "not after all those stories," and they looked at the others with knowing glances.

After everyone had left, Beryl and her family sat down together, tired and drained by the afternoon's event. They had another pot of tea and a fresh plate of sandwiches, chatting together quietly about the people who had turned up and encouraging her to be positive. She needed to grieve, they all knew that, but she also needed to get on with life and that would take considerable willpower. She was to return home with Victoria for a few days but as she was fiercely independent Victoria knew that she would soon be driving north again to take her back to Leeds.

"I've arranged for the flowers to be taken back to the church," said Bill.

"I was talking to a very nice chap and he said that quite often they place the flowers in church so that people can see them the following Sunday. I hadn't realised, but it seems that if we leave them here they are just thrown onto a big heap at the back of the building at the end of the day. I suppose that makes sense, what else could they do with them, I mean they need to start afresh tomorrow don't they? Anyway, it seems such a waste to leave them so someone from the church is going back to the crematorium and picking them up later."

"That's very nice," said Beryl.

"I didn't really see the flowers; I think I was too upset."

"Well you did have a good look at them; I think you'll remember them later. They were lovely mum, really lovely. I think I counted ten or eleven wreaths." Victoria was grateful to Bill for arranging things.

"Ten or eleven? That's a lot." Beryl was gratified to think that so many people had bought them for Maggie.

"How nice of people. I'm sure they were lovely. I'm glad my lilies will go to the church, I hadn't really thought about what happens to them afterwards. Thank you Bill."

It was late evening before Libby eventually arrived home. She went to bed but couldn't sleep. She couldn't rid her mind of the image of Maggie laughing hysterically as they all gathered around the black cat as its small coffin went into the incinerator at the crematorium.

L ibby began to live when she left home for university. This should not be taken as a criticism of the first eighteen years of her life but she looked back on the day that she left home as a defining moment. It was a movement into a new society, a new culture, a new way of looking at things and a new way of understanding herself. Up to that time she had never really thought about who she was and why she was as she was. From the moment she stepped onto the train and headed off in the direction of Birmingham she knew that a whole new world was opening up. It was 1955 and she was almost nineteen years old. No-one in her family had ever been to university before and whilst later it would be commonplace and Victoria's three children would all progress to university without a second thought, when Libby made the move it was not only uncommon it was also regarded as being slightly dangerous. What these dangers were was never spelt out, but she knew that the rest of the family thought she was setting out on a perilous adventure.

She was the same age as the three-penny bit. She remembers being excited when she first discovered that and although everyone else born in 1937 could make the same claim, Libby had always regarded the fact as relating to her alone. It had become a part of the family tradition, this identification of Libby with the oddly shaped coin. She was also born in the same year as the Billy Butlin Holiday Camps began business, but somehow this event passed the Arkwright family by, perhaps because they could never afford to go. No-one ever associated Libby with Butlins in the way that they associated her with three-penny bits.

Perhaps this coin of modest value was well suited to the Arkwright girl because she came from a family of modest means. One of three girls she had been brought up by her widowed mother and could barely remember anything about her father. She knew him, of course from the small black and white photograph showing him with her mother. Beryl was pushing a small baby in a large pram along some seaside promenade and Libby was to learn that she was the little baby and that this was the first picture ever taken of her. She also knew her father from the sepia photograph of him in army uniform, taken shortly before he left home in 1940, never to return. There were no other pictures, no items of daily living that she could look at and say 'that was my fathers', not even any books with his name written in them. It was as though he had never existed apart from the two photographs and the two girls. It was a long time before she discovered that Victoria had a different father and there was even less evidence of his life. She remembered how, when they were small the two of them would sit under the table and weave exotic stories about their absent fathers.

"Oh look, be careful, there's a lion coming towards us."

"Have no fears my beloved, I've dealt with lions before. I have no fear of them, nor of snakes or beetles or even of the dark."

"Oh, you are so brave, how I wish you could stay with us here and defend us in this terrible, wretched and frightening place."

"Yes, yes, that would be perfect, but I have a wife and family at home and I must return to them, they too need me and even now they will be shedding a tear for me for I have been away too long. But I will always remember you Hermione, who could ever forget such ravishing beauty."

At other times their stories focused on the war.

"Zo, tell us Herr Arkwright. Vy are you a spy?"

"I am no spy," he gasped, as he hung from the prison wall, his arms pained by the cruel chains.

"Then how did you know vhere ve vere? How could you save so many men wizout knowing? You blew up the bridge saved the lives of a zousand prisoners and allowed zem all to escape, sacrificing yourself."

"I just did my duty, as any Englishman would."

With those final words he would die and the German guards would say that they had never seen such bravery.

Their mother was always reluctant to give any information and would quickly change the subject whenever they raised it. 'Those days are past' she would say 'there's nothing we can do about them, we must live for now and not feel sorry for ourselves'. It was always the same response and it used to puzzle the girls as they were not feeling sorry for themselves, they just wanted to know, but 'those days are past and there's nothing we can do about them' was just about all the information they ever got. 'Those days are past' would become their favourite phrase when growing up and discussing happening in their past.

L ibby and her sisters had little idea about the world into which their mother was born. It was a society so far removed from their own that it was almost beyond their powers of imagination to think about. As troubles began to mount for them in different ways they would each begin to reflect upon her life. Perhaps it was her powers of endurance that helped to make them the people that they were.

Albert and Lizzie Skinner already had three children when Beryl was born, or five if the two who had died were included, one at birth and the other aged two. She was the youngest of three sisters, soon to be followed by two brothers and another sister. They lived in a four-roomed terrace house; each terrace forming the side of a square, the houses looking outward, whilst in the centre of the square was a shared toilet block, eight lavatories serving the twenty four homes and the hundred and thirty eight people living in them, although that figure was always changing because of deaths and births. Albert worked in a local foundry where the hours were long, the work physically demanding and the pay poor. Lizzie had been in service when they married and had remained so until the first of their many children came along. Whenever possible she earned a little extra money taking in washing from some of the larger houses nearby, but the demand was not great and, if the truth be told, she didn't really have the time or energy to do much more than care for the family, make their clothes and feed their bodies.

Albert was a good father and although he could be strict the children were genuinely fond of him, none more so than Beryl with whom he seemed to have established a particularly strong rapport. She would run to meet him as he returned home at the end of the day, and although tired and dirty, he would hoist her high above his head and bring her home sitting on his shoulders and squealing with delight. There would be family expeditions to the woods, where Albert would often trap a rabbit or two and then Lizzie would make a wonderful stew which they consumed with delight and speed. They would go down to the river and bathe and in the summer they would stretch out on the grass and soak up the sunlight and the warmth, rare commodities during the long winter months. Beryl would look back on those days with a sense of balmy nostalgia, remembering the warmth and not the cold, the light and not the darkness, the laughter and the times of happiness rather than the times of sorrow, especially when an older sister died of pneumonia and a younger brother drowned. The times of sadness could be recalled, but basically when Beryl thought about her childhood she remembered her father; his rugged strength and his great tenderness towards her, it was always her father that she remembered. Even when she alone was left many years later, all the others having died, it was her father who filled her memories, long before the images of her mother, her sisters or brothers emerged from the distant past. Late in life, when she lay in a nursing home, she often thought that he was there, at the end of her bed, standing smiling and beckoning her to get up and go over to him. This is precisely what she eventually did do in 1992, fourteen years after the death of her youngest daughter Maggie had so affected her and left her in a state of prolonged and numbed bereavement. She got out of her bed, held out her arms towards him as he smiled and called her over. When she was discovered much later, she was dead, but she had a beatific smile on her face. After years of struggle she had found peace.

The turmoil that Beryl was born into mounted up in her early years as conflict with Germany became inevitable. Albert and Lizzie would discuss the worsening situation night by night as they sat in front of the fire which provided both heat and light in the long winter evenings.

"George's two lads have volunteered," Albert passed on the news to Lizzie and watched her face as she absorbed it. "He says that before long everyone will be going. Every day at the foundry there's news of people leaving, I'm not sure how we'll manage if many more go."

"Well just you make sure that you stay there, they need your work, it's no good everyone going off to fight and leaving no-one behind to run everything. Anyway, your work's important, what would the army do if all the foundries stopped working?"

Lizzie was quick to seize upon any argument that served to divert Albert's thought from possible volunteering.

"Aye, that's true enough Lizzie. We can't all be going off. Who would do the work? Still, it's a difficult thing this war, I mean it's something that we've got to win and we won't win it unless men enlist."

"Yes, but don't you go getting wild ideas in your head Albert Skinner, you've a house full of bairns who need you around. Let them go to war as haven't got your sort of responsibilities."

Young men were volunteering for the army all around them. They were spurred on by a sense of adventure, by the opportunity to escape from the confines of their working and living environment and by a call to patriotism that was probably as unfounded as it was ill-considered. Patriotism became the order of the day and posters were displayed on all the bill-boards about the town and in shops and post offices. It was all very confusing to Albert and Lizzie. They were afraid of what was happening, they didn't understand the subtleties of European politics, but they did have an inbuilt sense of what was right and what was wrong and it did seem to them that Britain was right and Germany was wrong. Beyond that, it was difficult to know what to believe. They were anxious to maintain some security for their family, and to gain a little more prosperity, but how those objectives could be achieved was beyond their fathoming. What they didn't want though, was for the comforts that they had, and in reality these were small enough, to be taken from them. It was important to stand and fight to retain their freedom argued Albert, but Lizzie wasn't so sure that she had much freedom to defend. A new child each year for the past nine years had left her exhausted, but she maintained the home, fed her family and slept at night, although not for long periods since there were usually one or two of the babies awake. It was different in the summer when they could go out into the fields and the woods, but for the long winter months she was more aware of the cold and the damp than of any freedoms which needed to be defended. Hunger, poor health, illiteracy, poverty and a fear of unemployment hung over their home like a constant cloud, dark and menacing, blocking out the possibilities of brightness. Lizzie didn't say much but she feared greatly. She feared for Albert, she feared for the children and she wondered what would become of them all if the war persisted. But persist it did and as the war progressed more and more single men from the locality volunteered for action. They would leave their street cheered on by those who remained behind. They left as heroes, many never to return.

"Did you hear that Lloyd George is coming to the Corn Exchange next week?"

Albert was sitting by the fire drinking a mug of tea. It was the only time of relaxation he ever seemed to get. He had finished his meal, the children were in bed, and he sat each evening and reflected on his life and his work, and occasionally on his wife and children. "I thought I might go and hear him. They say that he's a fine speaker and I think we need to hear from men like him just what's happening in the war, there are so many conflicting stories. If anyone can tell us about it, it will be him."

Lizzie felt an involuntary shudder go through her body, like some kind of premonition.

"Now Albert, please don't get talked into going to meetings. I know he's been the Prime Minister but why should he be coming to a place like this? It seems a strange thing for him to do, unless he's trying to whip up enthusiasm for the war."

Despite Lizzie's attempts to dissuade him, Albert and many of his colleagues at work went to hear Lloyd George. They returned home deeply impressed. He spoke with a passion that roused them, he was eloquent, forceful and convincing. Those who were more perceptive than Albert and his workmates were also more cautious and sceptical. They had heard about the power of his rhetoric and they were more critical of his assessment of the situation. They thought his arguments commonplace and lacking in conviction and they were worried by his ability to draw passionate response from those who listened. For men such as Albert, Lloyd George held out a noble and honourable challenge and he returned home knowing that his duty as an Englishman and as a father, was to enlist and join with the thousands of others who were determined to ensure that right would prevail and the values of his society should be maintained and preserved. Values which had assigned him to a life just above the poverty level, which denied his wife the right to vote and which seemed determined to ensure that his children would follow in his stead as second class citizens working, if they were lucky enough to secure and keep a job, to maintain their place near the bottom of the social hierarchy. Albert returned home convinced that it was his duty to volunteer.

"How can you do such a thing? What about the children? What about me?" Lizzie was distraught, her worst fears were being realised.

"But can't you see it's for their sake that I need to go? I don't want you to suffer; I want a better life for you and for them. It's my duty Lizzie, can't you see that I could never live with myself if I didn't enlist and do what I could to safeguard my country. That's why I'm doing it. It's for you and the bairns."

It was his basic goodness which led him to such a conclusion, and Lizzie damned the day when he was born with such a sense of moral responsibility. Her tears proved no opposition for the sense of righteous duty that had taken seed within him and within a matter of days he had signed up. It was some comfort, but not very much, for Lizzie to learn that so had most of the men in the neighbourhood. There was a new sense of camaraderie developing for the men as they looked ahead to the adventures that lay before them. But for Lizzie and for most of the other women there was a deep sense of foreboding, a fear which was impossible to articulate but which dried out their very souls. She reached the stage where she could cry no more and with a deep sense of sorrow she watched as Albert and the other men began to adapt to life in the army.

The last night that he was home Lizzie cooked his favourite meal and watched as he spent more time than usual with the children. He helped to put them to bed, something he had rarely done before and she watched silently as he spent time looking at each one of them as they fell asleep. It was difficult to speak about what was in their hearts and minds as they held each other closely that final night. Albert lovingly chided Lizzie for being so silly for being so upset.

"Now Lizzie, don't get so het up. I won't be gone for long and then when I get home we'll have a better and a safer future; something for us to look forward to, for you and me and the bairns."

"How can I not be upset?" complained Lizzie. "How are we going to manage without you? How will the little ones fare? And what about you Albert? You've never done anything like this before. You're not a soldier, you're a foundry man, how will you cope? And in any case, how can I think about you going and killing people, that's not you Albert, that's not the sort of man that you are."

"I'll cope right enough and so will you, now don't be getting so upset. I won't be gone long. There's lots of us going and we should soon teach them a lesson they won't forget and then we'll be back. Honest, I'll be back before you've realised that I've gone. And as for killing people, well I'll only get nasty if they get nasty with us. In any case, I probably won't be anywhere near the fighting."

He reminded her how important it was that the children should be cared for, he promised to write and assured her that all would be well. In the end, through sheer exhaustion he fell asleep, but not before Lizzie had noticed quiet tears trickling down his cheeks as he slipped into what would prove to be a restless and disturbed night.

Morning came and it was an early start. The uniform was proudly donned and the neighbours all came to their doorways to look at Albert and wish him well. The children, unsure what all the fuss was about, stood by slightly perplexed, but were happy to join with all the others as they went out into the town centre and saw vast numbers of the men of the town line up for duty, for King and country. Albert looked ahead proudly as he set off and seeing Beryl in the waving crowd, he gave her a wink and a special smile, a smile that Beryl remembered to her dying day. Albert who had never been more than twenty miles away from the place where he was born was now en route for France and, unwittingly, for the battle of the Somme.

Nothing could have prepared him for what he was to experience. He was to find friendship and trust amongst men that he had never known before. Men like Albert usually kept their feelings to themselves. He was to discover depths of endurance and courage in himself that he could never have imagined and he was to witness a brutality and a senselessness that went beyond anything that even the concept of blasphemy could ever conjure up. He was to discover the best of things and the worst of things and the worst would triumph over the very best. If he had been told about what he would discover he would never have believed what was said. If he had believed what was said he would never have enlisted. After a brief settling-in period near the front line Albert's company moved forward in early July. Wounded men and frightened prisoners met them coming the other way, as they marched on. What surprised him most and he was totally unprepared for it, was the number of dead horses and mules; mutilated, emaciated, rotting in the fields and by the roadside. He was expecting to see corpses, he had seen a number already although not on such a vast scale, but had not reckoned on the animals. It seemed strange to him, as he marched on, that he should be more upset by the sight of the dead horses than of the dead soldiers. The Germans had been using tear gas shells and they had to march through great patches of mist which attacked their throats and eyes. It was a journey into hell and they had not yet reached their destination. They went through a wood and it seemed as though not a single tree had been left unscathed and everywhere there were bodies. English bodies and German bodies bizarrely mixed up and left to rot together, almost as friends, whilst their luckier comrades had made it back to base, ready to fight-on on some later day, in the hope of moving the front line forward a matter of yards. They marched and marched and had still further to go. Albert was tired, his legs ached, his feet hurt and he was uncomfortable in his uniform. He sometimes felt faint and sickly, he wanted to stop and rest but they marched on. He felt a physical wreck and he hadn't even started fighting.

He exchanged his small, damp and overcrowded house in England for an even smaller, drenched, sodden, stinking and overcrowded trench somewhere in France. "Welcome home" were the first words that greeted him as he settled into his allotted space. The wonder was that it did become a sort of home, a place of relative security in a totally alien and insecure environment. A place where there were men who would be willing to die for you a moment or two after cursing you to the outer limits of existence. A place where a cigarette became a feast, and a few moments of shallow, uninterrupted sleep became the equivalent of a holiday.

It was a good thing that Albert was no great writer. Not only had he always been unable to acknowledge and express his emotions without great difficulty, he was also unable to communicate them in writing. It was a sign of their determination to better themselves that both Albert and Lizzie had learned to read and write but his letters home conveyed nothing of the hell that he was experiencing. That was a comfort to Lizzie who had heard that some of the men were living in unimaginable conditions. He sent his love to them all, he thought of them constantly and he looked forward to the time when the guns would stop and he would be back home playing once again in the woods with them all. But even as he wrote such words he wondered whether he would ever be able to go into a wood again without seeing the dead lying all around. Day turned into night, night turned into day, days turned into weeks and weeks turned into months. It seemed to rain relentlessly, turning the trenches into quagmires. The noise was intolerable and the silence was even worse. Deep and surprising friendships were established over a mug of tea only to be terminated by a sniper's bullet or by another bombardment causing total mayhem, confusion, pain, suffering and carnage. Albert lost count of the number of bodies he had pulled across the muddy fields, lost count of the number of deaths he had witnessed, lost count of the number of times he had gone 'over the top' fearing for life and limb. He was numbed, his conscience was anaesthetised, he had virtually stopped thinking and was becoming an automaton, a cog in some vast unyielding enterprise, a number, a statistic. It was a statistic, an official statistic, that he became the day the German mortar blew him into the air and left him impaled on the rounds of barbed wire that were spread out in front of the German trenches.

It was almost a year before Lizzie discovered how Albert died. One Sunday afternoon there was a knock at the door and standing there was a young man, a young man with the eyes of someone much older. He had a limp and was of an extremely nervous disposition.

"Excuse me, but are you Mrs Skinner, Albert's wife, or rather widow I should say?"

Lizzie nodded and wondered who this person was and what he could possibly want with her. She was suspicious; the years of want and struggle, particularly this last year had taken their toll. Children emerged from the shadows and Beryl, now a seven year old, stood and clutched her mother's long skirt.

"Pardon me dropping in on you like this, but well, you see, I promised Albert that if anything happened to him I would search you out and let you know how much he talked about you." He glanced down, "You must be Beryl, or am I mistaken?" Beryl was embarrassed that a stranger should know her name and she looked up into her mother's face enquiringly. "Forgive me; I've not introduced myself, have I? I'm Neville and me and Albert sort of palled up and spent a lot of time together. Then, after he copped it I was hit myself and I've been in hospital for months, but as soon as I could I've kept my promise and here I am. I'm sorry Lizzie – is it alright if I call you Lizzie, it don't seem right saying Mrs Skinner when I've always sort of known you as Lizzie?"

Lizzie smiled, feeling grateful to this man who had suddenly turned up from goodness knows where. She invited him in and they sat and talked for several hours. He willingly accepted sharing a simple meal with them and spent time with the children, playing and making them laugh. It was from Neville that Lizzie learned about life in the trenches, the horror, the enormity of the suffering and the danger. She learned about the bloodshed and the injuries that the men sustained. She learned about the rain and the sludge, the mud and the problems they had with keeping the walls of the trenches intact. She learned about the rats and how they came and ate the eyes and the livers of the corpses as they lay in the trenches. Brown rats and black rats, but it was the brown ones that grew and grew until they were the size of cats. She learned about the lice, the nits and the outbreaks of trench fever. She wanted to know, she was desperate to know what it was really like. Slowly but surely she built up a picture of Albert's life since the day he marched off with all the others, proud to be doing his duty and walking off to build a better world for her and the children.

She wanted to know how they fought from the trenches and Neville explained how word would get passed down the line – 'Watch out, Fritz is on the move'.

"So what happened? What did you do?" Lizzie was anxious to understand what it must have been like for Albert.

"Well sometimes, we just kept our heads down low and did nothing, just hoping that they would go away. There was a strong temptation to climb up and have a look over the top of the trench, but when you've seen your mate have his head blown off for doing that, when you've been splattered with his blood... Oh, it was terrible, it really was. I shouldn't be telling you all this. I don't want to remember it, how I long to forget it, but when I go to sleep it's there, it won't go away and I wake up screaming and covered in sweat. Sorry Lizzie, I shouldn't be telling you all this."

"Of course you should Neville, can't you see that I need to know it. I want to know what it was like for Albert. Knowing it somehow brings him closer to me, can't you see that?"

Neville nodded. Yes, it made sense to him but he still wasn't sure if he was doing the right thing. There are some things that should remain hidden and he wasn't sure if he was telling all this to Lizzie for her sake or for his. He could not escape his memories; they haunted him night and day. Perhaps telling Lizzie was an attempt to offload them onto someone else, but all that happened was that they returned with the additional burden of her pain and tears. He felt himself trapped and damned, whether he spoke about his experiences or not.

There was a long pause. Neville seemed a long way away, Lizzie was having difficulty coping with all this new information.

"Tell me about when you had to attack. What did you say – 'going over the top'? How did that happen? You must tell me, I need to know how it was for Albert, I've thought about it so often but have no idea what happened, I just think hard and harder, but can never come up with anything. Tell me about it, please Neville, tell me."

She moved closer to him and looked straight into his face. Neville could not bear the intensity of her questioning and he looked down at the ground, his hands forever active, rubbing against each other. It was a long time before he spoke.

"We all got ready, helmets, guns, boots... everything that we needed. We all gathered together right along the trench, three, four five or six deep. Then we waited, I don't know how long we waited but it seemed an eternity. We waited, sometimes there was an eerie silence, it was as though the whole of life had stopped. No guns, no bombs, nothing, just quietness. Once or twice one of the blokes would start crying, they were soon shut up, you can't cope with that when you're about to go over. Then suddenly the platoon officer would blow his whistle and he'd clamber over the top of the trench, often with a cigarette in his mouth and we would all follow. We climbed out and ran, we ran like bloody hell though we often didn't really know where we were running to, we just ran. Then, as we ran, the guns would explode, or the field would have been mined and we just blew up. Oh Lizzie, it was terrible, terrible."

Tears filled his eyes and he began to shiver. Lizzie leaned across and held his hands.

"Just take your time, take your time, there's no hurry. Shall I get you something to drink?"

"We lost so many men, Oh God they were just blown up. It was unbelievable, one moment he was your mate and the next moment there was a bloody big bang and he wasn't there any more... So many men were lost, good men, brave men. They didn't deserve to die... and I didn't deserve to live either. Why am I here and the others aren't? Oh God, I feel so guilty. I feel as though somehow it's my fault, I should have saved them and I didn't know how to. Honest Lizzie, I would have done if I'd known how to, but I didn't."

"Don't blame yourself; I'm sure you did everything you could. You're a good man Neville, look how you've come to search me out, that's a good thing to do. You wouldn't have done that if you weren't a good man. You would have saved them if you could, no-one is blaming you, no-one. And anyway, I'm glad that you came home alive or how else would I have known about Albert?"

He spoke with tenderness about his friends and it was clear that something deep and extremely important had taken place to bond these men together, shared experiences which they alone could understand. He spoke about many of the officers with pride and admiration, but he was also angry. He was angry about the tactics, angry about the so-called leaders, angry about the politicians. There was a huge reservoir of anger within him that welled up when he spoke.

"There was so much waste," he said, "so much waste of talent, waste of lives, waste of everything that was good and wholesome and honest. I can't tell you how good some of those men were and they died, they all died, and for what? Was it worth all the sacrifice? Was it worth it?"

"Yes, yes, it was worth it. How could we live with ourselves if we didn't believe that? I'm sure Albert believed it was worth it, he was so proud you know, going off to fight for a better life for me and the bairns. And look, now the war's over, the fighting has stopped. They didn't die in vain Neville, they didn't. Look at me, look at me, they didn't die in vain."

Neville was unable to look Lizzie in the face. He knew that it was important that she believed that it was all worthwhile, but he didn't. No, he had long ago reached the conclusion that it was all in vain, a waste, a massive waste. But the generals and the politicians weren't wasted. No, they received medals and decorations and ate with Lords and Ladies, but his mates, where were they? They were left in the fields, most of them blown to smithereens.

Then he told her the story of William Stones, a miner from County Durham whom he and Albert had met in September. He was small, a mere five feet two inches tall and weighing nine stone. Married, with two daughters he was deemed to be too frail when he first volunteered but as the number of casualties grew, so the criteria for acceptance were relaxed. Bill was delighted to get into uniform and couldn't wait to be posted to the front so that he could play his part in what he believed to be an honourable and just war. He was a brave man and Neville recounted some of his heroic actions. He was promoted twice, to Corporal and then to Lance Sergeant. One night in November he and a friend were ambushed and his friend was shot and killed. Bill ran for his life, dodging a hail of bullets. He didn't know where he was and he was almost paralytic with fear when he was found, a gibbering wreck of a man. Neville's eyes glazed over with concern and with anger as he described to Lizzie how Bill was taken away and tried by court martial, being found guilty of 'casting away arms in the presence of the enemy'.

Lizzie listened, not saying a single word. She saw that there was a compulsion within Neville that was driving him on. He was oblivious of her, of where he was, he was living in a trance, he was somewhere on the battle-field in a world that she could never really imagine, despite all that he had told her.

"They took him away and shot him, Lizzie, his own people took him away and shot him. After all that he'd done, after all that he suffered, his own people took him away and shot him. These are the people who are running the war; these are the people for whom we are losing our limbs, our sanity and our lives. Our own people took away this slip of a lad, who had volunteered to fight for his country, and they shot him. It wasn't even the German's who shot him, it was our own people."

It was late into the evening when he explained to Lizzie how Albert had saved his life. Risking his own life Albert had climbed out of the trench, crawled on his belly some two hundred yards to where Neville lay wounded and pulled him back, slowly but surely, with enemy fire all around. He was wounded, bleeding badly when Albert reached him but not badly enough to be sent home. He had to stay and continue fighting after a couple of days when they had managed to bind him up and stop the bleeding. He was then ready for the next call to go over the top. Tears filled his eyes and Lizzie wondered if he would be able to continue.

After a long silence he told her how Albert had died. Neville was exhausted; he had talked about the war for the first time since he was invalided home. No-one else had heard his story and today he was re-living those days and weeks. He was experiencing once again the pain, the sadness, the anger and the sheer futility of it all. He broke down in tears, shaking all over. Lizzie went over to him and held him, talking quietly and gently she slowly calmed away the shaking. The tears flowed, from her as well as from Neville, and they clung to each other united in grief. For a long time neither of them spoke, they wept and held each other tightly. It was not sensuous, it was not unfaithful, it was not wayward, their night together was a time of healing and restoration for both of them. Neville left the following morning and Lizzie never saw him again. It was the following spring that Beryl's young brother Albert Neville was born and Lizzie always referred to him as God's parting gift from her brave and dearly loved husband.

Many years later Libby was to search out her grandfather's name on the civic war memorial. It had been erected in a large private cemetery which had been closed to new burials for many years now and the only people who visited the site now were middle aged women walking their dogs, young people finding a quiet spot to inject themselves and others of an indeterminate age who stretched out on the gravestones to sleep off their alcohol induced stupors.

B eryl learned two things as she grew up. She learned that her father Albert, killed on the Somme, was a hero and she learned that all would be well if the family stayed together. This gave her a secure foundation in a world that was changing very quickly. She never doubted that she was loved; she never doubted that things would not turn out alright and she never doubted that she would not live forever. She was right on the first count, many people would question whether she was right on the second and she was definitely wrong on the third. But when she was young, blossoming into a young woman, life seemed so very exciting and she was almost intoxicated by all the possibilities that were opening up for her.

She discovered dancing. It was a moment of great surprise and utter joy. She had natural rhythm, the beat and movement seemed to spring from her innermost being, she just loved it. When the Charleston became the rage, Beryl was supreme and people would stop their own dancing just to look at her. She was not the prettiest girl around but she was certainly the most attractive. She had an innate love for life, an easy and relaxed manner with other people and although she was not rich in monetary terms she was a millionaire in so many of the things that money was unable to buy. Lizzie watched her daughter growing up with pride, admiration and perhaps even with a little envy and she often thought how Albert would have delighted his favourite child. What was so admirable about Beryl was that she was totally unaware of the fact that she was attractive and a joy to be with. There was a degree of naivety about her which merely added to the overall sense of wholeness and joyfulness that exuded from her and filled her surroundings.

At home she was a second mother to the children who came after her and an adored sister to those who came before. In many ways the house revolved around her, not in any self-centred way but rather in the way that light and happiness seemed to radiate from wherever she was and when she moved away it was as though the sun had temporarily gone behind a cloud.

Christmas 1927 was very special. A blizzard hit Britain and snow fell at Christmas making the outlook almost magical. Two days later Beryl and a group of friends went to a local dance and soon after they arrived a young man, tall, smiling and neatly dressed, walked across the hall straight up to Beryl. He gave a small bow to her to which she responded with the sweetest of smiles and said: "I noticed you as soon as you walked in. You are the most beautiful girl in the hall and I would be honoured if you would have this next dance with me."

Beryl was lost for words, not only did she have the next dance with him, but practically every other dance that evening. She had never met anyone like George before. He was serious beyond his years but with a flash of humour and his face would suddenly light up when something amused him and his laughter was infectious. For George it was love at first sight, but Beryl was far from sure. She liked him, of that there was no doubt, but she was not yet eighteen and was not looking for a steady boyfriend, she had too many other friends and was reluctant to focus on just one person. And yet, she was never happier than when she was with George, never more content than when walking out with him. To begin with the rest of the family teased her mercilessly and Lizzie was apprehensive, but as time passed George became an accepted part of the family.

He was a few years older than her, not many, but enough for him to know that this friendship was something special and, in his eyes, long-term. He lived at home with his mother, who worked in a shop, and his father who was now unable to work having suffered greatly in the war. Blind and with one leg amputated, George's father took a special liking to Beryl and often talked to her about his experiences. She liked this because it made her feel closer to her own father and slowly, over the months, a special bond built up between them. George used to claim that he was jealous, that he was sure she was only going out with him so that she could visit his father. But it was friendly banter, his father provided the father that she had lost and she gave him the daughter that he had always longed for.

George worked in a local factory; he was a foreman and confessed to Beryl that he had ambitions of moving up in management. He had seen the damage that the General Strike had done within the community and was saddened by the antagonism and animosity which had grown between the two sides of industry and he used to talk excitedly about his ideas for bringing workers and management together, so that they could discuss their concerns without fear and see if it was possible to find a way forward which was to everyone's advantage. As time went by it was clear to everyone that she and George were made for each other but it took her quite a long time to reach that conclusion.

He was patient. He was also kind, generous and in love. She knew all that of course but what she didn't know was whether she was in love with him. She talked to her mother a great deal about it and hardly ever a word about it to her older sisters and yet they were forever falling in and out of love and could be said to have been experts in the matter. Lizzie said that the time would come when she would know, beyond a shadow of a doubt, whether she wanted to marry George or not. Better not to rush things, she counselled, but also not to fight against fate. Lizzie was a great believer in fate.

A few months had passed since George last asked Beryl to marry him, it was the fourth time he had asked her and the fourth time she had declined. One bright Sunday afternoon they walked over the fields and alongside a stream towards a small wood.

"That wood always reminds me of my dad," confided Beryl.

"We used to go there and play. He used to chase me through the trees and when he caught me he would lift me up, high in the air and swing me round and round."

Her eyes clouded over and George could see that she was re-living those childhood memories.

"He must have been a good man, to spend time playing with his children."

"He was, he was a marvellous man, and I still miss him even though he's been dead for so long. I think I was his favourite though, I'm not sure if the others remember him in the same way that I do."

She looked at George and smiled.

"He was quite right to favour you," George whispered. "He could clearly see something special in you, in the same way that I can."

"Oh George, don't be so serious! Anyway, if you want me you will just have to catch me," and with that Beryl was running off into the wood, darting around the trees and shouting out with pleasure. George chased her, he was amazed at how nimble she was and how difficult to catch. It was several minutes before he caught up with her and when he did he lifted her off her feet and swirled her round in the air. They fell to the ground, exhausted and full of laughter. George turned to her, caught hold of her hand and for the fifth time asked her to marry him.

"Please, please say that you will. I won't take 'no' for an answer, I'll pursue you until you agree or until I die and I don't intend dying for a very long time, so you had better agree quickly and stop running."

"Oh George, you're so sweet. Sometimes you remind me of my dad, he would say things like that, all very serious just after we'd been laughing, you are an absolute treasure."

"But Beryl, that's not enough, I don't want flattery and believe me, I am flattered when you say that I remind you of your father, but I want your love, I want you to marry me."

Beryl smiled, she took his hand to her lips and kissed it gently.

"Yes George, I'll marry you, I can't run away from you forever can I? But I can try."

With that, she leaped up and ran through the woods again, shouting out with joy. George ran after her and then ran with her; eventually they came to a stop and embraced.

"Beryl, you have made me the happiest man in the world."

George's eyes were full of tears and Beryl was quite amazed by the enormity of what she had just agreed to. They held hands and walked slowly home, along the path that Albert used when he carried her home on his shoulders.

They moved into George's parent's home, occupying the back bedroom. It made more sense this way as they had extra room and Lizzie's small home was already overcrowded; nonetheless it was a difficult transition and she missed the noise and banter of her family. She visited them most days and was always reluctant to make the short return journey to her new home when the time came. Whether becoming pregnant made the situation better or worse was difficult to tell. Beryl needed more time to rest, she wasn't finding it an easy experience, and she craved for the support and comfort of her mother even more.

Victoria was born in the autumn, named after Queen Victoria. Never was a child more welcomed. George was ecstatic about his daughter and Beryl was profoundly moved by the whole experience. It was as though there had never been a baby quite like Victoria before, every movement was analysed and celebrated, every gesture was imbued with significance and meaning, every little development was heralded as unbelievable and evidence of superior intelligence and every little cough or cry was reflected upon in case it was a portent of approaching doom. Victoria was the centre of attraction of everyone around her and would not experience this again until her final days.

This scene of domestic bliss and contentment was rudely shattered one afternoon when a young lad suddenly banged mercilessly on Lizzie's door.

"Goodness me, whatever is the matter," cried out Lizzie as she hurried to the door, "the baby will be woken by all this noise and then we won't be able to get her back to sleep again for ages."

She opened the door and saw a young boy, about eight years old, scruffy, dirty and with a sweaty face. Beryl recognised him as she looked over her mother's shoulder at the door; he was one of the young tear-aways who lived next door to her at George's parent's home.

"Me mam says you've to get back home straight away," panted the boy, "there's been an accident at the factory."

The colour drained away from Beryl's face and she felt as though she had been thumped in the stomach by an icy fist.

"Whatever's happened?" she asked frantically, "what sort of accident?"

"I don't know Mrs." said the young lad, "I was just told to run as fast as I could and tell you to come home."

Beryl scooped up all her belongings, dumped them in the pram alongside the baby and accompanied by young Albert, her brother, she ran down the street and across the two main roads before reaching her home. George's mother was standing at the door waiting for her, her face streaming with tears. She grabbed hold of Beryl and clutched her as though she might never let her go again.

"Oh my love, thank God you've come. There's been an explosion at the factory, George has been injured, badly, he's been killed."

Beryl let out a stifled scream and rushed into the house. Albert stood by, feeling both awkward and intruding but also necessary as he lifted Victoria from the pram and cuddled her. George's mother turned to him, seeking consolation and comfort and he was embarrassed, not knowing what to say.

That evening Beryl returned home to Lizzie, never to stay the night again in the house which had been her home for almost a year, until George's parents themselves died. She took to her bed and Lizzie nursed her, cared for the baby and ensured that the rest of the family was supportive and understanding. Lizzie then went round to visit George's parents to discover what had happened and to plan, with them, some strategy for survival as the world collapsed in on them all.

In many ways Beryl's life went into reverse after George died. She now stayed with her mother but every day would take Victoria to visit George's parents. His death lay heavily upon them though and they were never to recover from the shock and their grief. It was his father who crumpled first, unable to face yet one more death in a life that had become top heavy with death. He lived for Beryl's visits and loved holding the baby although his blindness prevented him from seeing her, but his spirit had gone. Within a year he too had died and George's mother lost all appetite for living although she was to struggle on for another two years. Beryl was dutiful in her visiting although for much of the time she lived as in a dream, not remembering much, not responding to much, just going through the motions. This young woman, who had been such a radiant star, bringing life and laughter to every situation and warming the hearts of all whom she met, had withered emotionally and often seemed unable to focus upon people or to hear what they were saying. It was as though she no longer belonged to the world and if it hadn't been for the presence of Victoria she would almost certainly have melted away into non-existence. The baby to whom she had given life now ensured that her life too should continue. They were locked together in mutual need.

She took to walking a great deal, through the woods that she used to explore with her father, along the paths that she used to roam with George. Sometimes she walked with a purpose, striding out as if determined to reach a defined destination, though she had no idea what this destination might be. At other times she walked slowly, almost in a trance, oblivious of other people whom she might meet along the way. She seemed to lose all sense of time, sometimes going out as dawn broke and not returning until the afternoon, at other times not setting out until the evening. There seemed to be no reason or logic to her activities. Victoria accompanied her wherever and whenever she went. Lizzie was frantic with worry, the others tried to interest her in things that they were doing or divert her attention by pointing out people and places beyond the confines of their home but Beryl had withdrawn into an inner world of grief from which there appeared to be no escape. Her marriage seemed too brief to remember, the future too enormous to contemplate, there was only the present moment and that had to be endured.

It is difficult to know just when precisely she began to recover. Perhaps it was when more sorrow was added to the heart that was already grief stricken to breaking point. George's mother had a stroke whilst hanging out the washing and died a few days later. Beryl visited her every day, sitting by her bedside whilst Victoria played by her side. They did not speak much, George's mother unable to and Deryl lacking any desire to. In her will George's mother left everything to Beryl. The small house, in which she had lived her year of married life and the small savings that they had accumulated over the years did not amount to very much but such an inheritance held out to Beryl the possibility of independence and the chance to create a new life for herself and Victoria. The new house served as a kind of overspill for the old house, a place where Lizzie's other children could find a bed or create some personal space. After all these years Beryl could now offer something, she could once again be a giver rather than a taker and slowly, very slowly, she seemed to emerge from the depression that her grief had triggered.

It was like the way that snow melts when spring is in the air. It was like the way that green shoots spring out of barren earth after a long winter. It was like a flower opening out from a tightly closed bud. It was the re-birth of Beryl. She had been lost to them all for the best part of three years. She was never to regain the joyful exuberance of her earlier years, but what was emerging was a young mother, mature beyond her years, who was slowly and surely creating a home not only for her child but also for her mother, worn down by hardship and financial insecurity. Lizzie was tired from the years of raising her family without the support of a husband and she was tired, almost exhausted, by the additional anxiety that Beryl's situation had brought in the last few years.

Beryl went back to work a few months later, leaving Victoria with Lizzie. She enjoyed it, she was beginning to feel at ease with people again and she came home in the evening with all the office gossip and with a view of the world that was a breath of fresh air for Lizzie.

One evening when she returned home there was clearly something on her mind; she seemed preoccupied as though troubled by something that must have cropped up at work. It was late into the evening before Lizzie broached the subject.

"Is everything alright my love? You seem a bit distant, as though something is bothering you."

"No, I'm fine thanks mum, no, there's nothing troubling me. Well, not really, and it's not troubling me, it's just that I've got a bit of a problem, that's all."

"Well are you going to tell me about it or would you rather that I left you alone? I don't want to pry, you've got your own life to live, but if it's anything you want to talk about then just carry on. A problem shared is a problem halved, isn't that what they say?"

"Oh, it's nothing really," replied Beryl, "it's just this man at work."

"Is he giving you trouble? Isn't there someone you can complain to?"

"No, it's nothing like that. It's just that... Well, you see... he's asked me out and I don't know what to say."

"Well that's wonderful," exclaimed Lizzie, "is he nice?"

"Yes, I suppose he is. I've had a feeling that he's been looking at me for several weeks now, I suppose I was quite flattered really, but then this afternoon he came over to me and suggested that we might go out for a walk on Sunday afternoon."

"That's lovely for you," said Lizzie, "of course you should go, it'll take you out of yourself for a bit, give you something to look forward to. You need some time with people your own age, don't worry about us, I'll look after Victoria. But here I am, getting ahead of myself, what did you say to him?"

"I said that I didn't think that was possible as I have my little girl to look after and then he said he knew that, that was why he suggested going for a walk as I could bring her with me. That took me by surprise, I thought when he knew I had Victoria he would run a mile."

"So what did you say then?"

"I said that I would let him know tomorrow. You see, I just don't know what to say or what to do. It's come as a complete surprise to me and I don't think I ought to be getting into things like that, with George only being dead such a short time."

Lizzie was unsure how to proceed. This chance for Beryl was the answer to prayer as far as she was concerned. She had longed, through all those hard years of Beryl's depression, for there to be the possibility that her life might be re-created and that she might, at some stage, find another husband. She didn't want to presume too much, too quickly, but her looks may have betrayed her inner feelings a little.

"Oh, I know you think this is just wonderful, but just remember, you didn't go off on dates after dad was killed did you?"

"Don't be so silly," replied Lizzie, "that was entirely different. I was much older than you are now and I had seven children and there was a war on. You can't compare our situations at all."

"But you can," argued Beryl. "You loved dad and when he wasn't there anymore you didn't rush out to find someone else to take his place did you? The same thing applies to me and I'm not rushing out after someone else."

"Who says anything about rushing out? You have been asked to go for a walk with what seems to be a nice young man – that's all. He's not asking you to marry him, for God's sake. Don't be so foolish, accept the offer and see if you enjoy it. Anyway, a walk would do you good, you don't get enough fresh air. And another thing, it's well over three years since George was killed and in all that time you've never once been out with any of your friends, with anyone your own age. You need some younger company my love, honestly and truly you do."

Beryl frowned and said she would see what she felt like in the morning, but she knew that she was going to say 'yes'. What she hadn't told her mother was that she had noticed him soon after she began working in the office and had immediately taken hold of herself and put all thoughts of any sort of friendship out of her mind. Well, she had tried to, but clearly without much success.

Sunday's walk with Frank and Victoria was the prelude for another walk the following week. The next week there was a walk without Victoria and the week after that the walk finished with him coming home and having tea with Lizzie. He was tall, a good six inches taller than Beryl, with dark curly hair. He had an easy, approachable manner and was extremely funny, with an endless stream of jokes. It was clear from the start that they had something special in their relationship. Beryl used to reflect that she had loved George, but it had taken her a long time to discover that love and it was a quiet, undemonstrative sort of love. With Frank it was different. She didn't yet know if it was love, but she certainly enjoyed his company, was amused by his conversation, felt completely at home with his family and knew that he had brought something into her life that had been lacking for a very long time. He seemed to adore Victoria and she him and Lizzie felt that Beryl was happier than she had seen her for years, since before George even.

On May 6th 1935 Beryl and Frank were married. It was the same day as the King and Queen celebrated their Silver Jubilee. All the streets were decked out with red, white and blue bunting, there were flags everywhere and he tried to convince her that it was all in her honour.

Two years later, in 1937, the year of the three penny bit, Elizabeth was born, named after the young princess but with more than a passing thought being given to her grandmother. Although she was baptised Elizabeth, she soon became known as Libby, because that was how Victoria referred to her. So Elizabeth became Libby in a way that Victoria never became Vickie; that was the privilege, or burden, of being the firstborn.

If life was coming together again for Beryl after several years of turmoil, it was coming together in the context of growing worries within Europe over the emerging power of Germany. Whilst close at hand, within the immediate family, there was much to rejoice over and signs of growing economic prosperity, all was not well beyond the family. People were looking across the channel and seeing the growing strength of Hitler. It was difficult to know exactly what was happening, what was true and what was propaganda. In Spain a civil war was taking place and Beryl, like so many other people, wasn't quite sure what it was all about. She disliked the stories of war and tried hard to push all thoughts about what was happening in the world out of her mind. She was happy with her two children; she loved her husband and was pleased to have her mother living close by.

"I can't believe how lucky I am," she said to Frank one evening as they chatted by the fireside. "I think I must have had a difficult time after George died, to be honest I don't remember much about it. Then you came along and sort of rescued me, like a knight in shining armour."

"Nonsense, you didn't need rescuing, you just needed loving. I'm no good at rescuing people but perhaps I know how to love someone, especially if that someone is you." He smiled and put his arms around her.

"You know, it's me that's the lucky one."

"Well, perhaps we've both been lucky, we found each other and I'm very glad that we did. But I'm afraid Frank, afraid of all this talk about Germany. I'm not sure what's going on. Do you think Mr

Churchill is right, he keeps saying that we are not prepared that we should be more wary of what's going on in Europe?"

He had a feeling that before long he would be in the army, but he never voiced that feeling as he knew that Beryl and Lizzie were both emotionally scarred by the death of her father in the earlier war.

Those fears were justified. As Hitler began to march into the countries of Europe there was a very real possibility that England too would be invaded. Over the next twelve months hundreds of thousands of men were enlisted as Britain declared war on Germany and Frank was to be one of them. He had a photograph taken of himself in uniform, one of only two photographs in which he appeared that were to survive. The other was taken one summer's day at the seaside and showed him with Beryl pushing a pram.

"Don't leave me Frank, don't leave me," Beryl sobbed as she spent a final night with her husband. "I can't bear to let you go, promise me you'll look after yourself, promise me."

"Beryl my love, of course I'll look after myself. None of us wants to go but we have to, no-one is safe with that lunatic marching round Europe, we've got to stop him. For the sake of you and the girls I've got to do my bit. But I'll think of you all a thousand times a day. You'll be in my thoughts when I go to sleep and in my thoughts when I wake up. I will be with you, very near to you every moment of the day, even though we are apart, nothing will be able to separate us, believe me."

When Frank eventually left the house Beryl was distraught and Lizzie had a terrible feeling that history was repeating itself. Libby was three years old when her father went off to war, Victoria was ten. They were still the same age when he was killed. The evacuation from Dunkirk was later to be heralded by many people as a miracle, a sign of God's intervention. It never seemed so for Beryl. Her life changed irreversibly the day the telegram arrived.

"DEEPLY REGRET TO INFORM YOUR HUSBAND FRANK ARKWRIGHT REPORTED MISSING PRESUMED KILLED ON ACTIVE SERVICE."

What Frank didn't know on that fateful day was that Beryl was pregnant, and later she gave birth to Margaret, named after the younger princess, but known from her earliest days as Maggie.

From the day she received the telegram Beryl set her face resolutely towards the future, refusing to allow herself to look backwards. She developed her philosophy of 'those days are past – there's nothing we can do about them, we must live for now and not feel sorry for ourselves'. She did, of course, feel sorry for herself, but she was never, ever, heard to express such feelings. She developed an iron will. With her family she relaxed and was warm and caring, but beyond them she appeared hard and resolute. Neighbours kept their distance and the few friends she had treated her with a considerable degree of circumspection. Beryl lived for her family, particularly for the new-born baby whom Frank had never known. The relationship between the two of them was intense and all-absorbing. Victoria and Libby were loved deeply, there was no doubt about that, but the bond between Beryl and Maggie was different and was to remain so until Maggie's untimely death.

The three men whom Beryl had loved all died violent deaths in early manhood and she was never fully to recover from the shock and horror of those deaths. In their place came three daughters, bringing life and hope. She cared passionately for them, brought them up with pride and dignity, lived her life for them and through them, but never again regained the joyfulness and radiance that had made her such a dynamic and vivacious person in her earlier years. The family became the centre of her world, it was the one thing to which she was committed and it was a commitment that never wavered.

F or as long as Libby could remember there had been four of them, Victoria, Maggie, herself and their mother. She and Victoria shared a room and Maggie slept with her mother. Even when they grew older and Victoria got married when Libby was thirteen, Maggie did not come into her room but stayed with her mother. She much preferred having her own room to which she used to retreat and read whilst Maggie played records on the old gramophone in the downstairs living room and generally made a lot of noise and created havoc. Both Victoria and Libby had gone to the local girls' High School, Victoria leaving when she was fifteen, to work in a bank. Maggie had shown no inclination for learning whatsoever and happily passed her time at the local Secondary Modern School which she left as soon as she could to work in a reoord shop in town and, at the same time, Libby left school to go to university.

Before she could begin she was called for an interview at the local education office. She was ushered into a room and had to stand in front of a table behind which sat seven or eight elderly people who peered at her, none of them smiling. She thought they were probably councillors but really had no idea and none of them introduced themselves.

"So Elizabeth, you want to go to the university to study English?"

"Yes sir," she replied.

"And you have applied for a grant to cover your costs whilst you are away from home?"

"Yes sir."

"You know that you will have to work really hard whilst you are away don't you? I mean I hope you don't think that it will be easy. You are not going away on a holiday are you?"

"No sir, certainly not. I know that it will be hard work, but I am prepared to work hard."

"The thing is, Elizabeth," the only woman spoke, she looked about ninety and was dressed very smartly, "the thing is, you are asking the people here to pay for you, the money comes from the ordinary people here in the city and it is our responsibility to make sure that it isn't wasted. So what have you got to say about that?"

Libby wasn't sure that she had anything to say about that but felt that she needed to say something.

"I am very conscious of the fact that my studying will cost a lot of money and I am very grateful that I have this opportunity. I can assure you that I will work hard and will be very careful."

Libby stood there whilst the people behind the table put their heads together for a few minutes and whispered to each other, occasionally looking up at her and giving her a stare. After what seemed to be a very long time the person who spoke to her first coughed and put his hand through his hair.

"Well Elizabeth, we have thought about your application and you have assured us that you are prepared to work hard. On that basis the city is prepared to give you a grant of seventy pounds a term. What do you think of that?"

"Oh that's wonderful, I am very grateful to you all, thank you so much."

Libby meant every word that she said and she left the room determined to work hard and more than a little anxious about whether they would call her back, when her studies were over, to say how she had spent it.

The first term passed quickly enough. Libby coped with the work and quickly and easily made friends. She enjoyed the new freedom; no careful eye of mother, no Maggie chattering incessantly. Opening a bank account for the first time was quite a challenge but she went home with enough money saved to be able to buy small Christmas presents. Like most of her friends she arranged to work for the Post Office sorting mail for the two weeks before Christmas. This meant that she was able to make a contribution to the family finances which, together with the money that Maggie was now handing over week by week enabled her mother to provide extra provisions for Christmas for the first time in living memory without running into real financial difficulties. Maggie at work and Libby at university meant that life was changing for Beryl as well.

It was during her second year that the world changed for Libby, until then she had lived her life in black and white and suddenly, in the autumn of 1956 she discovered Technicolor. She also discovered her capacity for joy and pain in ways that she could never have imagined. The cause of this seismic shift in her life was Paul.

Maggie could never remember a time when she was not loved. She grew up with a sense of being someone who was naturally and universally both loved and liked. She knew that the two did not always go together, but in her case they did. She felt herself to be the most fortunate of all people. She knew her sisters were also loved, especially by her, but she also knew that they did not share her sense of spontaneous pleasure at the start of each and every day. For Maggie, each new day brought possibilities of new adventures, new experiences and always opportunities for basking in the warmth of people's love and admiration. They delighted in her presence and she delighted in theirs. She woke up each morning with a sense of wonder and she went to bed each night with a sense of gratitude. She clearly knew that there were upsets in life, times when things didn't go according to plan, but these experiences never seemed to remain in her consciousness, they just slipped away. She didn't harbour grudges; she seemed to lack that capacity in her psychological make up. Her cup was always half full, never half empty, but even that would be an understatement, it was invariably nine-tenths full and that would be on a poor day. Maggie was unique and people loved her.

Of course, such a personality did not come without drawbacks. It tended to create misunderstandings within other people, all of whom felt that they had a particularly special relationship with her, unaware of the fact that this was the effect that she had on almost everyone. As she danced her way through life she tended to leave behind her an unusually large number of casualties but she appeared to be totally oblivious of this and none of those so wounded ever dreamt of blaming her for their troubles, that was certainly never part of the equation. It was as though people were rather proud of having been marked, in some way, by their encounters with her.

She progressed through school with ease. This was not because she was the brightest of pupils but because school-work made little impression on her and certainly was not something to get worried about. She had no interest in examinations and so she was never disappointed when her marks were only moderate. Her mother could never understand that whilst both Victoria and Libby were concerned to do well and make the most of their education, she seemed to live in a completely different world. It was not that she wasn't bright, it was just that school and formal learning were not areas in which she had any interest.

She left school at the first opportunity and found herself a job in a record shop in the city centre, which she loved. She was meeting people all day long, she was listening to the latest records, she liked Tony, her boss, and she was earning money. She was able to pay for her keep at home and still have sufficient money left to spend on clothes, especially jeans which had just arrived in the country and were seen as being the latest word in teenage fashion. She also was able to spend her earnings on music, the cinema and hours spent in local coffee bars and pubs although legally she was not allowed in the latter but no-one seemed to mind. She was wonderfully, totally, happy and brought this sense of the sheer enjoyment of living back into the home with her and everyone seemed to benefit. Beryl used to wonder how she, who had known so much sorrow over the past twenty years, could have given birth to someone for whom life was so overwhelmingly ebullient. She was either forgetful or unaware of the fact that when she was Maggie's age she too brought light and laughter into other people's lives, in fact, in many ways Maggie was a carbon copy of her mother at that age.

Maggie's favourite place to hang about in was *Le Macabre* coffee bar. It was a converted cellar in a large warehouse. There were a number of small rooms, all dimly lit, with imitation skulls hanging on the walls, imitation cobwebs hanging from the ceiling and small loudspeakers in all the different alcoves through which the latest hit records were piped. Low seats, settees and low tables were invariably filled by people of her age or slightly older. Thick glass coffee cups, thick glass saucers were littered all over the place and occasionally cleared away and cigarette smoke permeated the whole place. Maggie loved it; she loved the frothy coffee, the sense of the macabre, hence its name, and most of all the people who congregated there every day and through until closing time at eleven o'clock at night. Before long she had talked herself into a part-time job there, supplementing her income from the record shop and meeting more people, new people and all those who, in her eyes, were the trendiest people in town. Beryl went there one evening to have a look at the place and came out after two or three minutes feeling very foolish and out of place. She was at least thirty years older than anyone else there, she couldn't hear any conversation because of the noise, she couldn't see where she was walking and she thought the coffee was outrageously expensive, especially since she didn't really drink coffee and they didn't serve tea. Maggie was greatly amused by her mother' reactions and assured her that she didn't have to worry because it was so dark that no-one would have recognised her. But that wasn't Beryl's concern, it was not her own welfare or reputation that was at stake but her daughter's; this was something completely beyond Maggie's understanding.

Elvis Presley fever was sweeping through England and Maggie played his records incessantly at home, almost driving Beryl to distraction.

"Maggie, will you please turn that record player down, I can't stand that noise any more, it just goes on and on and it's giving me a headache."

There was no response from Maggie who just sat there, staring at the record player, swaying with the beat. "Maggie, will you please turn that music down. Don't just sit there like a moron, turn it down, it's driving me crazy."

Again there was no response from Maggie and Beryl saw that she was now chewing gum in time to the beat as well as swaying. She waited a few minutes but there was still no response. When she could bear it no longer Beryl walked over to the wall and pulled the plug from the socket, the loss of power meaning that the record immediately slowed down to a halt and the voice of Elvis Presley sank through his boots.

"What the fucking hell do you think you're doing?" screamed Maggie, who turned on her mother with fury in her face, her eyes flashing and her lips trembling.

"Maggie!" responded Beryl, amazed and shocked by her language.

"Don't you ever dare do that again." She turned on her mother with a rage that was completely out of character and totally unexpected.

"If I want to listen to my music what's it got to do with you? I'll do what I bloody well like and you won't stop me. Do you realise what you've done? You've probably ruined my record and if you have I'll never forgive you." She glared at her mother and stood up and ran upstairs.

"Maggie, don't let me ever hear you using that gutter language in this house again. What on earth has got into you? I make a reasonable request for you to turn the volume down, you ignore me and then you come at me with the language of the sewer. Just stay upstairs and get into your bed, I have never been so humiliated in all my life. I never ever want to hear such language in this house again, do you hear?"

There was the sound of a door banging. A few minutes later Maggie came downstairs, glared at her mother and walked to the front door.

"Just bugger off mum and leave me alone." With that she was gone, slamming the door behind her.

Beryl was stunned. It was the first time they had ever fallen out and she was appalled, horrified by the intense rage and cruelty that Maggie had displayed towards her. She sat down and cried, something that she rarely did, having learned long ago that tears got you nowhere; you had to face up to life's trials, put on a brave face and move forward. But she could put no brave face on after this outburst; she was stunned and felt that all her inner resources had suddenly evaporated. The situation worsened when Maggie didn't come home and Beryl was frantic with worry when she stayed away the next night as well.

The following evening the door opened and in walked Maggie.

"Hi mum, sorry I didn't get back last night."

She walked over to Beryl and gave her a big hug and a kiss on the cheek.

"Did I ever tell you that you are the best mum in all the world? Anyway, you are."

She was full of smiles and made no mention of the altercation over the record player. It was as though it had never happened. Beryl was uneasy; she was delighted that Maggie was back, she loved receiving such love and affection but nevertheless she had been through a bad few days.

"Maggie, your language the other evening was just terrible, I..."
She had no time to finish the sentence.

"Oh mum, can't you see, I was just winding you up, you don't need to get serious about it. Anyway, I'm off to the cinema in a few minutes and I'll be late back, I don't want you worrying about me."
She blew Beryl a big kiss and then ran upstairs to get ready to go out, emerging a few minutes later all dressed up and rushing out, giving her mother another quick kiss as she went. This was Maggie all over, she had the ability to leave a crisis behind her and get on with life as though nothing had happened. She was apparently oblivious of the hurt and chaos that she left behind her, she lived for the moment and although it was hard to admit, she lived for herself.

There was to be a 'demo', something completely new to Libby. The university's Anti-Apartheid group arranged a mass rally and demonstration and just about everyone she knew was affected by the enthusiasm and excitement of it all. Different departments were urged to march, carrying banners and placards, to a central location on the campus where there was to be an African band and dancers and then a speech by Trevor Huddleston, a monk who had recently written a best-selling book *Naught for your comfort* about his experiences in South Africa. She was entering a new world of international affairs and developing a social conscience. Huddleston was a tall thin man, with his head shaven and he wore a long black cassock. He spoke for almost an hour, no notes, no visual aids, just a passionate recounting of what it was like to live in a township and he made Sophiatown come alive, as though it was just along the road.

Paul Crozier believed, for the rest of his life, that he fell in love with Libby that afternoon. She was tall and slim with long black hair, she was wearing a pink jumper and cardigan, her eyes were large and she was totally absorbed by this monk from Africa. Paul wanted to hear him but could remember nothing he said; he was simply distracted, totally and unnervingly by the sight of this girl. He just had to find out who she was, nothing was more important to him, and he spent the remainder of the rally working out how to do it. It took him three days to find out who she was and what course she was on and where she lived. When he set out on a course of action he invariably got what he wanted and now he wanted Libby.

He was a final year student, but getting a degree in music was not his major concern, he was interested in politics and he had ambitions to get into parliament. He was a great talker, had grand ideas and regarded himself as something of a visionary, a radical visionary. He was very bright and his commitment to his course was, to put it mildly, secondary to his principal purpose of getting to know people and getting known by them. The more important and influential they were so much the better.

"God mate," he said to his flat-mate when Bruce returned to Birmingham after a few days away, "I've met this fantastic girl, she's quite out of this world."

"Not another one Paul, what's happened to all the others?" Bruce was cynical, to say the least.

"No, this time it's for real, she's something special, different from the others."

"OK then, tell me all about her, but remember, you always say that they are different." Bruce slumped into an easy chair, opened a bottle of beer and settled down to hear about Paul's latest infatuation.

"Who is she, when's she coming round? Do I need to make myself scarce again and if so, for how long?"

"No, it's not like that, in fact I've not yet spoken to her, but I'm on course for doing so, yes siree, I most certainly am."

"I don't believe this, you've met her, she's wonderful and yet you've never spoken to her. This doesn't sound like you."

"Well, this is different. I told you she was something special. Don't laugh Bruce, but I wouldn't be surprised if I've just met the woman I shall marry."

"Bloody hell Paul, you have got it bad. Are you feeling alright, I mean you're not going out of your mind or something are you? It's hard enough living with you when you're sane but if you're breaking up in some way I'm not hanging around, sorry but I've got my finals coming up."

"Hey, I thought you were my friend. You come back, I tell you this great news and you go on about clearing off and leaving me. I tell you Bruce, this is for real, you just wait and see."

"Yeah Paul, that's just what I'll do, I'll wait and see."

To Bruce's surprise Libby did seem to be different. It was some time before he met her; Paul was treading very cautiously, almost as though he wasn't quite sure how to proceed. That was different. Having tracked her down, he then stalked her for a few days before getting ready to pounce. But this was not the usual Paul, this was a cocksure young man who suddenly found himself out of his depth, not quite sure of things. After slowly getting himself involved in a group of people around Libby for a few days he gradually moved in and invited her out one evening to go to a concert with him as that seemed a reasonable thing for a music student to do. She was a little hesitant when he asked her, explaining that she had never been to a concert before.

"That's splendid; then it will be my pleasure to introduce you to the wonders of the orchestra," enthused Paul.

"It's a good programme and I think you'll enjoy it and I'll talk you through the pieces so that you know something about them and what to listen out for."

The day after the concert a bouquet of flowers was delivered to Libby – "from Shostakovitch, so glad you like me." Shostakovitch was one of the composers she had listened to. It was the first gift of flowers she had ever received. That first evening was followed by many others, sometimes to concerts, sometimes to jazz clubs and often to little cafes where they would eat bacon and eggs at all sorts of times of day or night. The attraction was mutual, the pleasure they experienced in each other's company was something very special.

"Paul, you're a reformed character since you met Libby," commented Bruce one evening as they sat and chatted into the early hours.

"What's happened to that rakish way of life? I do believe that you've been with her for a couple of months and yet, if I'm not mistaken, you've not yet enticed her into your bed."

Paul grinned.

"Well, it's not for the want of trying, I can tell you. But yes, I've thought all along that this was special. I told you right at the start that she was different."

"Well make sure you keep it that way, you have a habit of ruining things when they seem to be going well. If you ever make it into parliament I hope you never become Prime Minister or God help the country, you'll have us into a war in no time or into some sort of messy scandal."

"Come on, come on, those days are behind me. You see, I'll make it in politics, provided you don't make a fortune out of spilling the beans on my student days."

"Don't tempt me, just don't tempt me you blighter."

"Yes, I know, people like you are prepared to sell your soul for a quick buck. No principles, no vision, no passion."

"I agree that I don't have your passion, but then I don't have all your experience do I?"

"Sod off!"

"Libby, how much longer am I going to have to wait? Can't you see I'm crazy about you? I want to show you how much I love you and I can't do that when you pull away from me every time we get really close?"

They had returned to her room and were lying on her bed and Paul was unsuccessfully trying to undress her. He was getting more and more frustrated. This was not how it usually went with the girls he took out. He admired Libby for her stout resistance but he was also annoyed by what he perceived as an outmoded puritanical streak.

"I mean, it's not as though you're religious or anything is it? Why won't you make love? It's the most natural thing in the world, unless of course, you don't really like me. Perhaps you're having me on and there's someone else. Yes, of course, why hadn't I thought of that before? You're happy to be with me here in Birmingham but you've got someone else back home in Leeds, is that it?"

He pulled away from her and stared into her face. She didn't know if he was angry or what. It was a new experience for her, a new and different Paul that she hadn't come across before.

"Of course there isn't anyone else, surely you know that?"

Libby was indignant and she sat up.

"You don't think I would have let you go this far if I had another boyfriend do you? Paul, don't push me, this is all a bit new to me, I'm not sure what's happening – to me, to us – I'm confused. Don't go on about it. The more you press me the more frightened I become. I love you Paul, really I do, but I'm not ready to go as far as you want. I'm not sure that its right, Oh I don't know, just leave off a bit."

"Well when will you be ready? When will you know? I mean, I've been patient haven't I?"

He moved away and took out a cigarette. He was playing a dangerous game and he knew it. Keep focused and she would give way, he could sense that, but one false move and he could put things back weeks, even months.

"Look Libby, I don't want to upset you and I'm sorry if I'm pressing you. It's not easy you know, holding back when you love someone as much as I love you. Perhaps we need a few days away from each other, you know, a little break. It will give me time to cool down a bit, I don't want to be a burden to you, make you unhappy and all that jazz."

"Oh Paul, you're not a burden, don't ever think that."

"No, I think I am, I'm causing you some distress, you can't deny that can you? Look, let's leave it for tonight and I'll be on my way and let's meet up again on Saturday. Anyway, with my finals coming up perhaps I ought to be doing a bit more work."

He leaned across, gave her a chaste kiss on the cheek, picked up his duffle coat and left. Libby felt utterly deflated. From the intensity of their passionate embrace to being left on her own had taken no more than fifteen minutes. She felt guilty, not sure if she was being unfair to him, putting extra pressure on him when he was already pressurised enough by his approaching exams. She loved him; she had no doubts about that, so perhaps she was being unreasonable, even selfish. She decided that perhaps the time had come for her to take the next step in her journey into adulthood, which is precisely what Paul was gambling on.

Bruce sensed that there was something different the moment he walked into the flat after a weekend away. Paul was working at the table but he looked up as soon as Bruce entered the room, a huge smile on his face.

"Don't tell me, I can guess. You've not spent the weekend alone have you? Now I see why you were not put out by my going away again, in fact you actually encouraged me to go. Well, was it worth waiting for?"

Paul stood up, did a little dance round the table and slapped Bruce on the back.

"It was worth every moment, every day that I had to wait. I tell you man, she's terrific."

"Well I just hope that you don't bugger this one up Paul. In all honesty, I think she's too nice for you."

"Well, thank you very much. You're a great pal I must say."

Paul was clearly annoyed by Bruce's comment.

"Now don't get me wrong," explained Bruce, "but you know what I mean."

"No I don't, damn you. I think that's a bloody awful thing to say. What do you mean? That I'm not good enough? I'll show you whether I'm good enough, you just wait and see. I tell you man, I'm going to get somewhere, you wait and see, and when I get there I'll remind you of your patronising manner, if I'm still in touch with you that is, which I very much doubt."

Bruce rolled his eyes up to the ceiling. Here we go again, another of Paul's outbursts. But he was right, Paul wasn't good enough for her if his assessment of the situation was correct. On the other hand he was probably stupid to say so out loud, especially when Paul was so euphoric. He unpacked his things and stayed in his own room feeling that the flat had somehow become sullied in his absence.

The term sped by very quickly. Libby was working hard and so was Paul as his finals approached. When they were not studying they went out together to occasional concerts or just to walk through the parks or, once or twice, taking a bus out to the Lickey hills and spending the afternoon getting some fresh air. Although Paul was committed to getting his music degree he was more and more passionate about politics and spent many hours discussing nuclear disarmament or the evils of apartheid. He was trying to get a job as a researcher for a labour MP, having decided that this was the best way to meet the people who might open doors for him. When he spoke about world issues or about his concern for the poor and under privileged Libby listened with pride and it never occurred to her to comment on the fact that he had lived a life of privilege. He came from a wealthy family, had a public school education and holidays abroad whilst she knew, from firsthand experience, just what it was like to struggle against poverty. Nor did it ever occur to him to ask her about life in working class Leeds or what it was like in a one-parent family. He was too bound up with his own rhetoric and convictions about poverty and inequality. He was the expert and she was the grateful recipient of his wisdom and understanding.

She felt guilty that she seldom made contact with her mother, but when she was away from home it was like being in a different world and she felt little inclination to assimilate the two. She received letters from Victoria and they always urged her to write home more often but, despite her good intentions, she did little to keep in touch. She gathered that Maggie had been in trouble or something but never followed this up and when she was at home nothing was ever mentioned of it. She lived in Birmingham and she lived in Leeds, the two lives co-existed but did not overlap. She said very little about her life in Leeds when she was in Birmingham and even less about her life in Birmingham when she was in Leeds.

A few weeks after her dramatic walk out Maggie seemed to spend the whole evening playing the latest hit record, Pat

Boone's 'Love letters in the sand'. She returned the stylus to the outer edge of the record as soon as it reached the centre. Beryl who was busying herself around the house had to admit that this one at least had a tune, when Maggie called out: "Mum, can you come here for a minute, there's something I want to tell you."

"Hang on for a minute," called Beryl, "I'll just finish what I'm doing, make myself a cuppa and come and put my feet up for a bit."

"Well, what is, my love?" she asked, a few minutes later as she put her legs up and stretched out on the settee.

Maggie hesitated for a moment or two.

"I'm not quite sure how to put this," she said, "and you're not going to like it, but I'm pregnant."

"Oh my God," gasped Beryl, and suddenly the room seemed to be spinning and she found it difficult to focus upon Maggie and what she was saying.

"You're dead right, I don't like it. Are you sure?"

Maggie nodded.

"I've known for a few weeks, I wasn't sure how to tell you but I thought you would want to know. I'm sorry."

"Maggie, you're sixteen, you say you're pregnant and I didn't even know you had a boyfriend. Have you told him? What does he say? What's his name?"

Beryl had no idea what to say, how to respond to such news. What was the right thing to do and say? She had no idea. It wasn't very often that she felt sorry for herself, but now she became aware of a great burst of anger towards Frank. How could he die and leave her to sort this out all by herself? At the same time she was glad that he wasn't around to hear such dreadful news.

Maggie was silent, looking at the floor and twisting a handkerchief round and round in her hands.

"Well come on," urged Beryl, "tell me about him. Oh God, what are we going to do?"

"Well, it's not quite like that," whispered Maggie. "I don't have a boyfriend, that is, I don't have a special sort of boyfriend."

"But you must have if you're pregnant," insisted Beryl. "What do you mean you don't have a boyfriend, you must know who the father is."

Maggie blushed.

"Well, mum, it's not quite as easy as that, life is different now from when you were young."

Beryl sensed that things were going from bad to worse.

"Maggie, have I got this right: you don't have a special boyfriend, you are pregnant and you don't know who the father is?"

Maggie nodded, tears welling up in her eyes.

"Well how long has this sort of thing been going on? You know, how long have you been playing about with boys?"

Beryl couldn't believe that she was saying these things.

"How long? With how many?"

"Oh mum, don't be angry with me, it's not as bad as you think. Things aren't like that, really, honestly."

"Well tell me then? How long? How many?"

There was a long silence.

"Maggie, answer me. How long has this been going on? How long? How many?"

"For about three years."

Maggie saw Beryl's jaw drop in disbelief.

"Three years? Oh Maggie, how could you? Since you were thirteen? I don't believe what I'm hearing. How many?"

"I'm not sure, quite a few I suppose?"

"For God's sake you must know how many boys you've been with," retorted Beryl. "Three? Four? Or more?"

"More" whispered Maggie.

Beryl was incredulous.

"More? Well how many more? A dozen?"

Maggie was crying now.

"Mum, it's not the sort of thing that you keep count of. Don't keep asking me these questions. I've told you now, I knew you would be cross. Don't go on at me... I'm sorry... it's just that I don't know what to do."

She looked up and saw that Beryl was crying. She moved over to the settee and put her arms around her mother.

"I'm sorry mum, perhaps I shouldn't have told you. I don't want to upset you."

They hugged each other, both of them crying.

"Don't be so silly, my precious. Of course you must tell me. It's just that I feel that I must have failed you somewhere, I've let you down, not been a good mother. Don't worry about it, we'll get it sorted somehow. The important thing is that we stick together, we'll find a way through it. Don't worry my little angel."

And so it was that Maggie consoled her mother, held her tightly as she cried, soothed and comforted her, assured her that she had nothing to blame herself about, that she had been a wonderful mother, the best a girl could ever hope to have. They remained together on the settee for a long time, each holding the other and drawing a mutual strength from their unconditional love. The sun had set and the room darkened, before either of them made a move. 'Love letters in the sand' was put back into its sleeve and was never played again.

Maggie's pregnancy was confirmed by the local GP who was also able to give them advice about the pros ands cons of adoption and what options were available to them. He said the fact that mother and daughter were tackling this together made the whole thing much easier. Beryl was adamant that she wanted the whole thing kept secret; it was for her a matter of considerable shame. Maggie was less sure; she didn't feel the same degree of shame and wondered how it was possible to keep such a thing secret anyway. No, argued Beryl, it was important that they kept this to themselves, she was sure that this was the best way forward and she was also sure that Maggie was far too young even to consider keeping the child. So plans were formulated and arrangements made. Maggie gave up working in the coffee bar but remained in her job in the record shop. She spent much more time at home and didn't go out nearly so often in the evening. This curtailment of her freedom, as Maggie saw it, was not particularly welcomed but she was reasonably happy to be guided by Beryl and spent a lot of time thinking about all the things that she would be enjoying again in six months time, once this little problem was sorted out. Nearer the time, when her condition was beginning to show a little, Maggie left her job and went to live for a while with Victoria and Bill where she was able to help them out with their growing family of three young children. Beryl was satisfied that she had managed the whole situation with no-one at home being any the wiser. It made sense to people when she was able to say that Maggie was helping her sister out for a few months, but she missed her presence in the house terribly and longed for the time when she would return. It was the first time they had ever been separated.

They were separated again when Maggie arrived at the mother and baby home run by the Church of England in a large house with a big garden, out in the country. Although based upon strict religious foundations it actually provided secure and loving care for up to eight girls who, for one reason or another, found themselves in Maggie's position. Staffed by a social worker, Mrs Briggs, with two other helpers it taught girls the rudiments of caring for their babies, managing a budget, providing a home and, of course, preparing them for childbirth. It also arranged for adoptions.

Maggie was interested in the other girls; there were six of them altogether. Two came from very poor backgrounds, with little education, they seemed slow to understand what was happening, what they were being taught and why. Another girl was loud and brash, always talking, always swearing and determined to have her own way in all things. She was cocky, looked down on the two simpler girls and had already had one child who had been adopted the year before. Maggie found her difficult and tended to keep away from her as much as possible. The other two were extremely friendly, one came from a rich middle class family and she had run away from home and lost contact with her parents, the other had very strained relationships with her family and her father had refused to speak to her when he heard about the pregnancy.

At night, when the other girls were sleeping, Maggie often lay awake; she missed not having a father. Even though she had never known him, there was a sort of father-shaped space in her psyche. She reasoned that it was not that she didn't have a father, it was just that she hadn't known him. She thought about him a great deal; even spoke to him in her mind. She knew that he was nice, that he loved her and was not judgmental towards her. She decided that she had a better relationship with the father she had never known than most of the other girls seemed to have with the fathers they did know. She missed her mother, she missed their whispered conversations before they fell asleep, and she missed her friendship and having her around. She would have loved her to be there at this time, so that she could talk to her about how she felt and about how frightened she was when she thought about the impending birth, but she knew that was not going to be possible. As she looked around her, Maggie came to the conclusion that out of all the girls in the house she was probably the happiest and the most contented in her relationships with others, particularly with her family.

Mrs Briggs had a long conversation with her about adoption. In fact she had several such conversations. She was puzzled by Maggie's attitude, by her views on her situation and by the apparent calmness and certainty that she displayed over her decision to have the baby adopted straight from birth, or as soon as practically possible. She was not callous, not uncaring, in fact quite the opposite. This is what puzzled her. She seemed to be extremely secure in her sense of self-worth, she had an excellent relationship with her mother and sisters and an apparently good network of friends. Her work record was good and she was sociable and easy to relate to, in fact she was good fun and a pleasure to have around. In many ways she was quite different from the majority of girls who came to the House. She was adamant however that she wanted the baby adopted and this clearly thought-through view didn't seem to be accompanied by any sense of regret, guilt or embarrassment. It was a relatively easy case for Janice Briggs to handle as far as the adoption procedure was involved, but she wondered how Maggie could have such clear views about what she wanted without apparently having any moments of self-doubt. Although she was soon to give birth there appeared to be no development within her of a sense of motherhood, no excitement about the new life that was developing.

Maggie eventually gave birth to a little boy, it was a relatively straightforward birth as those things go, with no complications. She was in hospital for four or five days and she left for home without the baby. The re-union with Beryl was an emotional occasion, each tearfully delighting in the other's company. Maggie was tired and slept a great deal but when she was not sleeping she was talking, telling Beryl about the other girls, about Mrs Briggs and all the other people she had met in this enforced separation. On the third day after she returned home Beryl suddenly said "Well, that's enough of all that now, we need to look ahead not backwards" and not another word was said about the whole affair by either of them for the rest of their lives, although for a long time Beryl grieved for the grandson she had never seen.

L ibby and Paul discussed what would happen during the summer and where he would be when she returned to the university the following year. He had a long-term commitment to visit America with the orchestra that he played with in his home town. His parents were going out to join him later and they were then going off on a family holiday. He wasn't sure when they were returning but thought he would be away for a couple of months. If he couldn't get a research job he might return to Birmingham, he wasn't sure, the future was uncertain and he was despondent about leaving Libby. The earlier excitement of the American trip had evaporated and more than anything else he wanted to stay in Birmingham with her.

"But that's impossible, and you know it is," reasoned Libby. "In any case I have to get back home and earn some money. I can't afford to remain here and even if I could it would be no good, I need to get back and see my mum. By getting a job back home I'm able to give her a bit, you know, pay for my board and lodging as it were and that helps out quite a lot."

"I know," interjected Paul suddenly, not really listening to what she was saying and having no understanding of the family's financial frailty, "why don't you come over to America and have a holiday with us all?"

"Paul that's ridiculous, it really is. First, I've no money for that sort of thing, second I've never been abroad so I don't even have a passport, third I need to help my mum out and finally I've never even met your parents. Just imagine what they would think if I trotted along with you. You do have the most silly ideas."

Paul grinned, she was right and he knew it, but it was a good idea nonetheless.

"No, you go off and enjoy yourself and leave me to work in the drapers shop in Headingley. You can write to me. Anyway, it will do us good to be apart for a while, it's all getting rather intense isn't it?"

She couldn't continue what she was saying because he was kissing her, his hands all over her and she had to fight to free herself from him.

"Paul Crozier, what do you think you're doing? I'm a respectable young woman, now stop it!"

"Oh no you're not, not any longer."

Libby went bright red with embarrassment and they both dissolved in laughter.

They duly took their exams and decided to stay on together in Birmingham for as long as possible before they went their different ways. She thought Paul was rather subdued and wondered what was on his mind, but he insisted that everything was fine. It was clear to her that everything was not fine and she had a chat to Bruce one day when she had turned up at the flat and found him there alone.

"Is Paul alright Bruce? I mean, is he bothered about something? He seems to be a bit low, you know, sort of depressed. I've asked him but he says he's fine. Have you noticed any difference?"

Bruce reflected for a moment or two, to be honest he had never given it a thought; he was getting on with his life and was rather fed up with Paul with his wild enthusiasms and his sense of self-importance. In fact, Bruce was quite looking forward to Paul leaving; he had already found someone else to share the flat with him.

"Well, I'm not too sure Libby. I can't honestly say that I've noticed any change but we don't really get on all that well these days you know."

"Don't get on? Well I'm amazed," exclaimed Libby, "Paul has never mentioned that, have you had a row or something? I'm so surprised."

"No, we've not had any particular disagreement, we just get on with our own lives and sometimes it's probably a day or two before we meet up, we tend to have different clocks, you know, I'm an early to bed and early to rise man and I'm usually out before Paul gets up."

Libby screwed up her face in thought.

"It's not me, is it? I mean have I come in and spoilt things between you? I never thought of that, I'm sorry Bruce, I never intended to break up your friendship."

"No, no, it's nothing like that. In fact you've been good for Paul, he's been much more bearable to live with since you came on the scene. No, it's just that I don't share his political convictions and I get a bit tired of him lecturing me about them all the time. Anyway, we've come to the end of our course, his mind is already on what he's doing next and I'm staying here in Birmingham so I suppose it's quite natural that we should drift apart a bit. Having said that, I hope that I still see something of you next session even though Paul will have left, I mean I've got used to you being around."

"That's so nice of you Bruce; of course I'll keep in touch with you. I'm pleased that you haven't noticed anything strange though, maybe it's all in my mind, but he sometimes seems to drift away and I'm not sure what he's thinking about."

"Perhaps he's a bit bothered about this musical school he's going to in the States, you know he hasn't really been doing enough practice for it and I think some of the people back home are a bit annoyed with him."

"Yes, I can see that might be the case. There have been several times when he said he was going home and then he's pulled out at the last minute because he wanted to stay here with me. Perhaps I'm not a very good influence on him."

"I don't think you should ever think that Libby, everyone in the department thinks you've been a huge influence for the good on him. The thing is, has he been a good influence on you?"

"What on earth do you mean by that?" She was quite taken aback.

"Oh nothing, I don't mean anything, it's just the sort of thing that slips out sometime, think nothing about it. I'm sorry."

She looked at him quizzically but decided not to pursue the matter.

At that moment the door swung open and Paul came in with a great smile on his face.

"Hey, guess what? I've got a research job with an MP. Well, it's not really a job, in fact I won't get paid for it but my old man says he'll support me for a year, so I'm on my way. Westminster here I come!"

She rushed up to him and flung her arms around him.

"Oh Paul, that's wonderful, it's just what you wanted, well done."

Even Bruce was moved to congratulate him and suggested that they all went down to the pub and he'd buy them a drink to celebrate. They linked arms and set off for the Gun Barrels.

M aggie soon found another job. It wasn't as exciting as working in the record shop but that job had now been taken by someone else and in any case her mother was not too keen on her returning to her old work and friends. She did see them, of course, but was careful to keep this part of her life out of Beryl's sight. She had calmed down a little though and was no longer involved with any boy who just happened to come along, on the other hand, at times she was more than a little bored. Still, it was important that she didn't put her mother through that sort of crisis again. This is not to say that she had embraced chastity as a new way of life but she was more discerning now and more prepared. Just occasionally flashes of the old Maggie returned. There was the time when she was off work for a few days with a throat infection. Half way through the morning, when she was lazing about listening to records there was a knock at the door and she opened it to find a man who had come to read the electric meter. She beckoned him in and, without speaking, showed him where the meter was. He was rather taken aback by this silent beauty but in his job he met all sorts of people and he busied himself looking at the meter reading. When he turned round he saw that Maggie had written him a note, smiling she passed him the piece of paper. "I'm sorry but I've got a bad throat and I'm not supposed to use my voice." The meter-reader took out his pencil and wrote in reply: "Oh dear, poor you, and you've not been using much electricity either." Maggie burst out laughing when she read his words and began to speak. It was over an hour later before he left; they were both very warm by then but hadn't been using the electric fire.

Libby returned home and quickly found her job in the local shop. A postcard came showing the Niagara Falls. Paul was settling in, the weather was wonderful and he was about to have a rehearsal. Another came a few days later, all was going well, America was wonderful and he was developing a taste for sweet corn. Eventually a letter arrived. He was having a good time but was missing her, it was only two or three sides and Libby wanted more. She realised that this was the first letter she had ever received from him and quickly concluded that he was not up to much as a correspondent. It was a week before the next letter arrived. Another postcard arrived and then another letter. Plans had changed and he was to stay out there for a further three weeks and would be back in Birmingham the second weekend in September. Could she drop a note to Bruce and let him know?

She was approaching her twenty-first birthday and Victoria wrote suggesting that as a birthday present she would pay for Libby to visit London and go to two shows with her, one in the afternoon and one in the evening. Libby was to choose whichever she wanted and she would book the tickets. They decided on the first weekend in September when Libby had just finished her summer job and she spent time looking through the papers to find out what was on. *My Fair Lady* at Drury Lane was receiving rave reviews and they managed to get tickets for a matinee performance and then Libby decided she would like to go to a concert in the Festival Hall. Victoria was not entirely enthusiastic about going to a concert but it was her gift to Libby and she tried to convince herself that it might be an enjoyable new experience for her. She was transfixed and began to realise why Libby had become such an enthusiastic convert. For Libby, the music brought back so many memories and whilst she was concentrating on the performance she was also thinking that it would be just one more week before she and Paul were re-united and he would be delighted to know that she had made this trip and enjoyed it without his reassuring presence.

They had a great evening; it was a birthday present that she would always remember and linking arms they moved through the foyer of the Festival Hall making their way to the exit to go over the bridge to the underground station. As they walked and talked Libby saw someone who reminded her of Paul, coming down the stairway with his arm round a girl who was busy whispering something into his ear, they both smiled and he gave her a quick kiss. It was almost as though fate had conspired for this to happen, because within a matter of seconds Libby and Victoria were face to face with a young man who was turning a deep shade of red and beginning to splutter.

"Ah, Oh, well, hello, how amazing to meet you here..."

The girl on Paul's arm looked nonplussed and turned to Paul for an introduction.

"Ah yes, Amanda, this is Libby a friend from college and this is?"

"This is my sister Victoria," said Libby "how strange that we should meet up in this way, I thought you were still in America, what a surprise."

Paul looked more uncomfortable than Libby had ever seen him before. His face was full of guilt, his eyes failed to connect with Libby's and he had let go of Amanda's arm.

"Er, yes, well, er, we, that is I, came home a couple of days ago and Amanda's father had tickets for tonight's concert, so we thought we'd make a trip into town."

Libby stared at him and then at Amanda.

"What a lovely ring you're wearing," she said as she glanced down at the girl's left hand.

"Well thank you," gushed Amanda, "isn't it just too lovely for words, and do you know, Paul gave it to me exactly a week ago today when he proposed to me at the top of the Empire State Building."

"I hope you'll be very happy together, you are probably well suited," said Libby icily, "now we must go, I'm afraid we don't have time to stop and talk."

She grabbed Victoria by the arm and turned away, then suddenly she stopped and turned back to face Paul.

"Oh by the way," she said, and before anyone knew what was happening she gave him such a slap across the face that he stumbled and almost fell. By the time he'd gathered himself together Libby and her sister were out of the Festival Hall and making their way over Hungerford Bridge.

She had little recollection of the next few days, they were spent in bed, sleeping a great deal and eating very little. Victoria and Bill had been supportive but not intrusive, caring but not demanding. Victoria felt guilty, if it hadn't been for her invitation this encounter would not have taken place, but Bill argued that it was much better for it to have taken place when Libby was with her rather than at some other time when she would probably have been without the love and support of her family. She could see the logic in that, but just wished that it could have been otherwise. Anyway, life with a small family meant that there were plenty of distractions and Libby's crisis inevitably had to be pushed to one side for much of the time, which was a good thing for them all.

Back in Birmingham a week later, shopping for essentials took her out of the flat and into the evening sunshine and Libby began to feel at ease for the first time. She was pleased she'd made the effort to return and whilst in many ways she had dreaded returning she knew that she had to face it and overcome it. She remembered how, several years ago, she had gone on a thirty mile walk over two days. Towards the end of the first day she developed blisters on both feet so that on the second day, although walking through the most beautiful countryside, she was aware of nothing but the pain of the blisters. Now, in a similar sort of way, she was conscious of very little apart from the aching void within her.

"It's ridiculous," she explained to Fiona and Celia, her flatmates, "it's not as if we were married or engaged or anything, I feel so stupid being so upset. For goodness sake I'm not the first girl to have been ditched am I?"

Fiona remained silent and Libby continued, "I've just got to sort myself out and get on with things. I'm not going to let this destroy me, I've just got to move on and try and forget him. It's ridiculous that I'm being so weak and silly. I'm sorry to be such a misery. I'll go and sort my room out, give myself something to do."

She left and closed the door behind her but Fiona could hear her crying, the door unable to hide the immensity of her distress.

A semblance of normality was gradually establishing itself when a letter arrived from Bruce inviting all three of them over to the flat for a meal a few days later. Libby was adamant that she couldn't face going there again but insisted that the others should go. Bruce was a good friend and it was important that the upset between her and Paul should not get in the way of other friendships. She was happy to meet up with Bruce on another occasion and in another place, but it was too much for her to return to the flat where she had spent so much time with Paul and which was so full of memories. It became a matter of considerable discussion as to whether the others should go, but Libby argued that it was fine to leave her alone, she was doing well and in any case there was some reading that she needed to catch up on. She would be fine, they must go, and so they went.

Midway through the evening, to her annoyance, the doorbell rang. Libby ran down the stairs irritated that she should be disturbed just as she was settling into her book. She opened the door and found herself face to face with Paul.

"Oh God," she sighed, "I could do without this. What's brought you here? I don't think I really want this. Do you have to arrive unannounced and break into my evening?"

"I'm sorry Libby, I just felt it was important to come and see you and to say that I'm really sorry about what's happened and I wanted to see you before I left, you see, I'm moving from Birmingham tomorrow."

The words tumbled out and he looked uncomfortable; he was uncomfortable. Deep inside himself he felt a profound sorrow which was making him feel decidedly queasy; he just hoped that he wouldn't throw up on the doorstep.

"Er, are you going to invite me in or do we have to converse through this half-open door?"

Libby hesitated. She didn't know whether to slam the door in his face or invite him in. She knew that what whatever she decided to do she would regret later. To invite him in was to intensify her inner pain; to turn him away was an action that she probably didn't have enough strength to sustain. Whatever she did would only serve to add to the memories that she would always have of him. In the end she did nothing, she just stood there looking first at Paul and then way beyond him into the distance, her eyes focusing upon nothing tangible. There was a long silence.

"Libby," Paul began again, "I do think it is important for us to talk and I'm not sure that standing out here is the best location for either of us, can I come in?"

Libby nodded, opened the door a little wider and led the way up the stairs and into the sitting room of the flat.

"Fiona and Celia are out," she began, "but I expect you know that. I expect that Bruce's invitation was part of your planning now that I come to think of it. How silly of me not to have tumbled to that straight away." Paul grinned in a sheepish sort of way.

"Well, let's say it was partly my doing, but Bruce really wanted to see you all again and didn't know how to get in touch. I knew the address and, well, the rest you know."

"You're so devious, you'll make a good politician," retorted Libby, "now say what you've got to say and get out. Don't you think you've caused enough trouble already?" Despite all her efforts Libby couldn't stop tears trickling down her cheek, she sniffled, wiped her face and sat down. "OK, tell me all about it and then get out of my flat and out of my life."

Paul took a big breath, this wasn't going to be easy, and seeing Libby there in front of him made it all the more difficult. Seeing her again just reinforced what he already knew, that he loved her, loved her deeply, but he was unable to say it. Even to admit it to himself was both painful and humiliating. He knew that he was a wretched coward but somehow he had to find the words. There was no doubt in his mind that he had caused her immense pain and he couldn't bear to think about it. He knew that he'd landed himself in an enormous mess and that whatever he did merely increased the level of his stupidity and ineptness. He looked at Libby and wished that he was dead, God how he wished it.

There was a long pause. The window was open wide and the evening sunshine gave the room an almost transcendent feel. The song of a bird came through loud and clear as it courted its partner, turning the attention away from the distant hum of traffic on the nearby road. For both of them the silence seemed eternal, it was as though it was easier to say nothing than to break into strained and inadequate language. They both sat there, having so much to say and yet saying nothing. It was Libby who broke the silence, almost whispering words which she had to force out.

"Well, come on then, what is it that you want to say?"

Paul took a big breath and began.

"Libby, first of all I owe you an apology."

"You owe me nothing, nothing," broke in Libby. "You're a free agent and you exercised your freedom. I had no claims on you and I am a fool for thinking otherwise."

"No, no, you are not a fool. You had every right to think that you had a claim on me, as I had for thinking I had a claim on you. It's just that I... Oh I don't know... it's just that I have behaved abominably and I've let you down, I've hurt you and I will never forgive myself for that."

"I don't think that will be a problem for you," responded Libby. "You clearly have a very short memory and you have a convenient way of manipulating it."

"I know that's how it seems," Paul whispered.

He was finding this far more difficult than he had anticipated, and goodness knows, he was anticipating a difficult time.

"I know that's how it seems, but believe me it is much more complicated than that. Hurting you was the last thing in the world I wanted. I can't believe that I've made such a mess of things."

"If you're looking for sympathy I'm afraid you've come to the wrong place, I've none left. Anyway, aren't you talking to the wrong person, surely it should be your fiancé who gives you understanding and sympathy, in return for the ring that you gave her on the top of the Empire State Building. Don't tell me that you've forgotten her already." The tears began to well up in her eyes again. "Just for the record, how long has all this been going on or did you meet her in Syracuse and the experience was so overwhelming you couldn't be bothered to write?"

"You don't make things easy for me, do you? But then, why should you? I'd better try to tell you the whole story but I'm sure you won't understand it, it's not really as it sounds. I'm not looking for sympathy; I know I don't deserve any. It's just that I don't want to cause you even more hurt. Oh hell, what a mess this all is."

"How sensitive of you not wanting to hurt me. Don't you think it's a bit late for that? Where was all your sensitivity when you were having a ball in America? You're an absolute shit, Paul, and now you come round causing more upset just when I'm trying to put my life together again."

"I met Amanda about five years ago. We became friends, nothing special, but we seemed to enjoy each other's company. I used to go round to her house and got on really well with her parents, in fact her dad is almost like a second father to me. Their home became a second home to me and one thing led to another and it was just assumed that Amanda and I would get together."

"Oh I see," commented Libby, "I suppose you were a little bit lonely when you were in Birmingham and needed to find someone to practice on, musicians need to practice a lot don't they? Well they don't come much more naïve than me, do they?"

"No, no, it wasn't at all like that."

Paul was now embarrassed and confused.

"I said that you wouldn't understand me. Believe me Libby; all the things that we said and shared together were true. You are the best thing that has ever happened to me, you must believe me. At the end of term I went home to tell her that it was all over between us, but…"

He stopped, not knowing how to continue.

"Sure I believe you. I'm the best thing that happened to you and now you can cast me aside and get on with your real life. Well, go!

Go, go, go, and get out of my life. I never want to see you again. I'm sure you and your second father's little girl will have a wonderful life together, but get out of my life. Get out of my flat. I can't cope with this anymore, I've cried too much over the past two weeks. I never want to see you again – may you rot in hell."

Libby was now screaming, the tears were flooding down her face, and she almost ran to the door and pushed him out, slamming it behind him. As he turned from the house it began to rain. He had no coat; he was in for a drenching.

T he engagement of Paul Crozier to Amanda Pettifer was the prelude to a society wedding. Engaged at the top of the Empire State Building in September, honeymooning in Rome in November and family and friends re-united for a baptism in March. The wedding itself had been quite a problem for Libby's friends to handle.

Bruce had refused to go. He replied to the formal invitation saying that, like Paul, he had a previous commitment. It took place in a fashionable London church with splendid music, flowing wine and great hilarity. Nearly everyone who attended decided that it had been a wonderful success, one of the best weddings they had been to for years. As Paul stood with his best man at the chancel steps, waiting for his bride to arrive, he looked behind, down the aisle and saw Libby beaming at him, her arm cradling a bouquet of lilies. His heart leaped within him and he experienced a rare moment of sheer joy. He blinked, looked again and saw Amanda's radiant smile as she walked down the aisle, her father by her side and five bridesmaids in her wake.

M aggie brought very few of her boy-friends home, probably because she never kept them for very long, so when she brought Mike back a second time Beryl began to suspect that he might be something special. It turned out that he was. Maggie had met him at a dance, he was a member of the band, playing a guitar, and he had come up to her during an interval and taken her completely by surprise.

"Hi, I'm Mike. I've been watching you from up on the stage. You're the best looker in the hall, how about having a drink with me when all this has finished?"

"Sorry, I can't do that," she said with a smile, "it will be too late and I've to be up early in the morning. But I'll see you tomorrow if you're not playing anywhere."

From such a strange beginning romance blossomed. He was totally captivated by her, and she, for her part, found that he provided her with a depth of friendship and understanding that she had not come across before.

Beryl was worried when Maggie said that she was going out with a guitarist in a band and she imagined the worst but was pleasantly surprised when she eventually met him. He was polite and he was clean, not at all what she had been expecting. He was also interesting to talk to and he explained that he was working in a band to earn some extra money as he wasn't all that well paid in his job at a local engineering firm. He seemed to calm Maggie down and she gradually changed from being a rather wild and precocious older teenager into what Beryl dared to hope might be an attractive and sensible young woman. She was proud of this transformation and reflected that somehow and at some time and she wasn't quite sure when, Maggie had changed from being a daughter whom she had to care for and worry about to being a friend. Friendship was a luxury that Beryl had never cultivated with anyone for a great many years. It was altogether very satisfying and pleasing.

On her nineteenth birthday Mike proposed and was overjoyed when she hugged him with pleasure and asked him why it had taken him so long. For her, it was a continuation of her life's experience of being the centre of attention and the recipient of everyone's admiration and affection. He adored her and she soaked up his affection as though she had never been loved before, although in reality she had only ever known people's unconditional love. In her own way she loved Mike, whether it was for himself or because of the affection he showered on her no-one really knew and it was clear, she was more than a little in love with the idea of marriage itself.

After a fairy-tale wedding which cost Beryl more than she could afford, Maggie and Mike moved in with her, an arrangement that suited the women well but one which Mike was never really comfortable with. He went along with it because he knew that it pleased Maggie, particularly as it meant that her mother continued to do most of the housework, the shopping and the cooking. He was keen to set up his own home and this became the subject of their first marital row, the first of many as Maggie had to adjust to the fact that not everyone who loved her was prepared to let her have her own way on everything. Although the actual row occurred when Beryl was out of the house, she very soon became aware of the changed atmosphere. It was the first time that she could remember Maggie not being the life and soul of virtually every situation. Instead of playing music, singing and dancing around the house she began to watch more and more television, Mike seemed to be away at work for longer, sometimes not coming home until after she and Maggie had eaten and although he was always perfectly civil and courteous to Beryl, she sensed that he was becoming increasingly unhappy, not at all the sort of behaviour that a newly married couple should be experiencing. When she tried to raise the matter with Maggie one evening she was more or less told to mind her own business and she felt a rift emerging between the two of them, mother and daughter.

"But Maggie my love, I don't like seeing you all subdued like this. You ought to get out a bit more. You and Mike never seem to go dancing or anything these days. You're both young, you should be enjoying yourselves especially since he's given up playing in the band."

"How many times do I have to tell you mum, stop going on so. I'm alright, we're alright, we don't need you interfering, so just leave off us."

"I'm not interfering. Is that what Mike thinks? I've never tried to interfere, ever since he first came here. Is that what he thinks?"

"No mum, he doesn't. It's me not Mike. Just don't keep going on at me."

"Well, I'm only trying to help."

"I know mum, but don't."

The tension eased somewhat when Maggie became pregnant. Mike was overjoyed, Beryl was happy for them both and Maggie seemed pleased that they now had something that they could all talk about and concentrate on after the difficulties of the last few months. It wasn't so much that Maggie was pleased to be pregnant, as the fact that it allowed her to be the centre of attention again and she liked it when Mike fussed over her in the way that Beryl had always done.

Eleven months after their wedding Ann was born, to be followed eighteen months later by Peter. It was clearly a great help having Beryl on hand to share in the childminding but once again tensions developed as Mike felt himself becoming more and more marginalised, apparently unneeded as the two woman talked, fussed, planned and lived babies. This time he was less prepared to sit back and pander to Maggie's wishes. He wanted them to create their own home and, much as he recognised Beryl's great generosity in housing them for all this time, he really thought they needed more space. After several heated exchanges and after many hours of discussion between Maggie and Beryl when Mike was at work, it was eventually agreed that they should put their names down on the housing list and hope to get a council house. They filled in all the necessary forms and began the long wait.

B ack in Birmingham, Bruce was introducing Libby to a whole range of music for the violin and she was involved in helping him out on the administrative side as he brought together three other string players to form the Coriolanus Quartet. He was particularly pleased by the name; he said he decided on it after seeing the play Coriolanus at Stratford with Fiona and Libby.

"You do realise that Bruce is crazy about you, don't you?"

Libby was taken completely by surprise by Fiona's words.

"Don't be so ridiculous, we're just good friends, there's nothing like that about it at all. You surely know me better than that."

"Oh yes, I know you alright but I also know Bruce and it seems pretty obvious to me that this is more than ordinary friendship as far as he's concerned."

"Please don't say things like that; you're not really serious are you? I've never, ever, thought in those terms. I think you're just imagining things – it's not a very good joke, Fiona."

"My dear Libby, I sometimes think that you have never met a man before! Of course he's mad about you, everyone can see it. It did just occur to me that you might be the only person around who wasn't aware of it, that's why I mentioned it. Ask Celia if you don't believe me."

That's exactly what Libby did, as soon as she came through the door.

"Hey Celia, be a friend, tell me that Fiona's talking through her hat, but she's been saying that Bruce has fallen for me. That's not true, is it?"

"Don't tell me you hadn't realised it," replied Celia.

"I was rather hoping that the feelings were mutual and that you had found someone else now that Paul is no longer around."

Libby turned pale and felt physically sick.

"Oh no… don't say that… the thought had never occurred to me and certainly I have no romantic feelings towards him. He's like a brother to me, I've never had a brother you know, and he's such good fun to be with and we get along together fine, but there's no question of anything more about it. Even if I was slightly interested, which I'm not, I hasten to add, it will take me quite a long time to get over Paul."

She was going to add "if I ever do" but stopped herself at the last minute.

She was appalled by the predicament that she inadvertently found herself in and wasn't at all sure what her next step should be. It was seven months since she had last spoken to Paul and every month, every week, every day she had forced herself to work hard to face the world and her work and get on with her daily living. She knew that everything within her, everything about her still yearned for him and without him she felt less than complete. She couldn't imagine life without Paul, she was aware of him throughout the day and most of her dreaming revolved around him. Her friendship with Bruce was quite therapeutic, with him she was able to revisit many of the places that she had previously been to with Paul, and he had continued the musical education that Paul had begun. She valued his friendship, it was important to her, but there had never been the remotest thought in her head that it could be anything more than friendship. She decided that the best thing would be for them to have a talk about their relationship, to bring these issues out into the open and Libby resolved to do that the next time they met.

It was over a week before such an opportunity arose. There was a note from Bruce suggesting that she went round to his flat the following evening and he would cook a curry for them. She made her way up the Hagley Road and arrived at the flat just as Bruce was coming out of the door to dump some waste into the dustbin.

"I hope that's not our meal you're putting in there," exclaimed Libby, "I'm really hungry."

"No, that was yesterday's left-overs, I haven't begun today's yet, but there's still plenty of room left in the bin if things go wrong."

They moved into the flat and Libby saw that the table was already set and there was a distinct smell of cooking in the air.

"You are one great fibber," she laughed, "everything looks ready and all so posh, is it a special occasion or something? Don't tell me you've landed a recording contract."

"No, nothing like that. Chance would be a fine thing. No, it's nothing really, but I thought I would try and do something special because it's my birthday today."

"Oh Bruce – how could I? I didn't know, or if I ever did I've completely forgotten. I haven't even sent you a card let alone brought you a present."

"There's no reason why you should have known. But you can put it down in your diary and send me a card next year. Anyway, the important thing is that you're here and that's the best present I could have. Anyway, it's not like I'm twenty one or anything special."

"I don't even know how old you are, let me guess."

Libby looked at him as though assessing a cow in the cattle market; if she had been near a walking stick she would have picked it up and prodded him.

"Well, you're certainly not in the first flush of youth are you? In fact I detect distinct signs of seediness and I do believe that you've got some grey hairs amidst all those dark curls. I would say that you are approaching thirty five... No, not as old as that, perhaps twenty five."

"Spot on," replied Bruce.

"I am approaching twenty five, I'm twenty three today! Now come on, let's eat."

She saw how much trouble he had taken to get the flat looking tidy, the table set, the food cooked and the music playing quietly in the background. She noticed, for the first time, his obvious pleasure that she had come round for the evening, and her heart sank. Fiona was right, this was something special for Bruce and she had never realised it. Clearly she hadn't been aware of the fact that she must have been sending out the wrong signals, and she wondered how on earth she was going to raise the subject with him – and on his birthday of all days.

"Bruce, I'm not quite sure how to put this and I suppose however I say it, it will somehow be wrong, but we need to talk about things."

They had eaten their meal and she knew she had to raise the matter.

Bruce looked genuinely surprised, he had no idea what was in Libby's mind and it was unlike her to suddenly get serious.

"Look Bruce, I love being with you, I enjoy your friendship and I think we get on together really well, but... but... well, I just hope that you don't fall in love with me or anything like that. I know that sounds silly, perhaps even presumptuous, but it's just that Fiona and Celia said that they thought that perhaps you were, just a little. I hope you don't mind me saying it, and please don't get annoyed with them, they're not trying to interfere or anything. I've never thought of our friendship like that. Anyway after Paul I don't think I could ever get involved with anyone else in that sort of way – not for a long time and, as I feel at the moment, perhaps never again. So please, please don't get hurt, I don't want to hurt you, you're too important to me, too nice... you are one of the best friends I have, but I don't want to mislead you. I'm not really sure what I'm saying, you know, it's just that I don't want you to think that I'm different from what I really am. Does that make sense?"

Bruce looked uncomfortable, he found it difficult to look at Libby and he looked at the floor and twisted his fingers in his hands.

"Thanks for saying that Libby. It just shows that you are a very special person. When you ask me, tell me, not to fall in love with you, that's a bit difficult for me. You see, I've been in love with you for ages. I think I probably loved you when you were going with Paul and I envied him so much. I was jealous of him, I suppose, that he could have you and didn't deserve you. Well, I don't deserve you, I don't mean that, but I know I would treat you better than he treated you."

It was now Libby's turn to look embarrassed, her face became flushed and her eyes became watery.

"Don't talk about Paul, please don't talk about Paul. I know that he hurt me terribly and I hear what people say about him, but it wasn't like that when I was with him, it really wasn't. I know it's all over now and he's married and I'll probably never see him again, but I can't accept that what was going on between us was somehow false. It was terrible what he did, but it was only terrible because it had been so good before. So, whatever else you say, please don't slag him off, I don't think I could cope with that."

"I'm sorry Libby, I didn't mean to upset you and I'm sorry for what I've just said about him. I guess you are right. He was my friend as well, you know, and I think I miss him more than I ever admit to myself. I suppose that's why I get angry with him. I get angry with him because of you – and that's because I love you and want you, and I get angry with him because I want his friendship and I miss him, I even miss his political lectures so there's a hole left in my life as well and realising that has come as a real surprise to me."

Libby smiled.

"I suppose we've turned to each other to try and fill the void that he's left in both our lives. But Bruce dear, I am not in love with you – though I do love you as a friend. Neither of us can satisfy the other in the ways that we have been bereft, but we've had some good times together this last six months and we've enjoyed each other's company, haven't we?"

"I know it's been a difficult time for you Libby and I feel almost guilty saying this, but for me I think the last six months have been the best six months of my life. I've loved being with you, we've got the quartet off the ground and some bookings are coming in. I do know that you don't love me Libby, but I was hoping that you might grow to love me, you know, bit by bit."

The conversation continued for the next couple of hours. For both of them, in different ways, it was a time of healing. For a start, for one of the few times in his life, Bruce had expressed his feelings in words rather than in music. He knew, of course, that Libby wasn't in love with him, but he had harboured the hope that she would forget Paul as she became more involved with him. In the light of this evening's conversation that now seemed unlikely. The evening had brought him closer to Libby, but it had also made him realise just how great the gap between them was. He would need time to come to terms with this new hurt, this sense of intense disappointment

The healing for Libby came in a different way. For the first time she had spoken openly and honestly about her relationship with Paul and what it had meant to her and what it continued to mean. She'd also recognised what was happening between her and Bruce, how they had both been seeking solace in the other for that which they had lost.

By the time she went home they had agreed not to see each other for a few weeks. It was a decision reached in a context of mutual fondness. It was late by the time she was ready to leave and, despite his protestations, she insisted on walking home by herself. They gave each other a hug as they parted. This was the first time that she'd been in his arms and although he had imagined, a thousand times over, what it would be like, it was not at all as he had envisaged it might be. She squeezed him and gave him a kiss on the cheek, and left. They parted closer than they had ever been before, but the truth was – they parted.

What Mike didn't know and what neither Maggie nor her mother told him, was that Maggie left the children with Beryl for long stretches of the day whilst she went into town, met up with old friends, found new friends, went to the cinema and generally began to liven up her life again. She found looking after two young children a bore and a tie. It was not that she didn't love them, she did, but she was more than happy for her mother to assume the major role in their care and upkeep. All this was threatened by the possibility of moving away into a council house in a different part of the city. No-one could accuse Maggie of being stupid and she made it her concern to find out more about how the housing allocation worked and who made the decisions. It took her some time, but eventually she found her way into the system, befriended the man who was responsible for allocations and had reason to believe that things would turn out alright before too long, at least that's what he promised when he was getting dressed.

Less than six months after they joined the housing list a letter arrived offering them a house on an estate quite near to where they were already living. Mike couldn't believe their good fortune and the fact that it was within walking distance of Beryl's would surely please Maggie even though he personally would have preferred it to have been further away. Maggie, to her surprise, was excited when the letter arrived and they set off that evening to have a look at the house, even though it would be a few weeks before they were able to gain the keys and have a look inside. Although, like all the other houses, it was a darkish grey on the outside, giving the impression of dreariness, especially on a dull day, it had three bedrooms and two rooms downstairs plus a kitchen. The road seemed to be quite a mix, with some houses neat and tidy with tight little gardens and well-kept lawns whilst other houses seemed very run down, with cracked windows and quite a lot of noise. All in all, they were both very excited. The extra space would be a real boon, even Maggie could see that, and there were possibilities for them to create a new home together in the style of the sixties rather than accommodating themselves to Beryl's rather old-fashioned furniture and wallpaper.

Mike was amazed that the offer had come through so quickly, he knew of people at work who had been waiting for more than two years.

"I suppose it's because we have the two young children," he reasoned with Maggie.

"Yes, I suppose that's the reason," she replied, "and I think that the way you treat people makes a difference as well."

"I'm sure it does," said Mike, although he couldn't remember Maggie being with him when he visited the council offices to hand in their papers.

They moved into their new home and Mike worked every evening and every weekend to decorate each room. Maggie enjoyed choosing new curtains, well, she chose the cloth and Beryl made the curtains and she was pleased with the way that they were furnishing it. They had a gas fire in the front room; it had a large wooden surround and a choice of different heats to choose from. There was an immersion heater, which meant that she could have hot water whenever she wanted it and Beryl gave her a new twin-tub washer as a moving-in present. For several months Maggie felt as though it was permanently Christmas. On the debit side she used to get annoyed that Mike was constantly working, or when he was not working he was tired. She wanted him to go out with her more often, Beryl would baby-sit she reasoned, so they could go dancing or spend a few hours in the pub. Mike was reluctant, partly because of the cost and partly because he had moved on from his band-playing days and now wanted to settle down and enjoy his home. It often seemed to him that Maggie was never satisfied, that she flitted around like a butterfly, seeking enjoyment and nourishment here and then leaving that space or place for something different, somewhere different. She used to chide him and say that he was unaware of the exciting times that they were living in; this was the sixties, a time of vibrancy and life, of colour and sound, of new experiences and possibilities. She wasn't ready to settle down and become middle-aged, she wanted to dance to the new music – the Beatles, Mick Jagger and all the new groups, it was all happening out there and she wanted to be part of it.

In 1964 their third child, Penny was born. They had been married for four years, had three children and Maggie was twenty-four. Mike was working hard; he had done well and now had a reasonable job in his firm. He adored his children and spent as much time as he could playing with them, caring for them, bathing them and putting them to bed. Maggie was happy for him to do so, she said that she was tired after having them all day and she wanted some space so she could relax a little and watch the television. She usually prepared the evening meal and this was about the only time that Mike wished they were still living with Beryl as she was no cook. He was aware of the fact that there often seemed to be great spaces between the two of them. He tried not to acknowledge this, he thought it was his fault and that he wasn't being sufficiently supportive of her and he longed for those times when they would catch each other's eye and experience a moment of sublime happiness. He loved Maggie, he was proud of how attractive she was, he was still amazed that she had agreed to marry him and he was constantly striving to ensure that he was being a good husband, caring for her, providing for her and ensuring that her needs were being met. What he didn't know and what Beryl suspected but never spoke about, was that she was looking to other people to satisfy many of her needs. For Maggie, one of the great things about the sixties was the emergence of 'the pill'.

It is difficult to know when he began to get suspicious that all was not as it seemed to be on the surface. Because he didn't want to know he failed to follow up one or two mistakes that Maggie had made, It was only later, as he thought about things that he began to see that a pattern had been emerging over several years. Matters came to a head when, whilst bathing the children one evening, they asked him to sing the song that Uncle Wally sang.

"Who's Uncle Wally?" asked Mike.

"You know Uncle Wally," laughed Ann, as she blew bubbles in her bath.

"You know, Uncle Wally, who plays with us in the afternoon."

His heart stopped, he felt a cold sweat of dread sweep over him. He could ignore it no longer. There was something happening, something that he had been trying to deny, ignore, blame himself for even thinking about.

"So what does Uncle Wally sing?"

"That funny song about the animals in the mud."

"Oh yes, I remember it, how silly of me to forget," said Mike weakly and he tried to launch into the Flanders and Swan song about glorious mud.

"No, not like that," squealed Peter, who was sharing the bath with Ann, "sing it properly, like Uncle Wally."

"Oh, I don't think I'm as good at it as Uncle Wally. What else does he do with you?"

"Well, we go to the park, we get ice-creams and once we went on a boat on the river."

"That must have been really good fun. Do you like Uncle Wally?"

"Oh yes, they both shouted out, he's very funny."

He tucked them up in bed and Maggie went up to kiss them goodnight.

"We've been telling Daddy about all the things we do with Uncle Wally," shouted out Peter.

"He's very funny isn't he?"

She nodded, gave all three of them a big kiss, took a deep breath and went downstairs. Things were never going to be the same again; she knew that as she walked into the front room.

"So you know," she whispered. "Well, it had to come out sometime. It's rather a relief, I suppose."

"What the hell's going on Maggie?"

Mike wasn't sure whether he was shouting or being very quiet. His head was spinning; he didn't know what to do, what to think or what to say.

"Who's this Uncle Walter character? Who is he? What are you up to? How long has all this been going on? What's happening Maggie?"

"Wally's a friend," she said. "He sometimes pops round on his way home from work. Nothing's going on, that's all there is to it."

"Don't give me that crap." This time he was shouting. "Do you expect me to believe that? I may be gullible, I may be too trusting, but I'm not completely stupid."

"Oh push off and leave me alone," retorted Maggie, as she moved out of the front room and went into the kitchen.

"Oh no you don't," he shouted, as he followed her into the kitchen and grabbed hold of her arm.

"Let me go," shrieked Maggie.

"It's nothing to do with you who my friends are. And it's nothing to do with you what I do with them either!"

"Oh yes it bloody is. You happen to be my wife and the mother of my children," and he swung his arm and hit her across the face. Maggie screamed and ran in to the other room crying.

He could not believe that he'd struck her. It was the first time in all his life he had been violent. Hitting Maggie was just about the last thing he could ever have envisaged doing. He adored her, worshipped the ground she walked on and here he was hitting her. He stayed in the kitchen for a few minutes before moving into the other room. She was sitting on the settee, a cushion up against her face, crying.

"Maggie, I'm sorry," he began, "whatever you've been up to, I've no right to strike you, I've never done it before and I'll never do it again. I promise you that. I'm truly sorry. Do you hear me?"

She nodded but didn't look up at him.

"Perhaps we need to sit down and talk this through, it won't do either of us any good shouting at each other."

She nodded again, but still did not remove the cushion from the front of her face.

"I take it that you've been having an affair with this chap, am I right?"

Another nod and still no sign of Maggie's face appearing. He sighed and sat down opposite, in an easy chair. He paused for a few minutes before resuming.

"Maggie, we're going to have to talk about this sooner or later, so why don't we start now?"

He was not prepared for her story of infidelity. It started soon after they were married and had been a constant factor in her life since then. Not just Wally, but a whole series of men whom she had met in the pub, in coffee bars and even at the supermarket. Maggie did not see these encounters as casual sex, for her, each one in its own way had a form of stability, was more than just a passing physical relationship. It was a way of trying to overcome the deep void that she experienced in her day to day life. It was not that she didn't love Mike, she did, she really did, but somehow it was never enough. She depended upon him, he was a wonderful caring husband and father, but when he had given his all and, she admitted, that was a great deal, there was still something missing in her life. She had hoped that when she had children they would provide whatever it was that she was looking for, but it hadn't turned out that way. She loved the children but they could not bring her the happiness for which she craved. No, that wasn't it, because she was happy, it wasn't a question of being unhappy. In fact, she felt that of all her friends she was probably the happiest, so that was the wrong word, it was not really about happiness, it was just that there was something lacking in her life. If she could find that then of all people she would be the most satisfied, because she had such a wonderful husband and children and a loving mother just a short distance away. She didn't know why she seemed to need these extra relationships, but the truth was that she did.

"I just don't understand you," sighed Mike. "I've tried so hard to love you and care for you and I thought you appreciated that, I thought that was what you wanted, but it seems I was wrong."

"No, you weren't wrong Mike, that was what I did want, what I do want."

"Then where did I go wrong? What more could I have done?"

"Mike, you didn't go wrong and you couldn't have done more. It's not you, it's me. I'm sorry, I don't know why I'm like I am but I just feel this sort of inner emptiness and I need to try and fill it. It's not you, it's me."

"But I don't know what you mean by 'inner emptiness'. No-one else seems to have it. It just seems to be another way of saying that you're sex mad, but you can't bring yourself to say it. I don't know whether I'm so angry that I can't think straight or just so sad that I can't get my head round it. But can't you see that this is no way to bring the children up. If you don't love me, at least you can love them."

"It's not about whether I love you or not or whether I love the children. Of course I love them and honestly Mike, I love you, I really do. I... I... Oh I don't know, I just don't seem to be able to live like other people. I think that perhaps mum is the only person who understands me."

Mike felt out of his depth with all this. Initially he had been angry, even furious, but as the story unfolded he recognised that being angry was not going to help either of them. He was surprised by how quickly those initial feelings of anger evaporated, to be replaced by a sense of deep foreboding and utter incomprehension. He felt totally empty inside, his mouth was dry, his heart was pounding and yet there seemed to be a great weariness spreading over his whole body. He looked at Maggie, his eyes full of love and tenderness but their focus distorted by the tears he was trying to hold back. He wondered if he had ever really known her, if he had ever really understood her. There must have been times when their lives fitted together, like a carefully crafted piece of machinery, but when he thought about it, he wasn't sure if he could remember when those times might have been.

Later, when they went to bed, they fell into each other's arm and their love-making was passionate, hungry and almost reckless. As they eventually settled down to sleep Mike was anxious in case he had been too rough, too demanding, and he felt slightly guilty and unsure about his motives and whether he had hurt or even abused Maggie. For her part, she went to sleep with a smile on her face thinking that if Mike was like that more often perhaps she wouldn't need to look elsewhere. Neither of them told the other what they were thinking.

A fter graduating Libby moved north, completed a Dip.Ed.and began her teaching career. She was pleased to be able to send money on a regular basis to her mother to enable her to buy special treats and she was generous in providing clothes and toys for Maggie's children as they began to appear. She spent three years in her first job which was deliberately within easy reach of her mother and then moved to London to a much larger school where she was given a promoted post.

Acting on Bill's advice she entered the property market and bought a flat in Offord Road in Islington, only five minutes walk from the underground, a couple of stops away from Kings Cross and she began to thrive living in London. With Victoria she went to concerts and the theatre and was proud to introduce her to the members of the Coriolanus Quartet when they played in the Wigmore Hall for the first time.

There were a number of men in her life during these days, but with none of them did she find a relationship that satisfied her. It was not a matter of great concern to her. She enjoyed male company and had a full and active social life but was never in any mood to settle down or even go steady. It was not that she was unattractive and she was never short of admirers, it was just that none of the people she went out with seemed able to communicate with her in a way which fed her soul or enlarged her mind. Occasionally she would take her latest boyfriend over to Victoria's and they would all get excited and, after they had left, discuss whether this was 'Mr Right', but she never took the same man back twice and Victoria began to despair that she would ever get married.

After a while she began to feel restless and unfulfilled. Many of her friends were settling down, getting married and having children. This didn't seem to be a realistic option for her, which was quite painful for her to admit to and she felt that she needed to do something to fill the void in her life. She began to explore the possibility of teaching overseas and there seemed to be a real chance that she could find work in Southern Africa.

Her mother was horrified. No-one in the family had every gone so far away and when people had gone abroad it was always with tragic consequences. Her father was killed on the Somme and her husband in Normandy. Now her daughter was thinking about going abroad. Whilst it would be unfair to say that Beryl was a racist it was a fact that she had never known any black people, she had never made any effort to know any and she was very worried about what might happen if Libby went to work with a lot of Africans. The thought even came to her that Libby might marry a black man and have mixed race children and she found the thought of that almost impossible to take on board.

"Mum, I just can't understand what the problem is. There's a tremendous need for teachers over there, the children want to learn and I want to teach them. It seems a very simple equation to me."

"Libby, you don't know what you're saying. Those countries are full of foreigners, their ways are different from ours and you'll never really be able to teach them anything; they don't think like us and do things in the same way."

"Oh that's absolute rubbish. Learning is learning wherever you are. These children want to learn to read and write, they want to grow up and earn their living and enjoy some of the things that we take for granted. You should see how keen they are about schooling."

"Only in the schools that they talked to you about. Can't you see that they are trying to kid you, they want to entice you over there."

"For goodness sake mum, of course they aren't enticing me, and they didn't talk about some specially selected schools. Anyway, I'm going ahead with it and exploring the possibility of going to Swaziland."

"Swaziland? Where's that? I've never even heard of it! What's wrong with teaching in this country, don't our children need to learn to read and write as well?"

"Of course they do, of course they do. But there are so many teachers over here and so few over there. And just because you've never heard of a country doesn't mean that it doesn't exist, and anyway, you've heard of it now. If you really want to know, it's just about to become independent. It's been a British Protectorate for years and there's a real sense of a new beginning and an excitement about its future. It's a wonderful opportunity to do something real and worthwhile in a new country."

"Well if, you ask me, there are too many countries getting their independence at the moment, what's wrong with them being British after all that we've done for them? Anyway, if there are so many teachers over here then tell me this – why are people complaining about the size of classes? Aren't there supposed to be too many children in our classes because there aren't enough teachers?" Beryl glared at her.

"In any case I'm wasting my breath, I suppose you'll just go and do as you please, you've always done that Libby, always been a bit selfish and concerned about doing what you wanted. Victoria didn't go on about wanting to go to university and Maggie has been quite content to find a job locally and stay around here and look after me if I needed anything, but not you, you needed to be away doing your own thing."

Libby was deeply embarrassed by her mother's views and attitude and also annoyed by the way she was twisting things. She also felt it grossly unfair as she had deliberately returned to Leeds for her first teaching job so that she could be near to her mother and quietly help her out. In the light of this exchange and of many other similar conversations, their relationship went through a difficult few months as Libby's plans began to take shape. Maggie showed little interest in the idea, in fact she showed little interest in anything that Libby or Victoria did, but she was not hostile and that was something to be grateful for. Victoria had very mixed views. On the one hand she thought it was a natural consequence of Libby's generous and caring approach to life and she was more than a little proud of her. Against this was the fact that she would miss her tremendously and she wasn't sure how her mother would cope, especially after all the arguing. Bill regarded it as a bit of left-wing idealism that she would grow out of.

Whatever everyone thought, Libby proceeded with her plans. By the time she was ready to leave her mother seemed to have reconciled herself to the fact and was showing a marked interest in where she was going and what she would be doing. Libby wasn't sure if this was genuine but genuine or not, it did mean that they parted company in good spirit and that was a relief to her.

The day of departure was such an occasion that Beryl and Victoria came to the airport to see her off, one of the very few times that her mother had ever been to London despite frequent invitations. They went up to the viewing platform on the roof of the terminal building and were able to wave to her as she walked across the tarmac to the waiting plane. The viewing deck attracted people looking out at the planes and waving to departing and arriving travellers. Victoria was particularly aware of a small group of women who were standing quite close to them, all of the crying. She noticed that, in their sorrow, they were trying to support each other although it was clear that they were total strangers.

The first woman, an elderly person possibly seventy or older was wiping the tears from her eyes and explaining that she was seeing her daughter off who lived in Australia.

"She comes over every two years, bless her. It's lovely to see her but saying goodbye is always so difficult, we both spend all the time crying. She has to get back to her family, I know that, but my health hasn't been so good recently and I suppose I'm afraid that I might never see her again."

"Oh your poor dear," commented one of the others.

"It must be awful for you. I know how you feel, well, I know a little bit. My son lives in America now, he comes back to England quite often, two or three times a year, but I can't help crying when he goes back. The house seems so empty after he's been there. Sometimes you're more aware of people when they've gone than when they're here."

"That's right," replied the first woman.

"I live quite easily without her for months and months, but when she leaves after a visit it always seems to tear me apart and I don't know how I'll get through the next day."

She looked across at the third woman who could hardly contain her sobs and was trying to camouflage them by blowing her nose into her handkerchief.

"Is it your daughter who's just left as well?"

"Yes it is," she replied. "I've never seen her go before, it's terrible isn't it?"

"It certainly is, I feel for you, especially with this being the first time. Where is she going, to Australia? Does she live over there now?"

"No," she whispered, trying to dry her eyes.

"No she's not going to Australia, she's going to Tenerife for a week's holiday."

For a few months normality returned and Mike began to half-believe that it had all been a bad dream. When things seemed to be going well it was impossible to imagine that Maggie had behaved in the ways that she had. He thought that by concentrating on being a good father and a good husband he would somehow prove to be irresistible to Maggie, just as, for him, she was everything that he could wish for. The children adored him, he adored them, he adored Maggie and clearly she adored them all as well. Things were certainly looking up. But they were also looking up for Phil.

Libby looked out of the small window, she wasn't sure where she was but was certainly aware of the fact that the flight was getting extremely bumpy. The earth looked red below her, there were quite a lot of trees but they were far apart from each other. She saw a bridge, with about twenty arches, but there was no water in what she assumed was a river bed. It seemed as though there were just miles and miles of scrubland, broken up by small clumps of what were probably bushes, but looked more like freckles from the height she was viewing them. She had not really slept during the night, her mind racing hither and thither, a mixture of excitement and apprehension, sorrow at leaving her family and friends and more than a little anxiety about how she would cope and whether she would make any friends. She thought about all that she was leaving behind and had a few moments of near panic as she wondered, not for the first time, if she was doing the right thing. She thought about the friends whom she would miss and allowed herself the luxury of thinking about the different men in her life and how she had never been able to sort out a satisfactory relationship with any of them apart from Paul, and that finished up as a disaster. She had tried to forget him, no-one could have tried harder she reasoned to herself, but it was clearly going to be impossible. She no longer felt angry about what he'd done. Anger was short-lived whilst love was eternal, or at least, that's what people said. She pulled herself up and decided this was a ridiculous pattern of thought to pursue and Africa was giving her the opportunity to create a new life.

She had remained in touch with Bruce and was delighted, and relieved, to have been invited to his wedding a few years ago when she met his bride Nancy for the first time. She had joined the Quartet after the original cellist had left and evidently at long last Bruce had found a soul-mate. Eventually, after being unable to sleep all night, Libby drifted away, accompanied by all her friends and their shared experiences, and she didn't wake up until the stewardess announced that they would shortly be arriving in Johannesburg where she would change planes there for the relatively short flight to Mbabane.

She was met at the airport, or at what served as an airport, by the two people she would be sharing a home with, both teachers at the same school, Patsy who came from Australia and Miriam from South Africa. They drove her towards Manzini, then turned off the main road and travelled into the countryside. She felt exhilarated, it was very hot but there was a refreshing breeze as they drove along, from the open windows. Patsy kept up a running commentary about all the places they passed. Miriam, behind the wheel, was much quieter and was concentrating on the driving, explaining that driving could be quite hazardous at times and that you had to be prepared for absolutely anything, from wild animals to drunken drivers, from holes in the road to army blockades.

"We thought we would take you home first," explained Patsy.

"You'll probably want to unpack and have a bath. Then we decided to take you straight away on a local tour to make you realise that you are no longer in England and then tomorrow you, or rather we, are invited to have lunch with the headmaster Mr Sithole and his wife. That should be nice, they're such sweeties."

Libby was to discover that virtually everyone was a 'sweetie' to Patsy.

"We were going to take you round the school straight away, but I think the Sitholes want to do that themselves. We've got a simple meal waiting for you when we get home, I don't know how hungry you are, anyway we've got something sorted out. Oh by the way, I hope you're not a vegetarian, I was when I arrived, but the idea of not eating meat is so incomprehensible to people here that I realised that I was going to starve as well as causing offence. You're going to have the room that Helda used to have. She's German, a real sweetie, but she left after about six months because she missed her boyfriend too much. I'm not sure if you are taking her class or not, I'll leave all that sort of stuff to Mr Sithole to sort out. Actually he's called Kislon but he likes to be called Mr Sithole, I think he likes the status and the dignity, but don't get me wrong, he's not pompous or anything and he's a very good head-teacher. We adore him, don't we Miriam?"

Miriam grinned and Libby detected a warm bond of friendship between them. She hoped that she would soon share in it rather than feel an outsider.

"You know, there are so many questions I want to ask, so many things I don't know, but now I'm here I can't think of a single thing to ask you, isn't that crazy? It's good to be here and I'm really grateful to you both for coming to meet me. I hope that you won't find me a difficult person to live with, you must let me know if I do things which annoy you. Anyway, I'm sure I'll settle in well with you unless you are both putting on a frightful act and beneath the surface you actually can't stand each other."

"We've had great fun trying to imagine you."

Patsy spoke whilst looking at Libby with a pronounced stare.

"We thought you would maybe have dyed hair, be overweight and frightfully proper, but I think you're a real sweetie, we'll get on fine. Do you play any sport? Miriam coaches netball and, would you believe it, I try and lead the soccer teams – I would be very happy to hand that over if you're a star centre-forward. The children know all about the English teams – Manchester United, Arsenal, Nottingham Forest and the like but they don't know anything about soccer in Australia."

"Oh dear, I'm failing at the first hurdle," sighed Libby, "I know absolutely nothing about football."

"Cricket?" asked Patsy tentatively.

"Failed again," sighed Libby, "although I do come from Yorkshire."

"Well what can you do?" asked Patsy pretending to be irritated beyond measure.

"What time does the next plane go back to England Miriam, we've got a hopeless case here?"

They arrived at a bungalow, set apart from the road and away from other buildings, it had a deep red roof and there were two large water containers one on each side to collect rain water. There was a dusty area all around, Libby supposed that it might be called a garden but such a word seemed to lack meaning in this context. There was a large veranda at the front, with a table and chairs and Patsy called this their 'drinking out' area. Inside, each of them had their own room; there was a large sitting room with a few mats on a wooden floor and a large fan hanging from the ceiling. All the windows were open, although they had bars to deter intruders. A reasonable sized kitchen, a smallish bathroom and a small junk room with cases and boxes piled high. It was hot and sultry inside, the air almost stale although that couldn't really have been the case with the windows open and the fan switched on. Patsy and Miriam had made some effort to give it a home-like quality with a few plants in the sitting room and one or two photographs dotted around.

"I'm afraid there's no television or anything like that," remarked Patsy, "but we do have an old radio which sometimes, and I stress the word 'sometimes' works and we can even get the BBC World Service if the wind blows in the right direction."

Libby could not envisage there being any wind, let alone imagine what the right direction might be, she was almost overcome by the sultry heat. They had prepared a salad, the main ingredient of which seemed to be green tomatoes and pineapple, but when she tasted them she was grateful for the juice and refreshment that they brought.

After a drive round in the afternoon which gave her some sort of idea of the size and shape of the place they headed back for the bungalow that she was already thinking of as 'home'. Once there she had an hour or two to herself as she sorted out her room, hung up her clothes and decided where to put the photographs she had brought with her. She had also brought a calendar with views of 'the English countryside' which she thought she might miss and she flipped the pages over to December and saw the snow scene, such a marked contrast to the heat that she was experiencing at that moment. Suddenly she let out a squeal and Patsy, who was passing by, popped her head through the door to enquire if everything was alright.

"Yes, yes," muttered Libby, "but look at that, what is it?"

She pointed to a large dark creature which was waddling across the floor. Patsy roared with laughter.

"That, dear Libby, is a cockroach. It's one of Africa's tamest wild animals and I'm afraid that you will have to learn to love them because we share our home with them, and with lots of other little creatures, not to mention all the moths."

Libby's heart sank.

The evening drew in quickly, there really is no dusk in Africa and the day moved from bright and sunshine to near darkness in a matter of an hour or less. The darkness reminded her of just how tired she was but she was also looking forward to sitting down with her two new companions and learning more about them. Miriam had cooked a stew, which they ate with great enthusiasm.

"We don't usually drink wine this expensive, but we thought we would tonight to celebrate your arrival," explained Miriam as she poured out a rather rich and fruity South African red.

"Perfect."

Libby stretched out on the settee and slowly sipped from the very full glass that had been poured for her.

"Well thank goodness you like wine," commented Patsy.

"We were rather afraid that you might disapprove. Actually, we do get through rather a lot, but only in the evenings. We find that it helps us to relax."

"I'm not quite sure who or what you were expecting, but you do seem to have been imagining me as some sort of an ogre. I'm afraid I am going to be a great disappointment to you. So, tell me about yourselves. I've so much to learn and come to terms with that I might as well begin at home."

Libby took another sip of wine and looked across at them to see who would begin.

"Well, I'm Patsy, as you know. I'm twenty seven years old and I'm from Manly which is a beach town just outside Sydney in Australia. I left school at sixteen, married at eighteen and divorced at twenty. After that I spent a year travelling, trying to sort myself out and then returned to Sydney to go to college. Eventually I qualified as a teacher and here I am. I was supposed to stay longer in Australia but my mum and dad split up and I didn't want to side with one rather than the other so I just took off. I love it here, I've been at the school for two years, the only problem with it is that it's rather a long way from the sea. I suppose I shall have to go home some time but I've no plans to do anything other than stay here and teach, it's a good school and the kids are just fantastic, absolute sweeties. Is that enough? What else do you want to know? As far as I know I don't snore and I'm quite friendly with cockroaches. As you know, I used to be a vegetarian but Miriam's cooking won me over."

It all seemed so straightforward, simple and matter of fact and yet Libby sensed that behind the smiling face and the outgoing personality there was a lot of hurt and a lot of searching. Perhaps they had much in common, time would tell. When the attention turned to Miriam the conversation seemed to change in character, she couldn't quite understand how but she experienced a different sort of mood or character. It was as if both she and Patsy were still trying to discover themselves, Patsy more so than herself, but Miriam knew who she was.

She was born in Soweto, in South Africa. Her father had been a minister and he looked after three large congregations. He was actively involved in community affairs and was a bitter opponent of apartheid and the way in which it restricted his movement and affected the life of everyone in his community. Her mother worked in a hospital as a general help, cleaning and helping to feed patients. She was very intelligent but had only received an education lasting three years. There were five children and Miriam was the youngest, and the only girl. Her mother was determined that she should receive a better education than she had and made considerable sacrifices to ensure that she did. Her father was seen as being a trouble maker by the police and had been beaten up on various occasions, so much so that his health began to deteriorate and he was unable to work, unable to earn enough to keep the family together. Her four brothers had left school and found work in local garages, and then two of them left Soweto, when her father became ill and went to work further away in the gold mines. She had never seen them since the day they left and had no idea whether they were alive or dead. Her father died shortly before she was married and she grieved for him for many months. Martin, her husband, had been a member of the church; he sang in the choir and had courted Miriam for several years. Her eyes smiled as she spoke of him and her words were soft and tender.

They had a son Reuben and a daughter Mary and all was well until one night the police raided their home in the middle of the night and took Martin away. It seems that he was beaten up and dumped on a road miles away from home and it took him many hours to walk home. The experience changed him, he became bitter and angry and began to associate with a group of more radical men, all of whom had fallen foul of the authorities in one way or another. His anger, she explained, was not towards her and the family, to them he remained devoted, but he was no longer prepared to sit and wait for change, he believed that it was necessary for the African people to fight for their freedom. She didn't know all the details of what he was doing but one day there were many cars screeching to a stop outside their house and men with dogs and guns jumped out and grabbed Martin and took him away. They said later that he was involved in terrorism and there was a trial. The prosecution wanted the death penalty to be passed but in the end he was given life imprisonment.

At this stage Miriam began to cry, very quietly. Patsy went out to the kitchen and made her a drink. She was amazed by what she was hearing for although they had shared a home together for about a year she had never heard the full story. After a while Miriam continued, it was as though she needed to talk, and she began to explain what Martin's imprisonment had meant for the family. Her mother had gone back to her own village, where she lived before she married, and she was now looking after Reuben and Mary. Miriam moved away from Soweto, which was not easy and she didn't explain how she managed to do it, and she found her way in to Swaziland and found a job teaching. She wasn't a qualified teacher but she had received a good education thanks to her mother and it was sufficient to enable her to get a job at the school. She was able to earn more than she needed for herself and was able to get money back to her mother to help with the children, whom she hadn't seen for almost two years.

"But how do you cope?" asked Libby, "how do you find the strength to continue?"

"God gives me the strength, God is my rock and my salvation. I sing a great deal and that gives me hope and encouragement."

"But I've never heard you sing," protested Patsy, "when do you sing?"

"I sing all the time, but I sing to myself. All the hymns I sang in my father's church, all the songs of my people, I am always singing. I sing to my children and they sing to me, I hear them in my mind."

When it was Libby's turn to talk about herself she felt shallow and disingenuous. She felt almost ashamed of the comfort and parochialism of her life.

Maggie met Phil on a blind date. She wouldn't have described it in that way but that's what it was. Her friend Sheila, whom she was in the habit of meeting a couple of times a week in the pub at lunchtime, engineered a meeting with her boyfriend's flatmate. Phil was tall, bronzed and handsome with long blonde hair in need of a wash. He immediately took an interest in Maggie as soon as she walked into the pub with Sheila and she couldn't resist his flattery.

"Hey Sheila, where did you find your friend? Where have you been hiding her? Why haven't you introduced us earlier? Come on, come on, let me get you a drink – I bet you're not on lemonade are you?"

He went off to the bar and returned, making sure that he sat next to Maggie, well almost *on* her, they were so close, their legs pressing against each other from hip to toe.

"I don't know who you are, but you look great, absolutely great."

Maggie blushed, smiled openly and winked across the table at Sheila.

"The first thing you need to know about me is that I'm Phil, I'm unattached, available and in love with life. All I need to know about you is whether you too love life, everything else is secondary."

Maggie didn't quite know how to reply, so she grinned at him, poked him in the ribs and said "Hey, I've met your sort before, all bullshit and no balls."

Phil was quick to reply.

"Well no-one's ever said that of me before, I've never had any complaints," and he shifted in his seat and put his arm round her shoulder.

"You don't waste any time, do you," retorted Maggie, making no effort to remove his arm.

"No, life's too short; you have to go for what you want. I know what I want, the point is, do you?"

"Perhaps I do and perhaps I don't, you'll just have to wait and see won't you."

She continued to go to the pub twice a week, whilst Beryl looked after the children and soon it was three times a week. It began with meeting Sheila, then with meeting Sheila and Phil and then settled down with just Phil. The pub was The Stranger's Arms (which proved to be an appropriate name). As the weeks went by she became besotted by Phil. He was physically attractive of course and he clearly found her to be the same, but there was more to it than that. It was as though he was uncluttered by anything and anyone; he seemed to have a freedom from cares, worries and responsibilities that Maggie found almost irresistible. He lived each day as it came, committed to enjoying it. What was past was past and seemed to have no hold over him, whilst the future was always offering something new, something exciting. Perhaps that was it. He represented an excitement that had all but disappeared from Maggie's life now that she had a husband, a home and three young children. She looked forward to her times with him because he never asked about her family, never asked about her past, he just seemed to relish the present moment. If he thought about the future, it was the immediate future that he thought about such as knowing when the flat would be free and when Maggie would be able to visit and spend time making love. He seldom thought ahead more than two or three hours and he offered Maggie an experience that she thought she had said goodbye to when she settled down with Mike. It was the experience of the present moment, disengaged from any sense of responsibility. It was focused upon self-gratification and as such it was a marked contrast to her life with Mike.

She knew, as the weeks turned into months, that she was building a new life for herself. She hadn't intended this and it came as a surprise to her when she realised it, but that was what was happening. Her realisation came just a few days before Phil brought the issue out into the open.

"Maggie sweetheart, there's something I've got to tell you. I'm leaving next week."

"You're *what?*" Maggie almost screamed at him. "What do you mean 'you're leaving'? You can't just sit there with a pint in your hand, rubbing your leg up and down mine and tell me that you're buggering off."

"Now don't get upset sweetheart, calm down. You know I've got work to do. It's time for me to be off again, the season is starting up again."

He was an entertainments manager in Benidorm. He had told her very little about what he did and to be fair, Maggie had shown little interest in pursuing the matter; in fact she had shown little interest in anything about him beyond the physicality of their relationship. It was as though she didn't want to be reminded that there was a world out there beyond the two of them. When she was with him she wanted to lose herself in the new reality which she supposed was being created, a reality which excluded the demands and responsibilities of normal adult life, a reality in which she stood centre-stage and only those who adored her had a part to play. The news that he was going to leave the following week devastated her; it was as though the very foundations of her being were slowly shattering. It was like an explosion in slow motion and she felt herself falling into the huge abyss which had opened up before her. It was suddenly dark and she felt dizzy as though she was spinning round and round and being sucked into a whirlpool.

"Now don't get all upset, that's just silly."

Phil had seen tears well up in her eyes. He leaned across the table and held her hands.

"I want you to come with me. Jack everything in over here sweetheart and come over to sunny Spain with me. We could have an absolute whale of a time. What do say? Will you come?"

This was not what she had been expecting, but then she had not been expecting anything. She had learned this attitude from him, it was one of the things that she found most attractive about him and it reminded her of how she used to feel as a teenager. The abyss seemed to spiral out of control and then suddenly there was hope, there was light and the possibility of life, new life, life more abundant than anything she had ever known before and Maggie felt herself reaching out and trying to grasp it.

She had never been abroad, she didn't have a passport and she knew very little about life in any other place apart from Leeds. The idea of leaving all this behind and making a new life in a new country was both exciting and frightening. She suddenly began to ask questions about his life beyond her and he enthralled her by his stories of wonderful beaches, constant sunshine, dancing through the night and a seeming endless supply of cheap drink. He painted a picture of life as a constant party of fun-loving people, sun-lit days and warm lazy nights. It was the most exciting scenario that she had ever envisaged and she was being offered the chance to be a part of it. She walked home that day quite intoxicated by the idea.

She never really made a conscious decision, she just knew, within a few days that she had moved into a state of acceptance of

Phil's suggestion. All she had to do was to work out how to leave. Even more problematic was how she was going to be able to leave her mother, but at least she knew that she could talk about it to her whereas she knew that she could never face Mike and tell him. She set in motion the process of getting a passport. Phil spent a long and sensuous afternoon with her before saying goodbye and plans were made for her to fly out to him at the earliest opportunity. She was once again alone, apart from her husband and three children and mother that is, but she felt that she was alone, and what Maggie felt determined what reality was to her, and so she was alone.

She spent the next ten days busying herself around the house in ways that she had never done before. She cleaned from top to bottom, she cooked meals that were rather more imaginative and she spent time with the children. Mike noticed the difference almost immediately. To begin with he thought that perhaps she was pregnant again, tidying up the nest was a feature of her days in early pregnancy, but there was something different about her this time. He wasn't sure what to make of it, but he was pleasantly surprised. She seemed to have more time. More time for him, more time for the children and more time for the home. She did of course have more time because she was not spending most afternoons with Phil, but Mike was not aware of this, he was just conscious of how much nicer it was to have her around with her mind focused on them rather than the often distracted manner that had seemed to characterise her in recent weeks and months. He knew that after the traumatic incident of a few months back their relationship had changed. In many ways it had changed for the better, but in other ways, which he could never really admit to himself, he felt that there was an invisible wall between them. He couldn't put it into words, he was not a man of words, but he knew it was there. There was a greater tenderness, more smiles and knowing looks and their lovemaking had become more passionate, but there was a strange sense of separation none the less.

Beryl was altogether more perceptive and, when needs required, more forthright. She had been aware of the bust-up between Maggie and Mike although no words had ever been said on the matter. She was aware of Maggie's new circle of friends; it could hardly have been otherwise since she did so much of the child-minding whilst Maggie was out. She was not proud of the way in which she was somehow involved in what was happening but, she reasoned, Maggie had come to her for help and, as always, she had tried to do whatever it was that Maggie wanted. But something was happening, she didn't know what it was, she feared it was another man, but didn't know for certain. Then, out of the blue, she didn't have the children most days and Maggie seemed somehow different. She certainly seemed happy, but if another man was involved and then suddenly she wasn't seeing him, surely this would have made her depressed or moody. She decided that the time had come to get things out into the open. A few days later the opportunity arose when Maggie turned up by herself one Saturday afternoon, she was free, she said, because Mike had taken the children out to the park.

"Sit down love and I'll make a cuppa," said Beryl when Maggie breezed into the house. "I've wanted to have a chat with you for quite a while."

Maggie went into the living room, looked at the photographs of the children on the wall and wondered what was about to be said. Was this, or was it not, the time for her to come clean with her mother? Maggie was still lost in thought about this when Beryl came back in. It must be serious, she thought, she's put the biscuits on a plate, she clearly means business so I guess the time has come for us to talk about everything.

"I know what you want to talk about," Maggie started before Beryl had even sat down, "I've wanted to talk to you as well, but didn't quite know what to say or how to say it."

Beryl looked at her quizzically,

"Surely talking to me has never been a problem, and goodness knows we've had enough talks about things that we don't need to go into again."

"I know mum, no, you're the best person in the world to talk to. I've never been able to talk to anyone like I'm able to talk to you. You're not only my mother, you're my best friend. I don't know what I'd do if you weren't there."

Suddenly and totally unexpectedly, she burst into tears.

"I'm leaving Mike; I'm leaving the kids with him as well. Mum, I've met this chap, he's really gorgeous, and I'm going off to live with him."

Beryl was expecting to hear about another man, but she was not expecting to hear that Maggie was leaving home.

"Leaving Mike and the children? Are you serious? You must be out of your mind. Why haven't you told me about this before? When did you reach this decision? Who is he? Oh Maggie, there are so many questions, how can you just turn up and say this to me?"

"Look Mum, I know this must come as a bit of a shock to you, well a big shock to you, but you must have realised that things haven't been all that good between me and Mike for quite a while now. It's just been so awful, I feel as though I've died when I'm at home and I just need to get away. Well I've got that chance now. Phil wants me to go and be with him and it's the best thing that's ever happened to me, honestly."

"Maggie, wake up," retorted Beryl. "You have a husband and three children. What do you mean you feel dead at home, you don't know the first thing about death and feeling dead? Pull yourself together. Even if you and Mike can't get on, you've still got three lovely children. You can't possibly want to walk out on them. For God's sake Maggie, you're their *mother*!"

"Oh I knew you'd go on at me, that's why I've not said anything before," replied Maggie. "This really is something that I have to do, it is, honestly."

"What you have to do is look after your children." Beryl was getting angry.

"Just who do you think will care for them, have you even thought what they will feel if you push off? What is that saying to them? That you don't love them? Leave Mike if you must, though I think you are crazy even to think of it, but take the children with you, sort out a sensible arrangement with him so that you both have them and share the looking after them, but don't for God's sake even think of leaving them. Mike can't cope, you know that."

"Mum, it's not like that. I can't take the children with me. I'm going to Spain."

"Spain? Are you completely out of your mind? Do you know what you're doing? You've never been abroad before; you don't even have a passport! Who is this man, a Spanish waiter that you've met, or what? And what sort of a man would expect a woman to leave her children behind. Maggie, you're crazy, you just can't do something like that."

"I can and I'm going to," shouted Maggie, and with tears streaming down her face she stormed out of the room, slammed the door and walked off. She had only fallen out with her mother once before and that was years ago, when she had stormed out as a teenager. They had gone through a difficult time when she was first married, before the children came along, but apart from those instances she could never remember a time when her mother was not always there, always fully supportive and always understanding. Why was she now being so unreasonable, that's not what she was expecting, her mother was there to support her and just when she needed that support her mother gets all difficult, it was most unfair.

She sat alone in The Stranger's Arms; it was a new experience for her. It was the place where she had met Phil, where his legs had crossed with hers in an electrifying manner at their first meeting. It was the place where they had discussed the future and made plans. Sheila had passed on a letter the previous day and it was full of exciting things and it sounded wonderful in Benidorm, though she admitted that she had very little idea what it was like. The main thing was that Phil was missing her and was asking her when he could expect her. The bed was ready and he was lonely without her. Maggie resolved to go as soon as possible, and that turned out to be less than a week away.

On her final evening at home she tried to remain calm and focused. She cooked a good meal, Mike's favourite, played with the children, insisted on reading to each one of them as they went to bed. She was kindly and affectionate towards Mike. He went to sleep happy, thinking that life was turning out alright after their rather troubled times. Maggie didn't sleep at all well. She was both excited by the prospect of seeing Phil again and also extremely worried about how she would manage the travelling, especially overcoming her fear of getting onto a plane. She congratulated herself on how she had managed to sort out getting a passport and arranging the travel, and she was pleased that she had saved the Family Allowance 'in case of emergency'. Well, this was a sort of emergency and she had enough money to see her through this great adventure, at least for a few weeks and she was sure there would be plenty of ways in which she could earn a living once she was settled there.

She had not given a thought to the Spanish language, assuming that everyone would be able to speak English. She thought about her children, each one in turn, and her eyes clouded as she looked up at the ceiling in the darkened room. They were good children, they would get on alright without her and they would understand why it was important that she was going, in fact she was sure that if they knew they would be encouraging her to go. Yes, the children were going to be fine, Ann was almost ten years old now, well able to look after herself, Peter was eight and he would be fine, he was a popular little fellow and never seemed to have much need for her and Penny was almost seven and had quite an independent little spirit. Mike would look after them and her mother would always be around to help out, as she always had been. Her eyes welled up again when she thought about her mother. She hadn't been back to see her since she stormed out of the house and she wasn't sure how things would go when she went round the next day, at all costs she had to keep calm, that was so important. Nevertheless, she was worried about leaving her, they had never spent much time apart, she relied upon her so much and, until that incident a few days ago, she had received unconditional love and support from her for as long as she could remember.

She was up bright and early the next morning; she was chatty, amusing and seemed to have time for them all. She gave Mike a fond kiss as he went off to work and then arranged for the children to go back to her mother's when they finished school. She sorted out all their school things, gave them each a big hug and watched them as they set off together. She cleared up all the breakfast things, tidied up the house, made the beds and set about doing all the washing. She went round to see her mother, calling in at a florist to buy her a bunch of flowers and rehearsing in her mind what she was going to say.

"Sorry about last week mum, I've brought you some flowers as a peace-offering. I don't know what got into me, anyway I'm sorry I upset you and I want to thank you for always being there."

Beryl was delighted to see her and thrilled to have the flowers, immediately busying herself and sorting them out in a vase. Beryl had hardly slept for the last week, though she would not admit such a thing to Maggie. Their argument and the way that Maggie had trounced out of the house had cut deep into her soul, it had been the most miserable week since she had heard the news of Frank's death. That Maggie could think of leaving the children seemed to her to be a betrayal of everything that was of value, of everything that was meaningful. Without the family there was no life, she could not envisage living without her relationship with her daughters, without them there was no purpose, no point in existence, no life. For Maggie even to think of leaving her children seemed to be the ultimate betrayal of everything that she had lived and worked for. She blamed herself of course. Even now it was difficult for her to apportion any sort of blame to any of her daughters; any perceived failings in them must ultimately be an actual failing in her. So Beryl had cried, for the children, for Maggie, for herself and once again for Frank whose counsel and friendship and support she had missed over the years more than anyone could possibly have imagined. Crying was a luxury that Beryl seldom allowed into her life, so when she did cry, there was so much to cry over, so many hurts, so many disappointments, so many things that had gone awry, so few things that had turned out as she had hoped for, except of course, for her three daughters and now one of them was opening up all the forgotten and suppressed wounds of many years.

"The flowers are lovely dear, there was really no need to buy them you know, it's just that we both got a bit upset. I was so appalled by what you said. I hope that you've come to your senses now."

"Yes, I've been giving it a lot of thought, I'm sorry to have dropped it on you, anyway, let's not talk about it anymore, it's too upsetting. Now tell me, have you heard from Libby recently, it's ages since she last wrote to me, I think she's given up on me because I don't think I ever replied."

"Actually I got a letter the other day, now where did I put it? She sent some photos, the children look absolutely lovely and there are so many of them."

They chatted on inconsequentially for another half hour or so before Maggie suddenly looked at the time and explained that she had to rush now. She had a lot of things to get sorted and was it alright for the children to come back here after school as she had to go to see the doctor.

"The doctor? What's wrong with you, you've never mentioned anything?"

"No, it's nothing important, I just need some advice about a twinge in my back."

"Your back? What's wrong with it? You've never said anything about your back before?"

"Well, as you know mum, I don't always tell you everything, but let's not start on that again!"

She went over and gave Beryl a big hug.

"Bye Mum, and thanks for everything," and with that she was gone.

Beryl looked at the flowers and heaved a great sigh of relief, thankful that that little drama seemed to be over, though she hoped that there was nothing seriously wrong with her back. Maggie was certainly quite a handful, but then she always had been. She decided to bake some scones for the children if they were coming over later.

Mike was surprised to find the house empty when he arrived back from work, usually all the lights were on and there was noise coming from every room, invariably some sort of argument between Ann and Peter, between Peter and Penny, between Ann and Penny, between all three of them together or between Maggie and any combination of the three. Today he was greeted by silence. He walked into the kitchen, surprised by its tidiness and saw a letter on the table.

Dear Mike

I'm sorry to write this in a letter but I couldn't face telling you. The children are at mums and I've gone and I'm not coming back. I met somebody six months ago and I've gone to live with him. I'm sorry but it just wasn't working with us was it?

I've tried to be a good wife and mother but I'm not very good at it and I'm sorry that I've let you down. You can't come and get me back because I don't no where I'm going but Phil will meet me when I arrive in SPAIN !!!

I no you will look after the kids and mum will help as well.

I've tried to leave the house nice and tidy and I've done the washing. We are running short of cornflakes and there's a bulb gone in Penny's room.

We had some good fun sometimes Mike.

Look after yourself

Maggie XXX

PS Its Anns parents day next Tuesday

W hen it rained, the heavens opened in a spectacular manner, the thunder crashed and lightning lit up the sky in ways that Libby had never seen before. Sometimes the night sky was illuminated so that, for a second or two, it was as bright as mid-day. She had also seen lightning plunging to the earth almost in a straight line and so it came as no surprise to her to learn that more people were killed by lightning in Swaziland than in any other country. She also knew that however torrential the rain today, it would be hot again tomorrow with clear blue skies or small puffs of white clouds. She loved it!

One day Patsy asked Libby if she would like to come with her to a Roman Catholic Mission way out in the bush in the south of the country. She had heard from friends that there was an Australian nun there who was related in some way to them and they wondered if she would be willing to go and visit her. Patsy went ahead and made the arrangements and they were invited to stay the night on the mission station. They drove south onto the low veldt and discovered that it was a completely different world from the area that they lived in. It was very flat, incredibly hot, arid and becoming desert-like because of top-soil erosion and the over-breeding of cattle. They moved off the main road and onto a dirt track and through the bush for about thirty miles. Libby was amused to see an old advertisement hoarding, rusting over and standing in the middle of nowhere with the words *Coca Cola* just about visible. They reached the mission station in its extremely isolated situation in the middle of the bush and were shown into the guest quarters, a small building with no electricity and the only water coming from a tank which collected rain water from the roof. As it didn't rain very often and they thought that they would have to make do with what they had until the rains came in about five month's time they were asked to use it sparingly.

The nuns laid on a magnificent meal and introduced them to another guest who was visiting his aunt, one of the sisters. Libby thought they were wonderful, they were an utter revelation to her and she was totally bowled over by their stories and their humour. One, a Scot, had been there for seventeen years another, from South America had been there for fifteen years and the other one, the relative of Patsy's friends was a relative newcomer from Australia and had only been there for seven years. The mission ran a clinic, a primary school, a secondary school, a sewing co-operative and a carpentry shop. They sat and ate and talked for almost four hours, accompanied by hundreds of flies, mosquitoes, moths and other leaping things, all attracted by the small oil lamp. The other guest was from New Zealand and was working as a civil engineer in Swaziland, but his aunt was the nun from South America. He was charming, attentive and amusing and here, in the middle of the bush, surrounded by flies and talking to nuns Libby found herself being mildly interested in a man she had never met before.

The Scots nun was a nurse and ran the clinic, which Libby visited the following morning, stepping over the people with malaria who were lying in the corridor waiting to be seen. She told them many amazing stories about her time in Swaziland, how one night she was awakened by a banging on the door to be told that there was 'a man with a hole' who needed the nurse's attention. She went out to find a man who had been stabbed by a spear. His three friends had put him into a wheelbarrow and pushed him almost fifteen miles, during which time his guts and intestines had spilled out into the barrow. She pushed them all back into the 'hole' and drove him to the nearest hospital, which was many miles away, and once there his intestines were washed, pushed back and he was stitched up. Not many days later he walked home. Libby could have listened to the stories all night, but they felt that they should retire and leave the nuns to get to bed. This became all the more important when they discovered that they got up half past four in the morning, went to chapel for an hour's private meditation from five o'clock, then they had mass at six fifteen and began work at eight. There was laughter when they admitted that they quite often felt tired later in the day.

They suggested that if the others wanted to go back to their quarters and talk further they should certainly feel free to do so, and in this way Robbie, as he was called, escorted Patsy and Libby to the small building where they would sleep and they sat out in the darkness, marvelling at the stars and drinking cold tea. It was midnight before Robbie moved off to his room by which time he had arranged to visit them the following weekend. Patsy gave Libby a knowing look as they moved inside, into what seemed like an oven after the relative cool of the outside night air.

"Well, you seem to have struck lucky, young lady, that chap is more than a little interested in you."

Libby blushed, although Patsy couldn't see her in the dark.

"Patsy, my love, I think I'm getting rather old for romantic ventures, I'm well over thirty you know. Perhaps I just felt in need of protection from all those flying things and creepy crawlies! Can you believe that those nuns have been here for all that length of time? No electricity, hardly any water, all this stifling heat and insects and things. I find it quite amazing; they must have a really strong belief."

"Yes, I know what you mean, but they could still be mistaken, after all Africa is full of people with funny beliefs."

"It's strange," reflected Libby "I don't think I've really thought of it before, but I suppose it could be said that the reason why I'm out here myself is because when I was younger I heard a monk talking about his work in South Africa. I wonder if Miriam ever came across him, I must ask her."

By the time they got up the following morning the nuns had been up for four hours and were already at work, their time in chapel behind them. Robbie had risen early, soon after six and was already well on the way back to Mbabane. Libby felt extremely lazy and rather guilty that she should be so relaxed and carefree whilst the mission was well into its working day. They had a look around the clinic and said their goodbyes to the sisters; Patsy said she would be writing to her friends with all the news as soon as she got home.

"Ask them to send me some picture postcards, will you please? I love it here, and I suppose I shall stay here until I die, but just sometimes I pine a little for the fresh air and the wonderful beaches of Queensland. Wonderful though Swaziland is, it doesn't have the Great Barrier Reef does it? You know, when I was younger, I used to work on tourist boats taking people out to the Reef and we would anchor off one of the islands and oh I just loved to swim and snorkel and see the incredible fish."

Robbie's visits became more frequent and he was a welcome visitor, always turning up with some special delicacy for them all to share. He was totally at ease with the three women although it was clearly Libby that he had come to see. It was obvious that they were now an established pair, enjoying each other's company and sharing many interests. They came into this relationship with distinctive histories which they were quite possessive about and it took a great deal of time before they could share with each other some of the details of their personal journeying. Both of them were outgoing whilst at the same time cautious, frank with each other without necessarily telling the whole story, enjoying what the other had to offer without probing too deeply, giving generously to the other but not unconditionally. They both sensed that there was something special about the relationship but neither of them was willing to look too far ahead or make any kind of assumption.

"So tell me more about your marriage."

They were sitting in a restaurant, a cool breeze being generated by a huge fan in the ceiling and they had drunk a bottle of wine. They were relaxed, well fed and enjoying each other's company. Robbie had told her early on that he was divorced, that he had come to Swaziland specifically to put time and space between him and his former wife. It was a mixed blessing though because it meant that he was not seeing his two young children as often as he wanted although for the last two years he had returned to New Zealand every three months to spend a week with them.

"Well, I thought it was pretty happy, I thought we were getting along together fine, but clearly we weren't. I suppose I was too busy to notice things, to pick up the clues. I was a bit of a workaholic and, in my sort of job you get big contracts and you have to be totally committed to them, to ensure that they are completed on time and to budget. I guess I was so busy with the work that I took my home for granted."

He stopped and reflected for a moment or two, Libby sat patiently, not interrupting and allowing him time to marshal his thoughts.

"We didn't have any rows or anything; there was no great falling out. It was just that I came home one weekend after being away for three weeks and Sally said that she wanted us to split up, that she had found someone else and wanted to move in with him. I was pretty devastated, as you can imagine, because it came as such a surprise. I tried to reason with her, tried to suggest that we talked it all through and found a way of sorting things out, but it was quite clear that she had made her mind up. I suppose she had decided on this weeks, probably months before, but I just hadn't noticed."

"Poor you." Libby stretched across the table and took his hand. "And what about the children, how did they take it?"

"Well that's a good question, how did they take it? I suppose I would have liked them to have burst in to tears and come running to me, but they just seemed to accept things. Of course they were still very young, just three and five and so they weren't really aware of what was happening. You see, my work took me away from home so often that there was nothing new in them being with their mother, I suppose it was the norm for me not to be there. I'm exaggerating, of course, but I can see that being alone with Sally was nothing new for them and they weren't likely to be imagining what life would be like without me, were they?"

Libby gave his hand a squeeze. He paused for a while and looked into his wine glass, swirling the remains around for a while.

"I suppose what I found most difficult was the fact that Sally had found someone else. I mean, in the long term, it is losing the children which is most problematic and hurtful for me, but in the short-term it was the fact that Sally had rejected me for someone else. I suppose that's always difficult for a person to come to terms with; there is this terrible sense of personal failure. You have been weighed in the balance and found wanting. So there was this great sense of inner emptiness, a sort of pain the location of which is difficult to place. It's not in the stomach or in the head, but it seems to be specific rather than general, but I never seemed to know where it hurt."

"So what's happened about the children? What's your relationship with them now?"

Libby was not sure how much she wanted to know, but this seemed to be an important time of sharing and she knew that if they didn't continue the conversation now that they had reached this point then there might not be another opportunity, not for a long time. They had spent many hours together, walked miles, driven for hours, sat in restaurants or in each others' home, but this was the first time that they had really talked about this in any meaningful sort of way. Why should there be a time when it seems to be 'right' to explore issues and other times when clearly it is not? It was not that either of them had set out to explore this topic, it just emerged.

"Well, as you know," continued Robbie, "I go back to New Zealand every three months and I either stay locally and see them every day or I take them away for a holiday and we go exploring and doing things together. In that way I ensure that I am still connected with them, that I still enjoy them and, I suppose, it's important to me that I know they still remember me and know that I love them."

"And what about Sally? Do you still love her?"

She knew that she was getting into deep waters here; they had never spoken before at such a level. He looked at her, smiled and then looked down at the table, turning his wine glass round and round in his fingers.

"I suppose the honest answer is 'I don't know'. I know that there is absolutely no chance of us getting back together again, although even after the divorce came through I had moments when I hoped that might be possible. I know that that will never happen and I'm reconciled to the fact. Whether I still love her or not is a more difficult question to answer."

He looked across at Libby.

"I think that since I met you my feelings for Sally have changed, she is not in my thoughts nearly so often, she is not in my dreams and I know that I have a future and a life without her and that it can be good, perhaps it might be very good, I just don't know."

It was Libby's turn to look down at the table. She was pleased to hear what he had to say and yet, at the same time she felt rather frightened, as though his words placed a burden on her that she was not yet ready either to acknowledge or to shoulder. She already knew that this friendship was different from all the others since Paul and recognised that feelings were being awakened in her, or perhaps re-awakened, that she had been neither expecting nor seeking. She looked across the table, smiled again yet said nothing. She could not think of anything to say, it was one of those moments when more is expressed by the absence of words than by their presence.

Robbie looked at his watch.

"We'd better go; I've an early start in the morning. Come on, I'll give you a lift home. I don't suppose I can persuade you to stay the night?"

"Your supposition is entirely correct," laughed Libby as they rose from the table and moved out in to the still night air.

"Just look at all those stars, don't you think they're incredible? I don't think I had ever noticed stars until I came to Africa. And do you know, there are stars here that you can't see in England, nor in New Zealand I expect."

Robbie took her hand and walked over to the car.

"And what you are looking at doesn't even exist now," he replied.

"You are looking at what existed years ago, it has taken all that time to reach us, things are not what they appear to be, we are looking at what no longer is. It will take time for us to see what is happening at this very moment."

He pulled her over and kissed her.

"It will probably take time to see what is happening to us at this moment as well. Come on, let me get you home or those house warders of yours will be calling the police and reporting you missing."

That is exactly what happened a few weeks later, but it wasn't Libby who was missing.

It was early evening and Victoria and Bill were washing up after the evening meal. It was a scene of domestic contentment, replicated in many, but not all, of the houses on this new executive estate in South London. It was a familiar routine, having a little time together, sharing a domestic chore before they each settled down into whatever activity was planned for that evening. It suited them well and they enjoyed the opportunity it gave them to chat over the day's events. Bill was now a director of his company, leaving the house early in the morning before the rest of them had really emerged from the bedroom, bathroom or breakfast bar in the kitchen. It was a way of life that had evolved over the years and it seemed to suit them well. Each morning was a highly ritualised routine bringing order from chaos with a sense of assured expectation. There was an air of predictability about their life and they liked it this way.

Victoria lacked the attractive vivacity of Maggie and the social commitment of Libby, she was altogether more reserved, preferring to be in the background rather than centre stage, but in that role she was strong and dependable. She was tall, slight and had auburn hair and was always smartly dressed. She regarded herself as rather plain and unattractive and would have been astounded if anyone had told her that she was good looking, but there were many men who thought she was. Her innocence in this area added to her charm.

It was this scene of classic British bourgeois domesticity that was so rudely interrupted by the telephone that evening. Bill answered it, annoyed that their conversation had been interrupted.

"Oh, hi Mike, you're a stranger... Yes, she's here, I'll just get her."

Victoria took the phone from him.

"Yes? Mike? This is a surprise... what? Oh no, I don't believe it! When did all this happen? Well how is she now?"

She looked shaken and sat down whilst still asking questions.

"Of course I'll come... I'm not sure what time I'll arrive but I'll drive up straight away, just give me time to put a few things together and I'll be on my way. Can I bring anything? Have you called the doctor? He's on his way... and the children? Oh poor you Mike, I don't know what to say... just get back to the house straight away and tell her I'll be there in a few hours, no, don't put any more money in, you can tell me all about it when I see you. Bye, then, and give her my love won't you."

Bill stood looking on anxiously, wondering what on earth was happening. It must be serious if she was going to drive up straight away; it was most unlike Victoria to do anything on the spur of the moment, she liked time to consider things, to assess all the options, to plan appropriately.

"It's Maggie," whispered Victoria. "She's done a bunk and left them all, and mum collapsed when she heard about it. Mike's called the doctor. The children are all at mums. I said I'd go up straight away. I'm sorry my love, but I need to go don't I? Mike says he thinks it's just the shock that's got to mum, but the children are all rather distraught. He said something about Maggie going to Spain of all places, but I'm not quite sure what he was saying, it was all rather garbled. Oh dear, poor mum, poor Mike – and those poor children. Whatever's got into Maggie? Oh dear, she must be crazy..."

"Of course you must go."

He moved over to Victoria and put his arms around her, giving her strength that she couldn't find within herself. Without her noticing it, Bill had led her over to the easy chair and made her a cup of tea.

She smiled, took a large deep breath and said "thanks for all that, I'll be alright now. I'd better get some clothes together and get myself off. You'll all be OK for a few days won't you?"

Within an hour of the phone call Victoria was driving north.

Bill was left at home to organise the family and sort everything out for the morning, which in all honesty, was not an onerous task. The children were well able to arrange things for themselves in fact, with a bit of luck, they would assume some responsibility for ensuring that he was alright. He had seen his role in life as making sure that he bettered himself, and this meant that he provided the wherewithal for his wife and family to enjoy more of the good things in life. He worked hard outside of the home and Victoria worked hard inside, it was a perfect partnership and it had worked well over the years.

It was a marked contrast to Maggie's experience and he thought about her self-destructive tendency. But it wasn't exactly 'self-destructive' as she always seemed to come through her crises apparently unscathed; it was the destruction of the people around her that was so hard to cope with. She seemed to sail through life leaving in her wake a trail of chaos and destruction. He thought about Mike and felt a great sorrow for him. Mike was not a person that he would normally have much time for. He didn't have his eyes on promotion; he didn't seem to have any sense of there always being something better just a little way ahead. He was what Bill would have described as a 'plodder'.

All those years living with Beryl; now he couldn't have done that, much as he admired Beryl and all that she had been through. The idea of living with her was quite unacceptable in his eyes. A man had to provide for his wife from the word 'go', not settle into some sort of second-class way of life. Even when Mike and Maggie moved into their own home, it was rented and they had stayed there ever since. He couldn't understand that either. He and Victoria were now in their third home, each one larger and better than the previous one. Mike and Maggie's garden was a tip, there was no other word for it, and they didn't seem to mind at all. It seemed to be a playground for all the children of the neighbourhood and when it wasn't full of children it seemed to be full of litter. He didn't blame them for the litter, that was the result of living by a bus stop, but he would have built a fence and made it much more private.

His attitude towards Maggie was ambivalent and complex. Part of him tolerated her, disapproved of her but accepted her as a member of the wider family. Another part of him was intrigued and fascinated by her, drawn towards her as a moth is drawn to the flame of a candle. That was a good analogy because Bill knew that he could quite easily get burnt and he had no intention of ever allowing that to happen. There had been one occasion a dozen years or so ago when, quite unbeknown to Victoria, that had very nearly happened. It was the occasion of a family Christmas, everyone staying with them in their previous house. At the end of Boxing Day, after two days of too much food and certainly too much drink, everyone had gone off to bed, it was well after midnight. Everyone, that is, apart from Maggie who stayed behind tidying things up, which was most unusual, and himself. She suggested that they had a final drink before turning in themselves. The coal fire was down to its embers, emitting warmth and light, and the Christmas tree provided the rest of the illumination, so the room was dimly lit and wonderfully warm. Maggie took her drink and curled up on the settee.

"Why don't you ever look me in the face Bill?" she suddenly asked.

Bill was taken aback.

"I wasn't aware that I didn't," he replied.

"Oh I think you are well aware. I think that maybe you're a little afraid of me."

"Now that's ridiculous," retorted Bill, "why ever should I be afraid of you?"

"I think that perhaps you find me rather attractive. Isn't that right? I know what men are thinking, you know, I've been around quite a lot."

"I find you attractive as my sister in law; I'm pleased that you are in the family, I like you and that's that."

"Then why don't you come and sit with me on the settee?" Maggie moved over and patted the space by her side. "Come on, bring your drink over, and sit here."

Bill knew that he was walking on thin ice. The truth was that he had felt a great magnetism towards Maggie all over Christmas. He didn't know why, it was that she just seemed to exude sensuality, and this was something that Bill had never really experienced before. Without wanting to, or perhaps because he did want to so much, Bill casually moved over to the settee and continued drinking his wine.

Maggie then leaned over towards him.

"Now kiss me," she whispered, "you know that you've been wanting to ever since I arrived."

"Don't be ridiculous," said Bill, trying to calm himself and wondering if he should get up immediately, but finding neither the will nor the strength to do so. Maggie made the move; she put her drink down, moved over to Bill, took the drink away from his hands, put it on the small table by the side of hers, put her arms round his neck, placed her lips on his and gave him a long, exploratory kiss. Bill was confused, but made no attempt to move away. Her kisses became more persistent and he responded and then her tongue forced its way into his mouth whilst at the same time her hand guided his to her breast. Bill broke away, furious with himself, yet directing his anger towards Maggie.

"Never, ever do that again. This is not what I want and it's not what I expect, either of you or myself. I am deeply ashamed that I allowed myself to be carried away, we both should know better."

Maggie was amazed; she had never had that happen to her before.

"Well, I thought that was what you were wanting, and you are a very attractive man Bill."

"It's not what I am wanting, and in case you have forgotten, I am married to your sister."

"Well don't let's fall out over it," sighed Maggie. "It didn't seem to me that you didn't want it. Anyway, I thought you were someone special, you are somebody special, and that's what special people want, isn't it?"

He had a moment of frightening understanding. He saw Maggie no longer as the sensuous young woman out to seduce him, and very nearly succeeding, but as a fragile and vulnerable child desperately wanting to be accepted and loved and wanting to reciprocate those feelings in the only language that she seemed to know. She was alone, drifting in a world which she didn't understand. Despite all her vivacity and her apparent popularity, she was wanting, needing, to relate to someone at a deep level, to be like other people, but not knowing how. Despite it all, he now saw so clearly, she was alone and she was lost.

He suggested that they made a cup of coffee and then he moved to a chair, opposite the settee and began to talk to Maggie. This was the first time that they had ever really talked to each other in all the years that he had known her, and he guessed that it might be the last.

"Look Maggie, that must never, ever, happen again – do you understand me? I know that we are both tired and have probably had too much to drink, but that's really no excuse. You know that I'm married to Victoria and I love her deeply, what we have just done would hurt her terribly. And you know how much Victoria loves you, you mean the world to her, and I'm sure that you never, ever, want to hurt her, do you?"

She was looking very tired. She was confused and the sudden end to her amorous designs had left her feeling empty and unsatisfied.

"Maggie, you are a most beautiful woman, there's no denying that, and men must find you incredibly attractive, especially when you give out those sort of signs and signals. But you know, there is more to life than that, and there is more to relationships and friendship than sex. What we were embarking on just then could have ruined the whole of our family forever – my relationship with Victoria and hers with you. Several lives could have been damaged forever by selfish thoughtlessness. Neither of us wants that, do we? I don't want this ever to happen again and I want neither of us to say a word about it to anyone – ever! Do you promise me that?"

She nodded, but she looked small and broken, a huge contrast from the sultry, sophisticated temptress of half an hour earlier.

"Maggie, you know that I'm very fond of you. I like you, I always have. Victoria adores you and if we are to keep things like that, so that we can all get on together well, and enjoy each other's company and all that sort of thing, then we are going to have to establish some basic rules. Rule one is that nothing like that ever happens between us again, and that is also rule number two and rule number three is the same."

She nodded her head, her tiredness disappeared and her spirits lifted. She realised that the reason why Bill was spelling this out so clearly and precisely was because he really did fancy her and he needed her to help him keep away from her. What he said about

Victoria was true however, and she didn't want to do anything that would hurt her, so it wasn't too difficult to agree to his terms, but she did wish that they had gone a bit further before he pulled away so abruptly.

Neither of them had ever mentioned the incident again during all the succeeding years. The difference between them was that she soon forgot all about it and he didn't. Many times over the ensuing years he remembered the scene, 're-lived' the scene would probably be more accurate. He was pleased, more than that, relieved that he had pulled back from the brink and thereby saved his marriage, because there was no questioning his love for and commitment to Victoria. On the other hand, he could not help himself wondering what it would have been like if he had not pulled back. He was both distressed and excited by the incident but had made sure that never again did he allow himself to get into such a situation with anyone, and certainly not with Maggie.

The phone call this evening revived these memories and they, in turn, reaffirmed his love for Victoria and his sense of sheer good fortune that their lives together had been so blessed. Whilst he and Victoria had gone from strength to strength, poor Maggie had continued to flounder and now this latest crisis seemed to surpass all the previous ones. He felt a surprising tenderness towards Mike, a man who had experienced one particular pleasure that that he hadn't, but missed out on all the others. He knew which of the two of them he preferred to be and he went over to the drinks cabinet and poured himself a whisky.

Victoria drove north as quickly as she could, but safely. She had never been reckless in anything but had always been competent and she drove as she lived. It was late spring, the days were getting longer and the weather warmer, nonetheless it was dark long before Victoria reached Leeds and drove up the road which she knew so well and which seldom seemed to change as the years went by. The front door opened as she approached, Mike was waiting for her, looking through the window and wondering why she had taken so long, though she could hardly have got there much quicker. He looked pale, his face drawn and his eyes larger than she remembered them; he seemed to have aged considerably in the few months since she had last seen him.

"Thanks for coming, you're a real brick."

He took her small case and ushered her into the living room.

"The kids are asleep – at least I hope they are – I've put them all together in the little bedroom, I thought they needed to be together and you can have your old room, is that alright?"

He was tentative, not sure whether he had done the right thing, not sure whether she would approve.

"The doctor's been, he's given your mum some pills to help her relax, I think she's probably dozing off now, but she wants to see you when you arrive. He said that he thinks she's OK, it's nothing serious, but he'll pop in again tomorrow. I told him that you were coming up and he nodded, I think you'll know what to say to him better than me."

"That's wonderful Mike. I'll just pop up and see mum, could you be an angel and make me a cup of tea and then we can sit down and have a natter. But no, first of all, what about you? Are you coping? Oh you poor dear, I can't imagine how you must be feeling. Did the doctor give you anything? I'm sure you probably need something to help you relax."

"I'm OK. It's just that it's all been a bit of a shock. I'm not sure what I feel really, and the kids... I just can't believe that she could leave them. Oh, it's such a mess. I'm sorry about your mum, Victoria, honestly I am. She's just been so wonderful; I don't know what I would have done without her being here. Oh dear, it's just so completely awful, I don't know what to do. It's good of you to come, I really do appreciate it. Were you doing anything special tonight – have I ruined your evening? Oh dear, what a mess it all is."

He sat down with his head in his hands and she moved over to him, sat beside him and gave him a kiss on the side of his face.

"Yes, it does seem to be a terrible mess, but I'm sure you'll pull through. You've got three lovely children and for their sake alone you'll find the strength to carry on, but I do see how awful it is for you. Anyway, I'm here for a few days and we'll try and get something sorted out. But now I must just pop up and see Mum."

She gave his arm a squeeze and left the room, going up the stairs to her mother's bedroom.

Beryl was lying there, quite still. For a moment or two Victoria wasn't sure whether she was asleep or not but when she became more accustomed to the gloom she could see that her mother's eyes were open but her face was motionless.

"Are you alright Mum? Can I get you anything?"

She moved over to the bed and gave her mother a gentle kiss. Beryl hardly stirred, she remained staring at the ceiling and didn't seem to register Victoria's arrival. She sat on the side of the bed and took hold of her mother's hand; it seemed cold and she began to massage it gently, trying to bring life back into this body which seemed to have slipped away into a different realm. Gradually she sensed that her mother was coming round, there was some movement in her face and after a few minutes she turned her head and looked at her. It was as though she was trying to remember who she was.

She stared at Victoria, looked away and then stared at her again.

"Hello, my love. What a surprise seeing you, I thought it was Maggie for a moment."

"No mum, it's me, Victoria. Mike asked me to come over and look after you. I think this business with Maggie has come as such a shock that it's given you a funny turn, but you'll be alright and I'll stay with you for a day or two until you feel a bit better."

"Thank you," whispered Beryl, and her eyes returned to the ceiling as though somewhere up there she had discovered a window, a window through which she could see things, events or people that others could not. Perhaps it was a world no longer accessible except in dreams. A world in which her father lifted her up on his shoulders and carried her through the woods. A world in which her husband kissed her goodbye as he set out for the factory, in which her husband donned his army uniform and set out for Normandy. A world in which Maggie came running towards her with outstretched arms and a smile of innocence on her face. Whatever it was, it held Beryl with a power that made her oblivious of everything else and she was totally unaware of the fact that Victoria had left the room, called in to check on the children and descended the stairs to talk to Mike.

Over the next two hours Victoria gained an insight into Maggie's life which she could never have imagined. Mike poured out years of grief and sadness, anger and incomprehension, but most of all, of love. She marvelled that he could be so forgiving, so non-judgemental, so desperately in love after all that he had endured.

Much as she loved Bill and he her, she doubted whether their marriage could have withstood the battering that Mike's had experienced. She began to understand, perhaps for the first time, why he had always seemed to lack ambition, why he lacked confidence. It took just about every ounce of his energy to keep the family together, to be both father and mother to the children, to live with Maggie's somewhat symbiotic relationship with her mother, and to forgive and accept and continue to stand alongside the wife whom he loved so dearly. There was little space or energy left for vision, for ambition or self-improvement. He deserved better, Oh so much better than Maggie ever gave him and Victoria felt ashamed that her sister could cause so much hurt to such an honest, decent and good man. She also suspected, although she didn't mention this to Mike, that her mother could not possibly have been unaware of at least some of the things that were going on. She experienced a great wave of sadness as she confronted things about her mother that she would rather have left dormant.

Later that night, when Mike had returned home, when she had ensured that the children and her mother were all asleep, she crept into her old bed and recognised that it would be a long time before she would be able to sleep. Before that could happen she would have to admit that for many years she had successfully repressed any critical thoughts and feelings about her mother. It had been the best way forward for them both but now, with Maggie's sudden departure, a whole new scenario was opening up. This family, so rigorously held together by Beryl's force of will, was now in danger of falling apart. Not because Maggie had made this dramatic move, although that didn't help matters, but because the great collusion into which they had all entered, was now exposed.

She was sure that Beryl was somehow involved in Maggie's infidelities and she saw now, for the first time, that the bond of love between Beryl and Maggie was as binding and restricting on them both as she had imagined it to be wholesome and liberating. She suddenly felt pangs of jealousy, feelings that she never knew existed within her, and she began to grieve. She grieved for the father she had never known, for the step-father whom she had loved and now, for the first time, she grieved for her mother. She felt that the relationship between her mother and Maggie had somehow had the effect of diminishing the relationship that she had with her and, quite probably, that she had with Libby as well. Perhaps Beryl's single-minded devotion to her family was not, after all, a thing to be admired but rather to be pitied. Perhaps it was a reflection of her own inability to grieve and goodness knows, she had plenty to grieve about.

Victoria realised that she must have been repressing a degree of annoyance and anger for many years because of the way that her mother always seemed to deal with difficult issues. She just refused to confront them out in the open and everyone had to play along with her, as though they didn't exist. It began to dawn on Victoria that those days were not past; they lived on and influenced the present. Why had they never really been able to talk about her father? Why had they never talked about Libby and Maggie's father? Why couldn't they explore the past, surely that would help them to understand the present and cope with the future? Perhaps this was at the root of all Maggie's troubles. This was a thought that had never occurred to her before and it began to make sense although she found it very painful. Perhaps this was why Libby had gone to live abroad; perhaps she too couldn't bear to live too close to her mother.

"Do you see what I mean?" she said to Bill when she got home. "Perhaps Mum's insistence on controlling how problems are dealt with has meant that, as a family we have never really dealt with them at all, we've just pretended that they don't really exist."

"Oh come on now my love," reasoned Bill, "don't you think that's going a bit too far? I don't see your mother behaving like that."

"Then why wouldn't she talk about Maggie all this week? I learned things about Maggie from Mike which made me feel sick; I could never have believed them. Mum must have known about some of them at least, but she has never mentioned them. She never really spoke about this latest episode, every time I tried to raise the subject and talk through just what has been happening, she just closed the subject down. We *never* really discussed it – can you believe that?"

"Perhaps it was just too difficult for her, perhaps..."

Bill never finished the sentence.

"But that's just my point." exclaimed Victoria. "Because it's difficult for her she won't discuss it, she won't share anything and the only way that she can handle things that are difficult is to bury them deep inside her. When I think back over the years I don't think we've ever really talked about anything. Do you remember years ago when Maggie got into trouble and came to live with us for a bit, well that has never, ever, been mentioned since."

"Oh come on love, there are some things that families don't talk about. That little incident with Maggie is best forgotten by everyone."

"But don't you see," argued Victoria, "if that incident had been talked through properly then perhaps Maggie might not have got herself into all these other messes. Perhaps mum's refusal to face up to things has had the effect of making things worse for Maggie. Oh dear, the poor thing, I wonder what goes on her in head."

Victoria thought that her relationship with her mother would never be quite the same again. I suppose, she thought, that I have suddenly grown up and it's taken me forty years to do so.

Maggie was terrified of the aeroplane. She boarded it with much trepidation, it seemed absolutely huge to her and she couldn't imagine how it could possibly get into the sky. For a brief moment she felt like turning round and running back home and she weighed up the images in her mind of Phil and Mike and knew that she wanted Phil. She took her seat and looked out of the window. It seemed very small and she wondered why she couldn't have been on a plane with larger windows so that she could get a better view once they took off. She was fascinated by the air blowing down into her face and soon worked out that she could switch the light on and off. A large elderly woman came and sat next to her, over-spilling from her seat and squeezing into Maggie. She was puffing and sweating and didn't seem to notice her at all. The air hostess welcomed them on board and Maggie felt slightly less frightened when the pilot spoke to them because he introduced himself as 'Captain Johnson'. Well, if he was a captain, reasoned Maggie to herself, he must be quite important and able to fly the plane alright. On the other hand, did the hostess know something about him because she was telling them all about the things they had to do if they crashed into the sea. Maggie looked around, she couldn't see where a life-jacket could be stored and she had no idea if she would remember how to tie the knot. That was alright for the sea, but would they have parachutes if it crashed over the land? The time for take-off came and the engine noise increased and the plane slowly began to taxi to the runway. Maggie looked out of the window and took a big breath. There was no going back now, her great adventure had begun.

Minutes later she was clenching the arms of her seat as the noise became intolerable and the plane began to gather speed. She was afraid that the pilot had done something wrong and the engine would explode. She watched the terminal buildings as they sped by them, getting faster and faster, but still on the ground. Perhaps they were too heavy and it wouldn't get off the ground. Perhaps they would plough on into the field at the end of the runway. She glanced at the woman in the next seat, who was sitting motionless with her eyes closed. I hope she hasn't died on me, frightened to death, thought Maggie. She could understand how that phrase had come about; you could actually die if you weren't strong enough. She looked out of the window and was amazed to see that they were in the air. It was a miracle and she wanted to tell the woman next to her that they were actually flying, but didn't. After a few minutes the sound of the engine changed and the plane seemed to slope over to her side and she saw all the land and was quite convinced that they were going to crash. She was terrified but hoped she wouldn't die, that would be so awful after all the planning she had done. She closed her eyes and said a prayer. When she opened them again they were much higher and then they flew into a cloud and she couldn't see anything. How does the pilot drive it if he can't see, how does he know where to aim it? Suddenly there was sunshine and a clear sky. How amazing, it had been very overcast when they set off and now it was bright and sunny, just as she imagined Spain would be. She looked down and was amazed to see that there was no land, only what looked like snow for as far as she could see. What an amazing thing flying is, she thought. She loved it when they brought her a meal. It was chicken in a silver box and there was a little bag of salt. She took the lid off the main course and saw the croquette potatoes and thought that she had never had such an impressive meal before. All this and a trifle as well. She decided that eating on aeroplanes must be one of the great luxuries of life, and here she was, enjoying it. She felt wonderful.

When it was time to land her feelings of fear returned, added to which her ears began to hurt. She looked out of the window and saw the sea below her with tiny boats and as the sea met the land she could see a thin line of orange which she supposed was the beach. The land didn't look very green, more a sort of yellowy brown and there didn't seem to be any fields. They were losing height and she began to worry in case they were dropping too quickly. The plane banked over and she could see nothing but sky, then it seemed to roll over to her side and she saw the land so much more clearly. So this was 'abroad'. She was very excited. She heard a great clanking noise below her and was worried that something had fallen off the plane, but no-one else seemed to have noticed it. Then they were close to the ground and the plane seemed to be a bit unsure of itself, wobbling from side to side and then suddenly they seemed to have hit the ground and there was a tremendous noise. 'Oh God', she thought, 'I've come all this way and now it's crashed' but it didn't crash, instead it slowed down and very slowly came to a stop. She felt triumphant but slightly bothered that she seemed to have gone deaf. Just her luck!

Nothing could have prepared her for the weather as she stepped from the plane. It was amazingly hot, but a sultry sort of heat with a gentle breeze, it was something that she couldn't describe; she just knew that it was very different. She walked across the tarmac with all the other passengers and felt extremely proud of herself for having made the journey.

It all seemed to be so chaotic at the airport, but very exciting. She queued up to have her passport stamped, and looked very closely at the big, blue and rather smudged stamp and then followed the others to collect her luggage. She looked up at the advertisements on the walls and loved the fact that they were in different languages. She instantly decided that she would learn Spanish but wasn't sure which of the foreign advertisements was actually in Spanish. Her case collected, she made her way into the vast reception area with seemingly thousands of people either coming or going and looked around for Phil. Everyone else seemed to be hugging people as they greeted them or said goodbye to them but there was no sign of him. She wondered if she was in the right place and after a while walked around to see if there was a more obvious place where people met up, but Phil was nowhere to be seen. Half an hour passed and Maggie began to panic. What should she do? Where should she go? The exhilaration of her arrival had now evaporated and she was finding it hard not to cry, out of pity for her situation. Was it for this that she had left her home and family? To stand forsaken in a foreign airport, knowing no-one? An hour passed, she needed to go to the toilet but was frightened to leave her spot in case Phil missed her. The crowd dispersed considerably as time passed, then new people arrived and there was another bout of busyness and then that crowd too seemed to disappear. It was two and a half hours before Phil arrived, sauntering across the hall as though he had all the time in the world.

"Hi babes," he said as he approached her and put his arms around her, giving her a long kiss and caressing her as though they were the only people around.

"You're early, I thought the flight wasn't arriving until four o'clock and I reckoned that it would take you a good half hour to get through customs and all that stuff. Anyway, welcome to Spain. Oh yes, this is Frank, he works with me and thought he would come over to the airport for a ride, get him out of the place for an hour or two."

Maggie was both delighted and angry to see them; she was also both relieved and apprehensive. This wasn't the welcome that she had been expecting. For almost a month now she had been anticipating this moment and now it had arrived she had waited two and a half hours and then had to share it with Frank.

"Phil, you idiot, the plane was on time. I told you it was arriving at fourteen hundred hours, that's what the ticket said. Fourteen hundred hours means two o'clock and I've been waiting here for almost three hours wondering where the hell you were. I was getting so frightened and I'm so hot and sticky and tired. You'll just have to wait here with my case and let me go and freshen up, I feel really dreadful."

"Yes, you do that. Me and Frank'll go over and have a beer. I must have mistaken fourteen hundred hours for four o'clock. Sorry, sweetheart, it's an easy mistake to make. Anyway, you run along and make yourself beautiful and we'll have a drink. By the way, did you bring any duty-free with you?"

Maggie glared at him, but by that time he had turned and was walking away towards the bar.

They reached the car and Frank automatically sat in the front with Phil and Maggie squeezed into the back where there was hardly any room on the seat, it was full of boxes, papers, shoes and various sorts of sticks and stones. She felt a little subdued but was pleased to be here and couldn't wait to arrive at Phil's home and have some time to herself with him. They drove for about half an hour and reached a sea-side town with large multi-storey buildings and lots of cafes and bars and a great many people wandering around in bathing costumes, shorts and big bright hats. They drove through the town to the other side, it was rather like a huge building site and then the car pulled onto some waste-land where there were three or four large caravans.

"Here we are Maggie sweetheart, home."

Phil leaped out of the car and strode off to the nearest caravan leaving Maggie to scramble out and get her case from the boot. Frank said cheerio and hoped to meet her later that evening and he walked off back towards the town.

Maggie ventured up the three steps into the caravan, it wasn't exactly what she had been expecting, but at least she was here, with Phil and alone. For the very first time they had time together without having to watch out for other people or hurry or get back to meet the children from school or collect them from her mother's. They had time and she was in Spain.

"Well, what do you think of the place?" asked Phil as he wandered to the far end of the caravan and opened a small door.

"This is our bedroom, come and see if you like it."

Maggie moved down to join him. The bedroom was extremely small, the bed was unmade and the caravan was scorching hot. It smelt of body odour.

"You didn't tell me that you lived in a caravan," protested Maggie. "When you spoke about home I assumed that you had a house."

"Well, house, caravan – what does it matter? They're all the same thing aren't they? Anyway it's home and I'm sure you'll love it. I'm not here a lot. I'm at work until about three in the morning and then when I've had a sleep I usually go down to the beach and have a swim. It's only just down the road and it means that you don't miss there not being a bath or anything in the van. Then we stroll over to the bar and have a few drinks and before you know what's happening it's time for work again. Sometimes I earn a few extra pesetas helping Frank with his pedalloes and he's got a couple of motor boats as well. So? What do you think?"

"Well, it's not exactly what I was expecting but I'm sure it's going to be fine."

Maggie didn't sound too convincing but Phil never picked that up.

"Look, I'm really hungry; it was ages since I had that meal on the plane. Why don't I get changed into something cooler and then we might go and get something to eat?"

"Sure, although I don't think many places will be open yet. It's siesta time in Spain you know. I've got a better idea. Why don't you just take off all those clothes and come over here and see how hungry I am as well."

Maggie felt in much better humour when they eventually went off in search of food. First they walked down to the beach and she walked along with her feet in the sea, marvelling at the warm water. She had changed into a blouse and shorts and wore a pair of sandals which seemed skimpy when she bought them in Leeds but now she seemed to be positively over-dressed. It was late afternoon and the sun was rapidly receding. The neon lights in the bars were shining brightly as they settled down for a meal on a terrace, underneath a bright blue umbrella. Music was coming from inside the bar and they looked at each other, laughed and ordered their food and a bottle of red wine. She was not used to drinking wine, despite the many hours she had spent in pubs back home. The tiredness from the journey, the hot sun, the wine and meeting up with Phil again all combined to make her feel extremely sleepy. They decided that she wouldn't join Phil that evening as he ran his disco, instead she would go back to the caravan and get some sleep. The thought of dancing through until two or three in the morning was beyond her, but she looked forward to it later. She had the feeling that everything was going to be alright. It was new, it was different, it was Spain.

The bedroom was extremely stuffy and she opened the windows but instead of getting a cool breeze it seemed as though only hot air came through. The bed was uncomfortable and she was almost too tired to sleep but eventually she dozed off and was fast asleep when Phil came in sometime after three o'clock. He had been drinking heavily and made a great deal of noise as he threw his clothes off onto the floor and then set about making sure that Maggie didn't continue in sleep.

When Maggie woke up at about nine o'clock Phil was still deeply asleep and so she lay awake and reflected on her situation. She was happy, she couldn't deny that, but even at this early stage there were forebodings that it couldn't last. Neither the happiness she felt nor the domestic arrangements she had fallen into, conveyed any sense of permanence. Nine o'clock became ten o'clock which became eleven and she could stay in bed no longer. She climbed over Phil and got dressed. She could find nothing which would serve as breakfast in any of the cupboards so decided to let herself out and go exploring. She made her way to the beach and walked in the shallow waters, just as she had done the day before. The sun was really hot and she decided that she must get some sun-cream on the way home and also buy a large hat. She stopped for a coffee and roll and slowly made her way back to the caravan only to discover that she was locked out. The curtains were all drawn and she concluded that Phil was still in bed and banged on the door. There was a lot of shouting from inside but she couldn't hear what was being said, which was probably just as well because it was not a pleasant sight or sound when Phil eventually opened the door.

"What the hell do you mean by waking me up at this unearthly hour? Are you crazy woman? No-one in their right senses gets up until after one and it's nowhere near that. Anyway, where the bloody hell have you been? What do you think you're doing walking round wearing a bloody stupid hat like that? God almighty Maggie, have a thought for others, I was working until just a few hours ago."

With that, he turned round and went back to bed, leaving Maggie furious and also somewhat bewildered as to what she was supposed to do each morning whilst he slept through until the afternoon. A couple of hours later he emerged and was a whole lot more civilised.

"Sorry I shouted sweetheart, you woke me up in the middle of a deep sleep. I'm not very good in the mornings after I've been working, but I'm OK now. Am I forgiven?"

He moved over and put his arms round Maggie.

"I guess it takes a bit of getting used to having someone around all the time. They don't usually stay more than one night."

He immediately realised that he'd said the wrong thing, he could feel her stiffen in his arms.

"I'm only teasing you, my love. Your surely didn't think I meant it did you?"

He looked straight into her face, winked at her and gave her a kiss. Maggie forgot that she was annoyed and allowed herself to be carried along; she was so pleased to be in his arms again.

That afternoon they went swimming and after another meal at the same bar as the previous day she accompanied him to the *Pasa Doble Bar and Disco* where Phil worked six or seven nights a week. As she was introduced to the staff there and to some of the regulars she was aware of the fact that people were casting a curious eye over her. Phil was well known as a womaniser and so it was a matter of local gossip when they learned that he was bringing a live-in lover over from England. What neither of them knew was that more than twenty people had set up a wager with each other as to how long it would be before she returned to England.

She stayed at the Disco until the early hours. She danced a lot, drank a lot and felt that she was seventeen years old again. As the night wore on the place became almost unbearably hot, the evening temperature being increased by all the lights and all the bodies. The place seemed to throb with the music, people either loved it or loathed it and the vast majority loved it and came back night after night. Phil was an accomplished DJ and Maggie was proud to think that, of all the admirers who thronged around him, it was she who would be accompanying him home and to bed.

Days were spent lazing in the sun, swimming a little, drinking a great deal, partying often and dancing the nights away. For a while Maggie loved it. She loved the music, the carefree way of life and her relationship with Phil. She wrote postcards to the children after six weeks saying that she missed them and asking them to give their father a kiss from her. They were torn up as soon as they arrived and the children never saw them. She wrote infrequent letters to her mother, saying little and breaking Beryl's heart in the process. She made no contact with anyone else and she received no mail because she told no-one her address, not even her mother. There were occasional times of crisis with Phil, especially when he never returned home some nights, but on the whole their relationship was reasonably stable even if it was not particularly deep.

I t was the long school holiday and Miriam decided that she would go back to her mother's village to see her children. It wasn't an easy decision for her to take as she knew that there was a certain amount of danger because of her husband's involvement with the ANC. She had never revealed the whole story of how she got from her mother's village to Swaziland but it was clear that it hadn't been all that straightforward. She was plainly nervous but also excited by the prospect of seeing her children again as she heard news of them only very rarely. She set off early one morning and said that she would be back in two weeks time. She gave them both a hug as they left her at the bus station. She wasn't all that clear how she was going to make the journey and there seemed to be too many provisional possibilities for Libby to be at ease, but she and Patsy reckoned that this was probably the way Africans made that sort of journey.

Two weeks passed and Miriam had neither returned nor been in touch with them. They bought in extra provisions so that they could have a great meal together when she turned up, but days passed and there was no sign of her. A week after she was due to return they became anxious, after two weeks they became very anxious and after three weeks they just didn't know what to do. Term was beginning again and Miriam still hadn't appeared. They discussed the matter with Kislon Sithole, the head teacher and he looked concerned and frowned deeply.

"Oh this is bad, this is very bad. I knew that she wanted to go there but I advised her strongly not to do so, I told her that I didn't think it was safe. There has been trouble in that region, much trouble. Oh dear, Oh dear. I will make contact with some of my friends and see if I can learn anything. Come back tomorrow and I'll tell you what I have found out."

The following day Kislon and his wife, Patsy and Libby and two other African members of staff gathered together.

"What I have learned is that Miriam's husband is still in prison but there was trouble at the prison and some men died. I don't know why or how many, but her husband was not one of the men who were killed. It seems that there was a lot of anger when the news broke out and there was a lot of tension in the district near to the prison. Miriam's husband is quite a popular hero-figure to many young people in South Africa and I think the authorities have been frightened by this."

Kislon got up and walked round the room as he spoke.

"I don't know the full story but I have heard that the authorities wanted to keep their eyes on Miriam's children and so they arrested her mother and took her and the children away. I don't know where they took them. But if Miriam went to see her children she would find that they had gone and I'm sure she will have been asking a lot of questions and stirring up some trouble. You see, Miriam was not supposed to leave South Africa when her husband was taken. She managed to get out and we on this side were able to help her a little. I don't know how much of this you know, but it has all been kept very secret. I don't know why she didn't tell me she was going, Oh dear, Oh dear."

Libby and Patsy were amazed at what they were learning. They had only grasped part of the story and they had lived with her for several years. Libby struggled with mixed emotions. Part of her felt deeply sad that Miriam had not shared more of her life, that she had lived with them but kept huge parts of herself hidden. On the other hand, she felt immense admiration that she could be so strong and single-minded.

"She must have been so lonely at times and we didn't know." Patsy was beginning to cry.

"How could we have been so thoughtless, so insensitive?"

Kislon's wife came over to them and gave them both a great hug.

"Now don't you two go blaming yourself for anything. Miriam was wonderfully happy with you both, she told me so on many occasions. She said that you treated her as a normal human being, that you shared things with her, that she felt she was your equal in every way. You can't begin to imagine what that meant to her. Only if you have lived the life that Miriam lived would you have any idea what that meant to her. Kislon and I know much about her but our lips are sealed. We have told you enough. Now go back to your home and settle into your work. Miriam may come back, but I think it is more likely that she won't."

"But can't we do anything? Shouldn't we tell the police, couldn't they search for her, make a request to the police in South Africa?"

Patsy was racking her brain to find a way forward.

"I shall do whatever I can," said Kislon.

"But the police here are not the same as they are in your countries. Sometimes it can create greater problems. I know people; I have ways of finding things out. Now I beg you, please go home now and don't tell anyone else what I have been saying to you. If anyone comes asking questions you must say that you know nothing, just that she went back to South Africa on holiday. And please, if anyone comes asking questions, you are to let me know, but do it carefully, not straight away, they may be expecting you to come straight over to me. We must all be very careful. Go and say your prayers for Miriam."

They were very quiet as they walked back home. It was difficult taking in all that they had heard and they both realised that they were strangers in a foreign land. A land where people thought differently, where experiences were beyond their imagination and where there was so much sorrow and pain co-existing with so much life and vibrancy. Libby sat and stared at a praying mantis as it went through its ablutions whilst standing on the window-sill. She felt a great loss and a sudden sense of fear, almost as though someone had been through the house looking through their personal possessions. What if they had?

Although only one person out of three was missing from the house, the effect was much greater than a third. Both Libby and Patsy felt diminished and they doubted whether life together in Swaziland would ever be the same again. They needed to spend more time together so Libby asked Robbie to join them on several occasions when earlier the two of them might have gone out together. The school term was in full swing again, there was work to prepare, lessons to give, extracurricular activities to lead and a whole range of social activities with other members of staff to occupy them and help them forget, at least for a while, the mystery that surrounded Miriam's disappearance. It was about three months later that Kislon Sithole came round to their home early one evening. They were surprised by his visit as he had never been before.

"How nice to see you, please do come in. Can we get you a cold drink or would you perhaps like a glass of wine?"

He smiled and accepted a glass of water. He looked at the two young women, one from Australia and the other from England, both places that he had never visited and probably never would and he felt himself fortunate that they should have wanted to come and teach in his school. They were good teachers and popular with both the pupils and the other teachers.

"I am afraid that I am the hearer of bad news," he began. "I have learned that Miriam is dead."

Libby and Patsy gasped in disbelief. Surely not? She was their friend, friends didn't die, friends were always there.

"I don't know the details and probably never will. I have heard that she reached her mother's village and collapsed when she was told that the children and her mother had been taken away. She was very poorly for several days but then regained her strength and said that she was going to find them. She set off walking, she walked for many many miles but then it seems there was an accident. I am told that a car hit her as she walked along the road, it did not stop and no-one knows who did such a thing. I am sorry, very sorry. I feared that such an outcome might emerge. I prayed for her safe return but she has returned to the Lord. I am so sorry to bring you such news."

They were utterly stunned and tears trickled down their faces even though they were trying to be very brave and strong. Kislon Sithole was embarrassed, he didn't want to make these young women cry, but he knew that he had cried himself when he had heard the news.

"I don't know how many of her belongings are here but perhaps you would be kind enough to tidy them up. Perhaps any clothes might be given to some of the mothers, do you think that would be a good idea? I'm sure that is the sort of thing that she would want. If there is anything precious then I should have it and I will see if I can save it for her children one day, provided of course, that they too do not have any 'accidents'. Now I will go and leave you to your grieving. We shall hold a special service in the school tomorrow afternoon. Thank you for your kind hospitality."

With that he stood up, smiled, bowed very slightly and left. They closed the door behind him then stood, with their arms around each other and wept.

Juanita was young, attractive, sultry and sexy. For all the Englishmen in the bar she was mysteriously different and they made a bee-line for her, competing for her attention. She was Spanish and spoke a form of English that was both amusing and endearing. She had knowledge of the country and its ways, she had stories to tell and could enchant people by her tales of Spanish history, its villains and its heroes, its folklore and its music. Ah yes, its music. Juanita could play flamenco guitar, she could dance and she could sing. Each night she sang, each night they applauded her, shouted for her and would not go home until she gave them more, which she always did. She flirted with the men, captivated the visitors to the club, earned a little extra money on the side and completely and utterly obliterated Maggie in the mind of Phil.

Maggie found all this difficult to come to terms with. She realised that, compared to Juanita, she was no longer young, the centre of attention and everyone's darling, and she didn't like it. The little princess was now over thirty and there were younger and more attractive people entering into her world. She was jealous and she didn't know how to handle it. In just about every encounter she had ever had with men it was Maggie who called the tune, it was she who played cool and hard to get or who upped the temperature and the stakes. It was Maggie who decided when to play and when to walk away. There had never been a Juanita before in her life and she had never developed the skills needed to fight off an intruder, a predator, from her territory. She was a loser; she knew it and she didn't like it. What she didn't know was how to extricate herself from the situation.

On the other hand, she loved the sunshine and the warmth of Spain; the sea, the carefree life with its parties and dancing. She loved meeting up with holiday-makers who were intent upon having a good time and spending money – often on her. She found work for herself in the disco, serving behind the bar and doubling up as a waitress when needed. It was all rather casual, money in hand at the end of the day, and she spent it almost as easily and as frequently as it came but she did begin to put some aside for when she needed to leave. She thought that she had it well-hidden. Coming home one night she found the box empty and she had an almighty row with Phil as a result. He denied all knowledge of the box let alone the theft and said that someone must have broken into the caravan. She could find no signs of entry and there was no evidence of anything else being taken or even of cupboards and drawers being opened. She was absolutely certain that Phil had taken the money, probably to buy drugs with. She discovered his drug-taking habit a few weeks after arriving and shared his practice of smoking cannabis each evening, usually just before work and once they got home in the early hours. She refused though to experiment with the other drugs he was taking. He was amazed to discover that not only didn't she want to use them but also that she actually disapproved. It was yet one more thing putting pressure and strain on their relationship. And yet, for every burden and problem there were also times of exhilaration and contentment.

With the arrival of Juanita she finally admitted to herself that there could be no long-term future with Phil. If it wasn't Juanita it would be someone else, she knew that. There would always be a Carmen or a Dolores, a Maria or a Juanita. She could hardly blame Phil because this was almost a mirror image of herself, this drifting from relationship to relationship with little thought for the future and even less for those who might be affected by it all. It was this sense of freedom that had first attracted her to Phil, but such freedom did not come unencumbered and she recognised that for each part of Phil that she was attracted to there were other parts which annoyed or pained her.

O n hearing of Miriam's death Libby realised that this was the first time she had really wept since she had broken up with Paul. It was also the first time she had really missed someone, the first time she felt that part of her was no longer functioning since that day, many years earlier. The service at the school the following day was memorable. She couldn't understand how something so significant and meaningful could be arranged so quickly, so spontaneously. There was an outpouring of grief and raw emotion such as she had never witnessed before and she felt she was an intruder, somehow thrust into the centre of the pain and emotions of a different culture. It was hard being English in Africa at a time like this. The singing was something she had never heard before, so moving and throbbing, pulsating with life. It was a music that seemed to emerge from the innermost being of the people, as though they could do no other. They became alive in a quite different way when they sang. She remembered how Miriam had told her that she always had a song in her mind, in her heart, even though no-one could hear her singing. Miriam believed that God could hear her and, despite her own agnosticism, Libby could believe that this was so. There were many tributes to Miriam, much weeping and wailing and yet also a sense of wholeness which she couldn't understand. She was touched, that among the many people from so many different areas who gathered together in the afternoon sunshine, she saw Robbie who had taken time off from work to pay his respects to someone whom he too counted as a friend.

She had now been in Swaziland for four years. She had only been home once and was beginning to feel guilty that she was not giving her mother more support. She had been deeply saddened to learn of Maggie's escapades and her flight to Spain. She'd heard nothing from her herself. Beryl had mentioned it in her letters but never said very much about it and she wasn't a great letter writer at the best of times. Virtually all of Libby's information came from Victoria and it was from her that she learned about her mother's deteriorating health. Victoria couldn't put her finger on anything particular but felt that the years of supporting Maggie were beginning to take their toll and the last couple of years had been extremely stressful for her. Victoria was shouldering the responsibility for ensuring she was given support and encouragement, and she had always been adamant that Libby should remain in Africa rather than come home as she suspected that once she did then she would be expected to be at Beryl's beck and call.

Libby knew that she was protecting her and she was grateful to her for that. Together, they had arranged for Beryl to have a telephone installed and they paid the bills for her. This meant that Libby could now phone up once a week to check out on her mother, but despite the thrill of hearing her voice her mother actually said very little, she gave nothing away and Libby was often left wondering if she had gathered anything at all from her phone call home. She gained much more, of course from Victoria.

One evening in the bar, quite early, before it filled up, Maggie struck up a conversation with a man who had visited several times over the past couple of weeks. He was clearly not on holiday, but she was attracted to him by his accent.

"You're a long way from home aren't you, with an accent like that?"

"Well it all depends what you mean by home, doesn't it?" He replied with a smile.

"Anyway, by the sound of it you're also not exactly from these parts yourself, are you? Whereabouts do you hail from?"

When Maggie told him Leeds he broke into a broad grin.

"Hey, I'm from Bradford, we're practically next-door neighbours."

"So what are you doing over here then if it's not a rude question, you don't seem to be on holiday and I've seen you pop in for a drink quite often but I've never seen you here at night?"

Maggie looked at him straight in the face, her eyes seeming to lock into his.

"No, it's not a rude question." He wondered who she was; she was certainly attractive and also forthright.

"I'm over here for a few months working. I work for a tourist firm back home and they're opening up the Spanish market so I'm here checking out different hotels and seeing if we can arrange anything with them. It's quite interesting, I get to stay in decent places and I have a big check list I have to go through to see if the places are suitable."

"Sounds a great job," remarked Maggie, "much better than working in a place like this all through the night."

"Well if you're interested I could probably take you on for a couple of months or so. I'm way behind with the work and I've got authority to get some help if I can find any, but it's not too easy to find people, they are all either working already or just bumming about and not wanting to work."

"Are you serious? I'd be dead interested. To tell you the truth I'm a bit stuck at the moment. I came out here to be with my bloke but it's gone a bit dead with him, I think he prefers the young Spanish dancers and singers. I've been wondering how I can break away. I need to earn a bit before I go back home and this is all that I can do, you see Phil works here so they give me a few hours doing this and that but it's all a bit unsatisfactory if I'm honest with myself."

"Well, if you really are interested, come and see me at the hotel in the morning and I'll talk things over with you and explain what's involved. I'm afraid it would mean that you'd have to live in the hotel, that's how we find out what they're like."

"That sounds even better. I'm cooped up in a caravan with Phil at the moment and it's getting too small for the two of us. I'll certainly come and see you tomorrow. I'm Maggie by the way."

"And I'm Stuart. Great, I'll see you tomorrow at about ten. I'm at the Hotel Matador, it's on the front. I'll see you in the lounge."

With that, he finished off his drink, shook her hand and left. Maggie felt as though a huge burden had suddenly been lifted and she settled into her work with a sense of eager anticipation.

The Hotel Matador overlooked the sea. It was set back in gardens, six storeys high and painted white. By its side was a large swimming pool and by ten o'clock in the morning there were already thirty or more people swimming or sunbathing on the blue loungers. Maggie was surprised, she didn't know that people got up so early when they were on holiday, it was certainly an early start for her as she hadn't finished work until well after two that morning and it must have been another hour or more before she eventually got into bed. Phil was still fast asleep as she let herself out of the caravan. The lounge was large and spacious, its wide doors and windows were all open to the sea and there were about twenty settees and even more easy chairs, a marked contrast to the caravan she had just left.

Stuart was waiting for her, he was dressed casually but smartly and had a briefcase with him and a great pile of papers on the table. He ordered cold coffee for them both and immediately got down to business.

"So, Maggie, you are definitely interested in this little job then?" Maggie nodded enthusiastically.

"Yes, I really am, in fact I'm quite excited by the idea."

"Great. Well I've been on the phone to England to talk to them and they are happy to take you on, on a temporary basis, provided that I am satisfied that you can do the job and that everything is in order. I don't suppose you've brought your passport with you have you?"

He then went on to describe what the job would entail and explained that Maggie would be paid into an account in England to make it easier to get round the employment rules. He would ensure that she received enough Spanish money to live on from day to day but the rest of her salary would go straight into her bank back home. He was somewhat surprised to discover that she didn't have one, but said that he could get it all sorted out. They sat for a good hour or more and found that they related to each other in a relaxed and easy manner and it was agreed that, barring any unexpected snags, she would begin work the following Monday. She would be given a room in a small hotel not far away and there would probably be enough work to keep her on the books for a few months. It was her first real paid employment for many years and she couldn't wait to begin. As she walked back to the caravan she felt that life had definitely taken a turn for the better. She was going to be able to stand on her own two feet, earn her way forward and move into a new phase.

She decided that she wouldn't tell Phil that she was leaving until Sunday morning and she spent a lot of time on Saturday working out in her mind how she would break the news. She didn't want to end the relationship in a blazing row nor did she want to hurt or upset him, because she still felt a great fondness for him even though she now knew it wasn't love. In the event she needn't have worried because he never came home on Saturday night. He turned up sometime in the early afternoon of Sunday and was in no mind to have any sort of rational conversation. Maggie explained that she was leaving, that she had found herself a job and that they might bump into each other as she would still be in the area but that it was time for their affair to come to an end. Phil looked at her rather quizzically but did little more than grunt. Maggie wasn't sure that he had understood what she was saying and began to explain it again.

"Maggie sweetheart, I'm neither deaf nor stupid, I heard you the first time. I don't know why you want to move out, is it something I've said?"

"Well no, not really, it's just a realisation that's been growing on me these last few weeks. But since you mention it, perhaps it might have something to do with what you've been doing. Where have you been all night? Or should I say 'who have you been with all night?"

"Well if you think I'm going to tell you that you must be dumber than I thought," responded Phil. "It's got absolutely nothing to do with you where I was or who I was with."

"No, I understand that Phil," she commented, "but can't you see that a relationship can't thrive when one of the partners feels free to swan off with other people, turn up much the worse for wear and then expect everything to be alright, as though nothing had happened?"

Phil grinned.

"You're right, of course sweetheart, you're always bloody well right! I can see that it's not very clever of me, but that's the way I am. Anyway, it's been good having you here, we've done quite well together haven't we, and you should be pleased to know that it's lasted longer with you than with anyone I've been with for years. So, when are you going?"

"Right now, actually. I've a room booked in a local hotel and I'm starting work tomorrow."

"Good God, you get a move on don't you. Well, do you have time for a final little fling, I've just about got enough energy, but it will have to be quick I'm almost out on my feet."

"Phil, you say the sweetest things and you really know how to talk your way into a girl's heart, but I'd rather not if you don't mind. Let's just remember the times when it was good and I'll get a move on and let you get some sleep."

"OK, as you like, but you know where I am if you ever want a little break."

Thus ended the relationship that broke up Maggie's marriage, which severed the deepest of links with her mother, which separated her from her children, that took her to a foreign land and which began the process of her growth into maturity.

She took to her new job as though she had always been waiting for this one opportunity. She was hard-working, reliable, committed and also very good at it. Stuart was delighted by her contribution and enjoyed her companionship. Six weeks into the work he arranged to meet her, saying that he had some good news so why didn't she join him for dinner. He took her, not to one of the hotels where he was able to eat 'on the house' but to a rather upmarket restaurant several miles away in the countryside. They talked easily about their work and when she thought they had spoken long enough about generalities Maggie brought the subject around to the whole point of the evening.

"So, Stuart, what is this good news you've got to tell me? Let me guess – I'm getting a pay rise or you're getting a pay rise or you've been invited to become the manager of the biggest hotel in Spain and you want me to help you run it? Now which is it?"

"Wrong on all counts I'm afraid," laughed Stuart. "Well, I suppose it just could be interpreted as a pay rise for you, I'm not sure. The thing is Maggie, you've done really well since you joined the company and I've let them know just how good you've been. They've been back in touch with me and they want me to ask you if you would be interested in working for us full time. That means a job back in England once this piece of work is over. I'm not totally sure what's involved but it seems that they are planning to develop things and they want to open up a new centre in Coventry and they wondered if you'd be interested in being part of it. You would have all the appropriate training, of course, so you need have no fears about not being able to do it. What do you think?"

Maggie was taken aback. She had never envisaged herself as a working woman and certainly no-one had ever approached her about a job before.

"Gosh Stuart, that would be absolutely brilliant. Tell me more."

He outlined what was envisaged. She would leave Spain once this piece of work was finished and they would put her up in a hotel in Manchester for a few weeks whilst she got to know more about the company and what the work would involve. Then, if all went well, they would set her up in Coventry in the new office they were opening. He didn't know what the salary would be but he suggested a figure that was far higher than she would have dreamed of.

"Maggie, this isn't very easy for me to say, so please don't take offence if it doesn't come out very well. I know it's nothing to do with me and with this job although in a sense it is. I've never pried into your life and I don't mean to be intrusive, but am I right in thinking that you have a husband and family back home? I mean, if you do have, might this mean that you wouldn't really be able to take up the job? You see, it would mean you living in Coventry and that's a big thing to ask someone to do. Please don't take this in the wrong way, but I hope you can see that it could make things a bit tricky, I mean the company wouldn't want to invest in your training and everything and then you pack it in a few weeks."

She was quiet for quite a while and then she looked up, smiled and put her hand across the table and squeezed his for a moment before withdrawing it.

"No, you are quite right to bring it up, in fact it's quite a relief to talk about it. I'll try and put you in the picture but don't be surprised if you get more than you bargained for. Can I talk to you as a friend, I mean you won't report everything back to your boss will you?"

"No Maggie, I won't report things back, well what I mean is that I will need to report back if I think that this is an idea worth pursuing, but I won't be discussing any of your personal business. Personal stuff is personal and that's the way it should be. I suppose I'm just covering my back, I don't want to send in a glowing report and then hear that you've left a month later, do you see what I mean?"

"Perfectly, I think we understand each other, it's just that I don't want to be embarrassed if everyone knows all about me."

She took a deep breath and gave him a quick resume of her situation, leaving out the more lurid parts. They talked on, sharing the stories of their lives. He was separated from his wife and he was trying to come to terms with her decision that she preferred to live on her own rather than with him. He had volunteered to do a few months in Spain to get him away from England and to give him time to think things through. He was making progress but confessed that it wasn't easy.

"I suppose we're in similar situations really," he said, "although you made the decision to leave and the decision was made for me. Anyway, it's been a good evening and I ought to be getting you back to the hotel. I've another hour or so to spend on paper work when I get back to my room."

He settled the bill and drove Maggie back to her hotel.

"Thank you so much, that's been a lovely evening, and on top of that there is the prospect of a job. I don't know how to thank you enough."

Maggie leaned over and gave him a polite little kiss on the cheek.

"You know, it's quite a new experience for me to spend time with a man without him trying to get me into bed. Thank you for paying me the compliment of talking to me as a person rather than as a body."

Stuart grinned.

"Well, it's nice of you to say that, but in all honesty I don't know if it's totally true. The idea had crossed my mind more than once. Off you go now and don't be late for work in the morning."

Perhaps if Miriam hadn't died then Libby might have moved out and set up home with Robbie, but that was never really considered as she knew that Patsy had been knocked off balance by the tragedy and all its implications. It was important to remain in the bungalow and provide her with the support she needed. They did lots of things as a three-some as well as enjoying times when they were alone together and Libby found it very easy to relax with Robbie, he was homely, undemanding and good company. One afternoon she was visiting his home and was busy preparing a meal whilst he sat at the table completing a crossword. After half an hour Robbie filled in the final blank squares.

"Finished it," he exclaimed triumphantly.

"Robbie, you're wonderful," Libby skipped across the room and gave him a kiss. He pulled her down towards him and they embraced as they somehow managed to fit together, albeit uncomfortably, into the easy chair.

"Am I really wonderful?" teased Robbie.

"Of course you are. Not only wonderful, but fantastic at crosswords, Victoria will be most impressed," and she gave him another kiss.

"Then will you marry me?"

It was as though time stopped still. Libby had the sensation of the floor giving way and she felt that she was plummeting downwards, faster and faster, so that she could no longer breathe.

"Oh Robbie, don't, please don't ask me that."

She felt the colour draining from her face.

"Libby dear, I've already asked you. I've loved you for ages. You've shown me how to live again, you've given me hope, and you've touched the innermost parts of me. I can't imagine living without you. Please, please say you will."

It was the question that Libby had been dreading. She had thought about it many times and wondered whether, or rather when he would ask her. Even more, she had many times wondered what she would say. When it came she was totally unprepared. She didn't know what she felt and what she did feel she couldn't interpret. What she could interpret she couldn't trust and what she could trust left her feeling exposed and isolated.

"Robbie my precious, you are so sweet. Do you know, that's the first time anyone has ever asked me to marry them and here I am thirty five years old. But I do wish you hadn't asked, please don't. I just don't know what to say. I suppose I just want the present to continue like this, I don't want there to be a future where we have to make decisions I just want things to stay like this – always."

"Things can't stay like this Libby, you know that. Nor can we. Look how we have come together this last year, we belong with each other. We have to create a new future, together. I want you to be my wife more than anything else in the world."

"I don't know what to say. I love you, of course I do, but I don't know about getting married, I just don't know. I'm so confused; I'm not sure what I can say."

"Just say yes, just say yes."

Robbie held her tightly, and whispered the words into her ear.

"I can't say yes, I can't, I can't… " and she began to cry.

They sat in a restaurant. The atmosphere was strained, but it was the sort of strain that love creates, when the desire to please the other conflicts with the desire not to hurt the other. They were both finding it difficult to express their thoughts and feelings in words. How strange that just a few hours ago they were laughing about a crossword puzzle and then, without warning, she was having to face up to one of the most difficult and important decisions of her life.

"Robbie, I just don't see how it could work. Your children are in New Zealand and you need to be near them."

"Yes, but I was hoping that you would join me there, so that we could set up a home and keep in contact with them."

"But all my family live in England and I've never even been to New Zealand. My mother is in her sixties, she's all alone, one of my sisters is in a mess and the other one is left with all the caring and the coping. I can't just leave Africa and go even further away. In fact, I'm not sure how long I can stay here anyway, my mum's not well... Oh, I don't know, it's just so difficult."

"But if we love each other then we'll find a way through these things. You could come to New Zealand and return to England every year. That would be more often than you are doing at the moment. Can't you see that if we are together in this then we'll find a way through all these difficulties? Libby, you're a very special person, meeting you has been one of the best things that has ever happened to me, can't you see, we are made for each other?"

"Oh, I just don't know. There are so many problems, so many hurdles to overcome. You say that I could go to England every year, but it's not as easy as that. Apart from the cost, I can't just leave my mother; you know what a wretched life she's had. I feel somehow that I have to give her something back, show her that I love her and appreciate all that she's given me."

"Honey, I appreciate all that, but you know, you don't actually owe her anything. I mean, you didn't ask to be born, it wasn't an arrangement that you entered into, you know – 'I'll care for you when you are young and then you can care for me when I am old'. That sort of attitude ruins people's lives, don't you see that?"

After her time in Spain Maggie went to Manchester for her training before moving onto Coventry where she soon settled into the city. Her flat had a sitting room with a wide window which looked out over the Memorial Park and the trees presented an ever-changing outlook. During the winter when it was windy or stormy they bent to and fro, forever restless. When the frost came their branches became sparkling and when it snowed they looked tall and majestic, but bending under the weight. In springtime the new leaves emerged from the buds with delicate vulnerability and in the summer the branches provided a canopy, providing a resting place in the shade away from the glare of the sun. She had never noticed trees before but she became fascinated by their life-cycle as she watched them from her window. She loved the flat and was happier there than at any other time since her childhood.

The work was both interesting and demanding and she had no regrets about taking the plunge and agreeing to join the company.

Stuart unexpectedly became the regional manager for the midlands and, effectively, her boss. It meant that they saw quite a lot of each other. To begin with this was work related as they both settled into their respective new work but before long they were seeing each other socially. He made no secret of the fact that above all, he wanted to return to his wife, but there seemed to be little prospect of that happening. He enjoyed being with Maggie and he wanted, perhaps needed, friendship and companionship as he settled into his new job and his new home in Birmingham about twenty miles away. They saw each other on a regular basis, but only once or twice a week. Occasionally he would stay over but showed little desire to make this a more frequent occurrence. Maggie had been to see him in Birmingham but she had never stayed there. It was a state of affairs that seemed to satisfy them both although she would have raised no objections had he decided to stay more often and for longer.

A s she walked along the street to the house in Leeds where she had spent so many years Maggie was more nervous than she imagined possible. She approached the door and just as she was about to knock it opened and her mother stood there, staring at her with tears running down her cheeks. There was a momentary pause, a mutual embarrassment and then Maggie rushed forward and hugged her, unable to speak, choking with emotion and almost gasping for breath.

"Mum, Oh mum, I'm so sorry, forgive me, please say that you forgive me, I'm so sorry to have hurt you, I've missed you so much, please say that it's alright, that you forgive me."

The words tumbled out, hardly making any sense.

"Mum, I love you, I'm so sorry. It's good to see you. I've missed you so much; I can't tell you how much I've missed you."

There had been little indication whilst Maggie was in Spain that she was missing her mother, but perhaps she had deliberately suppressed such feelings in her desire to start a new life. She was recognising a sense of loss which she had not realised until this moment. It was as though a dam had suddenly collapsed and a torrent of pent up emotion, of loss and love, of guilt and longing came flooding out.

It was several minutes before they separated, indeed before Beryl said a word. She had begun to believe that it would never happen, that she would never see Maggie again. She was tired, empty and lacking the resources to respond adequately. Her face was drawn, her health was deteriorating and she was losing interest in people, in life itself. She slowly disengaged herself and walked over to the settee beckoning Maggie to come and sit by her side.

"Maggie, Maggie, I can't tell you how good it is to see you. I thought I would never see you again..."

She found it impossible to continue; she just sat and wiped her eyes with a crumpled handkerchief. The silence between them more eloquent than any words.

"I never thought you would come back... never... you've been away so long, Oh Maggie, don't ever leave me again, don't ever leave me again."

"No Mum, I'll never go off again. I'm back now. I've learned my lesson, I'm here and we'll be together, I won't ever go off again."

"And Mike, will you come back to Mike and the children. They all miss you so much you know. Mike was terrible after you went, he was off work and didn't eat... it was awful. Have you come back to them as well?"

"No Mum, I can't do that. I really can't. I've caused them so much pain and trouble, I know, I know, but I can't come back. I could never settle down with Mike again, it just wouldn't work, and I can't bear to see the children, it just wouldn't work."

"Oh Maggie, how can you say that?" Beryl's tears came flooding back. "How can you say that?"

"Mum, please don't press me, I can't bear that. Look, I've come back, I need to be near you, but I can't go back to my old life, I just can't. I've got a job, I'm earning some decent money and I'm trying to sort my life out. It's a long and painful process. God knows, it's difficult enough, please don't make me feel even worse. I know what a mess I've made of things believe me, no-one knows that better than me, but I can't go back, I can't, I can't."

"But what about the children Maggie, what about the children?"

"Mum, don't, don't. I can't bear it, that's why I wrote and asked you to make sure that there weren't here today. A day never goes by without me thinking about them. I hug them each night in my mind before I go to sleep, but I'm not a good mother, I'm not. They deserve better than me. I can't help it. I'm not you. Mum. You have been so fantastic, all my life you've been such a wonderful mother. But I'm not like you. I just can't do it. I would like to be able to but I can't, I just can't. I've got to learn how to live again, to sort myself out, not to be such a trouble to everyone, especially to you, but don't ask me to do what I'm incapable of doing."

"But what about the children? What about Mike? Surely you'll be going back to them?"

Maggie realised that her mother wasn't really hearing what she was saying. She had aged such a lot since she'd been away, but it was less than two years, how could such a short time have made such a difference? She got up from the settee and tried to sort her face out. She went into the kitchen to make a cup of tea. When she came back her mother had barely moved. Her lips were moving but she wasn't saying anything. She seemed to be whispering and Maggie bent down to try and hear what she was saying. She fought back the tears when she heard the words "She's back, she's come back, Maggie's back." She seemed to be in a daze and Maggie was unsure what she ought to do.

"I think we ought to get you up into bed for a rest Mum."

Their roles were being reversed; she now had to look after her mother, the way that she had been looked after herself for so many years. She helped Beryl upstairs and somehow managed to settle her into bed. She made no comment, just stared ahead and occasionally whispered "she's back, she's back." Maggie sat with her for a while and then went downstairs to make another cup of tea. She was standing in the kitchen when there was a knock at the door. She was just moving to open it when she heard voices outside and she froze.

"I'm sure we weren't supposed to be coming to Grannie's today," said a young voice.

"I know, but I don't think it matters," came a reply.

"I'll knock again, but I think she might be out, I'm sure that's what dad said."

There was another loud knock and then silence. Maggie heard footsteps move away and she quietly moved into the sitting room and took a furtive look through the window. Three young children, happy, playing with each other, walked back along the road. She moved to the table to steady herself, nearly falling, weak at the knees. She sat down. She couldn't believe that there were any more tears left in her body, but there were and they came pouring out and didn't stop for a long time, a very long time.

Although she hadn't planned to, Maggie stayed the night with her mother and was relieved to find her in a much better condition in the morning. She beamed as Maggie brought her a cup of tea up to bed and then climbed in beside her.

"Oh Maggie, it's just like it used to be. I'm sure we are going to be alright aren't we? Everything will get back together again. I'm so pleased."

Maggie decided not to open up that conversation again, instead she lay down and they spent the next hour reminiscing, laughing at some of the situations they had shared in the past and catching up on news of Victoria and her family and of Libby. She went downstairs and prepared breakfast and then gave her mother a big hug and left, running for the train and arriving at work almost four hours late.

She fell into a pattern of going back to Leeds every three weeks, ensuring that the children were not visiting on those days. Beryl had spoken to Mike about her visits. He found it difficult to believe that she didn't want to see them. He had hoped that she would return, but he did recognise that it would be quite traumatic for the children to see her only for her to leave them again, also, there was the added problem of Jenny. Since Maggie left he had developed a friendship with a young teacher and she had recently moved in with him. Now, just as he was starting to live again, she was back. He wanted her and yet he knew that he was better off without her.

A new pattern of life was developing which suited her, bringing a sense of deep satisfaction. She loved her job and occasionally was sent back to Spain to check up on various hotels and interview possible temporary staff for the holiday season. She never re-visited the *Pasa Doble* and she never bumped into Phil again, nor did she want to. She walked around the streets of Benidorm and marvelled that she had once turned up there without a penny, lived in a caravan and worked in a bar and a night club. More often she was in other resorts, visiting tourist attractions and developing a way of communicating with the Spanish staff which was relaxed and yet, at the same time, conveyed a sense of purpose and determination.

The relationship with Stuart blossomed. They had a passionate weekend in Rome, a romantic trip down the Nile and a wonderful week in Paris. There were advantages working in the travel industry. One of the things that she liked about him was his honesty, although this was also the very thing that caused her the greatest sadness. From the first he had always made it clear that although he was very fond of her and loved her in his own sort of way, he also grieved the loss of his wife and was always hopeful that his marriage might be resurrected. Maggie often wondered if this was a possibility or whether it was fantasy, or even an unconscious device he had created to ensure that he didn't make a commitment to her. She was happy with their relationship but would willingly have moved into a more permanent and formal partnership. It seemed ironic that she, who had had so many partners over the years, was unable to settle down with the one she was most attracted to and at ease with. She was happier with Stuart, even though they were not exactly together, than she had been with Mike and he was her husband. She was also faithful to Stuart which was something that she certainly wasn't when she was married.

It was coming up to Christmas which was the worst time of the year for her, the time when she remembered her own childhood which seemed idyllic in retrospect, the time when she remembered her own children and felt deep pangs of loss and it was the time when she stopped and thought of Victoria and her family and of Libby. Victoria had, at long last persuaded her mother to spend Christmas with them in London and she had invited Maggie to join them and to bring Stuart. Maggie knew that he wouldn't go and she didn't want to go without him. The alternative, to spend Christmas together, just the two of them, seemed very attractive. Her thoughts about it received a severe setback the next time they met.

"Maggie, I'm not sure how to put this, but I've got a problem."

Maggie looked at him, surprised.

"What sort of a problem? Have you got a pain, are you ill or something?"

"No, it's nothing like that. It's just that I've had a Christmas card from Christine. She wrote a small note with it – look," and he handed a piece of paper over to Maggie.

Hi Stuart, I've managed to track your address down. How are things? I don't know what you are up to these days, but I wonder if it might be possible for us to meet up again sometime. I've had time to think things over and I just wonder if I did the right thing. I don't want to intrude if it's all over with you, but I just thought it might be possible for us to meet up again. I haven't found it easy to write this. Love, Christine

Maggie's heart sank, she didn't say anything, she just handed the paper back to Stuart and looked at him.

"The thing is Maggie; I don't know what to do."

Maggie could not believe what she was saying when she looked at him, took his hand gently and looked at him.

"I think you do know Stuart. It's what you've really wanted and been hoping for isn't it. Jesus, it's just about the last thing that I want, but you'll go Stuart, I know you will," and a small tear tricked down her cheek.

"Yes, I suppose it is," his voice was barely audible. "But now it's come I'm not so sure. We've got something going really special between us, haven't we? I never expected this when I picked up the cards from the floor this evening, I didn't even recognise the handwriting on the envelope. The thing is Maggie, I never wanted to split up from Christine in the first place. I fell in love with her years ago, fifteen, twenty years – I can't remember when, but she was always the girl for me. I was the happiest man in the world when we got married. I thought we were happy, I know I was, but I suppose I never noticed that she wasn't. We tried to have children, you know, but it just never happened. I suppose that was when I began to lose her…"

He was looking into the distance, he was speaking to Maggie but in reality he was speaking to himself and she knew that her chances of keeping him were disappearing by the minute. He had always been honest about the pain he felt about the break-up of his marriage and he had never made great and extravagant confessions of love towards her but, as he admitted just now, they did have something special going for them and it had been an extraordinary experience for her. She looked around the room, the lights on the Christmas tree were blinking on and off as they were an hour ago, but somehow they had lost their magic. The Christmas cards, with their colours and their messages of love and friendship now seemed rather shallow and false.

"I was going to discuss the arrangements for Christmas but now I'm not sure what the best thing to do is. I'm sure you will go and see her and I don't want to stop you, even though the very thought of it makes me feel sick, but you will have to do what you have to do. So, what does this do to our plans for Christmas?"

"Perhaps it doesn't do anything to our plans. I won't be seeing her until after Christmas if I do see her, so we can still go ahead with our plans. What were our plans, by the way?"

"Well, that's just the point, we don't have any. I was rather hoping that it could just be the two of us here, but this has put a bit of a dampener on that idea. I mean, I would hardly be having you to myself would I? There would always be a third person, however much we pretended that there wasn't."

"Maggie, I'm so confused. You know that I've always loved Christine, I don't think I've ever hid that from you, have I? But at the same time I realise that I've also fallen in love with you, I didn't mean to, I guess it just crept up on me and took me by surprise. How can anyone love two people at the same time?"

In different circumstances, six thousand miles away Libby was asking herself exactly the same question.

They spent Christmas in Mallorca. It was not what either of them really wanted but they decided that it would do neither of them much good to be cooped up together indoors for hours on end. Their problems went with them, of course, they both knew that, but they had different things to interest them and talk about. They stayed in a quaint old hotel and had a room with a balcony overlooking the sea. It was facing west and each evening, or rather late afternoon; they sat with a bottle of wine and watched the most glorious sunsets. Maggie thought it must be rather like waiting for someone to die, you tried to make the most of each day but were acutely conscious of some future date when all that you cared about would disappear.

Libby and Robbie had an unsatisfactory evening. The fact that they loved each other made it all the more difficult. They parted with an agreement that she would think things over and let Robbie have an answer at the end of the week. He had to be in

Lesotho for four or five days and they agreed to meet up the following Friday evening after he returned. Libby went home more depressed than she had been for a very long time. She should have been excited, even exultant, but there was a great sense of foreboding and unease, she was not at all happy.

Patsy looked up when she walked into the kitchen.

"Hey, what's wrong with you? You look as though you've seen a ghost. Is everything alright?"

Libby nodded and then burst into tears.

"It's Robbie," she said, "he's asked me to marry him."

"Why that's marvellous! Let me open a bottle of wine. Why on earth should that make you cry? You cry when they say that they don't love you not when they say that they do."

"No, don't open a bottle; I've already had too much to drink. There are just so many problems. He wants to live in New Zealand and that makes sense because his children are there, but I can't ever see myself living so far away. I'm more and more aware that I need to be thinking of going home. My mother's not well and there are all these family problems. Maggie left her children for this chap in Spain and now she's left him and is with somebody else, my mother isn't all that well, my sister's taking all the strain... Oh, I just don't know... I think I'm missing my friends. I need to go to a concert; I need to listen to music. I think I don't belong here anymore – Oh what a mess."

Miriam's death made her realise that, however much she tried, she would never really be at home in Africa and never really understand the culture and the life of the people she so enjoyed living amongst. She had to face up to her own 'Englishness' and in doing so she somehow felt a failure. She had wanted so much to be committed to Africa and its children but now she felt that somehow there would always be a gap, that she would always be a visitor and ultimately a stranger.

Two days before Robbie returned from Lesotho, whilst Libby appeared to be no nearer to making her mind up, a phone call from Victoria had a decisive influence upon her. She knew then, beyond a shadow of a doubt, that she had to return home.

Maggie had been home for three days when, as she was lying in the bath she felt the lump. To begin with she didn't believe it, pretending there was nothing, she continued to soap herself. She stretched out and let the water come up to her chin. In normal circumstances she would have relaxed and reflected on the joys of a deep bath, instead she raised her hand up to her breast again and began feeling all around. Yes, there was no mistaking it, there was a lump. A multitude of thoughts flashed through her mind, her life up to this moment compressed into a few seconds, her future stretching out endlessly before her into the darkness.

Dr Graham was the sort of GP who exuded old fashioned professional competence and charm. He sat behind a large desk, Maggie sat before him on a small chair. He had folders and papers all around him, he was clearly not a very tidy person. She sat with nothing in her hands, feeling extremely vulnerable. He was approaching retirement; his family had made a big issue of that over their Christmas celebrations. 'Not long to go now, Dad' his sons had teased him, but he didn't want to retire. Since his wife had died a year or two before he found that work was the only thing that kept him sane. He could not bear the thought of not having something to do each day, all set out for him and waiting for him to apply his mind and skills to.

"I don't think we've met before Mrs... Mrs... now let me see, Ah yes. Anyway, it's very good to meet you, I'm Dr. Graham. Now what seems to be the problem, what has brought you here today?"

He beamed at her, looked over the top of his glasses and weighed her up. She was a very attractive young woman, he thought. She was probably in her thirties and having to adjust to losing her youthful charm. There was a certain sadness in her eyes, he noticed, she's had some knocks over the years, I wonder what they were? Dr Graham was a skilled practitioner and he prided himself on his ability to make a quick assessment.

"Well, I hope I'm not wasting your time, although I hope I am I suppose. Anyway, I seem to have a lump in my breast and thought I ought to come and get it checked out. It's probably nothing."

"You've done exactly the right thing, my dear, and you're certainly not wasting my time. Now when did you first discover it?"

"Just a few days ago. To begin with I was too frightened to come but I knew that was silly. If it is something then it needs to be seen to."

She liked him, he was not overpowering and he wasn't making her feel small and insignificant.

"Just come over to the couch, slip your top things off and we'll have a little look. Now tell me exactly where you felt it."

She thought that she might feel embarrassed but she didn't. She indicated where she thought it was and the doctor looked, prodded and generally gave her a good examination, probing underneath her arms and muttering to himself as he made the examination.

"What about the other side? Have you felt anything there?"

Maggie shook her head.

"Well I'll just check it whilst you are here."

He took his stethoscope and checked out her breathing, tested her blood pressure and then told her to put her things on and return to her seat. He went over to the desk and began to make some notes.

"You are quite right; there is a little something there. I don't think it's anything to get too worried about but you were quite right to come and see me. I congratulate you on finding it. You should have become a doctor. These things are not always easy to locate, you have done well. I'm going to write a letter to Mr. Grimbold at the hospital and ask him to have a further look to see if he can sort things out. Now don't go worrying about it, we don't know what it is so there's no point in worrying."

"But have I got cancer, doctor, is that what it is?"

He looked at her and deliberated over his words. He didn't want to alarm her but he was not unconcerned. He had come across too many similar instances, too many young women looking at him with frightened eyes.

"Now you are an intelligent young woman, I can see that, and I don't want to insult you by not being frank, but neither do I want to alarm you unnecessarily. It is true that it could possibly be cancer but, on the other hand there are many other things that it could be as well, so there is a greater chance that it is something else. That's why I need you to see the hospital. Going there should not be seen as a bad step, it does not signify that things are bad. I want you to go there so that we can clarify what the situation is, so that we can eliminate some of the possibilities and try and get to the bottom of what it is. Whatever it is, you have come straight away and that is always a good sign. It is much better to sort these things out in the early days rather than let them develop."

Maggie thanked him and walked out of the surgery. She didn't know what she felt, whether to cry or be angry or just ignore it. She wanted to tell Stuart, to be comforted and supported by him but decided that this wasn't the right time. It was most certainly the wrong time, it was this weekend that he was going to see Christine. Thinking about that took over from thinking about her lump.

He let himself into the flat, looking anxious and uncomfortable. He suggested that they went out for the day and they drove over to Stratford and walked by the river for an hour. It transpired that he was still undecided as to what to do although the meeting had gone well. Maggie asked where they had met and he said that he had taken her out for a meal. She pressed him as to what happened then and he said that he had taken her home.

"Look Stuart, you are not making this easy for me. I'm having to prise information out of you. You went out for a meal, then you took her home. Was that it then? You took her home, dropped her off, said goodbye and drove back to Birmingham? Was that how it was, or have you something more to tell me?"

"I took her home and stayed the weekend."

"Right, I'm beginning to get it now. And when you stayed at her place, did you sleep in the spare room?"

"No."

"So, although you say that you are undecided what to do, you weren't apparently undecided what to do then? Come on Stuart, be honest with me. It's all over between us isn't it?"

He was silent as he walked along the path. He kicked a stone and saw it make a splash in the river. He looked at her then he looked away again.

"Maggie, I don't know. You say that I'm not making it easy for you, but neither are you making it easy for me. I feel that you are pressing me, forcing me along a path that I've not yet decided on. I honestly don't know."

"Well when might you know? Later today? Tomorrow? Next week? Next month? What am I supposed to do, sit around and wait for you to decide which woman you want to be with? What are you planning to do, sleep with us both for as long as possible and then decide who turns you on the most?"

He resented this remark and he turned on her angrily.

"I know this is bloody hard on you, I know that I'm messing you about, but I'm not doing it on purpose. I'm trying to sort things out in my mind and having you saying things like that doesn't help. If we are unable to resolve things together then perhaps we need to go back and we'll meet up again when we can be rather more civil. Can't you see that I'm in a hell of a mess? Don't force a decision on me that I might regret, that you might regret."

"Oh come off it Stuart, you've already decided. Just get back to the car and take me home only this time just drop me off and don't come in for the weekend."

They journeyed back in silence. Maggie got out of the car, slammed the door and went in without saying a word and without looking back.

She was right. He had decided, though whether she had pushed him towards that decision neither of them would ever know. He went back to Christine, leaving the company and getting work nearer to home. Before he left Birmingham he sent her a huge bunch of roses together with a letter.

My dearest Maggie

I am sorry that our friendship came to such a difficult and unsatisfactory end, it was unworthy of something that has been very important and precious to me and, I dare to believe to you. I want to thank you for all that you have given me and shared with me since we met up in Spain over two years ago. You have been very special to me. I know that my decision to go back to Christine has been difficult for you, actually it has been difficult for me as well although I don't think you believe that. If I wasn't already married and if I hadn't been in love with Christine for so many years then I would almost certainly have wanted to be with you for the rest of my life. I'm sorry that things have worked out like this and I hope that some day you will understand and forgive me.

It will be a wrench leaving the company, I have loved the job and, of course I have really enjoyed working with you. Maggie, you are a fantastic member of staff and we are very lucky to have you on board – or rather, they are (I'm forgetting that I've left!).

Thank you for everything. You are a super person and deserve to find happiness, a happiness that I've failed you in.
>*With love*
>*Stuart*

She read the letter through twice then took out her cigarette lighter, set fire to the corner of it and dropped it into the hearth when her fingers began to get burnt. Then she picked up the roses and thrust them into the waste bin in the kitchen. She put her coat on, went out without bothering to lock the door and walked to the local pub and sat there drinking for the rest of the evening. When she eventually left, at closing time, she was violently sick in the car park and with a very unsteady gait made her way home.

If she thought that things had reached rock bottom and couldn't get any worse, then she was wrong. Her appointment at the hospital duly arrived and they took her in overnight and performed a biopsy. She was very frightened and felt very much alone. She hadn't told anyone about this lump and as she lay in the bed after the investigation she felt drained of all strength and of all inner resources. She had radiated life and vitality, everyone else used to revolve around her and now she was in a hospital ward and no-one knew she was there apart from the medical staff who, in their own way, continued to revolve around her, but it was different.

Dr. Graham sat behind his desk and looked at her. She seemed to have aged in the few weeks since he last saw her. Although still attractive she was clearly in distress and he doubted that it was primarily her health problems which were distressing her. He was used to seeing people who had been for a biopsy, their anxiety was understandable, but in Maggie he saw a deeper inner distress which he couldn't quite understand.

"Well my dear, you've been to the hospital and they've had a good look at you, so how do you feel now?"

"I feel fine, thank you, the hospital staff were very good." Maggie spoke with a composure which surprised him.

"So what have they found?" she asked, leaning forward and looking straight at him.

Again he was surprised. People usually waited for him to speak but here was someone who was taking the initiative and asking him the questions. He admired her strength of character. She was clearly making great efforts to remain in control of herself and he decided that he would proceed along the lines that she was clearly wanting.

"Well, I'm afraid the news is not as good as I was hoping for. Now don't get me wrong, things are in hand, but Mr. Grimbold would like to see you again."

"What do you mean when you say that things are not as good as you hoped for? What exactly is the position?"

She was forcing the pace.

Dr Graham was quiet for a while, looking at her and trying to assess how best to phrase his words. She clearly wanted to know the truth about her condition but he doubted if she was as strong as she appeared to be.

"Before I answer that question and I am going to answer it, fully for you, but before I answer it tell me this – who have you got at home? Do you have a husband, a family? Who is there to look after you when you are not well?"

Maggie didn't like the way that this conversation was developing. What business was it of his to ask questions about her domestic situation?

"I'm not quite sure what you are trying to find out Dr. Graham by these questions, but if you really want to know, then I'll tell you. I am separated from my husband and family and I live quite alone. Is that what you need to know?"

He was interested by her rather aggressively defensive reply and concluded that he had touched a raw nerve. He decided that he would return to it later.

"No, no, no that's quite alright, quite alright. But you see, I need to know these things if I am your doctor and am going to help you. Anyway, back to the problem of that lump. Mr Grimbold tells me that they have done a biopsy and found out a bit about the growth that you correctly located. There seem to be two problems associated with it. The first one is that it is what we call 'malignant'. There are two types of growth, malignant and benign and I'm afraid that yours falls into the malignant category which is rather more serious than if it were benign. The second problem is that it is quite deep, which makes it more difficult to treat."

He waited for a moment or two to see how she was reacting to this news. She sat looking at him, apparently registering little, so that he was not at all sure how much she had understood.

"What this means therefore is that Mr. Grimbold would like to see you again."

"I see, I see," she said quietly.

"I have a malignant tumour in my breast and it is not going to be easy to sort it out. So what does that really mean?"

"Well, there are various options open to us and we are going to have to explore them one by one…"

Dr Graham was cut off as he spoke.

"Dr Graham, please don't beat about the bush. Why is it that men seldom say what they mean, why do they have to dither around to find words that don't exactly say what they mean? Please be straight with me, I'm not a little girl you know."

Ah, so that's it, he deduced. She's separated from her husband and she's been in some other sort of relationship that has probably come to an end since I last saw her. Come to an end not of her own choice by the sound of it. The poor thing, and now she has to cope with this as well.

"Very well my dear, I'll lay out the facts for you as clearly as I can. You have a malignant tumour that is deep rooted. It will be necessary to get rid of it as soon as possible, before it spreads. There are various methods of doing this, from a course of pills to destroy it chemically, to radiotherapy which is a form of burning it away from the inside. It is doubtful whether either of these courses is likely to succeed, although I cannot say that for certain. The third option is to intervene surgically and to cut it out and this would almost certainly mean the removal of the breast, or a mastectomy. That is a clinical decision and I am not the person to make that decision which is why it is necessary for you to see Mr. Grimbold again. I wanted to know who you have at home with you as clearly this is a distressing situation and it is better if you have someone with whom you can talk things through. I am here to offer you whatever support I can but people usually like to have friends or family to give them the support that they need. I have one or two small booklets here which I can give you which help to explain what is involved and I am always here to talk with you again if and when you might need that. Do you understand what I've been spelling out, is there anything that you want me to explain in a different way? Take your time to think this over, there is no great hurry."

"Thank you doctor, I appreciate your honesty and I think I understand what you have told me. Does it mean that I am going to die?"

"Well, if you don't get it sorted out it will probably mean that your life is shortened considerably. If you do get it sorted, and clearly nothing is certain in these matters, then I would expect you to have many years of life left. People are affected in different ways and it is difficult to be precise in these matters, but I think it would be foolish if you went home thinking that a death sentence had been issued, that would cause you unnecessary distress. I have not been able to give you good news today but the bad news that I have given you must be tempered with reality and there is much that can be done, a great deal, a great deal. Now take my advice and find a friend or a member of your family with whom you can discuss these things. Finally, just before you leave, forgive me for intruding, but am I right in thinking that it is not only your health that is causing you distress at the moment?"

Maggie looked at him and finally smiled and nodded her head. You are a clever old man, she thought to herself, but said nothing.

"I thought so. Well let me just give you a word of advice. We all have different sorts of pain, physical pain and emotional pain, and they often present themselves in the same way and we can't always sort the one out from the other. Sometimes it is easier to tackle the physical pain than the emotional pain. What I am telling you is that whatever else is bothering you, I think we can do some positive work sorting out the physical problems – the emotional ones may take longer. Well, goodbye my dear and keep in touch. I will be hearing from Mr. Grimbold after you've seen him."

As she walked home from the surgery she saw the first daffodils of the year, a sure sign that spring was on the way despite the cold wind. 'Perhaps I have to believe that there can be springtime for me even though at the moment I feel that I am in the deepest and darkest winter,' she said to herself as she quickened her steps.

It took Libby quite a time to settle her affairs in Swaziland. She worked until the end of term and then had a memorable send-off from the school, with much singing and dancing, many photographs and a gift of a large wall-hanging showing the school, trees and a clear blue sky. It was something that she was to treasure for the rest of her life. There was also a large book of letters and drawings from the children which she later had bound and to which she would return time and time again as the years passed by.

Parting from Robbie was much more complicated. Every move, every decision was analyzed and talked through endlessly. He could not accept the fact that Libby felt the need to return to Britain. He found it incomprehensible that she could say that she loved him and yet was not prepared to marry him; that she could enjoy his company and yet deliberately decide to withdraw from it. The only way forward seemed to be an agreement that he would visit her in six months time and until that visit they should consider that all their arrangements were provisional.

It was a time of many contradictions, of tension between being sure and clear and being unsure and befuddled. She couldn't understand how there could be so many ways of looking at the one issue, so many differing aspects and such a gulf between what she thought in her head and what she felt in her heart.

"Most people think things through and then reach a decision," argued Robbie, "you do the opposite, you reach your decision and then think out the reasons for it, I just don't understand the way you operate."

"I'm sorry, I really am. I don't do these things on purpose you know, it's just the way that I am."

"I know, I know and I suppose that's one of the reasons why I love you, but I can't pretend to like it, because I seem to be incapable of persuading you to accept what's good for you. You say you'll go back home. You've no job, you've a flat hundreds of miles away from your mother which someone else happens to be living in, you have more or less lost touch with your friends and you want to get back to see a sister who has never even written to you in all the years that you've been out here."

"Oh Robbie, we've been through this so many times before. Don't ask me why, because I can't tell you, I just know that I have to go home. I know that what I'm doing is causing you pain and that just adds to the difficulties that I have, but I know that I have to press on, I can't help it, I really can't. I don't know why, I just know that I have to go."

A few weeks later she left. Robbie insisted on driving her down to Johannesburg, making it a special mini-holiday as they took several days to reach the airport. They enjoyed each other's company, they ate well, they walked and found good overnight accommodation. Although they clung to each other as they eventually fell asleep, they both knew that there was a great gulf between them. Neither spoke of it but both were aware of it. Although Libby was physically there she was mentally elsewhere, in a world that Robbie neither knew nor understood. Their love for each other was real but it was not all-inclusive and Robbie knew that he had lost her, even as she gave herself to him.

V ictoria met her at the airport, she had insisted that she stay a few days with them before heading north to see their mother. There were so many things she wanted to talk through with her and anyway, she wanted to know all about Africa and especially about Robbie. The interrogation began before they had left the car-park.

"Goodness Victoria, let me take a breath," laughed Libby. "How am I ever going to answer all those questions? I can't even remember what they all were!"

"Well tell me about Robbie first. Is he coming over? Are you going to marry him? What's he like? When do we see him?"

"Oh how can I answer all those questions? You know, it's not quite as simple as you assume it to be. Yes, he's a real sweetie..." Libby laughed when she realised she had picked up Patsy's phrase, "and yes, he wants us to get married, but... well it's not so straightforward. He says he's coming over in six months but, to be honest, I don't think he will. I think it's all over really."

"So is that why you've come home? You need to get away from him?"

"No, no, it's nothing at all like that. I've come home because... because... well, to be frank I'm not too sure why I've come home apart from knowing that I just had to. I think I've been worried about Mum, and then all this upset with Maggie... I just felt that I needed to be back here. And somehow, things were never the same after Miriam's death, it has really affected me, I think."

She asked about Bill and learned that he was becoming much more active within the Conservative Party, which Victoria didn't seem to find at all strange whilst to her it was utterly incomprehensible.

Victoria filled her in on the news of Maggie and then continued.

"Libby, I need to tell you now, before you go up to see her, but I think you'll find a big change in mum. She's not been well, she's very depressed. Sometimes I think she's coming out of it but then it all seems to go to pieces again and she's back in her own private world and its hell for her. She can't communicate, she doesn't seem to notice that you're there, she just sits and looks – it's really quite eerie at times. I've got to warn you before you go, it's awful sometimes."

Libby looked at her and could see that she was plainly shaken. Her face looked drawn, quite unlike the relaxed and smiling Victoria of just an hour or so ago.

"I've tried not to worry Bill with it. I'm sure he knows, of course, he always does, but we don't really talk about it. It's funny really, because we talk about everything, but not this. It's as though he seems to feel that this is something very private, very personal to me and he shouldn't intrude. At first I was sad, it's the only thing we don't really share, but now I'm glad because it means that I can get on with life here without my worries taking over and getting in everyone's way. I didn't want to burden you with this whilst you were away and anyway you had your own worries and problems, but I'm so pleased that you're back. I can't tell you how pleased I am."

"I'm sorry, I didn't know. I suppose I should have done but I didn't. I knew that I often couldn't really communicate with her when I phoned and sometimes I thought I was probably wasting both my time and money even trying, but I didn't really put two and two together. Oh Victoria, you are so good. You've been carrying this all alone; you must have thought me terribly selfish."

"No, I never thought that," she protested. "I was just so pleased that you were doing something useful and something that you wanted to do. You know I really admire you, you've done so much with your life and I sometimes think that I've just wasted mine. Look at me, I live in considerable affluence, I want for nothing, I've got a wonderful husband and three lovely children but I haven't actually done anything, I haven't achieved anything."

"You really are incredible," said Libby. "Can't you see what an amazing thing you've achieved? Look, we grew up not exactly in poverty but not far from it, but you have created this lovely welcoming home. You've nurtured and supported your family in a marvellous way and helped to restore some faith in cynics like me when it comes to men and settling down. You've carried the burden of caring for mum and, on top of all that, you have been wonderfully supportive of Maggie. There must have been times when you were in utter despair, but you've always been there for her. Anyway, what you have done and achieved makes my life sink into insignificance. Despite everything, I suppose that much of the time I was running away. Running away from my past, running away from failed relationships and running away from mum and home because I can't bear the thought of ever having to return there. But you've stayed, you've stayed with all that's troublesome here and you've carried all our pains and all our burdens. I don't know what I would do if you weren't there, I really don't."

They watched the late news on the television and were just about to turn it off when an item appeared about an issue in parliament and Paul Crozier's face filled the screen. He was now an MP and had raised a question in the House which had created quite a stir. It was the first time that Libby had seen him since he had visited her flat and she had pushed him out, shouting after him as he left. He looked considerably older, his face lined, he sported a beard and his thick hair flopped untidily over his forehead. She gasped when she saw him.

"I don't believe it, I really don't. My first night back in England and who do I see but Paul. It's such a surprise."

"I'm sure I would never have recognised him. In fact it's only now, when you mention the name that I realise who it is. But then I wouldn't recognise him, I mean I've only ever seen him once and that took me by surprise."

"Not as much as it took me by surprise," laughed Libby. "On that note," she said, "I think we'd better get some sleep, it's been a very long day and I don't think I can keep my eyes open any more."

They gave each other a hug and made their way upstairs. Libby was glad that she was back. She was concerned about the news of her mother's depression and about Maggie's cancer, but as she closed her eyes and slipped away into sleep her thoughts were not focused upon them, nor upon the man from whom she had parted some twenty hours earlier, they were filled with memories of the man she had just seen on the television screen.

It was raining, she had forgotten how dreary Leeds could be. She looked at the people as she walked along the street; they looked old, they looked weary, their eyes cast down as though worn down by years of struggle. She walked up to the front door, not sure what she really felt and knocked. Her mother seemed surprised to see her and her welcome was muted, somewhat tentative; it was as though she was not expected. She quickly made a cup of tea and fussed about but Libby felt that she was not engaging with her, it was as though she didn't know what to say, what to ask her about. She found it was difficult to keep eye contact and felt an awful sense that her mother had somehow disappeared, that she was no longer there. Her voice was fainter and she spoke with a flat tone, the words lacking any variation in timbre. She received the gift of a lovely wall-hanging, made by some of the mothers of her pupils in Mbabane without enthusiasm.

Libby asked after Maggie, wondering if Beryl had been in touch with her since the operation but was met with a look of incomprehension as though she had no idea what she was talking about. It was a difficult time and she was relieved when her mother went into the kitchen and said she would get them some tea made. She left her for a while and then went in to join her and found her mother standing looking out of the window as though she had forgotten all about preparing the tea. Libby suggested that she should make it instead whilst her mother had a sit down and she set about creating a meal. To her amazement she found that there was virtually nothing to eat in the house and she could only surmise that her mother was slowly starving herself without realising it. She made an excuse about needing to go and post a letter and went out to the corner shop and bought in some groceries. She was ravenously hungry and put together a simple meal of eggs on toast with some grilled tomatoes but her mother ate very little, slowly toying with the food and taking an inordinate amount of time over it.

It was not long after seven o'clock when Beryl said she would go up to bed. She said she was pleased to see Libby and would see her again in the morning and then she left her. An hour later Libby crept upstairs, she could hear by the heavy breathing and occasional snore that her mother was asleep. She looked into her room and saw that she'd not changed into her night clothes but was curled up on the bed with an eiderdown pulled over her. The room looked empty, uncared for and Libby thought that probably nothing had been changed in it for at least ten years and possibly twenty. She went downstairs again and got herself something more to eat and then telephoned Victoria.

"Well the situation has clearly deteriorated," commented Victoria. "She certainly had more life in her when I was there ten days ago. I think you're going to have to get the doctor in. Oh I'm so sorry for you, coming home and finding her like this. I did try to warn you but from what you say things are worse than I imagined. What did she say about your coming home? Was she pleased?"

"I don't think she even registered that I'd been away," commented Libby. "She certainly wasn't interested in anything that I'd done and I don't think she was expecting me, she looked very surprised when I turned up. I suppose I can take heart that she knew who I was, but in the light of what followed I could understand if she had forgotten all about me and thought I was a complete stranger."

Libby went to sleep in her old bed. She was frozen, puzzled and slightly ashamed of herself for wishing that she wasn't there. The next morning Beryl was up early. She heard her moving around and got up and joined her. She wondered if she would startle her, just suddenly appearing, but needn't have bothered, her mother seemed to be waiting for her.

"I hope you slept well my love. I should have put a bottle in the bed to warm it up, I'm sorry. Now what do you want for breakfast, I don't think I've got any bacon left, I meant to get some for you but forgot it with all the other things I had to get in. Anyway, I'll make some toast then we can sit down and you can tell me all about it."

"All about what, mum?"

"Well, you know, 'it'. You just sit there and tell me all about it."

"OK, I'll fill you in on things but first of all tell me about Mike and the children. I hear he's got a new partner, I'm popping round to see them later, what's she like?"

Beryl frowned.

"Mike? Mike? Oh, you know, Mike is Mike."

"And the children?"

"Yes, yes, the children. Everyone is fine, Mike, the children, yes, everyone is fine."

"How often do you see the children mum?"

"Oh yes, I see them, yes, yes. Now, what about some toast?"

Libby realised that Beryl had no idea who she was talking about. It was as though they didn't exist. She didn't quite know how to move things on.

"I was thinking about popping into the surgery to see the doctor later on. Do you think it might be a good idea if he popped round to see you mum? You know, give you a once over?"

"Whatever for? I don't need a doctor. Why do you want one, aren't you feeling well?"

"Well mum, I thought you might be a bit low, you know, a bit depressed and perhaps he could give you something to give you a lift, bring a bit of colour back into your cheeks."

"Goodness me I'm fine. It's Libby I'm worried about you know. I saw her recently and she's lost so much weight. I don't think Spain was good for her at all. Now you run along and get on with your jobs and I'll busy myself with all my things, there's a lot to do you know, a lot to do. Now off you go and come back and see me again. If you see Maggie in the street tell her it's time she was in, she's been out far too long."

Libby went up to her room and sat on the bed trying to decide what to do. This wasn't the visit home she'd anticipated. The whole day stretched out in front of her and she was unsure how to fill it. She was calling round to see Mike in the afternoon but had nothing planned until then. She went downstairs and decided to have another chat with her mother.

"Hello my love. What have you been up to?"

"Mum, I thought I would go into town and do a bit of shopping. Will you come with me? It will be your birthday soon and I'd like to buy you a nice cardigan or something."

"Oh no, my love. I don't want to go into town again, I've only just come back. I was just going to sit down and have a rest."

She sat in the easy chair and within a matter of a few minutes she was fast asleep. Libby decided she would try and clean the house up a bit and began with the kitchen which didn't look as though it had been cleaned for months. Two hours later she moved into the living room and her mother was still deeply asleep. Although she was using the vacuum cleaner and making quite a noise she seemed impervious to it all and slept on.

The next day she left for Coventry. She was unsure what to expect when she arrived at Maggie's. It was more years than she could remember since they had been alone together and, try as she may, she couldn't recall a single occasion when they had really communicated at any depth. She felt it was as though she was going to visit a stranger, but a stranger about whom she knew a great deal. Victoria had said that Maggie's flat was nice and that was an understatement. Libby was astonished that she could have created such a lovely place for herself. It bore no resemblance to the home that she had set up with Mike. It was tidy, warm, comfortable and had pictures and flowers.

"I'm so pleased you like it. I've never lived anywhere so nice and to my great surprise I enjoy being at home and I like it being tidy and welcoming. Look at those trees, aren't they simply wonderful?"

Libby walked across to the window and looked out over the park, it was a beautiful view and she could understand why Maggie was so pleased to be there.

They looked at each other, both trying to weigh up the sister they didn't really know. There was a long pause and then they both burst out laughing when their eyes met and they knew exactly what was going on.

"Thanks for coming, I do appreciate it. I suppose I didn't really expect you to make the journey and I would have understood if you hadn't, but I can't tell you how pleased I am to see you again. I've had a difficult few years, well, that's putting it mildly I suppose, but I think I'm on the way back now – at least I thought I was until this cancer sprang itself on me."

"I'm just so pleased to be here," responded Libby. "I did wonder if we would have much to talk about after all these years, but I can see that I was being silly to be so apprehensive. It's good to see you again, Maggie, it really is. I'm afraid I've not been much use to you over the years; I suppose I've been too much concerned with my own things to bother overmuch about other people. I knew that things were bad for you but I didn't know how to respond, what to say. So, in the end, I guess I just did nothing. Was it as bad as I imagine it must have been?"

"Worse," laughed Maggie. "But don't get me wrong, I don't want sympathy. Almost everything that went wrong was my fault; I'm not blaming anyone else but myself. I think I just went into free-fall and didn't know how to stop. I'm afraid I've made a hell of a mess of my life, haven't I? Still, I've had a lot of fun as well, I really have," and she grinned wickedly.

Libby couldn't really disagree and didn't know how to respond, so she said nothing and looked into Maggie's face. She was still remarkably attractive and Libby thought that with looks like that you are likely to run into trouble. Of course she was no longer young, middle age was engulfing them all, but she was remarkably trim and vivacious and still had that wonderful smile and twinkle in her eyes.

"Tell me about Mum, how is she? Oh Libby, I've caused her so much trouble, not just over these last few years but for so long before that. She has always been there for me and I never really appreciated it. Now I can't even get over to see her, not for a few weeks anyway. How was she?"

Libby wasn't sure how much she should tell Maggie. She didn't want to hide the truth from her but neither did she want to burden her with additional worries.

"I think she's doing reasonably but she seems to be quite depressed, I think. She was pleased to see me again but somehow we never really connected, which I found a bit distressing. I really think she should be seeing the doctor but when I mentioned it she would have nothing to do with such an idea. Also, I think she doesn't look after herself very well, I don't think she eats enough. There was virtually no food in the house and even when I cooked us both a meal she didn't really want to eat. She's anxious about you, of course, and I'm sure that as you convalesce and get better then she too will perk up a bit, but I must confess I was rather surprised and saddened by what I found."

Maggie's eyes filled with tears.

"It's my fault Libby; I know I've caused her a great deal of pain. When it was all breaking up with Mike she was absolutely wonderful, so great with the kids. I'm not sure how much she knew, I didn't tell her very much but she's no fool. She was furious when I said I might go off to Spain, we had a huge row, it was awful. I managed to smooth it over and then I suppose I tricked her into believing that all was well when it wasn't. I was planning to run off and I just left her – Oh God, what a selfish cow I've been. Libby, I'm not proud of what I've done and I am trying to put my life together again, but I've caused her a lot of pain, I've hurt her so much."

"Yes, I can see that," said Libby, "of course I don't know the details or anything but I know that it came as a great shock to her. It came as a shock to all of us. Victoria was marvellous of course, as she always is, but I don't think it was easy for them. But whilst all that may be true, I don't think that's how mum sees it."

"Really?" Maggie was genuinely surprised.

"I suspect that she never thinks about the time when you were away now; she is just so pleased that you are around again. You know, she never stops talking about you. Of course, Victoria and I have always been aware of the fact that neither of us could hold a candle to you, but we weren't jealous of course. Not half! We both raged with jealousy but because we loved you both and you both seemed to love us as well we settled into a good way of living and accepting it."

"Oh gosh, was it as bad as that? I never realised, honestly, I didn't."

"Don't be ridiculous, of course you didn't," Libby was quick to reassure her.

"No, I think it's lovely that there is this special relationship between you, and I don't think that your troubles have wrecked it, quite the reverse probably. You both need each other just as much as ever, perhaps even more so. So don't feel guilty, just make sure that you enjoy what's left and keep in touch with her. If anyone can bring her out of this depression it will be you."

They talked with ease; they shared stories about their lives over the past few years. They had a good meal and turned in early to sleep. Both lay awake in their respective bedroom thinking over what the other had said and each one marvelling that they could be the daughters of the same mother, so different had been their experiences.

Libby was awakened the following morning by a song thrush, its wonderful call alerting her to the fact that the sun was shining and the day looked full of promise. After breakfast they had a walk in the park and then Libby went into the city centre to explore the cathedral whilst Maggie sat down to write to her mother. A string quartet was rehearsing in the cathedral prior to a concert that evening. It was a late Beethoven quartet and she sat at the back and listened as she contemplated the huge tapestry hanging on the east wall. The music stopped and the players had a discussion about a particular phrase and Libby suddenly recognised one of the voices. She jumped up from her seat and walked down to where they seated. The first violin put his instrument to his chin again and was just about to begin when he looked up.

"Libby, I don't believe it! What are you doing here?"

"I'm listening to some sublime music, please don't stop Bruce, let me sit back and enjoy it. I've only been back in the country a few days and here I am listening to the Coriolanus Quartet, it's as though I've never been away."

After the quartet's rehearsal they went off and had lunch together. He and Nancy now had twins, which meant that the quartet had to find another cellist, the third in their history but the other members had remained the same. He told her all about the development of the group, about their successes and their more scary moments and he spoke about their future plans with obvious pride and satisfaction. They were shortly to bring out their first recording. She recounted some of the details of her life in Swaziland and was gratified by the very real interest that he showed in her work and the questions that he asked. He remembered that she had been to the Trevor Huddleston rally, he was there as well, and they talked briefly about those days in Birmingham. She told him that she had seen Paul on the television on her first day back and he told her that they were still in touch. His marriage was over, both he and Amanda had been involved in extra marital relationships, as Bruce so quaintly described the situation and they had split up acrimoniously. She couldn't help feeling a degree of satisfaction that Amanda had reached her come-uppance and it seemed that Paul clearly hadn't changed.

It was almost time for the afternoon rehearsal when they left the restaurant.

"I'm so glad that you're back in circulation again Libby, I really mean that. You've been away far too long."

They parted, set off in different directions, walked a few paces, then they both looked back, smiled and waved to each other.

Maggie couldn't believe that Libby had met a friend when she arrived back several hours later than expected.

"I've been here for ages and hardly know a single person and you come along from the middle of Africa and meet someone you know within twenty four hours. You're quite amazing Libby, you really are."

"Ah well, it comes with age and experience," laughed Libby and Maggie smiled back at her.

"It's so good to see that smile again; I've missed your laughter. You know, one of the abiding memories of my childhood is your infectious laughter."

"Yes, well, that's not always a good thing is it? I suppose I've beguiled too many people by my smiles and I can't say that I'm proud of the result. Anyway, how do you smile at cancer? Do you think it will go away if I try and seduce it by my laughter?"

"Well, not exactly, but it has gone away, admittedly through surgery, but you've got a clean bill of health now, at least that's what we are all hoping, and surely that is something to laugh and rejoice over."

"Yes, you're right, of course," responded Maggie.

"That is something to smile about. I'll try and re-discover my youth, but I hope it's only my smiles that return, I couldn't cope with all the rest."

She looked pensive and licked her lower lip. It was requiring a great effort to lift herself from the sadness of recent months.

Back in London Libby began to re-create herself. Within a couple of months she was back in her flat in Islington and now that she was intending to stay she began to decorate it and turn it into her permanent home. Pride of place in the sitting room was the wall hanging given to her by the children in Mbabane. There were pictures, enlarged photographs showing some of the more exotic places she had visited and a brand new music centre with enormous speakers. She thought long and hard about what bed to buy, should it be a single or a double? Robbie was threatening to come over soon, if he made it then she would need a double bed, but if he didn't come – ah, that was a question to which there was no clear answer. In the end she opted for the double reckoning that she would probably get a better night's sleep in it anyway.

She quickly found a job supply teaching and although she had only been out of teaching in England for five years she found the contrast quite marked, especially as far as discipline was concerned but also in the attitude towards learning shown by the pupils. In Africa there was a hunger for knowledge and education was prized and sought after, whereas in London the thirst for knowledge seemed to have dried up long before the children came into her classroom. Education was seen as a boring imposition, whilst in Africa it had been an eagerly sought scarce commodity. She noted that no-one in the staff room seemed remotely interested in the fact that she had been teaching in Africa. It was not a happy school, it was not well managed and too many of the teachers seemed to have lost whatever spark they might once have had. It suited Libby well in terms of bringing in some money, getting her back into the English system and giving her the chance to look around for a more permanent position. This came about quite quickly when, to her delight she was appointed Head of the English Department of a large school less than half an hour's journey from her flat, just a few stops away on the underground. It was the first job she had applied for.

B eryl didn't improve and a phone call from Mike alerted them to the fact that someone needed to take action. That weekend Libby drove north with Victoria. Beryl agreed to see a doctor and Victoria stayed on into the next week to accompany her. She was diagnosed with clinical depression and admitted into hospital. She was to stay there for the next four months. It was a long haul but she gradually emerged from this inner world of despair and began to take an interest in people and events again. The hospital explained to Victoria that she seemed to have an inherent tendency to depression and they suspected that this was not the first severe bout that she had suffered. They knew nothing of the depths to which she sank after the accident which killed her first husband, nor did anyone else. She was determined to return to her own home and would not consider staying with any of the family, not even for a few days. She regained her stubborn streak and her resolute manner.

When she was not visiting her mother or phoning up Maggie or Victoria about her and when she was not immersed in her school work, Libby had to think through her relationship with Robbie. He telephoned at least twice a week and wrote almost as often, pleading with her to reconsider her actions and return to Africa to be with him. She enjoyed talking to him at first but as the weeks passed she found that she began to dread the calls. She knew that she was going to stay in England, that her work at the school was just beginning and that she was beginning to create a new life for herself. She also knew that she missed his company and the intimacy of their relationship. He phoned to tell her that he was taking leave and coming over to London and would be with her in two weeks' time, for her half term. She was full of foreboding at the prospect. She was not even sure that she wanted him to stay with her but felt that it was churlish to ask him to stay elsewhere. Supposing he was to stay with her, where would he sleep? She was full of uncertainties and yet, at the same time, she knew that she missed him and would enjoy showing him round. She was lost in thought one evening when the phone rang and it was Celia inviting her to her engagement party.

"That's fantastic Celia, many congratulations. You don't waste time do you, all these years as a confirmed spinster and then straight in, no messing. It's wonderful news and of course I'd love to come. Actually, Robbie will be over from Swaziland that week, will it be alright to bring him?"

"Even better," said Celia, "we've all been wondering what he's like. Is this the real thing for you as well? He must be keen to come all this way. Anyway, he's a lucky bloke if he's in with a chance for you. By all means bring him, one more won't make any difference."

"Hey, don't get any ideas about us, it's all so difficult – it's quite impossible really, he wants us to live in New Zealand and that's totally out of the question for me."

"Don't you dare go off to New Zealand, not now, just as we've got you back again. Anyway, I must fly now, great that you can come. Bye."

With that the phone went dead.

I t was raining the day he arrived and it continued to rain for the next three days. Not torrential rain like in Africa, but a miserable drizzle that meant you had to wear a raincoat but doing so made you too hot. She waited anxiously for his plane to arrive at Heathrow, wanting to see him and yet, simultaneously, wishing that he wasn't coming.

Another crowd surged through the entrance to the foyer and then she saw him and her heart skipped a beat. He was handsome, he was tanned and he was smiling as his searching eyes lit upon hers. He came through the barrier and flung his arms around her. He was strong and she realised that she had missed that sort of physical contact, that sense of being wanted. They spoke quickly, the words not really meaning much, just filling up the space as they adjusted to each other's presence. The flight, the food, the weather, aisle seat or window, the journey to the airport, whatever immediately came to mind. They looked at each other, looked away and smiled when their eyes met again.

"Oh, it's been so long Libby, I can't tell you how long it's been. But now I'm here and I don't want to waste a minute, I'm relying on you to show me London, show me what I'm missing. I see that you've already arranged some rain for me, that really is welcome as well you know. Now let me look at you, have you changed? Yes, I do believe that you have. You look lovelier than I remember, and younger too. It must be the English weather. So, tell me about everything. Will I meet your mother? What about your sisters, how are they? Do I get to see your school, I would love to see your classroom, I bet it's different from the one you had before? What are we doing today? Where can I take you out for dinner?"

"Robbie, hold back a bit! You've only just arrived, you must be tired out. All these questions, anyone would think that we hadn't spoken on the phone every few days for the last nine months, never written any letters. You must know just about all there is to know.

So, enough about me, how are you? I mean how are you really, beyond that bluff exterior, how are you deep inside?"

They made their way back into central London, not really answering any of the questions raised but enjoying each other's company. Talking about irrelevancies, totally oblivious of the fact that time was passing and so it seemed no time at all before they arrived at Libby's flat. Robbie was extremely complimentary about it, thought she had decorated it beautifully and loved all the things that she had bought and the ways in which there were traces of Africa in just about every room. She had a home-making instinct, he had suspected this from the bungalow she had shared with Patsy but now that she was in her own place he marvelled at what she had been able to create. She was slightly embarrassed, unsure how they should proceed now they were alone together in the flat. He sensed her unease and re-assured her.

"You're looking anxious my love. Don't worry, I know this is a big thing for both of us and we are going to have to get used to each other for a while. I won't pounce on you, much as I would like to, you've no need to be apprehensive. But what I would like to do is have a shower or a bath or something and get these travelling clothes off and then perhaps we can go out and you can show me things."

"Thanks Robbie, you are nice. Come on, I'll get you a towel and then we'll go off into the city and I'll show you the Thames and perhaps we'll go to the Festival Hall and have a meal overlooking the river."

They walked along the South Bank, looking at the boats moving up and down the river. As darkness came they looked at the illuminated parliament buildings and Robbie was amazed by it all and stood and stared at Big Ben.

"It's very strange to see it for real for the first time after all the years of knowing it so well but never having seen it."

Libby too began to see things in a different way as she pointed them out; the Tower of London, St Paul's Cathedral, Westminster Abbey and all the little streets around the West End. It was as though she too was seeing them for the first time. Together they enjoyed walking through the rain, splashing in the puddles and getting to know each other again. They had only been separated for a little more than eight months, in one way it was no time at all but in another way it seemed to be very much longer. Time had moved slowly for him as he continued in his work and moved around Swaziland and he missed Libby more than he could ever explain. She, on the other hand, was busy with her family, her old friends, setting up her home and finding work and then obtaining a worthwhile job. She seldom had enough time, Robbie had too much. These differing experiences were difficult for them both to reconcile. On the other hand, Robbie was a wonderful companion, she enjoyed his company immensely and she supposed that, if pressed, she would have to admit that she was still in love with him. Robbie knew or sensed all this. He had arrived wondering if her love had waned and he felt reassured by the ease with which they still related. The sleeping arrangements, which clearly were an anxiety for Libby when he first arrived had ceased to be a problem after just a few hours together; they shared her bed naturally. Yet he knew that the chances of her leaving London for New Zealand were so remote that it was not even worth them discussing the possibility. The only alternative, it seemed, was for him to move to England. As he pondered this option he realised the enormity of it and, for the first time, appreciated what he was asking of Libby when he was pressing her to move to New Zealand. If he wanted her then he was going to have to come and be with her, there seemed to be no alternative. He decided to think through what this might entail before suggesting it to her.

They went to Victoria's for dinner. They warmed to him immediately and Bill had a long discussion about politics, cars and engineering whilst the girls cleared the table and chatted on in the kitchen.

"He's the best one you've brought round so far, easily the best," said Victoria, looking into Libby's face to see if she could gain any further information.

"Yes, I know," she replied. "He's lovely and we get on so well together but – Oh, I don't know, there are so many problems. I can't really see how it can work out."

"Well if you don't want to go over there, and that is a great relief to me, I must say, speaking from a position of total self interest, why doesn't he come over here to live?"

"Yes, I've been wondering about that, I might suggest it to him. But the truth is, Victoria, I don't really know if I love him. More than that, I suppose I'm saying that I don't really know what love is. I thought I used to know but I'm no longer sure. How did you know that you loved Bill?"

"I've never really thought about it," laughed Victoria, placing the wine glasses in the cabinet.

"I suppose we just drifted into it, more a sort of extended friendship that just seemed to grow. I mean, there was no great revelation or anything, it just seemed to happen. It's not something I've given much thought to, strange really when you consider how important a thing it is. I suppose I just knew that I loved him and we got on with life. Perhaps you are expecting too much Libby. You know, you think that love is something different when in actual fact it's not different it's just an ordinary process. You grow into it, I suppose."

Libby frowned and Victoria knew that she wasn't really communicating.

"I don't want to intrude and I've never asked you about this before Libby, but are you still caught up Paul? I know it was absolutely ghastly for you when you saw him with that woman but have you never really got over it? I've often wondered. Forgive me; I'm just being silly, especially bringing this up when you've just arrived with Robbie."

"No, you're not being silly; you see I just don't know. It's clearly nonsense to think that I still love Paul, it was all so many years ago. He was a complete sod to me and hurt me terribly and yet, at the same time, I know that we shared something very special and I've never experienced it since with anyone else, not even with Robbie. Although Paul was so cruel, I suppose I still continue to believe that underneath everything he loved me – but then, I don't actually know what love is. I may be completely wrong and anyway, after all these years whatever he felt will have gone, but somehow it has left me marked, scarred I suppose. I honestly don't know whether that's a good thing or a bad thing, but it's there. So, in answer to your question, No, I'm not still hung up over Paul, it was all over and done with years ago and Yes, I can't erase the memory. Does that make sense?"

"Oh Libby, you poor thing. That explains so much." Victoria turned and gave her a great hug. "I can't say that I understand what you feel because I don't, but I do know that there's something within you that can't move forward and I've often wondered why none of your relationships has ever flourished. Anyway, you've got a lovely man here in Robbie, take care of him Libby, you won't find many more like him you know."

"I know that, I know that only too well. I think I love him, but I'm not sure because I don't know what love is. I don't feel for him in the same way that I felt for Paul, but perhaps that wasn't love and this is. Oh what a mess it all is. You know, I was dreading him coming over and now I can't bear to think that he'll be leaving in just a few days."

"Are we getting any coffee or do we have to come and make it ourselves?" Bill's voice drifted into the kitchen.

"We've established world peace, founded a new engineering firm and I've flogged Robbie an Aston Martin, if we don't get a drink soon the whole deal may collapse."

"Coming my dear, mustn't keep the men waiting must we?" trilled Victoria and the two sisters moved into the sitting room and joined them. Libby was surprised to discover that Bill seemed to be genuinely interested in what Robbie had to say about Africa and he was questioning him with an intensity that he had never shown when discussing things with her. I suppose that being a man must give his views more credibility she thought. She saw Victoria as being trapped into Bill's chauvinistic world, and yet she seemed happy enough, not subjugated, not oppressed, not in need of being liberated. Libby envied her apparently stress-free existence.

"Come on, tell us what you are thinking," said Bill, "you seem to be caught up in a world of your own."

Libby smiled.

"I was thinking how nice it is all being together here like this. I've told Robbie so much about you both and now you've all met and seem to like each other."

M aggie was out walking when suddenly the sky turned dark and a clash of thunder heralded a sudden storm with torrential rain, without a raincoat she sought shelter in the first available place, which happened to be a church. It had a notice board by the pavement saying "All Welcome." She ventured inside and was bemused by what she found. It was dark, despite the lights being on. There was a strange smell; she learned later it was incense, which seemed to hang around, a sort of staleness mixed with the smell of extinguished candles. She was puzzled by the coloured embroidered hangings. A large table, which again she learned later was an altar, had a beautifully embroidered green cloth reaching down to the floor. There were a great many flowers, lots of candles, some of which were lit and the sort of untidiness which suggested that the place was used a lot rather than being neglected. She wandered round, looking at the various plaques and stopped before a war memorial, reading the names of men, any one of which could have been the father that she had never known and she wondered if his name was on a plaque anywhere, she'd never thought about that before. There was a large table at the back and a screen behind showing photographs of a school in Africa, probably just like the one that Libby had taught in. It was clear, from the various notices, that the church sent money to the school and there were letters pinned up, written by the children thanking the people for their gifts.

Maggie sat down for a while and soaked up the atmosphere. There was a sort of other-worldliness about the place, she didn't know what it was but she was strangely attracted to it. She thought that the last time she had had any connection with anything to do with a church was way back when she was young and had spent time at the mother and baby home. She had quite forgotten the place and the memory of it suddenly flooded into her mind. That little baby would now be about twenty years old and she wondered what had happened to her tiny son. She was filled with an immense feeling of longing which was intensified by her thoughts about the three children she had left behind for Mike to look after. What a mess she'd made of her life, but at least things seemed to be better now. She no longer craved for sexual fulfilment, no longer believed that life without a man was no life at all. Indeed, her life was altogether richer and more contented without the complications of having a man around. She looked up and saw a priest approaching her from the front of the church.

"Hello there, is everything alright? Can I be of any assistance?"

Maggie looked at him, he was about her age, had deep intense eyes, thick black wavy hair and a kindly smiling face. He was wearing a cassock, a long black garment with lots of small buttons down the front. He saw Maggie staring at it in wonderment.

"Oh, I'm sorry about the garb, I just finished a service about twenty minutes ago and I've been clearing things up."

Maggie smiled at him.

"Forgive me for staring, I didn't mean to be rude. Actually I was miles away, lost in thought and you took me by surprise. But thanks, I'm fine. Actually, I just came in out of the rain, I hope that's alright. I saw the sign and it said 'All Welcome' so I came in and here I am. It's quite an amazing place isn't it? I don't think I've ever been in a church before."

"Never been inside a church before? Goodness me, where have you been all your life? I don't think I've ever met anyone who has said that to me before. Well, now you're here, what do you think?"

"Well, it's really rather nice," said Maggie. "It has a bit of a strange smell, sort of fusty but not quite and it's rather dark, but I like it, yes it's very nice. Anyway, who are you? Who am I talking to? I've always been told that I shouldn't talk to strange men!"

"I'm the vicar here. I'm Father Peter."

"Father Peter? Do you mean that's what people call you? How amazing. But you're only the same age as me, or perhaps even younger. I couldn't possibly call you 'Father'. Do you mean people actually call you that? 'Father Peter'? Well I never, you learn something new every day don't you?"

"You certainly do," he replied, "and who are you?"

"I'm Maggie," she said, holding out her hand and giving him a firm clasp.

Peter Hicks was rather taken aback. He was used to people drifting into his church, usually old ladies, most of whom he knew. Then there was a fairly regular flow of people who had some sort of mental frailty, people with problems, people who wanted to lie down and have a sleep, people who would come in and shout and create a minor disturbance and one man in particular who regularly came in and thumped the piano keyboards. Yes, he was used to people turning up, but he had never before been confronted by such an attractive and straightforward person as Maggie. She had looked him straight in the eye, had challenged the security that his title of 'Father' gave him and admitted that she knew nothing about churches and was obviously completely baffled by his cassock. He shook her hand and immediately felt a sort of magnetism run straight up his arm.

"Well Maggie, I hope it won't be the last time you come in and you don't have to wait until it rains next time. We are always here and we have our main service on Sundays at ten o'clock, you might be a bit puzzled by it if you've never been in a church before, but I can assure you, you would be very welcome."

"Thanks Peter, I might take you up on that. I hope you don't mind me calling you Peter, I really couldn't go round calling people Father, especially since I've never even called my own father that. Anyway, time for you to take your frock, or whatever it's called off, and time for me to move on, I think it's probably stopped raining now. It's been nice to meet you; no doubt we shall bump into each other again sometime. Bye."

Saying that, she turned and walked out, stopping at the door for a moment, turning and giving him a wave. She left behind one very confused priest.

The next day the sun shone. They went to Greenwich by train, walked around the park and returned by boat, Libby soaking up the sunshine and warmth and Robbie totally engrossed by the guide's commentary. They wandered around St James's Park, walked down The Mall, stood outside Buckingham Palace trying to see if they could recognise anyone in the cars which swept through the gates, but they couldn't.

It was time to get back to the flat and prepare themselves for Celia's engagement party. Robbie was pleased to be going, he would meet up with a group of Libby's friends, many of whom he had heard about but never expected to meet on this flying visit. When they arrived the place was already full of people, there was much laughter, a high noise level, a jazz band playing and a few people dancing. Celia looked radiant and she almost ran over to them when she saw them. She hugged Robbie, introduced him to Adrian her new fiancé, gave him a drink and vanished. Libby was delighted to see Bruce and Nancy and she pulled Robbie over to them and explained to him about the formation of the Coriolanus Quartet.

"That's absolutely amazing," exclaimed Robbie.

Celia returned and whisked him away saying that there was someone else from New Zealand, perhaps he might know him, and within seconds they were gone.

Libby moved around, enjoying seeing so many people whom she knew or recognised. She caught sight of Fiona talking with a small group and began to make her way over to her before she lost sight of them. For a moment she stopped and looked around, wondering where Robbie had been led off to, but as she looked she felt a strange sensation come over her, as though she was somehow becoming the centre of attention. She wondered what on earth it could be when she heard a voice.

"Well, well, at last we meet again, I can hardly believe it. Libby, it's wonderful to see you after so long, I can't tell you how thrilled I am."

She swung round and came face to face with Paul.

She was stunned, it had never occurred to her that he would be there, but on reflection, of course he would be there if he was free. Celia had remained in contact with him over the years and Libby suddenly remembered Celia saying that she felt Paul was going to need a few real friends as he moved up the political ladder. She looked at him, straight in the eyes. They were soft, with lines around them. He had a beard, his hair was thick but already showing signs of ageing, he looked slightly dissolute but he was clearly and unmistakably Paul. She remained silent, taking it all in.

"Of course, you don't have to speak to me," he laughed, "but I rather hoped that the pain and anger of our last meeting might have diminished over the years."

Libby blushed and looked down, then she looked up into his face and gave him a smile which would haunt him for years to come.

"I'm so sorry Paul, it was just such a surprise, I hadn't expected to see you. Anyway, it's lovely that you remembered me, it's been a long time."

"Remember you? God, I've hardly ever spent a day without thinking of you. Tell me, that chap you are with, is he your husband?"

"No, no, he's just a friend – well, not exactly, that is, well, he's quite keen that we should marry. But why am I telling you all this? Let's begin again. How's Amanda?"

"Oh Libby, that came to an end years ago. Of course, it should never have begun I know that and I knew it at the time but didn't know what to do. Believe me, I wanted you so much more than I ever wanted her. I'm married again now, to Julia, she's here somewhere. But what about you – God Libby, I can't tell you how glad I am to see you. I despaired of us ever meeting again. Haven't you been in Africa?"

"I came back home about nine months ago. Actually, on my first day back I saw you on the telly, that was quite a shock I can tell you."

"You saw me on the box? Did you recognise me or had you forgotten all about me?"

"Of course I recognised you, how could I ever forget you?"

"Oh Libby, I've so often thought that you might have forgotten me, and I would understand if you had, but I can't tell you how relieved I am to know that you haven't. Libby, we must meet, we must see each other again. What are you doing on Saturday, any chance of us meeting up for lunch?"

He moved closer to her, almost touching her, the whole length of her body. She could feel the tension in the air around them.

"Paul, don't! You don't know what you're saying. You're a married man, for the second time unless there's been another one in between and here you are, trying to chat me up if I'm not mistaken."

"Now don't get shirty with me, and what's all this about 'chatting up'? I don't even know the meaning of the word. Why don't you come over to the House of Commons and let me give you lunch and show you around. I always said I'd get into parliament, didn't I?"

"You certainly did, and you always got what you wanted didn't you Paul?"

"No, not always. I didn't get you did I? My God, how I wanted you. So come on, have lunch with me, let me show you around."

He moved slightly to put his arm around her shoulder.

"Paul don't! We've been through all this before, we are both much, much older and I hope, wiser. I think we ought to move apart now. It really has been good seeing you again, it really has, but I think Robbie will be wondering where I am."

She moved away but he followed her and caught her arm.

"Don't leave me, Libby, don't leave me. We must meet and talk."

"Paul, it's no use. Don't stir up old feelings. All that was a long time ago. You've got a distinguished career and a wife, and at least one child, I haven't asked you about your family, but give them your full attention; you are not being fair to them."

"But what have you got Libby? You've never married. I feel as though I might have wrecked your life, let's meet and talk, come on, it can't do any harm."

"Don't patronise me Paul, please. I have a good life, it's rich and interesting; I admit I haven't been married twice but sometimes marriage isn't all that it's cracked up to be, is it? Go back to your politics. I've loved seeing you again, I really have, don't spoil it, please. I would like to remember you kindly, and I will remember you, I promise, how could I ever forget you? Come on, let's go back to our people."

She leaned across and kissed him on the cheek, a little friendly peck and then walked away. This time he didn't follow her, and she experienced a great painful and ever-widening emptiness within her.

Occasionally during the rest of the evening Libby would catch Paul's eyes across the room, he always seemed to be looking at her. She was embarrassed, thinking that everyone would be watching them but of course they weren't, everyone was busy enjoying themselves. She was in turmoil, torn apart by the joy of meeting Paul again and knowing that he still cared, yet appalled by the consequences of such a realisation. She looked across at Robbie and he smiled and leaned across and took her hand. She looked around and knew that this was where she really belonged, here in England, amongst these people, many of them her friends and acquaintances. Could she see Robbie fitting into it? Perhaps Yes, if she hadn't met Paul again, but she had a feeling that her recovery programme had been wrecked and she was going to have to work through a whole range of grief and sadness before she could confidently say that she fine again.

They were both pensive as they made their way back to Islington. Robbie trying to decide whether to throw up his job and come to England, Libby trying to erase Paul from her thoughts and both of them conscious of the fact that tomorrow was Robbie's last day before catching a plane back in the evening. They walked along the Embankment holding hands and looking at all the lights reflected in the river. Big Ben struck one o'clock as they passed. They had decided to walk rather than get a taxi, neither of them was ready for sleep, both engaged in a tortuous exercise of mental clarification and Robbie wanted to soak up as much of London as he possibly could. It was an hour later before they arrived home by which time they were ready for bed and they held each other tightly as they fought off sleep for just a little longer. Robbie was conscious of feeling that Libby had somehow moved away from him, just as she had on the night before she left Africa. He wondered what it was all about but put it down to the fact that she didn't like farewells. They were both almost asleep when he suddenly sat up in bed, put the light on and said: "Libby, we must talk."

He had reached a decision. He couldn't wait until the morning; it had to be discussed now. Libby slowly came to, mumbled something about keeping it until the morning, and rubbed her eyes.

"Libby, why don't I go back to Swaziland, settle my affairs and come back to live in England? Then we could get married and I could find a job here. You could continue your work at school and we could even stay here in this flat if that is what you want. How about it?"

"Oh Robbie, this is hardly the time to be making these sort of decisions. We are both tired, we've had a good day, why can't we talk about it in the morning?"

"Because, my dear Libby, I have just made a huge decision. Can't you see that? If you won't come to New Zealand, then I'll come to England. Why hadn't I thought about it before?"

"Because you have two children in New Zealand who need you there, that's why."

"But I'll work on it so that I can go back to New Zealand every six months. We could even go together for a month each summer. Admittedly it's not the best time to visit such a glorious place but that's when you have the time. In that way, we can be together. We can get married; it makes such sense you'll have to agree."

"No Robbie, no, no, no. It just won't work. I'd thought about that as a possible option a few days ago but it's no good, it won't work. I just can't see myself getting married. I'm sorry, I really am, but I'd never make you a good wife. You deserve more than I can give you, honestly, believe me, you really do."

"But that's absurd," exclaimed Robbie. "We've had a glorious week. We are made for each other, surely you can see that."

"Robbie, it's no good. I've thought about it, I've tried to sort things out in my mind. In so many ways I've wanted it, but when the crunch comes I know that I can't face it. It's no use Robbie, I can't."

She burst into tears and he moved across and put his arms around her. She sobbed uncontrollably, her whole body heaving up and down as she cried.

"I can't Robbie, I can't. I'm sorry, forgive me. It's not you, it's me. You are just lovely Robbie, the best thing that has happened to me for years and years and years, but I can't love you enough, it would never work, I can't give you all the things that you deserve and want and need, I'm sorry, but I can't."

"But you already do, can't you see that? You already do. I don't understand what you mean. We share so much, we like the same things, we're at ease with each other and I love you more than I can ever put into words, can't you see that?"

"I know," sobbed Libby, "but I just can't go on. I love you too, I really do, but I know that I can't marry you, it just wouldn't work, it wouldn't, I know it, I know it. We are going to have to split up Robbie, it's breaking my heart but we can't go on like this. You are going to have to leave tomorrow and that must be it."

"I can't do that, I can't," exclaimed Robbie. "You must be out of your mind. How can we move from the point of getting married to splitting up in about three minutes dead?"

"Robbie, there's no other way. I've thought about everything, but I can't go on with it. We have to finish. You deserve better than me and I know that if we keep going on like this we will destroy each other. Come to me, hold me and love me. Oh Robbie, I'm so sorry."

They made love, tenderly and passionately and as they eventually drifted off into sleep Libby cursed Paul from the bottom of her heart. She cursed him for all the pain and destruction that he had brought into her life. Not only was she losing a husband, she was also losing the possibility of having a family and she knew time was running out for that 'To Hell with Paul Crozier' she shouted in her mind, 'I wish I'd never met you, you lousy rotten stinking bastard' and immediately she surrounded him with love and with longing.

Robbie left the following evening. He thought that by coming over to London he would win her back and he had almost succeeded, but somehow it all seemed to fall apart at the end and he had no idea why.

It was three weeks before he saw Maggie again. She turned up one Sunday morning, sat in the congregation and followed everything with attentive bewilderment. Part way through the service Peter came down to the congregation and shook hands with them all. He reached Maggie and looked at her, and shook her hand.

"The Peace of Christ," he said.

"Lovely to see you again Peter," responded Maggie giving him a great smile and completely putting him out of his stride so that he missed all the people in the pew behind.

They all wondered who this newcomer was. They didn't get many new people attending the services and they certainly hadn't had anyone as young and as attractive as Maggie for a long time. Sitting behind her they were able to observe that she had no idea what was happening, she didn't know when to stand up, sit down, kneel or join in the parts of the service that the congregation said. She didn't know the hymns and when it was time for people to go up to the altar for communion she went with them and did whatever they did. Peter came along the row of kneeling people with the consecrated bread and was surprised to see that Maggie was kneeling there, like everyone else. Rather than pass her by he decided to place a wafer in her hand although he was sure that she wasn't confirmed and probably had no idea what it was all about.

"The Body of Christ," he said as he placed the wafer into her hand.

"Thank you Peter," she replied giving him a great smile.

She had failed to notice that just about everyone else grunted when they received the wafer and kept their eyes down.

"That was really enjoyable," she said as she left the church at the end of the service. "I liked your little talk but wasn't sure about lots of the other things that were being said. Anyway, I'll come again, but it won't be next week as I'm off to see my mum then, so have a nice time, cheerio."

With that she left and walked home across the park thinking about the strange events that she had been sharing in for the past hour. "Who would have thought that I would ever go to church" she said to herself, "but actually it was really rather enjoyable. I'll go again; it will give me something to do on Sunday mornings."

After her fourth appearance at a Sunday service Father Peter spoke to her afterwards and suggested that he called round to see her. This was his normal practice, allow newcomers time to settle in for a few weeks and then pop round to have a chat and answer any queries that they may have and extend a welcome to them. Maggie was taken aback by such a suggestion although she didn't show it. What sort of a man was this who invites himself round?

Churchgoing was opening up a whole range of new experiences she decided. She couldn't recall the last time she had entertained a man in her home without there being a specific sexual agenda, spoken or unspoken. She wondered if this might be the same and decided that such an idea was ridiculous and she would have to adjust to relating to men in a completely different way. She had managed it at work so why not in her home and in her leisure time. Still, it did seem to be a strange thing to suggest and she wondered if he went round visiting other people in their homes. Friday evening came and he rang the bell just a few minutes after the time they had agreed.

"Is it OK to leave my bike here?" he asked before putting a chain around the back wheel. He grabbed hold of a bulging diary from his saddle bag and followed her up the stairs into her flat.

"Hey, this is lovely Maggie, what a nice flat. I've never been in any of the houses in this part of the street."

"Why, do you make a habit of going to people's houses?" asked Maggie.

"Well yes, of course, that's an important part of my job isn't it?"

"I've really no idea; I don't know what your job is. You forget, all this church stuff is completely new to me."

She gave him a coffee and put out a plate of biscuits and he sat down and began to ask her all sorts of questions. Where was she from? What did she do? Where had she been...?

"God, you ask a lot of questions don't you Peter?"

He was suddenly quiet, embarrassed, and rather flustered.

"Oh I'm sorry, I didn't mean to intrude, I was just trying to get a picture of who you are. You know, I like to feel that I really know the people in my congregation, that I'm not a stranger, more of a friend, that sort of thing."

"It's quite alright, I don't mind, it's just that I'm not used to being visited by a strange man and asked all sorts of questions. I expect you'll be asking me if I want double glazing next."

Peter laughed, apologised again, ate another chocolate biscuit and smiled.

"Well, you fire away, ask me anything you want to know about the church then."

"But I don't think I want to know anything," said Maggie. "I quite like coming, it's very friendly, people are nice and welcoming although I don't know any of them. I don't know any of the songs you sing and all that but some of them are rather nice. I like your talks but I'm not sure if I really go on all this God stuff, but it's interesting. Do you believe it?"

Again, he was surprised, taken off balance.

"Well yes, I do believe it. I mean, I could hardly be a vicar if I didn't, could I?"

"I don't know," said Maggie, "I've never met a vicar before. And is that your job then, believing? Is that what you do?" She laughed. "I'm in the holiday travel business, but you – you just believe. How very odd."

He sat and talked for another half hour or so and then said he would have to go because it was choir practice night and he needed to get round to see them before they finished. He got on his bike and pedalled away. That is some woman, he found himself reflecting. I don't think I've ever met anyone like her before. Maggie washed up the coffee cups. What a strange man, she thought, what on earth did he want? Just coming round and asking me questions and saying that he believed things. On the other hand, he's quite dishy, I could have made something of him a few years ago.

P eter Hicks had been vicar of All Saints and All Souls church for five years. Before moving there he had worked on a housing estate in Birmingham. He loved being a priest, it was what he had always wanted to be. He loved the services, the ceremonies, the smell of incense and the sense of mystery. When he was first ordained, fifteen years ago he wondered seriously about becoming a monk and whenever he could he would take a break from his parish duties and spend a few days in silence at a monastery. He was deflected from that when he met Angela. She was engaged to be married and with her fiancé had come to Peter for marriage preparation, but as their classes went on it became more and more obvious to her that the young priest was finding himself in difficulties, he would get flustered and lose his words.

"That priest's very odd," her fiancé Eric exclaimed as they walked away one evening. "Did you see how he couldn't keep his eyes off you?"

She protested, but she knew it was true, she had been aware of it herself but thought perhaps she had been fooling herself. She also felt enormously flattered. In comparison to Eric, he seemed exciting, mysterious, even dangerous. One day he telephoned her and asked if she would come to see him by herself and she found herself strangely excited by the prospect.

"Angela, it's good of you to come. I hope you don't mind seeing me by yourself but I thought it would be easier if just the two of us spoke. The thing is, you see, I'm afraid that I'm going to have to ask someone else to take your wedding..."

"But why?" she exclaimed. "We've got everything planned. Why can't you?"

"Well, the thing is Angela... the thing is... I have to be somewhere else on that day. I'm on retreat, so I shall have to find someone else to do it."

"What do you mean 'on retreat', what's that? I so wanted you to do it."

"It means that I am away for a few days in a monastery. I go there for prayer and reflection and I'm afraid that I need to be there when you get married."

There was a long pause.

"Is that the real reason? Is that the only reason?" Angela was surprised to hear herself question him.

"Well yes, of course," he replied, looking uncomfortable.

"Forgive me for saying this Father, I know I'm speaking out of turn and I'm not sure how to say it, but I don't think I believe you."

"Not believe me, but it's true, I'm on retreat on that day, I'm not available." He looked her and then looked away, unable to sustain eye contact.

"When did you arrange this retreat?"

"Oh, months ago, I can't remember when."

"But we've had this date fixed for over a year, so why do you need to be away now? What's made you change your mind?"

"Look Angela, don't make things difficult. The truth is that I'm going to have to ask someone else to take your wedding service. I can't do it."

She felt herself suddenly emboldened and walked across to where he was sitting and crouched on the floor. She stretched out her hand and touched him.

"Father, Peter... it's me isn't it, you want me don't you. All these weeks I've been aware of something strange, so has Eric, he says that you keep looking at me..."

He stood up and moved away. He was sweating, embarrassed and his mind was in a complete turmoil.

"Don't Angela, don't say those things. I don't know what's got into you."

He stood and looked out of the window; it was several minutes before he turned round to look at her.

"Gee, what a mess I'm in. I'm sorry, I don't know what to say, I really don't. The truth is Angela, I feel terrible, I've failed in my duty as a priest. I don't know what to do. Yes, you are right of course, I hoped no-one had realised. I'm sorry, I do seem to have developed this silly infatuation for you and I can't get rid of it. It's much better that someone else takes your service and I go away and try and sort myself out. I need to pray about it, I need guidance, help. You see, I've been wondering about becoming a monk and everything seemed to be heading in that direction then suddenly I meet you and the truth is, I can't get you out of my mind. I think I've fallen in love with you Angela and I don't know what to do. You won't report me to the Bishop will you?"

He looked at her with despairing eyes.

"Of course I won't report you, what do you think I am? What you've just said is so flattering, so beautiful that I'm taken aback. Eric has never said anything like that to me, he's never actually said that he loves me you know, we just seem to have drifted into getting married. Now I'm not sure what to do either. God Peter, if you'll excuse the expression, you've put me in quite a spot."

She moved over to him, looked him in the face, stretched out her hands and stroked his head and chastely kissed him on the cheek. It was a moment of sublime bliss for him. Then she suddenly put her arms round him and kissed him, this time with passion and eagerness. He had to break away, overcome by surprise and longing.

"You're lovely, you really are," she said. "I'm going now, don't show me out, I need to disappear, if I stay any longer I shall burst into tears."

Without looking back she hurriedly left the room. Peter stood looking at the rows of books that filled the shelves on each side of his room. He stared them for a long time and then took down a copy of *The Confessions of St Augustine* and began to read.

It is difficult to know just what factors combined to draw Maggie to the church but the undoubted fact is that over the next two years she attended regularly and became a committed member. It could have been a growing sense of guilt and remorse over her past activities, which she could now see would fall under the general heading of 'sin' and which the church said could be forgiven, although it didn't really seem likely. Maggie knew that she had messed things up but she didn't go round with a sense of guilt, she didn't feel 'sinful', not in the least. It could have been that in the Church she could build up a relationship with God the Father in a way that she had never been able to establish a relationship with her natural father, that was certainly Peter's view. It could have been that in having to face up to her cancer and subsequent mastectomy she had become aware of her own vulnerability and mortality. Of course it could also have been that she was flattered by all the attention that this rather dashing young priest was giving her. He visited her regularly, he was clearly fascinated by her, probably infatuated by her, but never overstepped the mark and never made a pass at her and for Maggie this was a completely new experience.

She also got to know a whole new group of people many of whom were friendly whilst others, quite unknown to her, were highly judgmental and rather catty about her, all smiles to the front and vicious when her back was turned. Peter was aware of this and he sometimes despaired of the attitudes and mindset of some of his congregation. He tried to reason with himself that the church was there for people who were not yet whole and Maggie's arrival in the church had certainly revealed the fact that the church was made up of sinners. Some were sinners in the way that she, in his view, undoubtedly was; whilst others were sinners caught up within their own moral rectitude. For him, Maggie's arrival represented the high-point in his ministry so far. He was amazed that he had been able to encourage a woman of the world to enter into the community of faith. Not only had she lowered the average age of his congregation considerably but she had brought laughter, colour and experience of the world into a rather closed, worthy but dull group of people. Her presence in church on a Sunday morning made him want to do better, when she was absent he felt a sense of profound disappointment.

The attention that Peter gave to Maggie did not go unnoticed. People were jealous, critical and leaped to conclusions; none more so than his wife Angela. Maggie became the focus of several blazing rows between them. She told him to grow up, to see what a fool he was making of himself and she bitterly resented the way in which, in her view Maggie was twisting him around her little finger. He was becoming a lap-dog, a poodle, she said and was running the risk of ruining his ministry. He responded by saying that she just didn't understand his work. He was ministering to someone in great need, such a ministry was costly and he had to bear the pain of people misunderstanding him. It was clear to him that preaching the Gospel and welcoming people into the church was always going to be a fraught business and the more in need a person was the greater the cost was likely to be for those who sought to be alongside them.

Such a spiritualised response made his wife even more furious. Instead of kidding himself that he was doing 'the Lord's work' (his phrase!), he should face up to the fact that he was besotted by this fading beauty who had revelled in her sexuality whilst he had spent the last twenty years repressing his. Stung to the quick, he walked out of the vicarage on more than one occasion, banging the door behind him. By a strange process of reasoning, the more his wife berated him the more sure he was that he was doing the right thing. For the first time in his ministry he was being confronted by a world which he knew from reading the newspapers existed all around him, but which he had never actually experienced himself. A world of casual sex, a world in which families were rent asunder, in which mothers left their children and other women moved in to take their place. At last, he thought, the church was being the church in the places where it was most needed. He built a fanciful strategy of mission around a chance encounter with an attractive woman in his church one rainy afternoon.

Maggie was able to get to see her mother every third weekend. She tried not to notice how much she had aged, how she failed to look after herself as well as she might and how confused she often became, although the depression seemed to have eased. To Maggie she was always the mother to whom she could turn for comfort and for Beryl Maggie was always the person from whom she could receive unconditional love. They had a symbiotic relationship and when they were together it was almost as though no-one else existed. During all those weekend visits Maggie never once saw her children and Beryl never once mentioned them.

Her working life progressed well, she was good at her job and enjoyed it. She was popular with her staff and they were as committed to her as she was to them. Apart from work, the family and her church commitments she had little time for anything else. She was not a great reader, didn't play any games and had out-grown her passion for popular music. She was, she reflected, growing into middle age rather serenely and sedately, which was a great contrast to her earlier years. After her time with Stuart she seemed to tire of men, finding the pain that accompanied her relationships with them increasingly difficult to cope with. Also, her mastectomy seemed to bring to an end her desire for physical contact with them, well if not her desire, certainly her readiness to seek them out. Perhaps that was why her friendship with Peter was so special to her, it was a relationship that made no demands and never crossed the boundaries into the physical. Although he was a priest, she did occasionally wonder why he had never made a pass at her. It was not that she wanted him to, in fact she decidedly didn't want him to, but she was intrigued to reflect on why he hadn't. She once made a slight reference to this when he was visiting her.

"You know Peter, in times past if a man visited me at home more than once without ending up in my bed I would have thought something was wrong. I suppose that thoughts like that never occur to you, you are too holy, too tied up with the church to feel things like that."

He looked at her and smiled. He wasn't sure if she was trying to take their friendship onto a different level and he wasn't sure how best to respond.

"Well I can understand the attraction. As you say, if I weren't a priest then perhaps I might have tried my hand, who knows, but you're quite a girl Maggie and I guess I wouldn't have stood much of a chance."

"Hey, don't say that. You would probably have got there on your first visit."

Peter blushed and didn't know how to respond. He decided that it was time to go and he beat a hasty retreat. Later that night, as he lay in bed with his wife he wondered what it might have been like.

What he saw as his pastoral care of Maggie was causing people in the congregation to whisper amongst themselves. A few of them moved closer to his wife and this enabled her to share some of her anger and frustration over what was happening. It was eventually decided that two of the leading members of the congregation should have a private word with him and a date was duly fixed for them to meet. It was not a successful meeting. Peter was angry and thought that they had no right to make such suggestions and impugn his integrity. How he handled complex pastoral issues was his responsibility and his alone and he told them that he would not tolerate such interventions again. They left, embarrassed and annoyed that they had allowed themselves to be placed in such a situation.

The more the pressure mounted, the more Peter denied that there was anything unwholesome about his relationship with Maggie. Tension rose within the vicarage and one evening after visiting Maggie to discuss some parish event he arrived home to find that Angela had left. He was devastated and quite unable to decide what to do. He sat down at the kitchen table, opened a bottle of wine and drank it all. Still confused and distressed he decided to go out for a walk and get some fresh air. He walked and walked for several miles and by the time he came to retrace his steps it was after midnight, but he didn't go home, he went to see Maggie to tell her what had happened and to seek some comfort.

When Maggie went to church the following Sunday there was a different priest taking the service. The Reverend Graham Whittingham told the congregation that Father Peter was unwell and consequently he would be taking the services for the next two weeks. He was an enormous contrast to Peter. Large and insubstantial, untidy in dress and thought and lacking in charisma. He took the service with a monotonous voice and although he wasn't playing the organ the hymns too were all sung at a much slower pace and the whole service gave the impression that decline had set in. If services were run on batteries everyone would have concluded that the battery was flat and needed replacing. A few weeks later the service was taken by the Bishop who informed the congregation that their vicar would not be coming back, he had reached a state of nervous exhaustion and after a much-needed break and holiday he would be moving to a different parish.

A profound sadness spread through the whole congregation. There had been no opportunities to prepare for his departure and there was to be no return for a bun fight and for a chance to give him a leaving present. There were many in the congregation who blamed Maggie for the whole debacle but she was unaware of this. Others, however, whilst recognising that she must have been a contributing factor, reflected that a more mature priest would not have got himself into trouble. There were a few who believed that it really was a case of nervous exhaustion and they could well believe that he might well have experienced such a state as he tried to hold together a demanding job and the problems that he faced in his personal and domestic life. Maggie was totally perplexed; she had never before worked in an environment in which a person's personal dilemmas meant that they were removed from their job. In her experience people were sacked because they had their fingers in the till. Some of the people explained that he hadn't been sacked, merely moved on to a different parish, but as far as Maggie could understand it he had been sacked. She was also disappointed that he never got in touch with her after he left. He had sent her a note after his visit the night his wife left – *Maggie, thank you so much. Sorry to burden you with my problems, I am so grateful to you – many thanks, Peter* – and she had heard nothing further. She thought it was a strange way for a friend to behave and she had no reason to doubt that they were close friends after all that they had shared with each other over the last few years. She continued to go to church, finding that it gave her some sort of base, some satisfaction and support although she would have been hard pressed to explain the reasons why. It was never the same again after Peter left, but she still felt the desire, or was it the need, to continue, added to which quite a number of the people were genuinely friendly and interesting.

It was a few months after the upset at church that Maggie began to feel unwell. She found it difficult to pinpoint exactly how or why, it was just a sense of lethargy and occasional but increasing feelings of sickness and nausea. She did her best to ignore them, continued her work and continued her weekends with her mother. She even achieved the minor miracle of persuading her mother to visit her for a few days in Coventry over Christmas, but it was not an unqualified success. She didn't feel well and her mother was clearly more than a little disorientated by being away from home. Maggie found it difficult to cope with her and one evening after Beryl had gone to bed she telephoned Victoria. She found it impossible to retain an upbeat sound to her voice and when Victoria began to ask her a few questions Maggie broke down and confessed that she was feeling dreadful and finding it impossible to cope with her mother's uncharacteristic behaviour. Victoria said that she would drive up the following day, take them out for lunch and then drive Beryl back home. In the meantime Maggie should make an appointment to see the doctor and should make the most of having a few days off work and get some rest. The conversation with Victoria was an enormous relief, she realised that she now had no-one with whom she could share her thoughts and think around different options. She supposed that, in many ways, Peter had provided that although she hadn't realised it at the time. He was someone who seemed to take an interest in her, as a person, rather than as an employer or a work colleague. She didn't often feel sorry for herself, but at the moment she seemed to be drowning in a sea of self pity and it didn't help being Christmas-time which was always painful for her.

Victoria was concerned to see how drawn she was, how lacking in sparkle. Looking around the flat she noticed that it wasn't really decorated for Christmas; admittedly there was a Christmas tree but very little else. There were about a dozen cards and that was all, it was a marked contrast to her own home which was buzzing with life, festooned with decorations and positively overwhelmed by the number of cards. She decided that, rather than take them both out to lunch, Maggie should go to bed straight away and she would take Beryl back home with her and make sure that she got some proper food inside her and build herself up a bit, she was looking ghastly and Victoria was extremely worried. Maggie was in bed almost before they had left her flat, she had an appointment with the doctor first thing on Monday and decided that she would stay in bed the whole of Sunday which she did, apart from the several occasions when she got up to be sick.

The rest did her some good and by the time Monday morning came she felt able to get up and make her way down to the surgery. Dr Graham her old doctor had now retired and been replaced by a much younger woman who listened to Maggie with great attention asking her a whole range of questions after giving her a thorough examination. She returned to her desk and looked thoughtfully at Maggie, choosing her words carefully.

"I don't want to alarm you, so you must listen carefully to what I am going to say. I want to get another opinion on how things are with you, get some further tests done, that sort of thing. I'll phone the hospital and ask them to admit you. Is that alright with you? Have you got things to do? People to sort out or anything?"

"Well, no, not exactly," replied Maggie. "That is, I'm supposed to be at work again tomorrow, what exactly are you meaning? Will they write to me? Do I stay off work for a day or two or is it alright to go back, although to be honest I don't feel up to it?"

"No, I don't mean that, I mean I'll telephone them now and ask if they can take you in today. You would have time to go home and get your things together but then, if they can take you, I should get a taxi and get there first thing this afternoon."

Maggie was stunned. She wanted to protest but didn't have the energy or the spirit to do anything other than just sit there, finding words difficult to come by. The doctor phoned and arranged for her to be admitted to Ward 32 that afternoon and then wrote a letter, folding it and putting it in a sealed envelope for Maggie to hand over to them when she got there. Maggie wondered what she had written. It seemed strange that she should be the conveyor of a letter presumably saying significant things about her condition without having any inkling of what it said, nor being given much by way of explanation.

"Now try not to worry, I've explained to you that I just want you to have a few more tests, so that someone else can have a look at you as well. It's much better that we try and get to the bottom of this now rather than let it drag on; you wouldn't want to keep feeling like this longer than necessary would you?"

She had been with the GP for over half an hour but it seemed more like two or three minutes. Before she could come to terms with what had been said Maggie was outside in the winter sunshine. The road was busy, people were walking along the pavement talking to each other and two mothers walked together with their pushchairs, even the birds on the road seemed to be in pairs or small groups. Maggie felt that whilst all the world carried on and shared its concerns she was alone, isolated, with no-one to care for her or care about her. She walked slowly back to her flat, she needed to phone work to leave a message and also let Victoria know. Was there anyone else in the whole world even remotely interested in the fact that she was terrified? She would normally have phoned Peter but he had disappeared, just as Stuart had buggered off when she was in a similar situation a few years previously. Men! She arrived home and after making a few essential phone calls packed her bag. She suddenly felt a wave of fear come over her, almost inundating her, and she decided to telephone one of her friends at church to see if she would be willing to accompany her to the hospital.

"Maggie, of course I will. Look, you probably don't feel like eating much but I don't like the idea of you sitting about for the next few hours waiting until it's time to go. I'll ask Jim to drive over and pick you up in about half an hour and you can come and have a bite of lunch with us and of course I'll go with you and see you settled in. I'm so pleased you thought to ring. No, it's no bother at all, I would have been hurt if you had thought that you couldn't ask. I'm so sorry you're not feeling well, what a worry for you and especially at this time of the year. Anyway, you know you've got some friends nearby and I'll make sure you get plenty of visits. Tell your sisters and mother that they can phone us at any time, they will be worrying about you, being so far away. See you soon, my love, Bye Bye."

She looked at her watch; it was barely half past ten. Her whole life seemed to have been tipped upside down within the last two hours.

Ward 32 was large and busy. Twelve beds on either side, each one occupied. Perhaps I should have waited until tomorrow before I went to the doctors, she thought, then they would have been too busy to have taken me and I could have just got on with my life. It was an admissions ward, people didn't seem to stay there for long, they went home after having specific tests or they were transferred to more specialist wards. There was an air of detached business about it, no-one was there long enough to build up any sort of relationship with the staff and they, on their part, seemed to make little effort to communicate with the patients. Helen, from church stayed with her for an hour or so and then left, saying that she would be back that evening. Maggie was grateful and she tried to get some rest but there was a sense of unreality about the whole experience until she was seen by someone who could give her time and assess the situation. As the afternoon progressed she had blood tests, was taken for X rays and had her heart monitored. She somehow sensed that this was the lull before the storm. Several hours passed before the curtains were drawn around her bed and a doctor came and introduced himself and asked if she minded a medical student sitting-in on their conversation. He asked a great many questions, about her original cancer, her mastectomy, her health in the intervening years and the precise nature of her present discomfort. He examined her, probing and pressing her in different places. In the end he said that he wanted her to have more tests and more X rays and that he would arrange for these to be done in the morning.

In the meantime she was to drink some rather obnoxious liquid although that was not how he described it and he was afraid that he was going to ask her to miss the evening meal and tomorrow's breakfast. When all the tests were taken he would come back and see her, which would probably be the following afternoon. He was also giving her some new drugs to take which, he explained, might make her feel rather drowsy. They certainly did and when Helen came to visit that evening Maggie could hardly engage in conversation. She went home extremely worried although she tried to sound upbeat and positive when she telephoned Victoria and reported on what was happening.

The doctor returned the following afternoon and explained to Maggie that they needed to do an investigative operation. They didn't think that the sickness bouts were necessarily related to her tiredness and they needed to undertake further examinations. Although he realised that this must be a great shock, it wasn't necessarily bad news, they just had to find out what was happening. When Maggie asked when she might be having the operation she was devastated to hear him say that if she was in agreement, they would do it that afternoon. He said that it was unusual to proceed so quickly but they had spare capacity in the theatre because of it being Christmas and New Year with many patients having gone home and others not yet admitted. There were more tests, nurses seemingly everywhere and it appeared to Maggie that the whole ward was revolving around her. Once again, she had become the centre of everyone's attention. The anaesthetist came to talk with her, she was able to telephone Victoria and her mother to let them know what was happening and she left a message with Jim for him to tell Helen that there was no need for anyone to visit that evening. By the time she had her pre med. she was already feeling physically, mentally and emotionally exhausted. She hadn't expected this, she had been doing so well for so long that she had reached the stage of almost believing that she was in total remission. Of course, she might well be, this could all be something else but she feared, that it probably wasn't.

For the first few days after the operation Maggie wasn't too sure what was happening. Each day the surgeon would come into the ward, she was now in a different one, sweep round visiting each bed for less than a minute and then disappear. He would ask her how her back was, was it any better? Before she could formulate a reply he had disappeared. To begin with she felt too weak to protest but after a while she became annoyed and asked one of the nurses if she could arrange for the surgeon to stay with her for a talk the next time he was in. The next day when he came, he pulled the curtains to around her bed, drew up a chair and began to talk.

"Well Maggie, you want to have a chat with me I hear. Good, please feel free to ask me anything you want and if you don't understand my answers don't hesitate to say so. But would you rather have a relative or friend with you whilst we are talking?"

"Thank you doctor," said Maggie. "I don't have any close relatives nearby and I live alone. I'm used to dealing with things by myself but thank you for giving me that option. Well for a start, can you tell me what you've done? I know that I've had an operation but no-one has told me what you've found, what you've done or anything. I think I have a right to know, don't you?"

She smiled sweetly, she wasn't being aggressive or rude, she just wanted to know.

"Of course, you have every right to know and I will begin to tell you. Not everyone wants to know about their operation and so we usually wait until they ask, if they want to know we tell them, if they don't want to know then we don't burden them further. In your case we were trying to establish just what was causing your sickness and your sense of lethargy. With your history of cancer it was important that we acted quickly if we were able to and it just so happened that we had the possibility of going ahead straight away although I'm sure that must have been quite a shock for you."

"Yes it was, I wasn't expecting anything like that when I came in."

"No, I can understand that. Well we opened you up and had a look around. I'm afraid that we had to remove your ovaries, we detected signs that the cancer had spread to them. I'm afraid that you may have a bit of backache as a result of some of our other probing."

Maggie panicked for a moment.

"Oh no, I hadn't realised that the cancer had spread. You see, I thought I had conquered it after the mastectomy. Was that everything then?"

"Well we didn't remove anything else Maggie if that's what you mean. You see if we had continued to remove the affected areas then you might not have survived the operation. We had a good look round so that we could decide what further treatment you should have."

"I'm not exactly sure that I understand you doctor," said Maggie. "What do you mean by 'other affected areas', has the cancer spread to different parts?"

"I'm afraid it has Maggie. It has spread to your bowel and liver. To be totally honest with you, there is not a lot more that we can do. We can obviously ensure that the quality of your life is as good as we can possibly make it, but I'm afraid that the cancer has spread to these other vital organs."

Maggie's eyes filled with tears and she bit back her lips, trying hard not to burst into tears.

"Are you telling me that I'm dying?"

He leaned forward and took hold of her hands.

"I'm telling you that the cancer has spread to different parts of your body and we cannot remove those parts. We will be assessing what help we can give you in terms of treatment but I'm afraid that we can't make you better Maggie. I'm sorry to have to tell you this."

"Well how long have I got?" Her voice was little more than a whisper.

"I can't give you a definite answer to that question because no-one knows. But let me put it this way, I think we are talking in weeks rather than months. Perhaps twelve, fifteen weeks, we can't be sure. We will do everything we can to support you and care for you and relieve you of pain. I wish we could do more but your condition has been developing for quite a long time, it's just that until now it hasn't resulted in your feeling unwell, I'm afraid that is often the case."

She felt overwhelmed, burdened by a huge sense of grief and felt herself travelling ever more quickly into a sea of despair. She looked up at the doctor's face and recognised that it couldn't have been easy for him telling her this. She opened her mouth but no words came out, her tongue felt dry and enlarged and her eyes unfocused.

"Maggie, I'm going to ask the nurse to come and stay with you for a while. I'll come back tomorrow and talk to you again and if you want me to meet up with anyone else to explain things again then I will, or if I'm not around I'll ask one of my colleagues to. I'll give you some time to think about things and I'll talk to you further tomorrow. I'm so sorry Maggie but we will do what we can."

He moved away and very quickly a nurse came and comforted her a little, washing her face, tidying up her bed, and talking to her, reassuring her and finding out what she would like her to do. Should she telephone her sister? Would she like the chaplain to come and see her? Did she want anyone else to come and visit? Maggie said she thought they ought to telephone her sister and let her know the news, she wasn't sure that she could do it herself, she might break down and that would be too upsetting for everyone. Yes, she would like to see the chaplain, but perhaps not today, she needed some time to think and she needed to be able to cry so that by the time other people came to see her she was more used to the idea. For the moment though, she felt desperately tired.

When Victoria and Libby arrived to see her the following day she was feeling considerably better. She was recovering well from the operation, looked more like her old self and had begun the long process of trying to come to terms with her situation. This didn't mean that she didn't burst into tears as soon as she saw them walking down the ward, nor did it mean that they too were able to refrain from crying as they put their arms around her. The nurse came down and suggested that they might like to go into the privacy of a small room at the end of the ward and said that she would arrange for them to have a cup of tea brought to them. They talked together quietly and tenderly.

"Have you said anything to mum?"

"No, not yet. Well, she knows that you are in hospital, of course, but we haven't said anything else about it to her."

Victoria took hold of Maggie's hand.

"We couldn't say anything until we had come to see you. But now that we're here, it's not going to be any easier, is it? I'm not sure how we ought to handle it."

"Well, give her my love, won't you. Best for her not to know too much, I think. Who knows what might happen. Let's just leave it in the air."

The news was too big for any of them to take on board straight away so they talked around the subject for most of the time, not avoiding it but not allowing it to dominate every word that they spoke, even though it was clear that nothing else was really on their mind. Victoria said that she would come up and stay with Maggie when she was discharged and, when they knew what was happening, she would take her back to London for a week or so for her to recuperate. Eventually it was time for them to leave; they walked back to Maggie's bed with her and helped to settle her down again. They re-arranged the flowers they'd brought and placed the grapes near to her so that she didn't have to stretch. They kissed her goodbye and fought back the tears as they walked down the ward. As they passed the sister's office she called them in and asked them if they were clear what the situation was.

"We shall probably keep her in for another four or five days and then she will be able to return home. We'll sort out some chemotherapy and see what else we can arrange. There are drugs around now which can relieve the pain although she will probably feel quite nauseous for quite a lot of the time."

They asked about the likely scenario and she explained what might happen but pointed out that because everyone was different there was always an element of uncertainty.

"Does that mean that there could be uncertainty about her condition, that she may not actually be terminally ill, just very poorly?"

"I'm afraid not," the sister replied. "Her body is very badly affected, there's nothing that can be done to extend her life beyond a few months, but we'll try and do everything possible to support her and minimise the discomfort."

They drove back to London in a very subdued frame of mind. Neither of them had expected this, they were devastated when they'd been told by the hospital the previous day. Nor had they any experience of coping with death or bereavement and they felt ill-prepared to take on the role of carers as they were surely going to have to do as the weeks progressed. They decided not to tell Beryl the whole truth to begin with, especially since she wasn't well herself.

When it was time for Maggie to be discharged, Victoria brought her mother up the day before, en route to taking her home. Beryl was very much improved after her stay in London and seemed to cope well with the visit to the hospital. Maggie put on a brave front and they were able to sit together in the small room Victoria and Libby had been in just a few days earlier. Maggie held her mother's hands in hers and tried to reassure her that she was making good progress but Victoria suspected that her mother sensed the worst and that this visit had not changed her mind. Later, as they drove north, Beryl raised the subject directly.

"I don't think things are good for Maggie are they?"

Victoria decided to proceed with caution, she didn't want to cause unnecessary pain and upset but neither did she want to mislead her mother.

"No, she's really quite poorly. It was a big operation you know."

"Yes, but it's not the operation that I'm talking about," continued Beryl. "She has that look about her, I don't like it, I don't like it."

"What do you mean 'look'?" quizzed Victoria.

"I don't really know what I mean," confessed Beryl, "but often people get a certain sort of look when they're very ill. I think there is more to this than I've been told. Are you being honest with me? I don't want you and Libby keeping things from me, you know. If things are bad I need to know, it takes time to get your head round these things, believe me, I know, I know. I've been there before."

Victoria felt a wave of immense admiration sweep over her. Here she was, trying to protect her, forgetting that she was tough, that she had been tested over the years and come through the sort of pain, tragedy and bereavement that Victoria could hardly imagine.

"Well, I think you're right mum, she is in a bad way. The doctor said that when he opened her up he removed her ovaries but the cancer had spread much more than he could have imagined. He said that it wasn't possible for him to clear it away."

She looked across at her mother who was sitting staring straight ahead, a tear gathering in her eye which slowly trickled down.

"I knew it. That's what I thought. I just hoped I was wrong but I sensed that you and Libby were trying to hide something from me."

"I'm sorry mum, we just needed time ourselves to come to terms with it and we couldn't face seeing you upset when we didn't know how we were coping ourselves."

"That's alright dear, I understand that, but I've had a feeling for quite some time that this couldn't last. I wasn't surprised when they took her into hospital, I'd been expecting it, I don't know why, but I had. Oh dear, dear, so how long have we got? A year?"

Victoria shook her head, she couldn't speak the words and her own eyes were tearful.

"No, much less than that," she whispered. "They said it was just three or four months. Oh dear, poor Maggie, she's had such a torrid time. I think I'm going to have to pull into the next lay-by for a few minutes, I can't really drive when I'm like this."

206

They pulled off the road within a few minutes and Victoria stopped the car and opened the driver's window. She stared out, not having the strength to face her mother. She let out a great sob, turned and somehow managed to hug her despite the constrictions of the car. They held each other closely for a long time, sharing their tears and their grief. Victoria couldn't remember the last time that she had been in really close physical contact with her mother; it was probably when she was a small child and possibly before Maggie was born.

Each member of the family tried to come to terms with their grieving in their own particular way. Maggie, who began life as the centre of attraction, the sun around which all the other planets seemed to revolve approached the end of her life in a similar way. She was grateful to Victoria and Bill for looking after her for a week or two soon after she came out of hospital but she wanted to get home. She had learned to love her flat with its view of the park and the ever-changing patterns of the trees outside her window. She felt secure at home, at peace with herself. She found it ironic that at last, after a lifetime of turmoil and unsatisfactory relationships, she had now reached a state of contentment and she wasn't going to be able to enjoy it for much longer. For all her life she had been a 'people person', never really at home unless surrounded by others. It was the affection and friendship of others which gave meaning to her life and without people around her she had always tended to wilt, to feel less than whole, unfulfilled and unsatisfied. Now, she was enjoying her own company and found that she needed space. Space to reflect on the past and space to prepare for the future. She greatly appreciated the care and concern of her family and without their daily phone calls and their frequent visits she didn't know how she would survive, but she didn't want their company all the time, she needed the quietness which was both external and internal.

She also greatly appreciated the way in which friends from church had organised a rota to do her shopping and cleaning and to provide so many ready prepared meals for her, although in truth she ate very little. Another thing which she valued were the conversations she had with a couple of people from church who had the courage and the sensitivity to be able to raise the question of death and dying with her and who were able to talk through some of the issues and some of her fears with her. She missed the support she knew Peter would have been able to give her, support in facing some of the ultimate 'God questions' but the people who did talk to her were a great help and encouragement. She didn't know what she really felt or believed about all these things but thought that if there was a God, and she thought that perhaps there was, then all would be well. She couldn't conceive of a God who wouldn't love her. She had always been loved. On the other hand, if there wasn't a God, then dying would be rather like falling asleep and there was nothing about that to frighten her.

At times when she came close to despair, when she felt frightened or felt that life was unfair she resorted to a little exercise the hospital chaplain had suggested to her. She wrote down in a small book all the good things that she could remember; good people she had met, good memories and experiences. Then she would read through these, often remembering others and adding to the list. To her amazement she had completely filled one small exercise book and was already half way through a second one. The memory of all that was good helped to stave off the temptation to focus on the painful or the disappointing. Of course, remembering all the good things made her all the more reluctant to leave them, but by focusing on all that she had received, she seemed to gain strength which enabled her to face a future of loss.

She missed her children more than she could ever admit but decided that it was better for them that she didn't make contact with them, reasoning that it would be a double pain for them, meeting her again after all these years and then losing her a second time within weeks. She had given this a lot of thought and decided that staying away from them was a gift of love that she was able to give them. She hoped that, in the years to come, someone would explain this to them and she asked Libby to keep in touch with them, for her sake, and to let them know that although she had not been a good mother, it was not through a lack of love for them. After a great deal of thought she plucked up the courage to ask Victoria if it might be possible for her to get hold of some photographs of them. In her own way, her love was every bit as real as Victoria's for her children; it was just that she was unable to find appropriate ways of expressing it. Now, with her life coming to an end, she would like to hold some photographs of them, so that she could tell them that she loved them.

There were days when she felt physically wretched, tired, nauseous and often dizzy. For much of the time though she felt reasonably well. It seemed both sad and ironic to her that she sat there with all the time in the world each day but without the strength to fill the time with activity. She tried to reflect on all the good things that happened each day before she fell asleep at night, and to her surprise and delight there were always things that she could find to be grateful for. When she woke up in the morning she tried to look ahead with hope and expectancy, willing herself to believe that each day could bring something to make her smile, something to make her love and something to experience with a sense of gratitude. Again she discovered that if she looked for these then she invariably discovered them. People around Maggie were amazed by the way she seemed to be coping with her illness. For someone who had made a mess of living she was coping with dying so much more constructively.

More than once she was re-admitted into hospital whilst they tried to balance her drugs regime and she was able to enjoy a relationship with the department and the ward in ways which would have seemed inconceivable to her just a few months ago. It was suggested that she spend a few days in a local hospice where more time and greater expertise could be given and she found this to be a really good experience. She knew that she was getting weaker. She slept more often, had less energy and her appetite often virtually disappeared. She was losing her hair, her face was turning a yellowish sort of colour, her hearing began to be affected and she was sometimes conscious that she wasn't speaking very clearly or fluently. When the pain and the nausea were under control she was content. She enjoyed watching the emergence of spring from her window overlooking the park and she loved all the flowers which had been lovingly sent to her. Sometimes, she tried to image what her end would be like, but looking forward and anticipating how things might be had never been her strong point and for the main, she was content to leave the future to look after itself and focus on the here and now.

As the weeks went by she was able to concentrate for only short periods of time. It was as if the very act of concentration was itself a disabling activity. She decided that, whilst she still had sufficient energy, she would write a letter and ask Libby to give it to Mike after her funeral. She'd thought of doing this for some time but kept putting it off until one day, as the sun lit up her room, she decided that the time had come and she made a great effort, surprising herself when she discovered just how difficult and demanding a task it proved to be.

Dear Mike,

I am asking Libby to give you this after my funeral.

First of all I want to ask your forgiveness for all the hurt I caused you. I no I wasn't a good wife to you and I'm sorry. I did try but I wasn't good enough.

I'm really pleased that you found yourself another woman. From what I here she is a good person and has been really good with the children which is lovely. I am very pleased that they have had somebody to look after them. You are a good dad, always have been and that was why I was able to leave them because I new you loved them.

I don't have much money, but I've got a bit because I've been working and I'm buying this flat. When I've gone it will be sold. Any money left over when all the bills are paid I'm asking Libby to give to you to spend on the children in the best way that you no. You don't have to tell them its from me but you will no and you will no that I've been thinking about them whilst I am poorly.

You won't believe this but I do love them and think about them every day. I hope they grow up very happy.

My mum was much better to me than I was to them. I'm sorry but I couldn't be the person they needed but I want you to no that I love them and always will.

> *Your a good man Mike*
> *Thank you*
>> *Maggie*
>> *Xxx*

A week later her condition suddenly deteriorated. She could hardly swallow, she felt dizzy, confused and disoriented. Victoria had already come to stay with her indefinitely, going home at the weekend when Libby took over. She sat by her bedside whilst Maggie slept. The GP came in each day, as did a nurse, and after a particularly disturbed night he recommended that Maggie be taken back to the hospice where they could monitor her condition and relieve her distress more immediately. Libby and Victoria were both with her as she was carried out of her flat. Her eyes filled with tears, she knew that she would almost certainly not return but said nothing. Libby accompanied her in the ambulance noting her slight winces as it bounced along an uneven road, whilst Victoria followed in her car. A bed was waiting in a small room, one that she had been in a couple of times before. The two sisters went for a cup of tea then, when Maggie was settled in her bed, Libby sat with her whilst Victoria drove north to fetch Beryl.

She slept most of the day and most of the night, drifting in and out of consciousness. Libby held her hand, stroked her forehead and moistened her lips by dipping her own fingers into a glass of water and tracing over her lips with them. She dozed spasmodically but awaked at the slightest sound. It was mid morning when Victoria returned. Beryl looked strained, she had been weeping but was composed as she moved to the bedside. She took Maggie's hands and, almost miraculously, Maggie opened her eyes. She looked up at her and smiled. She opened her mouth a little and whispered 'Mum', smiled again and drifted into unconsciousness. Two hours later she died peacefully, surrounded by the three women who had so delighted in her when, as a child, she had captivated them all by her joyful delight in life.

When a family member dies, it seems as though the whole of life stands still. There seems to be no future, only the past, and so it was for Beryl, and Victoria and Libby. And yet life does proceed, time doesn't stand still, suspended, it moves on relentlessly, and everyone has to face the new day, the new week and create a new future, and so did they.

The months following Maggie's death were pivotal for Beryl, she could have gone either way. Libby and Victoria were extremely worried that she would sink into another depression and indeed, for several weeks it seemed as though that would be the case. What happened was that she neither regressed nor made progress, for a long time she remained passive, almost motionless. She went through the motions of living but it was as though it was her body that did this whilst her being, her psyche, whatever it is that makes a person a person, seemed to be wholly absent. Libby and Victoria lived on a knife-edge, fearing the worst yet hoping that the depression might stay away. It took about six months before she began to live again but once that process had begun it was as though Beryl was emerging from a chrysalis in which she had been imprisoned for many years. Time went by, Libby was immersed in her work and Victoria in her family, it was a period of relative normality after the years of turmoil with Maggie and everyone just seemed to get on with living their own life.

"Has mum ever mentioned a Mr Braithwaite to you?" asked Libby one day as they were walking home from a concert in the Festival Hall.

"Why yes, now you mention it, she has. It's funny that you should mention it, I haven't really thought about it, but of course when I do, it seems rather odd because normally she never ever talks about anyone when I give her a ring."

"You don't suppose that she's found herself a man-friend do you?"

They both stopped, looked at each other and burst out laughing, the very idea seemed quite preposterous.

"You know, I don't think I can ever remember mum having a friend of any sort. All the years of my life, I don't ever remember her going out with anyone, man or woman. She always seemed to live just for us. She was either busy working, sorting out the house, cleaning, cooking or sewing. She never seemed to do anything else, just look after us."

"I suppose that Maggie was her best friend, if you can say that sort of a thing about a daughter. Poor mum, you know I've never really thought about it, about her, I mean. She's just always been there and I've never stopped to consider what her life must be like really. I suppose she's been terribly lonely. I wonder why she's never been able to speak about our fathers? I used to try and encourage her to talk but she never would. 'What's past is past' was all that I could get out of her."

They kissed each other goodbye and made their separate ways home. A few days later Libby phoned her mother to check out some arrangements for the following weekend when she was going to be visiting her.

"I called you earlier on Mum, just before afternoon classes began but didn't seem to get through. Were you having a sleep? I'm sorry if I disturbed you."

"No my dear, I was out. Actually I was having a bite of lunch out at that pub place down the road then I went to the pictures with Mr Braithwaite, we went to see *The Sound of Music*, it was very good, have you seen it?"

"No mum, I don't get to the cinema very often but I've heard that it's a good film. What did you have to eat?"

"Scampi and chips. They were very nice but they give you too much you know, I couldn't eat it all. Still, it made a nice change."

Libby couldn't wait to phone Victoria.

It all began a month or so after the sudden death of Mrs Braithwaite. Her husband called round on Beryl to ask for some advice about cooking. He had always left that to his wife so when she suddenly departed without so much as saying 'goodbye' he was not only wife-less he was virtually food-less as well. Completely out of character Beryl suggested that he might like to come round and have lunch with her the next day, she was cooking anyway and so one more mouth to feed wouldn't be a problem. After having lunch with Beryl three or four times he suggested that, as he couldn't return the compliment, could he invite her out for lunch and would she come to The Stranger's Arms with him. Beryl couldn't remember the last time she had been in a pub, certainly it would have been before the war, but she was happy to go with him. It was there, over steak pie and chips, that the next breakthrough was made.

"Look, I'm not trying to be forward or anything but do you think it might be possible for us to move onto first name terms? I mean, it seems a bit strange sitting here and always referring to you as Mrs Arkwright and you calling me Mr Braithwaite. We have known each other as neighbours for what – thirty years at least – and we still don't know each other's first name."

Beryl wasn't too sure.

"Now look, I'm very happy to give you lunch because I make it for myself and it's very nice of you to buy me this steak pie, but I'm not sure that I want us to get too familiar. I mean, I've always known you as Mr Braithwaite and it would seem funny to call you anything else."

"Yes, I do realise that, but you see, I never think of myself as Mr Braithwaite. It's not a case of being familiar, it's just plain common sense that if two people talk to each other then they ought to call each other by their proper name, and my name's Rupert. Would it be all that difficult to call me that?"

"I suppose not... Rupert... but you see, although my name is Beryl I've never been called that by anyone since my husband was lost in the war. My children call me Mum and to everyone else I'm Mrs Arkwright. I never think of myself as anything other than Mrs Arkwright. Well, actually I don't really ever think of myself as anyone. I'm just me, sort of nameless I suppose."

"But your name is actually Beryl, isn't it? That's what you were called when you were a little girl and when you were growing up and I assume that's what you were called when you got married. So why can't you become Beryl again? Why don't you allow yourself to be yourself and not just Mrs Arkwright, though I have to admit, Mrs Arkwright is a fine sounding name. Would it be too big a thing for us to call each other Rupert and Beryl?"

Beryl was confused; she was not expecting this great leap into familiarity.

"I don't know... I'll think about it. Let's talk about something else."

But the ice was broken, the thaw had set in. Within a matter of months they were on first name terms.

That autumn they went on a bus trip together to see the illuminations at Blackpool. Beryl was finding some happiness at last after all her years of sadness. Her home was brighter, she had redecorated the living room after almost thirty years and had a gas fire put in to save her the work of bringing in the coal each day. Libby and Victoria were delighted and relieved to see the changes taking place. She was very reticent about things when they visited, admitting that she occasionally went out for a meal or to the pictures with Mr Braithwaite but giving no hint of any developing relationship. However, after their friendship had been developing for two years it was possible for Rupert or Mr Braithwaite to the girls, to come over for the evening and join them after they had had their tea on one of their visits.

There seemed to be no end to the new experiences opening up for Beryl in the latter years of her life. She couldn't believe it when Rupert told her that to celebrate her seventy-fifth birthday he had booked for them to fly over to Holland for a day to visit the bulb fields. They could get a flight from Manchester, leaving at breakfast-time which would get them to the bulb fields by lunchtime and then they would fly back getting to Manchester at about nine o'clock that night. It would mean that she would have to have a passport; he already had one because he and Mabel, Mrs Braithwaite, had been on a coach tour to Austria a few years previously. Beryl was both delighted and afraid. She had never been abroad, never been on an aeroplane and never imagined that she might. On the other hand, 'foreign' was still a difficult concept for her. When she told Victoria about the suggested trip, wondering if she would mind, she was surprised by her enthusiasm.

"That's absolutely wonderful mum. Look, I'll come up and drive you both over to Manchester in the morning and home again at night. It will be no trouble and I can spend the day in Manchester having a look round and probably getting to the cinema in the early evening. How about if Libby and I bought you a new outfit to go in? We have been wondering what to get you for your birthday and that would be perfect."

The day was a great success and Victoria had never seen her mother as happy as when she came off the plane that evening, she had a huge smile on her face. She drove them home and could hardly believe that this was the same woman who just a few years ago was languishing in a mental hospital speaking to no-one.

A few months later Rupert raised the idea that they might go and have a fortnight together in Lanzarotte. Beryl was very subdued by the idea, which surprised him.

"What's the matter, don't you fancy it? It's a lovely place, a small island, all that sea and sunshine. It would be a great place to go to in the autumn, when the nights are getting long and the weather is getting cold, a bit of warmth would do us the world of good."

"I'm not sure," said Beryl. She looked down at her handbag and moved it a few inches nearer to her leg.

"I'm not sure that it would be right. Going away together for a fortnight. What would people think? Anyway, I don't want you getting any ideas; I don't want to start any hanky-panky or that sort of thing."

"You daft thing. It's not your flipping body I want it's your company, can't you see that?"

Rupert was quite indignant. He fancied the idea of a fortnight away and he knew that he would never go by himself. What was getting into the woman, he had behaved impeccably all the time they had been seeing each other. Of course he wasn't trying to develop a physical relationship, how could she think that? Anyway, Mabel wouldn't like that and he wouldn't want to do anything that would upset her, even though she had been dead for several years now.

The matter resolved itself and they did indeed go to Lanzarotte for a fortnight at the end of October. It was pleasant but somehow there seemed to be something missing and Rupert couldn't put his finger on it. They enjoyed walking along by the sea-front; they had a good hotel, with adjacent but not joining rooms. They even danced together one evening, enjoying the music and humming along to the tunes of their youth; it was the first time Beryl had danced since before she and Frank had married and she was surprised at how easily she remembered all the steps. She enjoyed exploring the island on the bus tour they booked and she even tried some Spanish food once or twice but didn't really take to it. On a couple of mornings she missed breakfast despite Rupert's knocks on her door and when she finally appeared she didn't seem to notice that anything was amiss. Two or three times Rupert was perplexed when she called him by different names, sometimes he seemed to be George and at other times she called him Frank, he let the moments pass but wondered what on earth she was thinking about. On another occasion she was writing some postcards home and seemed to get confused over Victoria and Libby and once she said that she needed to get a card for Maggie. These were but minor occurrences but Rupert really did get upset when, on their last full day she accused him of walking round her room in the middle of the night.

"What on earth are you talking about Beryl? I've done no such thing."

"But you have, I saw you. You came in through the wall and kept walking around and looking. You know, you shouldn't do that. It's not right."

"You're talking absolute nonsense. How could I walk through your wall? I've never been into your room, nor do I want to. Believe me, when I get into my room I'm asleep within ten seconds of my head touching the pillow."

"Yes, but you shouldn't come into my room. It's not right. If it happens again I'll tell Albert."

"Who the hell is Albert?" asked Rupert, getting quite annoyed.

"Albert? Who's Albert? What do you mean? My dad of course. Everyone knows who Albert is."

Rupert got up and without a word he left the table and went for a long walk by himself along the front.

The next day Beryl appeared to have no recollection of their little tiff. She was totally lucid, good company and very appreciative of their holiday. She was packed and ready for off and thoroughly enjoyed their journey home, suggesting that they might come again because it was such a nice place.

Rupert left her alone for a few days when they got home and then turned up and suggested that they went out for a meal. They had lunch in The Stranger's Arms and when he began to talk about their holiday Beryl looked at him with a blank expression. It dawned on him that she had no idea what he was talking about and seemed to have completely forgotten that this time the previous week they were on one of the Canary Islands. That evening he telephoned Victoria.

"Oh hello. Is that Victoria? Good, this is Rupert... Rupert Braithwaite, your mother's friend."

Victoria was totally non-plussed, she had no idea who Rupert was. He had always been Mr Braithwaite to her.

"Well, I don't want to disturb you unnecessarily, but I don't think your mother's too well. No, she fine, she's not ill or anything, but I think her mind's going a bit."

He described to Victoria some of the incidents that had happened on their holiday and then spoke about George and Frank, saying that he had no idea who they were.

"Oh No! George was my father. He was killed in a works accident when I was a baby and Frank was her second husband, Libby's father, but he was killed in the war."

"Ah, well at least we've got that cleared up. Then she accused me of walking through the wall into her room at night. I can assure you Victoria that no such thing ever happened – I mean being in your mother's room. I do hope you understand that my relationship with your mother is one of friendship, two rather lonely people enjoying each other's company. There is nothing more to it than that I can assure you."

"Oh please Mr Braithwaite, don't think for one minute that either Libby or I have ever seen your friendship with mum as anything more than that. We are just so grateful that you seem to enjoy each other's company. You have been very good for her, brought her out of her shell and made her laugh. It has been lovely to see her smiling again, she's had a very difficult time over the years. So have no fears whatsoever, we trust you implicitly."

"Well thank you, I am pleased to hear you say that. But I am very worried about her. Sometimes she seems just fine and then the next time I see her she seems, well, how can I put it – strange, that's the word, strange."

Victoria spoke to Bill about it and they agreed that she should travel north the first thing in the morning. When she arrived in the early afternoon she was surprised to see that her mother wasn't dressed. She was looking well after her two weeks in the autumn sunshine but her face had a strange sort of vacant look about it.

"Hello mum, my love. What's up, why aren't you dressed?"

"It's good to see you again my dear. It's nice of you to come. Where have you come from?"

"I've just driven up from home, don't you remember I telephoned you and said I would be here soon after lunch?"

"Did you? Well it's nice to see you. Where have you come from?"

"Mum, why haven't you got dressed, it's the afternoon now, aren't you feeling well?"

"Me? I'm fine. Why shouldn't I be? It's nice to see you again dear. Where did you say that you've come from?"

"Mum, have you any idea what the time is?"

"Time? Well it must be getting on a bit, mustn't it? What time did you say it was?"

"Mum, it's almost half past two, don't you think you should be getting dressed?"

"Yes, don't rush me, I was just about to go and get ready when you arrived. You've come earlier than you said haven't you? I wasn't expecting you until the afternoon. Where have you come from?"

Victoria felt totally out of her depth. She wasn't expecting this and she decided to change the subject.

"Did you have a lovely holiday Mum, was the weather good?"

"What holiday is that my dear? Have you been away?"

"No, I haven't been away, you have. Did you have a good time?"

"Don't be so silly girl, I haven't been away, whatever gave you that idea? I haven't been away since I went with your father, that was a good holiday, just your father and me and Maggie."

"No mum, you've just come back from Lanzarotte, don't you remember? You went away with Mr Braithwaite."

"Me, go away with Mr Braithwaite? Whatever are you talking about girl? You don't want to let Mrs Braithwaite hear you saying that, she'll be round here like a shot, I know her. She's quite a woman that Mrs Braithwaite. I think they call her Hilda, I'm not sure, no, Mabel, yes that's it, Mabel Braithwaite. Do you know her?"

"Mum, Mrs Braithwaite's been dead for six years. You've been away on holiday with Mr Braithwaite, just like you went to Holland with him to see the tulips."

"Tulips? Tulips? I've never liked tulips, you know I don't like tulips. They're just a waste of money in my mind. Daffodils are nicer, you can't beat a nice bunch of daffs. Anyway, don't sit around talking and wasting time, I've got to get the tea ready, your dad'll be back home soon and he'll want his food."

Libby went north the following weekend and whilst her mother seemed mentally alert she noticed that she was wearing clothes which didn't match and there were marks and stains down her blouse which her mother seemed totally oblivious of. The refrigerator was in a mess, half opened things left without being sealed up, food well past its best and the whole thing extremely untidy. She found a saucepan put away in a cupboard without having been washed and she found a pair of gloves and a pair of glasses in the bread bin. When she asked if Mr Braithwaite still came round to see her she was met with a look of total amazement.

"Mr Braithwaite? Why ever would he want to come round here? He's busy enough with keeping his bees. I suppose he'll be called up soon, they are all going off you know."

"Going off? Who's going off where," asked Libby.

"The war of course, didn't you know that? All the young men will have to go. I remember seeing Dad go off, he was so smart in his uniform and he smiled at me when he walked past. I was so proud of him, but he never came back, his friend came back and told mam all about it, he was very thin I remember and he kept shaking."

Libby went to see Mr Braithwaite who confessed that he didn't go round so often these days. He kept his eye on her but there was no longer the companionship that he craved for since his wife had died.

"Sometimes she knows me and at other times she doesn't. I took her out last week for lunch but I don't think I shall do it again, she clearly wasn't happy and to be quite honest Libby, it was rather embarrassing the way she gobbled her food. There was no conversation, she just tucked into the food as though she hadn't eaten for a week. I don't want to appear callous, but I'm not sure that I can cope, I just don't know what's happened to her, it all seems to have come on so quickly. I'm not sure if I should mention this or not – but before we went out I had to remind her to take her pinafore off and put her teeth in. Now, she never used to be like that, did she? But I promise you I'll keep my eye on her and get in touch if I think you need to know anything, that's just about all I can do though, it really is. I'm sorry."

Two months later there was a telephone call from him to say that the police had found her walking down the street in her nightdress in the early hours of the morning. She didn't know where she lived and it took them a long time to discover who she was and where she was from. Victoria went up immediately and this time she demanded that a doctor be called. By the time he arrived Beryl was quite lucid, insisting that she was fine and quite able to answer all the stock questions that doctors ask people in such situations. Victoria showed him to the door and asked his opinion.

"Well, she seems to be fine at the moment. From what you say there is clearly some memory loss but it doesn't seem too great. I can't explain the midnight walks through the streets, but whatever caused that seems to have passed now. I think we'll just have to keep our eye on her, won't we? Let me know if anything else crops up."

With that, he was gone, leaving a very annoyed, confused and near-despairing Victoria on the doorstep.

The next crisis came when the police broke into the house when no-one could make any contact, only to find her collapsed at the bottom of the stairs. She was taken to hospital and once again Victoria and Libby drove up from London as soon as they heard the news. When they reached the hospital they found that she'd broken her leg falling down the stairs and the doctors were undecided as to whether she had tripped, fainted or had a stroke, they were still undertaking tests. They sat by her bedside, feeling helpless. When she wasn't sleeping she drifted into some form of consciousness but didn't seem to recognise either of them. They stayed overnight at the house and were grateful to Mr Braithwaite for arranging for the door to be fixed following the police break-in. They took him out for lunch the next day, partly as a way of thanking him for his quick response to their call the day before and also to express their gratitude for the ongoing care that he had shown over the months. It was from him that they learned that she now had occasional delusions, that she often accused him of taking her money, of walking round her home when she wasn't there and once, of stepping into her room from within the television set. It was firmly his view that she was no longer safe to live alone and he feared that she might set the house on fire by forgetting to turn the gas off, or even that she might blow it up by forgetting to light the fire. She was, he thought, not only a danger to herself but also to the houses and people around her.

She was in hospital for over a month with her broken leg, seldom showing any signs of recognition when she was visited. Eventually the hospital asked to speak with Victoria and Libby to talk through a way forward.

"We can't keep her here any longer I'm afraid," explained the ward sister. "She's really blocking up a bed, there's not much more we can do for the leg. We're planning to move her in the next few days."

She then mentioned a hospital that had been a workhouse in former times; their hearts sank, and that was that. It was hardly a consultation with the medical staff it was more a signing off, an absolving of themselves from any further responsibility. They merely relayed to Victoria and Libby a decision that had already been taken. They went to see her in the ward; she was sitting in a chair by her bed staring out straight ahead, and apparently oblivious of everything that was going on around her. Occasionally she developed a slight rocking motion and would mumble a few words to herself which they could make no sense of when they tried to listen. Sometimes she would look at them, sometimes she would smile but most of the time she seemed to be living in some strange land far far away. They didn't know if she was heavily drugged but they suspected she was.

The next time Libby and Victoria came up together it was to an extremely large, rambling building set in expansive wooded grounds. The entrance doors were very high and very heavy. They walked through into a large hall with a highly polished floor and with corridors going off in three directions, making their way to the ward which had now become Beryl's home. Its door was locked and they had to ring a bell to gain admittance. They walked down the long ward; it had a distinctive and rather unpleasant smell. She was at the far end and they passed several beds with people leering at them, one or two shouting out and at least two old people curled up crying. It was a walkway through hell and they tried to remember what was said to them at the other hospital, that she wouldn't really be aware of what was happening around her. They hoped that was true, how they hoped that it was true. They sat by the side of the bed, watching closely as Beryl peered at them as though searching through an internal filing system for signs of recognition. There were none.

"Hello mum, it's Libby and Victoria come to see you? How are you feeling today?"

She looked at Libby with a wry half-smile on her face but said nothing.

Victoria busied herself wrapping a blanket around her, tidying up her hair and asking if she wanted a drink or anything. Beryl made no reply, she looked at her, almost through her, as though Victoria's face was the doorway into a different place. Libby brought some hand cream out of her bag and began to massage her mother's hands, noting how thin and marked the skin had become. They sat together bound by a silence which they hoped might have meaning because words seemed to be of no use. They were allowed to stay on after the visiting time ended because of the long journey they had made and were able to help with her food when it came. A plate of warm mince and mashed potatoes with a couple of carrots. Beryl could just about manage to feed herself and Victoria wiped her chin, to clear the food which had dripped down from her mouth. This was followed by a small dish of red jelly with some cut-up pieces of tinned peach. On the tray was a plastic beaker with a top on it, so that she could drink from it without spilling. That at least was the theory. Libby looked around the ward, it was deeply dispiriting. Some people devoured their food almost before the plate had been brought to them, others sat and looked, making no effort to eat; one or two were being fed by the ward staff. She wondered which category her mother fitted into when they were not there.

After an hour and a half, which seemed to be an eternity, they felt that they needed to leave. They wiped her face, gently brushed her hair, put their arms around her and told her that they loved her. She had not spoken all the time they were there.

Just as they were about to go she looked up and smiled and said "Where's Maggie?" She then looked closely at Victoria and whispered "You are the spitting image of your father, that you are."

Both of them had tears in their eyes as they walked back down the ward. Speaking to the staff as they left they tried to reach some understanding of what was likely to happen.

"Well your mother has settled in really well since she arrived. She's really no bother at all."

"Yes, but what will happen to her, how long will she be here do you think?"

The nurse looked surprised that they should have asked such a question.

"Well people usually stay here. I mean, they're not able to go home are they? They all have some form of senile dementia and we try to keep them safe here. They can't get out, so they're quite safe, I don't think anyone has ever escaped from this ward."

"But what about treatment?" Libby did not like what she was being told.

"You do realise that these people have dementia don't you? That means we can't really treat them, I mean they won't get better. We look after them until they die. They're quite happy with us and very few of them are much trouble. If they get restless then we can give them something to calm them down but your mother is fine."

"It's so difficult for us," said Victoria. "We both live in London and visiting is really difficult. Do you think we should try and get her moved to be nearer to us?"

"Oh I don't think that's necessary. You see, she's no idea where she is and she's very happy and settled here. Don't worry too much about visiting, just come when you can, but she won't remember that you've been, so in many ways it's just a waste of your time isn't it? You can always phone up to see if everything's alright."

They returned to London extremely depressed. It was as though the most important thing as far as the hospital was concerned was that Beryl should not be a trouble, either to them or to the hospital staff, and that she should not escape. She was neither treated nor spoken of as a person, rather she was seen as some sort of passive creature, no longer a living person with hopes and fears, relationships or even her own history. It was most unlikely that anyone in the hospital had very much idea about who she was or what she had achieved in her life.

"I'm sure they don't mean it in that way, but that's the way it comes over. It's just like a warehouse isn't it, a sort of transit camp between life and death."

Victoria put words to the thoughts that kept circulating in Libby's head. They had a conversation with Bill about all the possibilities. He was concerned about the effect all this was having on Victoria and she burst into tears.

"I feel pulled and pushed in every direction. It's like a sandwich, with me in the middle. I have responsibilities towards my children and grandchildren and I have responsibilities towards my mother, and poor Bill gets left out, it just isn't fair. I don't know what to do, I really don't."

Libby too felt herself being stretched beyond her capabilities. She wondered about leaving work and going up north to look after her mother full time but Victoria wouldn't hear of it.

"It would kill you my love. You would do it for a week, two weeks or a month, but you would grow to resent it, resent her and resent us all. It would cripple you emotionally. You just can't do it."

"The only thing we can do," reasoned Bill, "is to find a nursing home locally, so that you can pop in and out without having to journey up north every week. I'll ask around, there are bound to be people I know who are in that business."

Two months later Beryl was moved down to The Cedars a small nursing home about ten minutes walk away from Victoria. It was not ideal but then, none of them were and they had visited at least eight in their search for the right one

In the four years that Beryl lived in The Cedars she hardly ever spoke and showed no sign of recognising them. She never really recovered from her broken leg and although she was able to walk, it was with difficulty and as the months went by she walked less and less until eventually she was totally bed-bound. Victoria wondered if she was actually encouraged much to walk or if it was more convenient for the home if she stayed in bed. Libby wondered if she was having another depressive breakdown, perhaps that was why she was so uncommunicative, but when she raised the possibility with the staff they dismissed the idea out of hand.

"No, your mother has senile dementia, that's why she's like this," was all that she was told when she raised the issue more than once. In the end she thought she was becoming a nuisance and that this might backfire and have repercussions on her mother's care, so she never raised the question again although it stayed in her mind.

She just seemed to exist, nothing more and nothing less. She lost weight, becoming little more than a skeleton. The staff seemed to ignore her for most of the time as far as Libby and Victoria could tell. Clearly she was no trouble, she didn't shout and scream, she didn't throw things and she made few demands on anyone. One night she sat up in bed and saw her father beckoning to her with a smile on his face. She climbed out and walked towards him, stretching out her arms as though to embrace him. A few hours later the night staff went into her room and found her lying on the floor, her arms still outstretched and a smile on her face. It was 1992 and she was eighty two years old.

The death certificate said that she had died of a stroke but Victoria and Libby had no doubt that she'd died of a broken heart. They believed that her grief over the death of Maggie, although temporarily suspended for a surprising few years when Mr Braithwaite had befriended her, had returned and eaten its way into her very being. Although they were upset by her death, they also felt that it came as a merciful release. The funeral was very low-key, with just a few people attending. There was a short address in which the minister said that Beryl had 'died' several years earlier and what they were doing today was formally saying goodbye to a body which, although breathing until very recently was no longer a living human person. Libby wasn't sure that she agreed with him although it did seem to make sense to her, nevertheless it wasn't the last word on her mother's condition and it left her feeling dissatisfied, as though her mother had not been properly honoured. No-one outlined the formidable forces against which she had struggled all of her life. No-one mentioned the unconditional love that had poured out on her children and no-one really knew or understood the extent to which the deaths of her father, two husbands and daughter had sapped the will for life from her. It had been a life of service, against the odds, and the funeral failed to identify or acknowledge any of it.

It came as a huge surprise to Libby to receive a letter one day informing her that her name had been recommended for an honour and would she be willing to accept an MBE for her services to education if it were formally offered. She was thrown into an instant quandary and experienced a host of contradictory emotions. She had little time for the honours system, seeing it as a relic of a class-ridden society, the sort of thing she was working to transform. On the other hand, she knew that it was an honour, nor only for her but, more importantly, for the school. But was this an example of self-delusion? She had to admit to herself that she was greatly flattered, and she would have loved her mother to have known about it, but was it a betrayal of her principles? The family came from the humblest of backgrounds and now here she was meeting with the queen. It seemed somehow wrong that her father and grandfather should have given their lives for their country and received nothing and here was she, doing what she loved doing, getting paid for doing it and now being offered this sort of recognition.

Several months later, working in her room at school, the secretary brought her a great pile of mail. Most of it had been opened and a certain degree of sorting out had already taken place. Forms which had to be filled in, letters from parents to think about and reply to, catalogues from various educational firms and applications from almost thirty people who were hoping to be short-listed for a vacant deputy headship. At the bottom of the pile was a type-written envelope with the words "PERSONAL – please forward if necessary" written clearly along the top; it had been posted in America. Libby placed it to the side of her desk to come back to later when she was having a coffee break and she turned her attention to the people who were hoping to come and work with her. She quickly glanced through the pile and was encouraged to think that at least half of them seemed to be distinct possibilities. She would pass them on to her senior management team for comments; whoever got the job would have to work with them very closely so it was important that they were involved in the process. Two letters from parents caused her more concern. One was from a mother whom she knew quite well. She had three children in the school, and another two had already passed through, she was writing about the youngest who had just been diagnosed as having meningitis and it appeared that her condition was quite serious. Libby knew the child well and put the letter down for a moment or two whilst she conjured up images of a happy and boisterous girl, with lovely eyes and a cheeky way of looking at you. She thought how cruel life could be for some people. The mother was an absolute gem, her husband had left her several years ago and she had brought up her family with enormous courage and commitment. Libby decided she would call round and see them on her way home.

The other letter was to tell her that one of her fifth form boys was now in trouble with the police and was unlikely to be back at school for some considerable time. She wrote a note and clipped it to the letter and sent it off to one of her staff who dealt with pastoral issues. They would not abandon the boy and would set procedures in motion to give whatever support they could to him and his family. He was a good boy but easily led astray and it really came as no surprise to her that he should end up in trouble, in many ways he was an accident waiting to happen. The letter didn't say what the trouble was but no doubt she would soon hear the sorry story. She recalled that he had quite a disciplinary record within the school; he was one of the few whom they seemed unable to inspire or communicate with. She wondered to what extent it was her failure and that of the school, which meant that he was now in trouble with the police. She felt this whenever there was such a problem. The truth was that she and the school did their utmost for such children but nonetheless she always felt that perhaps they could or should be doing more.

She was lost in a train of thought when the bell went signalling break time. How the time went, the morning was almost half way through and she hadn't finished with the mail yet. Not that she would expect to finish during the morning, she always read through letters first thing and then would usually settle down to answer them sometime around five o'clock when the children had gone home and after-school meetings had come to an end. She seldom went home before six thirty, needing the few hours of quietness to get her head around the problems of the day and the work that needed preparing for the next day. She looked out of her window and saw groups of pupils standing around together chatting or chasing around and burning off some of the pent-up energy which seemed to accompany them to school every day. It was basically a contented scene and she was proud of what they had been able to achieve over the years. Even her room gave her pleasure. She always managed to have flowers as well as plants, she had several paintings hanging, done by pupils over the years and there was the wall hanging that she had brought back from Swaziland and given to her mother. Sandra, her secretary appeared with a cup of coffee and she sat down to drink it and open her personal mail.

The address was Riverside Drive in New York and Libby was taken completely by surprise when she looked at the handwriting, for a moment she thought it looked like Paul's and she had to stop herself feeling suddenly elated. She turned it over and looked at the signature, it was indeed from Paul. She didn't read it straight away, instead she closed her eyes and tried to remember the last time they had any contact with each other. It didn't take much effort, even after all these years; it was the occasion of Celia's engagement, the evening before Robbie left, when the course of her life took yet one more of those unexpected turns. What would she be doing now, where would she be if she hadn't literally bumped into Paul that evening? Even now, after some twenty years, she didn't know whether she was pleased that they had met up again or not. She took a big breath and returned to the letter.

Dear Libby,

I hope that this eventually reaches you as I'm afraid that I don't have your home address.

As you see, I now live in New York and so my news from England is both partial and fragmentary, but I have just heard that you have been awarded an MBE and Celia has sent me a cutting from your local paper with your photograph and pictures of your school. I am so delighted for you and wanted to send you my warmest congratulations. It was a real bonus seeing the photograph, you don't seem to have changed one iota – I wish I could say the same about myself.

I don't suppose you know but I now work in New York. I gave up parliament at the last election and landed a job with the United Nations which I am enjoying. I wonder if you would be willing to have dinner with me next time I am in London?

I hear occasionally from Celia and Bruce was over here a few months ago with the Coriolanus and it was good to meet up with him in the middle of a crowded schedule. You can't beat old friends!

I do hope this reaches you and I hope that it might be possible to meet up. Please let me know. And many congratulations, it couldn't happen to a more deserving person.

Cheers

Paul

She suddenly felt quite sick and for a few moments was decidedly unsteady. She put the letter to one side, decided that she needed another coffee and thought she would walk over to the staff room; once there she would be assailed from all sides and this would have the effect of concentrating her mind on her work rather than agonising whether or not to accept the invitation to dinner. She quickly walked from her room and along the corridor, but even as she walked she knew that she would meet him again. Whether this was a sensible course of action she didn't know, but damn it, she was in her mid fifties, a head teacher and an MBE not a starry-eyed teenager, whatever was she thinking of! She replied a few days later saying that she would love to have dinner with him.

No.127 was a very discreet little restaurant in Chelsea. From the road it looked nothing at all, in fact Libby wondered if it was the right place when the taxi stopped outside. As she approached the door it opened and she was welcomed by a middle aged man, probably French, who smiled at her.

"Miss Arkwright? Ah yes, Dr.Crozier is waiting for you, please come this way."

He turned and led her through a dimly lit room, which was rather dark even in the middle of June, through some double doors and into another room which had French windows leading into a garden which stretched down to the Thames. As they walked into the garden Paul emerged from behind some shrubbery and moved towards her with his hands held out. There was a huge smile on his face as he leaned forward and kissed her chastely on each cheek.

"Libby, how wonderful to see you again. You look absolutely stunning."

He put his arm gently on her shoulder.

"Come on down to the river, I've a table down there with some rather nice cool wine, I thought we would just sit out for a while before we went inside to eat. That is, if that's alright with you, I mean, you won't be too cold will you?"

He walked down the garden with her, making small talk and covering up his nervousness so well that Libby had no idea that he was far from confident about this evening. They sat down and Paul poured a drink, a beautiful refreshing light wine. She took in his features as he busied himself. He looked much older, strained and prematurely grey. He caught her eye weighing him up and smiled.

"I'm afraid I'm not weathering nearly as well as you are," and once again she blushed because he had seen her scrutinizing him.

"But tell me, how did you get this honour, I was so delighted to read about it?"

"No, don't let's talk about that, tell me about your work, what is it?"

"I'm tied up with the UN bureaucracy these days. It's all very boring but someone needs to do it and it pays well."

"I had no idea what you were doing. I was vaguely aware that you were no longer in parliament, I mean I never saw you on the box or read anything about you so I assumed that you had moved on, but I didn't know what to or where or anything. It was such a surprise to get your letter from New York." She laughed, rather nervously.

"What happened? Did you lose your seat?"

"Libby, how could you? No I most certainly didn't! I never lost an election I stood for, I'm rather proud of that. On the other hand, I have to admit that my majority was shrinking fast. I decided that discretion was the better part of valour and I got out. Just as well, my successor got trounced."

"So how was parliament? Did you do anything special? You didn't get to be a minister or anything did you? I seem to remember that you had your eyes set on becoming Prime Minister when you were a student."

"Don't remind me of that. No, I never got into the cabinet, although I should have. I'm afraid that my face didn't fit. It's an absolute jungle in that place, it really is and I'm glad to be out of it. I can breathe more easily now."

They paused for a while, both sipping their wine and looking out over the river. There was so much to talk about and yet neither of them seemed in any hurry to break the silence. Their eyes met and Libby immediately dropped hers as they smiled.

"Tell me what you've been doing all these years. I hear snippets from Bruce and Celia but really I have no idea what your life has been like. You went to Africa, I know that and then we met, very briefly at Celia's party when you very definitely gave me the brush off."

"Oh no, it wasn't at all like that. I wasn't expecting to see you, it was a great surprise, you were with your wife – how is she by the way? – and I was there with Robbie, it was the evening before he went back to Swaziland."

"Tell me about him. Did you marry?"

"No, no, we didn't. We nearly did, but in the end it didn't seem right. But what about you, how is your wife?"

"Which one are you talking about? Libby, I've had so many that I can hardly recall their names. Perhaps we should go in and eat before we get bogged down in a rather tiresome story."

They moved inside. The table was by a window in the corner. They both looked out over the garden and could see the river. It was a marvellous setting, quite the best restaurant Libby had ever been in and she was sure that the food would match the setting although she wasn't sure that she really wanted much to eat. They ordered, talked about trivialities and then Libby brought the conversation back to their earlier exchanges.

"So, you've had several wives. That's news to me. I knew you had split up from your first one – I'm afraid I can't remember her name – but I haven't heard about any others."

"Look, I promise I'll tell you my story if you first tell me about your life. After all, we're here to celebrate your MBE and I want to know why you've been given it, what you've been up to, where you've been..."

"Too many questions Paul, too many questions. I can't possibly answer them all, but I'll give you a brief summary of my extremely ordinary life, it seems a fair exchange for hearing about the life of an international politician."

He pulled a face, slowly shook his head and listened intently as Libby told him about her time in Africa, about the disappearance of Miriam, about Maggie and her death, about her mother's journey into dementia and her friendship with Victoria. She talked to him about her school and what she was trying to do, about some of the problems they faced and the difficulties of providing a good education for poorer children in a society which continually undermined them. She spoke with passion, with a fluency that surprised her and suddenly she stopped.

"Paul, I've done nothing but talk about myself for the last hour. I'm sorry, I just didn't realise how the time was passing. I'm afraid all this lovely wine must have gone to my head. I hope I haven't bored you."

"Bored me? Libby, I wish you would go on for hours and hours. Your life seems so rich, so much more worthwhile than mine. I can see why they gave you an MBE, but they should have given you a knighthood or whatever the equivalent is for women, you are quite extraordinary."

Libby blushed, she knew that she had been carried away, she couldn't remember a time when she had felt so at ease and so able to express her thoughts.

"That's quite enough about me. What about you? What have you been up to all these years?"

Paul looked very pensive. He twisted his fork round and round in his hand, had another drink of wine and looked out of the window, at the lights across the river. He was finding it difficult to know how to begin, what to say. Libby waited, not wanting to break into his thoughts.

"I'm sure you remember that evening when I came round to your flat in Birmingham after you had, quite justifiably knocked me flying in the Festival Hall. You said on that occasion and I can remember the words so well, indeed they have haunted me over the years. You said 'Paul, you're an absolute shit', and you were right, my God how right you were. Libby I've spent the last forty years screwing up my life and the lives of most of the people around me. You never said a truer word. You know, a couple of weeks before I went off to the States, when we were students together, I went to see Amanda to tell her that I wanted to finish everything, that I didn't want to see her again. When I got there she told me that she was pregnant and that she had already told her parents. She said that she was going to join me in the States and we could sort our future out whilst we were there. I was totally overcome; it was as though a great cloud had descended on me. It was a cloud which has never lifted. I didn't know how to handle it. I had neither the courage nor the moral fibre to be honest with everyone, to be honest with anyone, especially with myself and so I just gave in. It ruined my life, it certainly did her no good and our child finished up as a drop-out who has wanted nothing to do with me for the last thirty years. The marriage was over before it began. I had a series of affairs – you must understand Libby that I am not proud of all this, I am just telling you as it is. You were right, I was, am, a complete shit."

"Eventually I married again and it was alright for a few years but then we drifted apart. I think they call it an 'open marriage' we both had various lovers and eventually she found one that she wanted to settle down with. The divorce was a relief. Since then I've been married again but that hasn't worked out either. I had a fairly long-term relationship with a woman, she loved me I know that, but I could never commit myself to her. In the end she had a mental breakdown and I never saw her again. I am in a relationship at the moment, she's an artist, but whether it will last is very unclear. With my record, I would have to bet against it. And that is me; a very different story to what one would imagine from looking at the pictures on the TV."

"Oh Paul, that's so sad, you deserve so much more than that. You always had such a burning passion for justice and for making a better world, you were really inspiring sometimes. Do you still have that passion?"

"Well, I'm not sure," said Paul, his face suddenly looking much older, his eyes sad and his voice little more than a whisper. "I would like to say that I have but I suppose that if I'm honest I would have to admit to becoming rather cynical and, God I'm ashamed if this, of feathering my own nest. You see, I earn quite a lot of money now. I'm a sort of *salon socialist*, with the emphasis more on the 'salon' – or saloon in my case, than socialist."

Libby remembered the burning idealism of the young Paul and wondered just when and why it had disappeared.

"I'm sorry that my outburst that evening has stayed with you, haunted you over the years. I'm sure you're not nearly as bad as you paint yourself out to be and I can't believe that the fault was always yours. And whilst I clearly thought that you were, as I so graphically put it, a 'shit', I wasn't intending to pass a judgment on your whole life or to cast a spell over your future years. Perhaps I shouldn't have said it, but I was very upset and extremely annoyed with myself for falling in love with you."

"No, you shouldn't have been annoyed with yourself. The truth was that I was in love with you, and I suppose I always have been. There, I've said it."

Libby leaned across the table and took his hand in hers.

"Don't say that Paul, don't say that. It isn't true, you know it isn't true. You've become rather emotional because of the good food and the wine and because we've shared so much. Don't let's stray into areas that we can't cope with."

She removed her hands; she needed to because she knew that if she didn't then her life could fall to pieces.

"Let's talk about something else. I must be off home soon and I don't want us to part feeling sad."

"Don't go Libby, stay here for a bit longer. Meeting you again has been the best thing that has happened for years. Why don't we get together again, for real this time?"

He leaned over to take her hands and below the table his legs stretched out to hold hers.

"Paul don't! Please don't start raising your hopes or playing around with my feelings. You know I can't do that. The time is past for us, it just wouldn't work. You know it, I know it, so please don't make it difficult for either of us. We're no longer students, those days are long since gone."

"But that's nonsense Libby. We're both free, neither of us has commitments to anyone else, unless your situation has changed. Why can't we give it a go? I know I'm almost forty years too late, but better late than never, surely you can see that."

"No, I don't see that. Paul, we almost made it together but we didn't. Anyway, you told me just an hour or so ago that you have a partner in New York. Too much has happened since our student days, for both of us. It's just lovely seeing you again, I'm sure you can see that. It's something very special, and I believe we have a very special bond of friendship which clearly the years have not been able to break, for either of us, but that's what it is Paul, friendship. Don't let's play, let's be grateful for what we have, it's very precious and it does mean a great deal to me, so don't let's spoil it."

Paul looked across at her, his eyes peering deep into hers so that she had to look down after a moment or two.

It was time for them to leave, Paul wanted her to promise to meet him again, the next time he was over, but Libby refused to make any commitment. She argued that they had both carved out their separate lives and they should continue to try and excel at the work they had chosen. This was their first meeting for twenty years and she was unwilling to say that it would not be another decade or more before they met again. As she rose from the table she swayed for a moment, going very pale. She sat down and Paul thought she was going to faint. He rushed round to hold her. In a few minutes she revived.

"Oh, I'm so sorry about that, it's just one of my funny turns – it's quite ridiculous really."

He was very concerned and started asking her questions about her health.

"No, I'm perfectly alright, there's absolutely nothing wrong with me. I just occasionally get these moments of tiredness, dizziness... oh, I don't know... honestly I'm fine."

"Libby, now listen to me, there is absolutely no way that I am going to let you go home by yourself... no, don't protest... I am taking you home and that's the end of the matter."

Not only did he take her home, he stayed with her. She didn't know whether she wanted him to stay or not, but she did little to protest. But she did protest when he slipped into her bed beside her, but not very strongly, her resolve quickly evaporating. She vaguely thought of raising the question of his current partner, presumably in New York somewhere – but what the hell, she turned over to face him, smiled, kissed him and held him in a way that she had never held anyone for almost forty years. He left the following morning, saying that he would phone her the next time he was in London. Either he didn't come back to London for a long time or he did come and never phoned, but it was to be six years before she saw him again.

It was the third time that Victoria had driven up this ramp onto the fifth floor. She couldn't believe it when she saw the sign. She'd been shopping and had parked the car in the multi-storey car park. Even though she had made a mental of note of where she'd parked she was distressed when she couldn't find the car when she returned with her bags full and her mind on other things. It took her over half an hour of walking round and round before she spotted it. She opened the rear door, threw the shopping onto the back seat and wearily climbed into the driver's seat. She waited a moment or two whilst she found a CD to her liking and then slowly reversed out of her space and began the journey home. At least, that was her intention, but here she was, once again, driving up to the fifth floor.

She pulled into a space, switched off the engine and burst into tears. A few minutes later she pulled herself together and decided to try again, but panic set in when she realised that she couldn't remember what she was trying to do. She decided to telephone home but there was no answer. She phoned Bill on his mobile. After no more than two or three rings he answered.

"Oh Bill, Bill, where are you?"

"What do you mean where am I? I'm at work, where do you think I am?"

"Bill, Bill, help me, please help me. I'm lost. I don't know how to get out of this place. I want to be home but I don't know where to go, how to get there."

He was immediately concerned and it took some considerable time for him to discover that she was in the car park.

"Look, don't panic my love. Just sit there and listen to some music and I'll come over and fetch you. It will take me a little while, will you be alright waiting, perhaps for half an hour? Or how about this, this is a better idea. Lock up the car and go back into the shopping centre and go and get a cup of tea. I'll see you in the Copper Kettle in about half an hour. OK? Victoria? Are you listening?" The phone was dead.

Bill phoned back. No answer. He tried again. This time Victoria answered.

"Hello? Oh Bill, it's you. How are things? What do you want? I can't really talk now unless it's important, I'm just on my way home. I'm in the car park; I'll be back in about twenty minutes, is that alright or was it something important?"

"Victoria? Are you alright? What are you doing exactly?"

"What am I doing? What do you think I'm doing? I'm just on my way home."

"But you've just phoned me to say that you're lost."

"What on earth are you talking about? I've never phoned you. I've been doing some shopping and now I'm on my way back home. Are you alright Bill?"

"No, that's fine, that's fine. I'll see you at home. I'll finish off what I'm doing now and get back home. I should be there soon after you. Bye my love."

He placed the phone on the desk in front of him and sat and stared at it. This was the fourth or fifth time this week that Victoria had phoned him, each time she was in some sort of distress. Each time she later denied any knowledge of calling him. Something was going on; he knew that he couldn't deny it any longer. Something was wrong with Victoria and he would have to find out what it was.

Once he had reached that decision his mind seemed to clear. This wasn't a recent phenomenon; there had been something adrift for a long time. He tried to think back over the last year, over the last two years, and began to see that there were a whole number of little incidents, trifling in themselves, but when viewed together, they built up an almost irresistible case for concluding that something was wrong. He remembered the time when she had thrown her house keys away, thinking that they were the keys to their previous house. He remembered her saying that she was surprised that she had kept them on her key ring all these years. She simply took them off one day and dropped them into the dustbin. By the time they had worked out what had happened to them the bins had been emptied. Twice she had failed to meet up with Libby when they were going out. On one occasion she stood by the barriers at London Bridge underground station whilst Libby was waiting for her by the ticket office at London Bridge mainline station. On the other occasion she had gone into London and simply failed to turn up at all. When Libby eventually spoke to her on the telephone several hours later it transpired that she had decided to go to the National Gallery having completely forgotten that she was meant to be going to the Albert Hall. Then there was the time when she had forgotten to do any shopping and they ran out of some essential items, Bill couldn't remember what they were but he could vividly remember feeling quite annoyed although he had never expressed it at the time. The more he thought about things the more Bill realised that problems had been mounting up for months and months and he was annoyed with himself for being so blind. He made his way home very pensive, feeling anxious and fearful for the future.

When he reached home Victoria was sitting in the garden drinking a cup of tea. He made himself a coffee and went out to join her. She gave him a wonderful smile as he approached and as he leaned down to kiss her he realised just how much his love for her had grown and matured over the years. He could not imagine life without her, she was all that he had ever wanted. He smiled at her, wondering how best to raise the subject.

"Victoria my love, are you feeling alright? I mean, is anything wrong at all?"

"Anything wrong? Why of course not, why should there be? Really darling, you do sometimes talk in the most extraordinary way. Whatever makes you think that something is wrong?"

"Well, when you phoned me from the car park you said that you were lost, that you couldn't find the way out."

"Bill, what a strange thing to say. I've never phoned you from a car park. I've been here all day, sitting in the garden. Whatever made you think that I'd been out? And as for getting lost in a car park... I sometimes think that you are imagining things. You work too hard Bill, perhaps you should ease off a bit. I know, why don't we have a holiday, it would do you the world of good."

"But that's ridiculous, I don't need a holiday, we've only been back from Spain less than a fortnight, don't you remember?"

"Oh yes, of course. Whatever am I thinking of? Anyway, it's lovely that you have come home, I wasn't expecting you for hours."

"But I phoned you a short while ago and said I would be back within half an hour. Don't you remember?"

"Did you? Well, it must have completely slipped my mind, how silly of me. Did you say anything else?"

He frowned, he was moving into territory that he didn't understand and he was unsure how to proceed.

"Listen to me Victoria; listen very carefully because I'm not sure how to put this. My darling, I think there must be something wrong with you, you know, with your memory. You don't seem to remember that you keep phoning me up; you don't seem to remember what you've been doing. I don't know what's happening but something is wrong and we need to get to the bottom of it."

"What on earth are you talking about? There's absolutely nothing wrong with me, I can't imagine what's got into you." She was almost sharp in her response, almost angry, but not quite. "Look, sit down and have a rest and I'll go inside and get us something to eat. Really, I've never heard such nonsense."

She picked up her cup and saucer and made her way inside leaving him even more bewildered and feeling that he had made a complete mess of trying to get things sorted. He got up from his seat and walked around the garden. There was work to be done. They had just returned from two weeks in Spain and it was already showing signs of neglect. That was the problem of having such an immaculate garden, you noticed neglect after just a few days away. He thought about their time away and tried to remember if there had been any indications then that Victoria might have a problem, but he couldn't focus on anything. The problems seemed to occur when she was on her own, when he was away from home and she was left to fend for herself. He continued to walk around the garden and then, on his way back to the kitchen he passed Victoria's car. He had no idea what made him walk that particular route, but as he passed her car he glanced inside and saw four or five shopping bags on the back seat. He called Victoria to the car and asked what they were if she hadn't been out shopping. She looked at them in amazement.

"Bill, this is really weird. Someone must have come up our drive and put those things into my car."

"But how could they, the car is locked?"

"Then that's even weirder. There must be someone round here who has the keys to my car. What do you think we should do?"

"I think we should get your shopping out of the car and into the house and perhaps have a talk about it later."

Bill hoped that perhaps the trouble, whatever it was, had resolved itself, although he didn't think that Victoria was looking as well as she used to and he thought that she'd lost some of her sparkle and vitality. Perhaps it was that they were just getting older. Perhaps it was the fact that the grandchildren, although a sheer delight, were also quite demanding and tiring. Or again, perhaps Bill was imagining things; perhaps it was his mind that was playing tricks and not hers.

Meanwhile Victoria was growing anxious. She sometimes felt that her mind was slipping away. She couldn't quite explain it to herself and she certainly was not going to try and explain it to anyone else. At all costs she wanted to hide the position from Bill, she didn't want him to worry. It was just that at times she suddenly felt lost and couldn't remember what she was doing or where she was. She had to work hard and concentrate or else she found herself doing silly little things. She never told Bill, but one day she found that she had put the shopping into the oven rather than into the refrigerator. Once or twice she had completely forgotten how to cook a recipe that she had used for years and years and just recently, to her great embarrassment, she had failed to recognise her next door neighbour when she popped round to see her.

The children were all too busy with their own lives and families to notice anything untoward, although they had, quite often, laughed amongst themselves about how scatty she was becoming. Matters came to a head in a most unexpected way. Bill returned home from work one day and was surprised to find that Victoria was out, although the door was not locked. He looked around for a note and not finding one thought that she must have popped out to the shops in her car for something. When, an hour or more later she hadn't returned he became anxious. He had tried her mobile several times and got no reply, so he telephoned the children and then Libby to see if they knew where she was. Each enquiry drew a blank. By nine o'clock he was extremely worried and decided to telephone the police in case there had been an accident somewhere. Nothing had been reported but they took the details of her car and said that they would make enquiries. He was at his wits' end, he didn't know what to do and he couldn't settle. He didn't want to worry the children unduly but felt the need to talk to someone. As soon as he phoned anyone he quickly terminated the conversation just in case someone was phoning him with any news. It was almost a surreal state of existence and he had no idea how to cope with it. It was shortly before midnight when he got a phone call from Mike, Maggie's former husband, whom he hadn't seen or spoken to since Maggie's funeral fifteen or more years ago.

"Oh thank God you're there Bill," said Mike. "I was worried that you might have moved house again and then I wouldn't have known what number to ring. The thing is, we've got Victoria here. She seems very strange; she's been walking through the streets saying that she can't get into her house. She must have remembered where we lived and came knocking at the door about ten minutes ago. She doesn't seem to know who we are, but obviously knew the way here and had no hesitation in coming in when we managed to make ourselves decent and get downstairs. She seems to be staring a lot, to be quite honest I didn't recognise her at first, it was Jenny who saw who she was."

"Mike, that's wonderful. I've been worried sick since I realised she'd disappeared. I came back from work and found she wasn't here. I've been in touch with the police and everything. Is it possible to talk to her?"

Mike handed the phone over to her saying that Bill wanted to have a few words.

"Bill? Bill? Who's Bill?" she murmured as she took the phone.

"Victoria darling, thank God you're safe. How are you feeling? Look, I'll just put a few things in a bag and jump into the car and I'll be with you in time for some breakfast. Is that alright? Victoria?"

Mike took the phone back.

"I don't think she's able to recognise you Bill, and she doesn't seem able to talk."

"Mike, I'm sorry about all this, can you make her comfortable, settle her down, see if you can get her to sleep and I'll jump in the car and be with you in a few hours time. Better still, do you think you could call a doctor and explain what's happened? He might be able to give her something to make her sleep. Explain that I'm on my way. Oh thank God you've got her. I'll be with you in a few hours Mike. I'd better let the kids know what's happened and Libby, I suppose – Oh poor, poor, thing..."

He pulled himself together and phoned the rest of the family. Libby insisted that he make a detour on the way north through London to pick her up. She said he would need company; that she would be able to help with Victoria and, at the very least, she would be able to drive Victoria's car back. Bill's protest was weak and within an hour they were both together driving north.

She realised that this was probably the longest time she had ever spent alone with Bill and, despite the circumstances, she enjoyed the opportunity of talking to him at a serious level. She learned about his growing suspicions about Victoria's health and was able to share her own anxieties which had been growing over the last eighteen months.

"I think your mother's illness took a lot out of her," said Bill. "She was really very distressed and although the nursing home was a big improvement on where she was before, I think she was never very happy about the way your mother was treated there. She often used to come home and say that it was as though she'd already died, that the people there treated her as a non-person somehow. I remember one day she was terribly upset when she went in and found your mother in someone else's clothes; they seemed to have completely lost hers. I'm afraid I wasn't a great help to her, I didn't understand what was wrong with Beryl and I suppose I just opted out of things really. I was happy to see that all the bills were paid and was more than happy for Victoria to spend time with her, but I can see now that I didn't really appreciate what was happening and the toll that it was taking on her."

"Oh Bill, I don't think any of us realised. I know that I found it incredibly difficult, trying to see her regularly whilst keeping on top of my job. I think I felt guilty most of the time. Of course I knew that Victoria was doing the bulk of the caring and I suppose I was happy for it to remain that way. I feel terrible now when I stop and think about it."

"No, I don't think you should feel guilty," Bill responded. "You did really well and I know Victoria never for a moment felt that you were not pulling your weight. You had a job to hold down and, if the truth be told, Victoria did have the time and, when necessary the money, to go and spend more time with her. Do you think that she has the same thing that your mother had? I mean, is she going to lose her memory and not know us? It's a terrible thought; the children and grandchildren would be devastated, they all adore her. Yes, they adore her... and so do I."

Bill's voice became very quiet. Libby didn't say anything, there was nothing to add and they both needed some space to sort out their thoughts.

There was little traffic on the road at this time of the night and he was able to drive at speed in a car far beyond anything that Libby had experienced before in terms of comfort. They stopped at a motorway service station for a comfort break and a cup of coffee and the dawn was beginning to break by the time they were on the road again. True to his word, Bill drew up at Mike's house shortly before breakfast time and was relieved to see that Jenny was waiting for them, giving them a welcome which was heartfelt and re-assuring. The doctor had been and had given Victoria an injection which had the effect of sending her to sleep almost straight away and she hadn't stirred since then. Jenny had stayed up with her all night whilst Mike went back to bed as he had to be up and at work soon after seven thirty. Bill went upstairs and sat by her bed, holding her hand and gently stroking it. He spoke quietly to her but she remained asleep. Libby remained downstairs with Jenny and before long they both fell asleep, sitting in the easy chairs and grateful that the immediate crisis seemed to be passing, although neither knew what might happen when Victoria eventually woke up.

It was mid-day before she opened her eyes and saw Bill smiling and looking into her face with love and tenderness. She smiled as he squeezed her hand.

"Hello my darling, welcome back to the land of the living. How are you feeling?"

She was tired and rather confused as to where she was, but was able to speak to Bill clearly and sensibly. After half an hour or so, with his encouragement, she was able to get up and join the others downstairs.

"My, what chaos I've brought to you all. Whatever got into me? I've no recollection of driving up here, none whatsoever. Jenny, I'm so sorry. What a fright I must have given you, but thank you so much, Bill tells me that you were wonderful."

Three days later Bill sat with Victoria in Dr Shakespeare's surgery. He was a large, rather blunt man, coming originally from Australia but having worked in England for most of his life. He was not their normal doctor, he was away, and so they had to familiarise themselves with this approach which, to begin with, they found quite intimidating. He stared at them for quite a while, made several grunts and asked them to go over the story of the last few days one more time. Victoria was nervous, reluctant to reveal what she could remember about the events whilst Bill was talking too much, covering up his anxiety with too many words. Jim Shakespeare was used to this, he knew he had to listen with intense concentration and he didn't think that they were being completely honest or open with him.

"So let me get this right, you have not been aware of any previous problems?"

He looked straight into Victoria's eyes and she turned them away, unable to cope with the searching look that seemed to go right through her.

"No, I didn't say that," whispered Victoria. "I mean, I think I have been aware of getting things wrong for quite a time now. I suppose I didn't want to admit it. I didn't want Bill to know. He's so busy and I didn't want to be a burden to him."

"But surely he must have known, you can't live with someone for as long as you have been married and not notice these things. Didn't you realise that he was aware of something being wrong?"

"Well, yes, I suppose I was aware, but I didn't want to acknowledge it."

"But do you acknowledge it now? Do you accept that there is something happening within you that makes you act in ways that you would not normally expect to? Do you accept that there are problems with your memory?"

"Yes, yes... I can't really hide from it any more, can I?"

Tears came into her eyes and she turned her face away so that the doctor might not witness her distress, but nor did she want Bill to witness it either. She looked down into her lap.

"Excellent. I know that it hasn't been easy for you admitting this, and I'm sorry if I seemed to be pressing you harder than you wanted me to, but I had to hear you acknowledge that something is wrong. Admitting that you have a problem is a major step towards finding out how best we can address it."

Bill suddenly looked relieved. He was beginning to dislike this Australian doctor who had suddenly been landed on them but now he understood what he was doing. He had been almost totally unsuccessful in persuading Victoria that there was something wrong. He'd been trying for weeks, months now, but always to no avail. Even this last trip north and her disappearance had been brushed aside by Victoria once she had regained her strength. It had been unbelievably difficult to persuade her to come to the surgery. Dr Shakespeare had listened to his story, had listened patiently as he had recounted episodes small and large that had troubled him over the months. Bill was aware of the pain that this was causing Victoria and he felt that he was betraying her as he spoke. Nevertheless he pressed on, feeling that there might not be another chance and he needed to let it all pour out.

Victoria, of course, denied most of what he was saying, and he was aware of a huge sadness enveloping her. He couldn't believe what he was hearing when Victoria began to speak. She denied that there were any problems, she wasn't aware of getting things mixed up and even this latest episode seemed to be explained away by saying that she went up to settle a few things of her mother's. It seemed to him that she was in complete denial. Dr Shakespeare spoke to her with insight and firmness, never rude, never aggressive but insistently questioning her until she reached a point of admittance.

"Now that we have ascertained that there is a problem; a problem with your memory and a problem with some of your actions which you don't seem to be able to explain or understand, we have to try and find out what is causing that problem. This may well take us some time. There are many possible causes and we are going to have to work through them and see if we can eliminate them one by one. For instance, it may be because you are depressed. Perhaps you have a deep-seated depression, possibly caused by your mother's death, I don't know. Or it may be a dietary matter, sometimes we can eat certain things and these have an effect on the way that our brain works. What I am going to do is to begin a process which I hope will make things clearer for all of us. Now does that make sense?"

Bill and Victoria nodded, in agreement.

"Whilst we are doing these tests, I want you to try and keep a diary and just make a note of any little incident, no matter how trivial it might seem. Then we can begin to see if there is a pattern. Now it's important that you co-operate with me, I can't do this alone. If we all work together, then there is a better chance that we might discover what's at the heart of all this. I want to emphasise that there is nothing to be ashamed of, there is nothing to hide, and it's absolutely fine whatever you do. If we can adopt that sort of attitude then we shall almost certainly make good progress. I'll arrange for you to have some tests, nothing frightening, just routine things to get us going."

When they returned to the waiting room Bill realised that they had been with the doctor for almost an hour. He wondered how many people were waiting, irritated that their appointment time had been missed. He felt slightly guilty but not unduly so. His prevailing feeling was one of intense relief. He knew that their concerns had been heard, that the doctor had gone at a pace that they could both understand, and that they were now in this together, helping and supporting one another.

They kept their diary together, logging in the various little incidents that were both a source of amusement as well as being an increasing worry. The loss of the car keys – several times. The loss of the car – in the car park but on a different floor. The time Bill hunted for the kettle and found it in the fridge. Victoria twice forgot the birthdays of her children and occasionally couldn't remember the names of her grandchildren. Most of these incidents were relatively small but when logged together they began to look quite serious. What was not logged in the book, but was noticed by Bill with considerable sadness, was the fact that Victoria seemed to be losing interest in his world, she forgot to ask him questions about where he was going or whom he had met. Also, she left him to do most of the telephoning to their friends, something which he had always left to her, and he noticed that some days seemed to go by and Victoria had little idea about how she had spent her time. He was able to discuss this with Dr Shakespeare when he once went about a minor health problem of his own. He was careful not to exaggerate the situation, for most of the time everything proceeded in a normal sort of way and few people would have noticed anything amiss. The children were increasingly aware, of course and so was Libby, but apart from them he didn't think other people were aware of what was happening. It was several months later, after quite a lot of tests and after Victoria had been visited by a psycho-geriatrician that they were called back to the surgery.

Dr Shakespeare looked across at them and smiled, he could sense their apprehension and he knew that there was no easy way to break the news to them. On the other hand, in his experience, discussing a diagnosis rarely came as a surprise to people and sometimes it was almost a relief for people to have a definite name given to whatever it was that was troubling them.

"We have done all the tests that we can and as far as I am able to discern these things I'm afraid that I have to tell you that you probably have Alzheimer's disease. I say this very guardedly because Alzheimer's is a very difficult condition to diagnose, but I am satisfied in my own mind that this is what has been causing you these problems. I would go further and hazard a guess that you have probably had it for about five years, which is usually the case with Alzheimer's. Now I know that you must have been hoping that this wasn't what was wrong with you, and although it's a serious condition you must not lose heart. There is much that we can do to help and support you."

Victoria's eyes welled up with tears and she found it difficult to speak.

"I thought all along that it was probably that. It's what mum had, dementia, although no-one actually spoke to us about it, and I always dreaded having it myself and now it's happened."

She turned to Bill and grasped his hand as he moved over to her, pulling his chair up and putting his arm around her shoulder.

"Alzheimer's is a disease that affects the brain," explained Dr Shakespeare. "Perhaps the easiest way I can describe it is to ask you to imagine that the brain is rather like a sponge, you know, with lots of holes in it. With Alzheimer's disease it is as though these holes get bigger and bigger. The memory becomes affected, we are not totally sure how at the moment. We used to think that people lost their memory, but there is now a lot of evidence to suggest that the memory is still there, somewhere, and what we have lost is the way that we gain access to that memory. It's probably very difficult for you to take this on board at the moment. I've got a couple of booklets here which tell you more about it and there's also a card giving you the address and phone number of the local Alzheimer's Society. I suggest that you let the news sink in and perhaps give them a ring in a few days. You will discover that you are not alone, there are many others who are facing the same issues and I'm sure you can gain understanding and support from them. What I suggest is that you read through the booklets and make an appointment to come and see me again in three or four days time and I can try and answer any questions you may have and together we can try and agree upon a way forward for you both. I'm sure that it's all rather difficult to get your head round at the moment."

They made their way home without saying much, there seemed to be little to say. They had both been expecting it and yet, when it came it came with a sense of devastation. But nothing new had happened that afternoon, they were the same when they came back from the surgery as they had been when they went and yet it was as though their whole world had changed, that nothing could ever be the same again. They both had images of Beryl in their mind as they drove along. Beryl stretched out on the bed, with saliva running from her mouth and her eyes staring at them with frightened incomprehension. Beryl sitting in her room for hour upon hour with the shouting and screaming of the person in the other bed making the place intolerable for everyone, except apparently, for her. Beryl rocking to and fro for hours on end.

Libby came round that evening and they talked together about the future and about their fears,

"I guess that this is the beginning of a journey into a strange land," said Victoria as she made a valiant effort to eat the food which she had cooked.

"It's a strange land for us all," commented Libby, "but you can rest assured that you will not be making the journey alone, we shall be with you all the way, no matter where it leads or how long it takes."

After Libby had gone home Bill and Victoria washed up together and got ready for bed. She was soon asleep but he found sleep elusive and after an hour or more in bed he was still wide awake. He got up, went downstairs and made a cup of tea. Sitting down he began to review his life, looking back with immense gratitude for all that he had shared with Victoria. He looked to the future and a sense of dread overcame him. What would happen? How would they cope? How long had they got together before the illness took her away from him?

After the sense of sorrow, he felt angry. Why should this happen to Victoria? Why should it happen to him? Of all the people he knew she was the kindest, so why should she be the one to suffer? It wasn't right, she didn't deserve it. She was one of the best people, not fickle or irresponsible, not immoral or a burden to society. Why should good people suffer and others, who weren't a patch on her, get by without problems like this. He was not given to introspection, he was a practical man who liked to get on with a job and he was unused to thinking about things for overlong. Neither was he used to having to cope with upsurges of emotion. He was finding it difficult to handle the immense sense of loss and sorrow and realised that he was near to tears and couldn't remember the last time he had cried.

He hadn't cried when his mother died, nor when his father died; he had wanted to but the tears never came. He thought that probably the last time he was aware of tears was when his first child was born and he was totally overcome by the sheer miracle of childbirth. Now, forty or more years later he was overcome by the prospect of the loss of Victoria. He was going to have to deal with it and, being the practical man that he prided himself on being, he set about forming plan. He would make her illness a project, the most demanding and important project that he had ever embarked upon. He would plan it, share his ideas with her and together they would try and make the next few years the best in their lives. Once he had decided on such a course of action he began to feel better and he began to feel tired. He went to bed, put his arms around the sleeping Victoria and sank into a deep sleep.

They decided that they would be completely open about her diagnosis and arranged a special dinner party for the whole family a couple of weeks later. Victoria felt enormously heartened and comforted and Bill felt that, in some strange way, it had brought him even closer to his family. For their part, the children felt proud of the way their parents were handling things and their natural sadness and grief was tempered by a sense of rediscovering the heart of the family again. It had been a long time since they had all met for a meal together and Victoria felt that, in some way, they had transformed the awfulness of the diagnosis into an opportunity for celebration. She went to bed happier that night than she had been for a very long time.

For the first year after her diagnosis they set about doing many of the things they had talked about doing in their retirement. They went on their cruise, they went to Spain, to Florida, to the Dutch bulb fields where Victoria felt a great sense of her mother's presence. They went to the theatre, to the cinema and spent time walking around those parts of London that people who live there so often take for granted. Libby went to art galleries and concerts with her and enjoyed meeting up for afternoon tea in Harrods and the Ritz. The grandchildren visited more often, the children phoned more often and Bill spent far less time at work, just going in when it suited him. To the outsider Victoria seemed the same as ever although Bill was aware of subtle changes. It was more difficult to plan ahead, she would get her dates mixed up and he became a very proficient diary secretary. She would forget birthdays and he was the one who kept an eye on the calendar, and she often got confused when the telephone went and would quickly hand it over to him, even when it was the children who were phoning. They laughed together at some of the more bizarre things that she did. Did they really need the twelve new saucepans that she ordered and was putting two pairs of shoes into the washing machine really the best way to clean them? She lost her watch on an almost daily basis and Bill decided that it made sense to have a duplicate pair of glasses because she often had no idea where they were, even when she was wearing them!

The following year it was more difficult to leave her alone in the house. Bill came back from work one day to find her walking around the house in her thick winter coat carrying a suitcase. When she saw Bill she asked him where she was and where was it that she was meant to be going. He decided that it was time to retire and after that he seldom left her alone. Going out together was still a pleasurable activity although it was occasionally problematic when she wanted to go to the toilet and sometimes he had to ask someone to accompany her as she became disoriented and occasionally panicked when she went by herself. He was aware of the fact that her world was beginning to diminish. She was less interested in things that were happening, she seldom asked about his concerns nor did she speak about the children on her own accord, only when he raised the subject.

There were regular routine medical checks. These revealed a progressive decline in her cognitive functions. She was advised to stop driving and her licence was taken away. Fortunately this didn't prove to be a difficulty and for this they were immensely grateful. Nor did she develop any aggressive tendencies, the changes in her personality being more in the direction of a greater introversion. They were never quite sure when her memory loss really gave cause for greater concern but the whole family seemed to recognise that the deterioration was quite sudden and distressing. Speaking to Libby one day Victoria asked her what her name was.

"Oh Victoria, you know who I am. I'm Libby."

"Yes, but Libby who? What's your full name?"

"Libby. Libby Arkwright."

"Really? Libby Arkwright? I used to be called Arkwright. Fancy that, we had the same name, although I don't think I was ever called Libby, was I?"

"But of course we had the same name, we're sisters. We grew up together, don't you remember?"

"Sister? Oh no, you're mistaken there. I've got no sisters. If I had sisters I would know them and they would come to see me. I don't think you're my sister. You're my friend, my best friend. You and my mother should meet, she would like you. Where do you live?"

Libby looked at her in amazement. This was the first time that Victoria had failed to recognise her and she found it really distressing. Talking it through with Bill afterwards he confessed that this had been going on for some time. She often didn't know him, confusing him for someone else. On one occasion she thought he was her father and was horrified when he climbed into bed with her. He said that he had to go and sleep in a different room; in fact he often slept alone now as she seemed to get very confused when he was there. On other occasions everything was fine and she would cuddle up to him and tell him how much she loved him. At first it hurt him, but he realised that it was all part of the illness. The main problem, he said, was the unpredictability of it all. He never knew from one day to the next, from one hour to the next, if she would recognise him.

Two days later Bill lost her. One minute she was in the garden whilst he was preparing a meal and when he came out she had disappeared. He looked all around, walked up and down the street and looked everywhere for her, all in vain. He was in a state of near desperation when he received a phone call from a neighbour living about ten houses away.

"Bill? It's Sandy here. Look, I hope you don't mind me calling you but I've just looked out of the window and I can see Victoria in our garden. She's swinging on the children's swing and singing in a very loud voice. I know that you've mentioned that she's ill so I thought I would let you know rather than go down to her myself in case I frighten her. It's no problem to us that she's in the garden, so don't be embarrassed, but I thought you might be worrying."

"Oh thank God for that Sandy, thank you. I've been going mad trying to find her – I've been up and down the road, past your house, of course, but I never thought to look into people's gardens. I'll be with you in just a couple of minutes. Thank you so much for phoning."

Bill had to erect a gate across the drive with a combination lock so that Victoria couldn't just walk out. She was beginning to decline quite markedly now and the family were increasingly concerned. Although at first she didn't want to go, they managed to persuade her to accept the doctor's advice that she attend a local day centre. At first she went just one morning a week, then it became two and within six months she was attending three whole days a week. It gave Bill some space, allowed him to sort out many of the domestic issues like washing and shopping and also it enabled him to play golf again, the first time for about eighteen months.

It was now four years since the dementia was diagnosed. It seemed both as yesterday and also as though it had always been the case. There is no space for time in dementia, time stands still. Time is a commodity for those who are busy, who live by diaries, calendars and clocks. You need none of these things when you just exist, when your days pass almost unnoticed, each one there to be lived through, full of incidents full of pauses. Time becomes irrelevant, what is it but the passing of days, the journeys of the earth around the sun, the changing of the seasons? Time is not life. Life is something entirely different. Bill knew that, so did Victoria. Life was about the smiles that they exchanged without the need for words. Life was about the way Bill massaged her hands with cream, brushed her hair, cleaned her teeth and ensured that day by day she continued to look good and wore clothes which suited her. Life was about having a grandchild on your knee even though you did not understand the relationship or remember the name. Life was being surrounded by people who loved you and whose love was unconditional.

Three months after their Golden Wedding Victoria moved into a nursing home. It was the most difficult decision that Bill had ever had to make. He felt consumed with guilt even though everyone around him had been advising him to do it for many months. Life had become increasingly difficult for them all. He knew that he was lucky in as much as Victoria hadn't undergone a personality change like some people do, she was still, essentially the same as she had always been, but the deterioration in her condition was proving to be more and more demanding and basically Bill was physically and emotionally drained. He had agonised over it, spoken to people whom he'd met through various Alzheimer support groups and had long discussions with the family. In the end it was a psychiatric nurse who persuaded him, arguing that it could improve the quality of Victoria's life and, paradoxically, give her more freedom, more independence than staying in her own home.

Albion Lodge seemed to offer the type of care that Bill was looking for and arrangements were made for her to have a room there. Some of their own furniture was moved into the room, her favourite pictures, her chair, photographs of all the family and many of her CDs. The care staff understood that she liked music and a list of CDs was drawn up so that they could play her the music she liked. They created a great scrapbook of photographs of all the family, with their names and little stories about them. It also contained photographs of some of their favourite places. It was to prove to be a marvellous help to visitors and care staff as they had something to look at and share with Victoria. The whole family was told that this was now her home and they were free to visit her at any time of day or night. They were to make themselves at home just as they would have done at her family home. There was a hairdressing room, which she went to every week, several lounges and a programme of activities ranging from keep fit to visits to art galleries. Victoria was free to mix or to remain in her room, she could join in activities or she could refrain from doing so. She had a choice. In fact, it was made very clear to Bill that the whole ethos of Albion Lodge was to allow people to make as many choices as possible. The intention was to empower them rather than to disempower them and every effort was made to encourage residents to take as much control over their lives as was possible. Bill could see that, by being there, Victoria had more opportunities than he was able to provide for her at home and this gave him great deal of comfort.

Early in her retirement Libby set about learning more about her family's history. She began by seeking out information about her father. Her mother had consistently refused to talk about him and although this was hurtful to the young Libby she intuitively understood that this was how it had to be. Now, she appreciated much more just how difficult her mother's life had been. It was only now, with her mother dead and with time on her hands that she knew it was permissible, at last, to search out her father and learn more about the influences that had shaped her mother's life. Knowing that her mother was born in 1910 she decided to begin about then and see if she could imagine the world which her mother and father frequented.

She knew nothing at all about her mother's family apart from a vague recollection of her grandmother. She remembered her as a small, very elderly woman who visited them every week for a bath. She knew that her mother came from a large family but she had never heard her speak about any brothers or sisters apart from one reference when she was young and learning to swim, to a brother who had apparently drowned as a child. She knew absolutely nothing about her father's family, she had no idea where he was born what he did or what sort of a family he came from. She had never thought much about it before, but now, when she did think about it, it seemed extraordinary just how closed her mother's mind had been about any matters relating to the past. It was as though the past no longer counted for anything, it was only the present that mattered and the future mattered only in so far as it was a continuation of the present. She had resolutely turned her face to look only in one direction, the past was the past, she used to say, and there is nothing that we can do about it, we must live for the present.

Libby however, wanted to know about the past. She wanted to know where she had come from and what forces, what circumstances had combined to make her the person she was. She realised, as she spoke with her friends that few of them knew anything about their families beyond their grandparents, that was about as far back as anyone went. Within two generations all that we are and all that we have done are forgotten, lost, as though we never existed. She wanted to know who the people were who gave her her name and her character and what they did. Perhaps it was witnessing the decline of Victoria that made Libby realise that she was the last of her generation in the family and when she died there would be no-one to keep alive the remembrance.

She discovered things about her grandfather's death during the battle of the Somme and then she set about trying to discover if there was a memorial to him anywhere. Her search came to an end in an almost derelict and overgrown graveyard. She stood there one autumn morning; the sky overcast and a touch of drizzle in the air, and looked at a large Memorial Cross, set up on a plinth above four steps. She read the inscription *To The Glorious Dead. Their Name Liveth For Evermore*. Beneath were listed the names of over a hundred young men, all of them cut down before their time and included in the list she found the name of private Albert Skinner, her grandfather. She looked around. The graveyard was in a state of serious decay, it was clear that no maintenance work had been done for several years and before too long the tall proud monument, with its boast of everlasting remembrance, would topple to the ground. Already it leaned forward at an alarming angle, and no-one appeared to care. Grass and small shoots were growing from the spaces between the parts of the masonry which once would have been as upright as soldiers on parade. She saw two women standing talking to each other a short distance away whilst their dogs relieved themselves among the gravestones. Beyond them she saw a young man, dishevelled and dirty, collecting broken branches and piling them on top of the small fire he had lit at the back of large family monument, an angel leaning forward with the top of its left wing broken off. Was it for this that her grandfather had died? She left the cemetery with a deep sense of sorrow and as she walked back, through the graves her eyes caught sight of a small headstone commemorating the life of a nineteen year old boy who had died shortly after her grandfather, 'following wounds received in battle'. She read the inscription:

> *Father, in thy gracious keeping,*
> *Leave we now thy servant sleeping*

Her heart went out to the grieving parents, themselves now long dead, who had buried their son here, in a burial ground which had been opened up especially at that time to cope with the wounded and the dying and the grieving. How many of them were now remembered? She pulled her coat together more tightly to stave off the coolness of the air and she yearned to be back home in London.

Her researches found that her mother had been born into a large family but she was puzzled by the fact that the youngest child, named Albert, presumably after Lizzie's husband was born some two years after the battle of the Somme and the death of Albert Skinner. Libby felt annoyed that her mother was no longer around to answer the growing number of questions that were being raised as she delved into the family's history.

Further work revealed facts about her own father that she'd never known. He had a brother and sister, but she had never heard any mention of them by her mother. Perhaps there had been a family crisis and that was the reason why they were never mentioned because, try as she could to remember, Libby had no recollection whatsoever of ever having heard anything about her father's family. Perhaps it was another example of her mother's ability to close her mind to things that she didn't want to be reminded of.

She worked her way through a great many regimental papers and was able to put together a reasonably coherent description of what happened on the fateful day when her father was killed. She decided to visit Dunkirk, to see for herself just where he had been, to see the sea from that perspective and to breathe the air that he might once have breathed. She prepared herself well for the trip but was unprepared for what she found. Grave after grave after grave in the cemetery, and then, the seeming endless list of names on the memorial tablets, each one representing the hopes and aspirations of families and friends, wives, mothers, lovers, fathers... and there, amongst them all she saw her father's name; Frank Arkwright. More than four thousand five hundred names were engraved on a series of rectangular slabs which formed columns on either side of a large avenue. She walked slowly along this broad pathway until she came to a small chapel or shrine which contained a beautiful engraved window showing scenes from the debacle of Dunkirk. She stood and could not stop herself from weeping. Why had she never been before? Why had her mother not been? Why had she not spoken about it? Why had he been killed? So many questions and no satisfactory answers. As she stood there she became very conscious of Maggie and wondered how differently her life might have turned out if she had ever known her father.

Throughout her illness Victoria maintained her interest in crosswords although she was no longer able to compile them. It was something that she could do with Bill and they spent many a happy hour together filling in books full of puzzles. As time went by they moved away from cryptic puzzles which she could no longer do and moved to easier puzzles with larger letters and more obvious grids. She sometimes completed them herself in the earlier days, and the family gained a poignant sort of loving amusement when they sometimes looked through the books and found that she had occasionally put more than one letter in a box in order to write an incorrect seven letter word into the spaces provided for a five letter answer.

Before too long she was unable to recognise different members of the family. Sometimes she thought they were her mother, her father, her school-days friends or people from books or television programmes. But even when she didn't know who they were, she often knew that they were people of importance to her, significant people. She failed to recognise Bill, but knew that he was very nice. She welcomed his visits but was unaware of the relationship between them, or so it seemed. The children found this distressing but curiously enough Bill didn't. He had a deep belief that she always knew him, even when she looked at him with a vacant expression, or failed to speak. He invariably found some little look, gesture or sound which convinced him that she knew who he was, even though he accepted that she probably no longer understood the concept of husband or lover or friend. He listened intently to her jumbled words and often could find meaning in them. He recognised that the words often didn't mean what they usually meant, that she spoke with a sort of poetic freedom.

The end, when it did come was unexpected and swift. She caught a cold and it developed into pneumonia. Bill was given the option of her being sent to the hospital or staying in the home and he opted for her staying where she was secure, known and at ease. He realised that her life might be extended by a few days or even a few weeks if she was sent to hospital, but he reasoned that life was about the quality and not the quantity of days. He wanted her to remain in her room, surrounded by her music, her pictures and the familiar sounds and smells of the home. It was a decision the whole family approved of and when, a few days later they were all summoned early one morning, they felt that they were indeed going to her home and not to an anonymous hospital ward.

She died peacefully, her husband of fifty-two years holding her hand and her sister and children surrounding her. They had shared her journey, as they promised they would, and although their grief was real so was their relief that her sojourn in this strange land had come to an end.

She would have been amazed by the number of people who attended her funeral, she had no idea of the impact and influence that her life had made on others. The vicar took the service with great sensitivity. He had visited Bill earlier in the week and spent several hours with him building up a picture of the sort of woman she had been. He closed his address with these words.

"It is often said, when people suffer from a dementing illness such as Alzheimer's Disease that the person actually died several years ago and that when the time for their funeral comes, we are saying goodbye to the body but the actual person has long since departed that body. Those who knew Victoria know that this is not the case. She remained a full person, in every sense of that word, until the very end. A sick person, of course, affected by the illness which so cruelly afflicted her, but a person right to the end. A person who could receive and soak up the love which unstintingly came from her family, a person who could rest in the assurance of her husband's love and who, in her own way, could still communicate with him until just a few days ago. For this, and for so much more, we today give thanks."

Libby couldn't help but reflect what a contrast Victoria's living and dying, even her funeral, had been compared to their mother's.

L ibby was having a bad week. She couldn't say exactly how or where this sense of being ill was located, but she knew that something was wrong. For over eight years now she had struggled without telling anyone, but this was worse, she could no longer hide it. Celia argued that she was depressed, that she needed to see the doctor and get some valium or something but she was quite clear in her own mind that she was not depressed. It was therefore with a certain degree of resignation that she made an appointment with the local surgery. The visit set in motion a long chain of tests, hospital appointments, further tests and a further hospital appointment before the news was given to her that she was suffering from a virulent form of acute leukaemia. The prognosis was not good. This alone, however, did not fully explain what some of the tests were throwing up and further investigations were deemed to be necessary.

After several months of relative stability or slow decline the deterioration in her health suddenly became marked and Celia or Bruce or someone, must have mentioned it to Paul because she was amazed to receive a telephone call from him in New York asking if he could come and see her.

"When are you next in London then?" she asked.

"No, not when I'm next in London, can I come and see you now?"

"I don't know what you mean Paul, when are you coming over?"

"Tomorrow, if that's alright with you?"

"Tomorrow? Wow, that would be lovely? What are you doing here, is it a conference or something?"

"No Libby, I'm coming to see you," and the phone went dead.

He had been to her home only once before and was slightly nervous when he rang the bell. She opened the door, saw him standing there, burst into tears and fell into his arms. He was horrified to see how thin and drawn she was, how unstable on her feet. He knew that she was ill but had somehow never expected to see her in such a condition. He almost carried her into the flat, she was so slight, so weak. Nevertheless, despite the illness and despite the effects of the treatment she was so clearly and unmistakeably the Libby of his heart and dreams. He held her with gentleness, finding words difficult but there was no need for words, they would have been an unwelcome intrusion.

"Oh Paul, it's so good to see you. Thank you for coming. I've been longing to see you again but never thought I would. It's been so long, so long..."

Her voice was little more than a whisper and her eyes were still full of tears.

"I'm afraid you've caught me on a bad day, I'm not usually as weak as this." She smiled at him. "Would you mind if I just stretched out on the sofa, I'm feeling very tired. If I drop asleep, don't take offence, just stay there, I'm so very pleased to see you, I can't tell you how much. How ridiculous, now that you're actually here I can hardly keep awake. Make yourself a cup of something, I'll be alright in half an hour or so."

She fell into a deep sleep. For a long time he never moved. He just sat looking at her, overwhelmed by sorrow when he thought of the years that they had wasted by being apart. He watched every small movement that she made in her sleep. Instead of the pale, rather emaciated face, the thinning hair and the dark patches under her eyes, he could see only a youthful radiant face, full of smiles and innocence. He looked at her and saw only the object of his love and his eyes filled with tears as he thought of the pain that he'd caused her. It was two hours before she woke up. She slowly opened her eyes and seemed to have difficulty focusing them on him. There was a momentary pause and then she recognised him.

"Paul, you are still here. I'm so pleased. Have you had anything to eat?"

"Anything to eat? I haven't moved all the time that you've been asleep. I've been like a guardian angel keeping watch over you. But I'm so pleased that you've woken up. You need to remind me where the bathroom is, I'm bursting."

Libby burst into laughter.

She was much better after her sleep. She recovered strength and vitality, her eyes sparkled and words rushed out as she tried to share her news with him and learn about his. It had been his intention to take her out to an expensive restaurant for dinner but they settled on telephoning for an Indian carry-out, although in fact she ate virtually nothing. She lit some candles and opened a bottle of wine, but was unable to drink any.

"Libby, I've not made any arrangements to stay anywhere, I hope it's alright with you if I stay here. I'm happy to stay in your spare room if that makes it easier for you."

"That would be lovely," Libby whispered. "But there's no need to stay in the spare room, I mean it's not as if it's the first time we have stayed with each other is it? It would be lovely to be with you, but I need to warn you, I'm afraid that I shall be unable to do more than go to sleep in your arms, if you would allow that, I no longer have the strength for anything else."

"I could think of nothing that I would like better. Thank you, you have made me the happiest man in the world," and he spoke the truth.

"So, when are we going to make the decision to be together for good? There's no point in denying that it makes sense. I want to be with you Libby, and now that you are not well you need someone to be alongside you and who better than me?"

He had slipped from being a genial and amusing companion to becoming a serious, ardent and insistent suitor. He was in deadly earnest, he wanted Libby and he had no intention of letting her slip away again.

"Don't press me Paul, don't let's go over that ground again. I can't make a decision like that. I've too many commitments, I can't do it, I just can't."

"Nonsense. Just tell me one commitment that keeps you away from me, just one."

"I can't, you know that I can't Paul. I want to be with you, believe me I do, but I just can't. It's too late, too late."

"I can't understand you, what do you mean 'it's too late'? It's the simplest thing in the world to say that you'll come. There are specialists in leukaemia in New York, we'll have you up and well within a few weeks, well months, I'm sure of that. New York has some of the very best cancer specialists in the world and I can afford to go to any one of them. In fact, we could go to all of them, one by one until we found the person who can cure you."

Libby wanted this time to last forever, but she knew that her days were limited. What their lovemaking, if such a word was appropriate for their tender chaste embraces, lacked in passion was more than compensated for by its compassion. Despite her weakness she embraced Paul and with great tenderness and unimaginable devotion he responded to her; they looked into each other's eyes, there was no need for anything further. The years disappeared and in their imagination they recapitulated the fierce intensity of their student lovemaking, whilst in reality they were experiencing the remaining embers, just as hot, perhaps, but without the flames of their earlier encounters. It was a night suspended in time, belonging to the two of them alone and satisfying every fibre of their being and transcending all the difficulties and problems that lay ahead of them. She slept, she woke, she slept again and all the time Paul remained awake, looking at her.

The next morning she was very much weaker and he was alarmed. He telephoned the surgery and a doctor came round within the hour. He wanted to admit her into hospital but she refused, she wanted to stay at home. He gave her an injection, arranged for a nurse to come round later and said he would call back at the end of the afternoon. Paul telephoned Celia and Bill, who was amazed to get his call, but said he would leave right away and be with them in about an hour.

"Libby darling. Why don't we just get married? Why not now?"

He meant it when he said it, but didn't stop to think about the complications of such a suggestion considering that he was already married and had been for the last seven years.

"Paul, dearest, I've something further to tell you. I haven't told you the whole truth about my situation. I have more than leukaemia and I'm afraid I am sinking fast, I don't have long to live now. Do you think I could ask something of you, I'm almost afraid to ask..."

"Ask anything, my darling, anything. I will do anything in the world for you, you know that."

"Paul, I'm not afraid of dying, but I am afraid of dying alone. Would you stay by my side, I don't think it will be long now, I have a sense that everything is drifting away from me – will you stay – please?"

Paul leaned over and cradled her in his arms. She looked up into his face and smiled, and slowly slipped into a state of unconsciousness. He didn't register the time passing. Bill's presence, visits from Celia and Bruce, more nurses. Time was suspended, the present moment stretched out eternally. One day, two days? He didn't know how long he sat there with his arms around her but he knew that when he finally let go she was dead. So was he, the only difference was that he was still breathing and she wasn't.

H e arrived back in New York looking tired and strained.
"Darling, whatever's the matter, you look ghastly?"

Veronica looked genuinely concerned.

"Oh it's nothing. I think I've caught a bug or something. There was a chap at the conference from the Far East or somewhere and he was sneezing all over the place. I think I must have caught something. It's quite irresponsible, it really is."

"Well at least you're home dear and you can forget all about work for a few days. It really is thoughtless of them to send you off at such short notice, and for almost a fortnight as well, and then for the telephone system to break down, it's just too bad, especially when we were having the Chamberlains over for dinner. Anyway, I managed to cancel them and they're coming over next Saturday."

"I know darling, it's a real nuisance but that's what international politics is all about, here today, there tomorrow, you never know what's going to crop up. I've really missed you."

She smiled and he gave her a kiss.

About the Author

Malcolm Goldsmith has worked in parishes in Birmingham, Nottingham and Edinburgh. He has been a university chaplain, a chaplain to a hospice and a research fellow at the Dementia Services Development Centre at the University of Stirling. He is currently active with groups addressing issues of ageing.

His book 'Hearing the Voice of People with Dementia' was short-listed for Age-Concern's Seebohm Trophy 'for the book which best promotes the well-being and understanding of older people'.

Working with Michael Kindred he has devised a great many board and card games which have been sold worldwide.
www.kindredgamesandbooks.co.uk

Printed in the United Kingdom
by Lightning Source UK Ltd.
133269UK00001B/7-48/P